FALL APART

ON THE SLOPES
BOOK 2

DAKOTA FOREST

DAKOTA FOREST

To the ladies that have been told you're not enough or you're too much. Screw them. You're perfect just the way you are.

PROLOGUE
LIZZY

August
Dayton, Ohio

"DO you want to fly out to Denver with me this weekend?" I know the answer is yes, even if I'm just venting my rage. It's a hot August day in Ohio and I probably look unhinged judging by the expression on V's face right now. I'm standing on her porch while she looks back at me with a confused expression on her face standing in her doorway, letting out a low, questioning groan. Veronica Perry has been my ride or die since college and would drop everything if I needed it. That's just the way she is. She's always cared so much about the people in her life.

"Why would we need to go to Colorado this weekend? It's not even ski season." She's still wearing a skeptical expression. I love that she's not even phased by the question itself and didn't shrug this off as some silly offhanded joke.

Instead, she's just looking back at me, curious to know why I just showed up on her doorstep this evening completely unannounced.

We hang out all the time - workout a couple nights a week, and see each other every day at the office - so normally she'd have some idea if I was going to drop by. But judging by the look on her face, I think she can sense my jumbled mess of emotions. Everything I'm feeling is making my voice go from defeated to frantic to purely angry in a chaotic flurry.

"Because I'm going to go cut off Johnathan's balls and someone will have to bail me out if I get caught." I rarely drop my *always on* battle armor. The bubbly, sassy outgoing version of myself is what everyone else gets to see. But she's my best friend and I can see it in her eyes that she knows something is wrong.

"Wait. What happened? What did *he* do?" In an instant her tone shifts from questioning to compassionate. She's sweaty in yoga pants and a sports bra showing off the mountain peaks tattoo on her ribs. The one I always tease her about for being such a *bad girl*. I clearly interrupted her evening workout, but I know she'll understand. As much of a routine junky as she is, she'll drop it for me. That's just how we are.

I steady myself, feeling the skin along my nose start to scrunch and tingle. It's the unfamiliar sign of tears welling up.

I'm Lizzy Frank.

I don't cry.

I'm a boss bitch and I keep it together.

So the foreign, burning feeling in my eyes is in stark contrast to the tension in my jaw from all rage and hurt coursing through me since the events of this afternoon.

"That fucking prick. He's been cheating on me. All these trips to Denver for that *long term project*? He's been hooking up with someone in his office there."

"What the actual fuck? And how did you find out?" She pulls me into a hug and I let my walls fall completely down. The first tears fall down my face onto her shoulder. Screw it. I guess I can cry for once.

"Eww. You're so damn sweaty. What were you doing, hot yoga or something?" She lets out a snort of laughter before letting go of me, looking me in the eyes, raising an eyebrow. I know this is her way of telling me to be serious and stop deflecting.

A long, ragged breath escapes me. "Fine. He's such a dumbass. He forgot his iPad at our apartment. I was trying to read on the couch and it was just blowing up with all these notifications. I read their entire conversation." She palms her face and shakes her head.

Our apartment. I cringe at those words. We've been together for years and shared that apartment for the last two. Now I don't even want to go back even though it's my name on the lease.

"Jeez. What. A. Dumbass. Like in so many ways. I'm so sorry." She looks back to me for a second, her kind hazel eyes scanning my face. "How about you come inside first? I've got pints of ice cream with our names on them. We can eat right from the tubs or I can dish some out while you dish out the latest from bookstagram. You can tell me about whatever, unhinged smutty book is your latest obsession." She rolls her eyes and laughs. "And after I stuff you full of ice cream, if you still want to go to Denver, sure. I'm your girl. But maybe revenge can be a little bit *less* intense than removing organs or appendages?"

I snort a laugh between tears. "No promises." I run my arm over my face before pulling her back in for a hug. "But thanks, V. You're my girl too."

CHAPTER 1
LIZZY
DIVE BAR - 6 MONTHS LATER

I LEAN over the marble vanity in the bathroom and pop my lips in the mirror. I love this shade of red lip stain. It might be a bit much for a Wednesday night out at a crappy dive bar, but I think it's perfect.

I've been looking forward to this President's Day trip to Aspen Valley and Park City, Utah for months. Originally it was just going to be a February girls trip, sort of like the trip V and I had originally planned in Jackson Hole over the holidays.

Spa days, late nights out on the town, living it up on Old Main Street in downtown Park City for a long weekend. That was until V lucked out over that Jackson Hole trip and fell in love with the man of the century, Tanner Chapman. So now he's crashing our President's Day girls trip and bringing his best friend Collin, V's brother, who also happens to now be my friend too.

But even if there will be more people than we originally planned, they don't get into town until tomorrow morning and I have the condo to myself tonight. And that's exactly why I'm going out on the town. All winter I've been enjoying my *Tour de Lizzy*. Just because I have no idea what I want long term doesn't mean I don't have *needs* right now. I'm a grown ass woman. Meaningless one night stands, especially over a thousand miles from my home back in Dayton, Ohio, are totally doable for me right now.

Sure, spending the long weekend with the group should be a blast. And I know my family's condo at the Aspen Grove Club will be a bit more cramped than we originally planned. I'm guessing we'll meet up with Tanner's younger siblings, Clay and Grace, who both live in the Park City area too.

We'll probably have time to ski both resorts, Aspen Valley where the condo is, and Park City, closer to the old ski town and only ten minutes away. It will be a great time.

And I'll gladly take all the distractions I can get. Sure, that trip over New Year's with V, Tanner, and Collin was fun. I even had my first threesome, sort of.

But I still have a bitter taste in my mouth.

I'm still angry.

I'm still hurt.

Johnathan, that dirtbag, left a hole in my heart six months ago. I wasted so many good years with him. Years that I spent trusting him, thinking he loved me. All of that time, that energy, thinking of our future, only to see him wash it down the drain, like it was nothing to him. Like *I* was nothing to him.

He even managed to spoil the peace and quiet of the stupid apartment, which now just reminds me of him.

So having a free night to myself, away from home where I can just get out and let loose is something I desperately need.

And besides, I haven't been out to Park City in months and the first thing I'd love to do is stop into Roxy's, the old dive bar a block off of Main Street.

Looking in the mirror in the bathroom at the condo, I can almost convince myself that I'm not still hurt. The confident face staring back at me feels like it's finally resembling the sassy bitch everyone thinks I am, the one I want them to think I am.

I feel like I look good.

No.

I *do* look fucking good.

Black tights, my trusty low cut black sweater dress, my favorite gold necklace with the ice cream cone charm pendant, and my hair back in a pony tail. I love this outfit. I feel like a catch.

Yep. Screw Johnathan. His loss.

AFTER HOPPING off the shuttle from the condo to downtown Park City, I walk South towards Main Street. Along the way, I pass the Town Lift, the chairlift that comes from the slopes straight into the center of town. I stop and watch for a minute as some of the resort employees are still riding it down. It's connected by a skiers' bridge that lets skiers come right into the center of town. This place is really unique with how the town and the resort blend together. Some of the ski runs at the base of the mountain even run right along the houses a few blocks off of Main Street.

Striding up the street through historic downtown Park City is something that feels timeless yet modern all at once. My pink cowboy boots I bought in Jackson Hole are cute as hell, but they probably weren't the best choice for the sloped street that I'm trudging up now. Even with the salt scattered on the shoveled pavement, it's still slick and I definitely don't want to fall and break something before I even get to ski tomorrow.

I carefully walk my way up Main Street, which is at the center of the old Western mining town turned ski paradise. It's lined with charming two and three-story brick buildings with a mix of old, brightly painted wood facades. There are bars, restaurants, art galleries, chocolate shops, all of the things it seems like every ski town has. If it wasn't dark out, I could even see the mountains surrounding the town on three sides.

Turning the corner, I walk another block away from Main Street towards my destination, Roxy's.

It's a dive. And that might be on the generous side. It's old, with a nondescript, wood paneled façade painted white that's been fading for years. Topping off the charming, dive bar vibe is a small red sign over the door with "Roxy's" stenciled in white. It vaguely resembles most of the old buildings right off the main drag, just a bit more... *grungy*.

On the inside, it's not much different. The wood paneled walls are raw and worn. There are pool tables along the back wall and a cozy bar with a dozen or so seats surrounded by a few high top tables.

It's definitely not a place Meredith Frank, my mother, would approve of. At first it was my secret escape and I'd lie about where I was going every now and then on our family ski trips. When I was older, I stopped hiding it from them, but they'd still always wonder why I'd come here. It's not the swanky, posh place the Frank family would go to. No espresso martinis or Chablis here, that's for sure.

It's a place I've been coming to for ages whenever I'm in town at my family's condo, ever since I was old enough to drink. Maybe even before I was old enough. Not that my parents ever need to know about that. And not like they'd really care either. They would be busy at some swanky place for dinner or at the condo with my younger sister, Charlotte.

No. I liked to come here to just get away, to *let my hair down*. Ok, maybe not literally, I'm wearing a ponytail. But no, just a place to get away from what I'm expected to be and relax. A place where my mother or my boyfriend couldn't tell me to tone it down a notch on the rare occasions he came on one of our family trips. A place to unwind and be me, unapologetically Lizzy.

Am I a little overdressed for this place? Probably. But whatever, I'm always overdressed. As my best friend says, I'm *always on*. So what, I enjoy looking good.

Even on a Wednesday night close to nine o'clock, the bar is busy. The sounds of all the people and their glasses clanking reverberate through the room. The wolf shaped neon light along the wall hums with the country songs in the background. All of it vibrates and courses through me, bringing me to life.

I work my way up to the bar and grab a stool at the corner. Getting a seat in prime position for people watching is practically a hobby of mine. Is the drunk guy over there going to get slapped or score with the woman he's been buying vodka sodas for the last hour? Are those two guys at the pool table going to fight or bro hug? All I know is that this is better than reality TV. People watching at these places is always a must for me. On a weeknight? Even better.

The bartender, a sweet girl probably barely old enough to drink herself, comes my way.

"Nice day out on the slopes today. You make it out there?" She tilts her chin towards the windows on the front of the building where you could see the ski slopes if the sun was still up. I always admire the politeness of local Utahns.

"Unfortunately not. Just got back into town today." I shrug, turning my palms up, jealous that I'm not here full time and can't ski when I feel like it. I swear V and Tanner rubbed off on me too much over the holidays.

"Bummer." She takes her bar towel and wipes the spot in front of me clean. "So what can I get you tonight?"

"Well bourbon, neat, and a glass of water. Thanks!" I hand my card over to her to start a tab, noting her raised eyebrows. Why does everyone act surprised the 5'3" blonde likes bourbon? Sure, I love me a mimosa or tiki drink. But sometimes, this is what I want. I just need to burn the tips of my nerves off. Just a *teensy* bit.

"Alright. I like your style." She nods before turning to the back bar to throw my card in the glass with the other tab cards. My metal card hits the bottom with a nice little clink and I hear a laugh from her.

A few songs later and I can feel my worries start to drift off. Who needs Johnathan? And why should I care what my mother thinks about me? And let's not even get started with Dad. We were close once, but somewhere along the way we grew apart. It was especially bad after Charlotte took more of their time when she got sick and was in and out of the hospital. I know she needed their time, but so did I and I still want to fix that chasm that grew between all of us. I just don't know where to start. At least Meredith Frank actually has an opinion about me, unlike him. It's not my problem I don't want to live up to her expectations, meet a nice boy in finance with a trust fund, and get married and pop out 2.5 kids. Johnathan was exactly who she wanted me to end up with. He was respectable, smart, and a safe choice. And if she had her way, we would have *patched things up,* stayed together, and done exactly that.

Zero chance, Mother.

If it was up to her, I'd have been defined by the man I was with just like her. And I've worked so hard to do things on my own. Instead of working for my dad, I got my own internship. I worked for a great startup on the West Coast. Sure, I did come back home to Ohio to work at another company, but I wanted to be closer to my friends and sister. And the opportunity was in fact a career advancement with some big, remote working perks.

I just want to be me. My own person, living my own authentic life.

The problem is I don't exactly know what that means any more. I always wanted to make my own life, but I was also with Johnathan for so long that I was ready to settle down and do what I thought was expected of me. It just felt like that was natural next step. We were even shopping for engagement rings, even though he hadn't actually asked me yet. Months removed from that now, I don't know if that's what I want any more. I don't know if that's ever what I really wanted. What I know for sure is that I don't want to be defined by someone else.

AN HOUR GOES by while I watch the crowd, enjoying the distraction from thinking about the life I thought I wanted, listening to the music on the juke box, and letting the stress of the travel day go by. When the bartender comes back with my second round, I feel a cold breeze drift through the bar, sending a chill up my legs through my tights. I turn to see the door open and watch as a tall, imposing figure walks in.

Just looking at him, I can feel the hair on the back of my neck stand. His hair is a dark, inky brown, tousled on top but pushed to one side. Below the shell of his ear I can make out a couple tattoos on his neck coming above the collar of his worn black work jacket. The features of his face are striking and defined, from his high cheek bones to his square jaw.

Jesus. Where did this guy come from?

I've always gone after the pretty, preppy boys. The ones I'd meet at my fancy private school or at my parents' parties or country club. The ones like my ex. But on my *Tour de Lizzy* of no strings attached fun, I've never come across someone like this guy. Yeah. There was that cowboy in Wyoming. But this guy is different. He's rugged, imposing, and raw.

He looks right at me, his brow furrowing and his jaw tightening into a scowl before he looks past me to the bartender, walking right towards us. He looks younger, maybe in his late twenties? But there's still something so intense and masculine about him.

"Hey Mandy," he says to the bartender while organizing a stack of coasters, "I'll take the usual."

"Sure thing, babe," she says, heading down the bar towards the fridge. He takes his jacket off, folding it neatly and laying it on the bar revealing a plain black t-shirt that hugs him in all the right places.

"What are you doing here?" His deep, irritated voice catches me off guard as he continues to look down the bar watching Mandy, facing away from me. I look around, noticing no one is within ear shot of us in the loud bar.

"Are you talking to me?" I look to him, but he's still watching Mandy and waiting for his drink, drumming his fingers along the wooden counter. I watch the way the corded muscles of his tattooed forearms tick with each motion of his hand.

He lowers his head, letting out a long sigh before turning to me.

His dark green eyes are so piercing as he looks right into mine. He does look young, but at the same time I get a glimpse of something behind those eyes that looks soulful and worn. I swallow hard and my mouth go dry as his eyes still rake over me. It takes all my willpower to hold his gaze and not rake my eyes over his body.

Who the hell is this guy and what's his problem with me?

"Yeah. I am talking to you. What are you doing here?" His tone is slightly less irritated and I can see one corner of his mouth quirk up into a playful smirk.

"I'm trying to enjoy my bourbon without being bothered. What about you?" I lift my glass to my lips, taking a long slow sip as I maintain this unusually intense eye contact. He's certainly handsome and confident. And he knows it. I'll give him that.

He huffs a laugh as he rests against the bar, propping himself up on his elbow. He leans toward me, leaving almost no space between us. "I'm waiting for the pretty little tourist princess to get out of my seat so I can enjoy my beer when it gets here."

Pretty little tourist? His seat?

Yep, he's definitely cocky.

I let my eyes run over him, admiring how the t-shirt hugs his toned arms and reveals more of his tattoos. He could certainly be a fun *distraction* tonight while I have the condo to myself before the others get to town tomorrow.

OK. I can play this game.

I roll my shoulders and flick my ponytail back, flashing a playful grin at him and looking at him with my best doe eyes. "Oh. I didn't realize you could reserve seats here. Silly me." I mockingly clutch at my heart. "I'm such a *tourist* after all."

His scowl disappears and lifts back into a smirk. Through his five o'clock shadow I can see his dimples now, softening the intensity of his striking features, making him somehow even more irresistibly delicious.

"Well, for a pretty little *tourist* like you," he pauses, his grin widening, "I guess I can make an exception. You can keep it." He turns and walks away, returning with another bar stool and sliding it right next to me.

The air between us already feels charged, buzzing and heavy with tension as our eyes linger on each other. It feels like an eternity passes before Mandy returns with his beer.

"Here you go, babe." She leaves the stubby yellow labeled beer on a coaster before heading back to the other end of the bar. He tips his chin to her and grabs the beer.

I can't help but notice his hands. They look worn and rough, like he works with them everyday. They look like the kind of hands that would feel good wandering over my body and gripping me. On the back of his hand holding the beer, I can see a horseshoe tattooed and some letters that I can't make out on the knuckles.

"Thanks," he says gruffly, getting my attention back from thinking about what his hands would feel like on me. But he doesn't move, still turned to face me, his eyes shamelessly lingering.

I feel my cheeks heat and my skin itch with anticipation. I look down away from his gaze trying to collect myself for just a second, but that only heightens the feeling. He's sitting with his knees open, inches from mine. His jeans hug his tree trunk thighs and my mind goes straight to thinking about how it would feel to be pressed against him.

He would definitely be a fun distraction for a night.

Even if he's young, everything about him screams *masculine*. The kind of man that would be rough and fuck me through the headboard.

OK, yeah. Maybe I overdid it on the flight and went a little too hard with the extra spicy books.

I look back up at him with a new sense of resolve taking over me. Yes, I deserve to have some no strings attached fun while I have the condo to myself tonight.

When I look at him, his eyes narrow and he lets out a low laugh.

I cock my head and raise an eyebrow at him. "What's so funny?"

He shakes his head and lets out another low huff of laughter, extending a finger towards me. "You. You're funny."

"How so?" I smirk at him, taking a sip of my bourbon before letting my tongue dart over my lips, licking a stray drop. I don't miss the way his eyes drift to my lips before he looks back at me. I know my lips look extra pouty with the stain I put on before heading out.

"You've got this whole little polite, pretty princess thing going on but you're sitting here at a dive bar drinking bourbon neat and eyefucking me. You're something else."

A breathless laugh escapes me and I reach to cover my mouth. I feel the blood rush to my cheeks as they go redder than my lips.

I pause before letting out an amused, thoughtful hum. "Well, I am just a pretty little tourist. I figured I'd take in *all* the sights." I let my eyes roam over him again and the approving grin he gives me is downright feral.

His deep laugh rumbles through me. I clench my thighs together, trying to dull the ache growing there.

He looks down at his phone for a second before looking at me and rasping his knuckles against the bar. "I need to check on something, but I'll be right back." He stands and as he takes a step past me, he looks back. "Enjoy *the sights*." He winks before turning away and walking towards the back hallway.

He fucking winks?

You've got to be kidding me. This guy is so damn cocky. And looking down, watching the way his Wranglers mold to his ass, fine. Yeah. I get it.

As he turns the corner, I get up, following him before I lose my nerve or let the sane part of me talk myself out of this. I stride across the bar, towards the hallway.

I turn the corner in a hurry and walk into what feels like a brick wall, startling myself and knocking me off balance.

Except it's not a brick wall. It's the cocky local.

He's there.

He's there and he's smirking at me.

"Something you need, *princess*?" he says, playfully and clearly pleased with himself.

Screw it. He's cocky, but the confident, bad boy act is doing it for me tonight. I step towards him, straining my neck to look up at him.

"Yeah. You." I push my finger into his chest. "You are exactly what I need tonight." I flatten my hand and run it over his muscular chest. His eyes are breathtakingly intense. A deep shade of green that feels like it goes on forever, like an alpine lake reflecting the forest around it.

"And why do you need me?" His voice is deep and gravelly. He leans forward, erasing the little remaining space between us. I realize just how much he towers over me.

"I need a man that can play rough and you seem like the type. Maybe fuck me until I can't think straight." A muscle flicks in his jaw as he cracks a wide, sinful grin that's only sexier with his dimples. I run my hand up his chest over the rose tattoo on his neck to cup his jaw. The feeling of his stubble under my thumb sends shivers through me as I imagine how it would feel between my legs. He seems like a guy that would be so eager to please.

"If I fuck you, you won't be able to walk straight, much less think straight." He reaches up towards my hand on his face, pressing it against his jaw as he steps further into me.

"Is that a promise or a threat?" I tease him, running a finger tip down his tattooed neck over his collarbone. His throat bobs as my nail traces the outline of the roses.

His hand grips my hip, pressing my body into him. "There's two things you should know about me. I was raised that I'm as good as my word. If I make a promise, I'm going to keep it or die trying."

I feel my heart pound as he crowds my space. His presence is intoxicating, more intoxicating than the bourbon I was just drinking. And he clearly isn't phased by my teasing. But I'm not backing down from him. I manage to get out the words, albeit with a little less conviction than my earlier taunt. "You said there's two things?"

His nostrils flare and his muscular chest fills out as he inhales a deep, irritated breath. His lips part when he leans forward, his grip on my hip tightening. His mouth is so close to me as he whispers into my ear. "I'm all action. I don't make threats."

The feeling of his warm breath on my neck, matching the heat pooling low in my core.

His words.

His voice.

A hushed whimper escapes me and my restraint snaps.

I fist his shirt, pulling him down to me. He slants his head and our lips meet. His kiss is hungry, piercing and devouring. I wrap one leg around him, drawing our bodies together and I can feel his bulge through his jeans.

He pulls away, both of us practically panting.

"You want to get out of here?" he asks. His eyes meet mine and I can see the eagerness in them. He reaches for my face, tucking a stray strand of hair behind my ear. I grab his hand, desperate for more skin to skin contact.

His hands are strong and rugged and mine disappears into his palm. I can see the horseshoe on the back of his hand more clearly and now I can make out the letters on his knuckles that spell out *COME.*

But it's the other tattoo that I can't look away from. The one on the inside of his wrist. It's a jagged little line forming the outlines of mountain peaks. It's the same one I've seen over the years on my best friend's ribs. It's the same tattoo that her boyfriend, Tanner, has on his wrist. The same one even Veronica's brother Collin has on his wrist. The exact same spot as this guy.

I look back into those eyes, suddenly very aware of the familiar, intense green hue. The mischievous smile with perfect dimples. The tall, mountain man build.

Oh god.

No. No. No.

This has to be a joke.

CHAPTER 2
CLAY
FRU FRU SHIT

WHAT IS a woman like *her* doing in a place like *this*? She smells so fucking good. Like all that fru fru shit that girls are into. Maybe coconut and citrus? All I know is that this close, I can smell her shampoo over the stale bar and I just want to breathe her in.

She was sitting at a bar drinking bourbon, not some girly cocktail. Where the hell does a woman like this even come from? Sure, she might be some annoying little tourist. But she's such a firecracker and so sassy.

And why is she looking at me like that now? The sexy, hungry look in her eyes is completely gone. It's replaced by something I can't quite place.

Maybe a hint of panic?

This sudden look of shock on her face is killing me.

Fuck. Maybe I read this wrong asking her to leave so quick.

"Everything ok?" I pull my wrist out of her hand, tilting her chin up with a curled finger towards me to look into those beautiful sapphire blue eyes. I playfully flick an eyebrow at her, trying to lighten the sudden change in her expression. "Cat got your tongue?"

Her worried look doesn't change. She looks like she's seen a ghost.

"Hey. What's wrong?" I look into her eyes, frantically searching for what could have gone so wrong so fast. I rest my hands on her shoulders. "Shit. I'm sorry"

"We can't do this." Her words are a muted whisper, lacking any of that early sassiness and conviction that was so sexy. She brushes my hands off her shoulders, rubbing hers down her front and smoothing out the hem of her dress.

"Hey. Did I do something?" I don't know what went wrong so fast.

"I just... I have to leave. I'm sorry." I stand there, dumfounded as she walks past me, heading towards the front of the bar. She snags Mandy's attention and gets her card, grabbing her jacket from the stool and turns to head towards the exit.

As she reaches the door, she looks over her shoulder, back at me. She bites her lip before her eyes flit away.

And like that, she's gone.

My heart is pounding. Who the fuck was she? This little spitfire that has my skin burning.

I guess this tracks though.

This is the kind of shit that always happens to me.

I HANG my keys on their hook just inside the door to my kitchen from the garage.

Fucking hell. What a rollercoaster. This is not how I thought my night would go.

No. Not at all. I was going to go and just grab a beer. My usual Wednesday after work routine. Nothing special.

Then I ran into the insane little blonde that got under my skin in all the right ways and clearly wanted to have some *fun*. Or at least I thought so until she ran off and I have no idea what I did. She just stared at me in shock before she dashed out of the bar leaving with zero explanation.

I hear a familiar rumbling coming from across the living room into the kitchen, instantly brightening my mood a bit.

"Oh hey, bud." I kneel down as Ani runs up to me, tail wagging. "Have you been a good boy while Daddy was gone?" I say in a deep, playful voice. "Or were you my bad little shit starter?"

I smile when he rests his head on my shoulder and licks my ear. I'm 6'3", but he's big for a Belgian Malinois and I love how he can still jump up on me like this when I'm kneeling down.

"Thanks for the kisses. It's been a rough night." That's an understatement. I left the bar without even finishing my beer. I figured I might as well get home and get a good night's sleep after that cold shower at the bar.

Fuck. I need a *real* cold shower now. I'm still so wound up after that.

I stand up, patting Ani and head over to the coat rack, putting my jacket on its hook and my work boots neatly in their tray. Ani follows me in his perfect heeling position, the one I spent months perfecting and still work on every day with him.

Walking through the hall along the polished concrete floors to my room, my mind is racing. I still can't get over this.

Who was that and why did she leave like that?

Was it something I did?

I know I can be a domineering, cocky asshole. But I'm still respectful. I pride myself on being respectful. That's how we were raised to be. That's what Dad expects from me, what Mom would have expected from me. I thought I was reading her signs right and we were going to have a good time.

She followed me and seemed to be calling the shots. *She* was touching my chest. *She* kissed me. *She* pulled me into her with her leg. Fuck. Just thinking about it is sending a rush of blood below my waist.

She was so gorgeous too. I wanted to do unspeakable things to that snarky little mouth of hers. She was clearly down for it. Or at least she was until something changed.

I don't know why I'm surprised though. That's what these tourists chicks do. Come into town, have some fun with the locals, then disappear until their next trip. But they usually aren't hanging out, alone, at Roxy's on a Wednesday night.

When I get to my bedroom, I toss my clothes in the hamper and head to the en suite bathroom to start a cold shower. I really need it. Work has been hell lately.

The project at the Aspen Grove Club has been going smooth, but remodeling an entire floor of a giant condo building in the Utah winter is less than ideal. I've been there night and day trying to stay on top of it. We've been doing demo for weeks and finally have the place stripped down to the studs, but the job site is cold even with our portable heaters and wrapped windows. At least the project at the Grand Lodge is almost done. I remind myself that this is why I just got promoted, because I can handle these things and not get distracted.

When I finally get in the shower, the cold water feels amazing. Between beating myself up at work, my constantly sore and stiff knees, and the raging hard on I still have from thinking about my mystery woman, it's exactly what I need.

I rest my head against the glass, finally feeling like I can exhale and let the tension fade away.

This is just how my life is.

This is nothing new.

Every time something good seems like it's finally about to happen, life comes in and snatches it away.

Even the sting of a one night stand running off before it even got started is brutal, but also just feels normal at this point in my life.

This is why I don't let myself get attached to anything. This is why I don't let myself think about the future.

Focus on the now.

Focus on what I can control.

CHAPTER 3
LIZZY
CHEEKY SEXCAPADES

I WAKE UP, squinting at the morning light sneaking in through the curtains. Groaning, I bury my face in the pillow. I'm a girl that needs a solid eight hours of beauty sleep to feel my best. And right now, I do not feel my best. I feel like death. I slept like shit.

I really need to give Dad a piece of my mind. I doubt he'd think anything of it, but I want to on principle alone. When I asked if I could have the condo this week with Veronica, he left out the tiny detail about the top floor of the condo building being remodeled. I'm guessing that's why he hasn't been out here yet this winter. Our unit was done last summer, but now apparently the entire floor above us is being remodeled and expanded.

I shouldn't be surprised though. Dad has been focused solely on his business since I was a teenager. If something doesn't impact him, it's out of sight and out of mind. I know it's not out of spite. My dad loves me and I'm grateful for that. He's just always so busy. It feels like me, his literal firstborn, hasn't been a high priority in his life in a long time, especially after Charlotte. I get it, she's almost ten years younger than me and needed extra care growing up. And he's self made and came from literally nothing and built his company. I just wish I could get more of his time and energy, even now in my thirties.

I just want to be the priority to someone in my life. Ever since I moved back to Ohio, at least I had V, my ride or die, always by my side. Someone that always made me a priority, like the day I showed up on her doorstep six months ago. I know I might just be in my head, but I feel this more now that V has moved out to Wyoming with Tanner and I don't see her everyday. I'm worried I'll lose that.

Maybe when my dad retires we'll finally spend some quality time together.

I close my eyes, trying not to think about that but also trying to look away from the light coming in from the window. To top it off, one of the contractors thought it would be funny to get here at seven in the freaking morning. I swear this guy thinks it must be fun to start stomping around like a one man wrecking crew.

But no, that's only a small part of why I barely slept last night. No. There's definitely one very *big* reason. One big, handsome, dark and brooding reason.

Clay. Fucking. Chapman.

Even thinking about him makes my entire body tingle remembering the way his eyes shamelessly devoured me last night. I mean I definitely did the same thing to him, but still. He was so intense it was somehow both unnerving and deeply satisfying. It felt like I was *his* priority last night.

Did I stay up all night looking at Tanner's frustratingly limited social media trying to find a family picture to confirm my suspicion?

Yes. Of course I did.

Was he as hot as I remember from the dimly lit bar? Also, very much yes.

So. This is great.

Cool. Cool. Cool.

I made out with Tanner's younger brother, Clay, in a bar last night. I felt his impressive erection against me through his jeans. I was this close to going home with him, and as he put it, *getting fucked so hard I wouldn't be able to walk straight.*

Thinking about those dimples. That smile. Those rough hands

gripping my hips. I'm sure it would have been rough and hot as hell. It would have been exactly what I wanted, what I needed.

Ok. Let's be real. *Way* more than that.

And if it wasn't someone I have an outside connection to, someone I could just have a one night fling with, I would have done it. I can't do strings right now.

And getting involved with Clay? Yeah, there's a lot of strings there.

So I did what I never do.

I'm cool. I'm confident. *I never panic.*

But last night, I panicked. I panicked and ran out of the bar barely saying a word to him like a crazy person. He probably thinks I'm insane too. At least I don't have to see him today since he won't be with us on the slopes. That's a win.

GROANING, I flap my arms around and rock back and forth like a helpless, waddling penguin. "Geez, V. Call your boy off. He's going to squish me to death." I manage to wriggle out of Tanner's bear hug, which I learned is a customary Chapman family greeting from Tanner and his grandmother. I give my best friend a playful scowl when she laughs at me. "Couldn't you have fallen in love with someone slightly less mountain man-y?"

She crosses her arms and shakes her head at me before stepping over and bringing me into a hug. A much gentler, less possibly deadly hug. "Missed you too, Lizzy."

We're all here, bright and early as Veronica always insists, about to get in the ski lift line for first chair at Aspen Valley Resort. They drove down from Jackson at god only knows what hour to get here at eight in the morning. They took Tanner's Sprinter van with V's brother, Collin.

Even though Tanner's helped her a lot with her anxiety and compulsive need for planning, she still always wants to be in the lift line to snag the first chairlift of the day and ski the fresh, untracked snow. I have to admit, after skiing with them in Jackson over the holidays, I can't blame her. I always enjoyed skiing as a kid. But for my parents, skiing was just a status symbol that they used for socializing - a way to entertain their friends and business contacts. But seeing the way my friends love it, the way they love the mountains, reawakened a joy for it in me that had been missing for years.

Tanner looks down at me in his red ski jacket and black helmet, towering over me. He makes me think of Clay last night. With his goggles resting on the brim of his helmet, I see his green eyes which are so frighteningly similar I almost have to look away.

Yep. They are definitely brothers.

How did I not immediately realize this last night?

Nope. I need to get that thought out of my head. Stop thinking about last night.

Tanner chuckles. "You know the Chapmans give big bear hugs. You weren't complaining when it was my grandma dishing them out after dinner over the holidays."

I roll my eyes and shove his shoulder, only knocking myself back. I forgot. The Chapman boys are built like brick walls, because of course they are. "That's different. She was feeding me and I was hangry. You, on the other hand, are just trying to crush me to death so you can have V all to yourself."

He snorts a laugh. "Ok. You're not entirely wrong. But we all missed you."

To be honest, I missed them too. Veronica has been my best friend since we met as college roommates. And to see her this happy, after she struggled with burnout at work and a miserable dating life, brings me so much joy.

Watching Tanner and her, it's like they were made for each other. I mean I know they've been friends almost their whole lives, but they're so in sync. So happy. They remind me of everything I'm slowly realizing I've never had in a relationship. The trust, the palpable and visible chemistry, the undeniable love. It melts my heart seeing my friend this happy.

A different, deep voice instantly gets my attention. "Well, well, well. There's my new bestie." I instantly look up, grinning wildly when I see a familiar face walking over from the ski rack.

"Collin!" I walk to him as fast as I can in ski boots, bringing him into a hug. I've only really gotten to know him over the last few months, but it feels like we're almost as good of friends as Veronica and I are. Before our last ski trip, I was worried that he might try and make a move on me. She assured me I wasn't her bisexual brother's type and she was right. We instantly hit it off and bonded over tormenting Veronica and Tanner about being so nauseatingly cute together.

"Sup, trouble?" he asks.

"Oh, not too much *co-bestie*. Went out last night. Slept like shit, got woken up by an ape stomping around the floor above me, and didn't have time to stop at Finch for coffee this morning." Since Collin is Veronica's twin and practically my bestie, he's been given the co-bestie title. I let out an exaggerated sigh. "So yeah, the day can only get better from here."

Collin grins and shakes his head. "Geez. Sounds like it. Oh. Walker says hi too." He gives me a sly wink after letting me out of his arms.

I feel my cheeks heat. Walker was the cowboy that Collin and I shared on New Year's Eve. Is *platonic threesome* the right name for when two of you don't actually touch each other and make a sandwich out of a hunky cowboy? I don't know. Who cares?

"Oh," I say playfully. "You guys still *hanging out?*"

And that's when I hear Veronica clear her throat. "You two know the rule. No details about that night. Tanner and I would be perfectly fine living the rest of our lives never hearing about that again."

I glare back at V, cocking my head and rolling my eyes. "Fine, V. But if I hear you and Tanner fucking in the guest room at the condo, I'm spilling the tea whether you like it or not."

And that's when I notice someone I don't know, walking up behind Tanner from the ski rack. The brunette, wearing all light blue ski gear and a black helmet, grabs Tanner from behind and tries to *tickle him* with an impossibly charming smile and giggle.

"Hey!" Tanner whips. "What the-" He instantly smiles when he turns around, flashing those Chapman dimples. "Grace! I should have known it was you."

He puts her in a head lock under his arm. "You're never gonna be able to sneak up on me. Never gonna happen."

She gets out of his grip, and shoves him. "You're just as bad as Clay. You're supposed to let your little sister win sometimes, remember?"

From what I remember that V told me, Grace is the youngest of the Chapmans. Tanner's our age, but Clay and Grace are both in their mid to late twenties. And having met all of them now, well not formally, *damn*. They grow them differently in Wyoming.

"Whatever. If you want to win, you gotta be better. We're not just going to let you win." Tanner teases back at his sister before looking over to me. "And, Grace, this is who you've been dying to meet: Lizzy."

She immediately looks at me before running right at me. Before I can even react, I'm being pulled into another hug. "Oh my god! I have heard so much about you!"

"Um. It's nice to meet you too." I pat her half heartedly on the back, only prompting her to hold me tighter. I was warned that Grace was *extremely* friendly and outgoing. "V, what the fuck? Do they really all hug like this?" I say, peaking around Grace's frame.

Tanner comes over, wrapping his arm around his sister's shoulder. "Come on. Lizzy hasn't had thirty years of practice with Chapman hugs like the Perry twins have."

She punches her brother on the shoulder before looking back at me and pointing a finger. Looking at her again, I notice the purple and pink strands of hair hanging out of her helmet. "We're going to have a good time! I just know it."

"Ok guys. This is fun and all, but can we get in line? If we don't-". Veronica starts to talk before her brother cuts her off.

"We know, we know. If we don't get in line now, we won't get first chair." Collin pats his sister on the back and leads us towards the chairlift line.

WHILE SKIING in Jackson with the group over New Year was fun, being back at Aspen Valley in Utah feels right. It's like I'm on home turf. Veronica was right, that mountain was fun but insanely challenging. I get it, they're all thrill seekers. I'm pretty sure they might even have death wishes. But Aspen Valley has always felt like an escape from my family life, even if they were here with me. I was always allowed to explore the mountain on my own while my mother was at the spa or back at the condo reading and Dad was on a business call, or taking investors out on the mountain. When I was first learning, Dad would take me out for lessons. But as I got older it felt like as far as they were concerned, sending me out into ski school was as good as daycare. But, as I got older, I explored more on my own. But I still craved the rare times that Dad and I got to ski together when he wasn't distracted.

This is the first time I've been here this season and being out in the cool, crisp winter air is exactly what I needed. Unlike Jackson, with its steep, rocky terrain, Aspen Valley has long flowing groomed runs or *groomers*. They're perfect to just free my mind, focus on the scenery around me, and ski at a relaxing, leisurely pace.

Sure, there is some more difficult terrain and we'll hit that eventually. But it's the first day out and Veronica and Collin have only skied here once before when they were visiting the Chapman family. So this time, it's my turn to be their tour guide on the mountain. And we're lucky to have nearly perfect, late February weather. Cool, crisp mountain air, blue skies, and hardly any wind. A perfect bluebird day.

Well, almost perfect until Tanner spots something I dread.

"Is that the mogul course?" he asks from beside me on the chair-lift, pointing at the slope below us.

I look down at the steep, pitch, noticing the large mounds of snow covering every inch of the black diamond ski run. I'm a good, competent skier, but even I don't enjoy skiing over or through the large bumps that put your body through hell.

"Yes, it is. It was actually the Olympic course when they were here in Utah." I still remember watching the event on TV with my dad, stunned that skiers could go that fast and that precise through the large bumps and still keep their balance.

He looks back down with eager excitement. "Can we ski it?"

"We?" I let out a laugh. "I'm not taking any part in that, but you can."

AFTER A FEW MORNING runs and avoiding the mogul course, we make our way towards the Jordanelle Express Gondola. I normally never come over here, avoiding this area because one, I hate gondolas and two, this side of the mountain doesn't have my favorite terrain to ski.

When we reach the line and wait for our turn to load onto the gondola cars, Veronica leads the way when Tanner steps in front of me, putting himself between Grace, Collin, and me.

"What gives, Chap?" I lower my eyes and glare at him. Not that he could see it through my ski goggles, but still. I want to make the point.

He leans down towards me while V talks with the liftie behind him. "Can you pretend you still don't know how to get on a gondola?"

I'd cross my arms and huff at him, but I'm holding my skis and poles so all I can do is continue to glare. "Pretend? I literally still hate getting on gondolas. I don't even know why you wanted to come this way."

He looks at me, but he raises his eyebrows and tilts his head back towards his girlfriend. "I want to ride up *alone* with her."

"Oh no. I'm not aiding in your cheeky sexcapades this time." I say quietly, remembering the outcome of their solo gondola ride back in Jackson that set their entire relationship in motion.

He raises his eyebrows again with an urgent, pleading look in his eyes. "No, it's not *that*." Tanner reaches into his pocket and pulls out a velvet box just far enough for us to see it.

I gasp and cover my mouth. "Oh. My. God. Say no more. I'm on it."

I look up just in time to see Collin grab Tanner's shoulder and bring him in for a hug. Meanwhile, Grace looks like she's about to squeal and is doing everything in her power to hold it in.

When Tanner and Veronica get into the gondola, I drop my skis on the ground right in front of the liftie before he can grab them to load them into the rack. That buys us just enough time to miss the gondola car, forcing us to take the next one.

Mission accomplished.

I watch as Veronica stares back, shaking her head as their gondola car goes up the mountain. I grin, raising my goggles to my forehead, waving and winking at her.

"Smooth." I hear Collin behind me, patting me on the back.

I shrug my shoulders and laugh. "What? I'm terrible at this. I seriously don't have to pretend."

After the three of us step onto the next gondola car, Collin sits next to me and Grace sits on the bench across from us. Thankfully it's just the three of us and we can chat without random strangers in the car with us. She takes her helmet off, pulling her earbuds out. I look at her and yet another, no surprise, set of stunning Chapman family eyes.

"What are you listening to?" Collin asks, pulling a protein bar from his pocket and taking a bite.

"I'll give you one guess." She smirks at Collin.

"Oh my god. You're as bad as my sister. You're like eight years younger than us. How did you even start listening to Teal Tigers?" Collin shakes his head before taking another bite of his bar.

Teal Tigers is the band that Veronica has been obsessed with since high school. Even in our apartment in college she had their poster up. I'm pretty sure even with Tanner in her life, she still has a crush on the lead singer, Tommy Jacob. On our Jackson trip, we got to use his hot tub because Tanner manages and takes care of his ski property there. I swear she hasn't stopped talking about how cool his house and kitchen were since then.

She shrugs. "It's not my fault your sister and I have excellent taste in music. I just wish they still made new music. It's been years since they released an album."

After a minute of quietly enjoying the view from the gondola, I feel Grace's eyes drifting back and forth between Collin and me.

"Ok. I feel like I'm missing something here. What do you guys know that I don't?" She grabs her helmet and goggles and wipes them clean before looking back at us. "And what was with the sexcapades joke? And they're getting engaged? Holy shit! This is amazing! I always wanted a sister after growing up with those two ogres."

I look at Collin. "You want to tell her or-?" I tilt my palms up in a questioning gesture.

"Oh no no no." He shakes his head at me. "That's all you, girl."

"Fine." I look over at Grace. "The last time those two were alone on a ski trip in a gondola..." I pause, pressing a finger to my lips and humming. "Let's just say Tanner got on his knees for a *different* reason."

She closes her eyes and shudders, prompting a chuckle from Collin.

"Ok. That's sort of romantic in my brother's own fucked up way. But, Lizzy, for the sake of our new and hopefully very long friendship, please don't say anything else." She looks up, with a contented and stunned look on her face. "I still can't believe he finally did it. He's been such a mopey bitch for years. We always wondered when he'd grow a pair."

I grin at her sitting across from me in the gondola. "I like you. You're spunky."

Collin groans and leans his head back against the gondola window. "Oh my god. I should have realized you two were gonna hit it off."

I pat Collin on the knee. "Don't worry, co-bestie. You're not getting replaced already."

I hear the whirring of the gondola car passing the upper tower.

I gather my gloves and pull my goggles back down over my face. "Ready? Time to celebrate with the newly engaged couple."

CHAPTER 4

CLAY
PRISSY LITTLE BLONDE

"SERIOUSLY MAN, CONGRATULATIONS." I raise my beer and reach across the hot tub to tap it against my older brother's. "It's about time." I'm wearing an ear to ear grin that doesn't feel forced for a change. Tanner deserves to be happy and I'm glad it's with the girl, the woman, he's been in love with almost his whole life.

"Thanks," he says, smiling back at me.

When my brother called me and confirmed he was coming to town with his girlfriend, he invited me to hang out because he had something we'd need to celebrate. My brother isn't one for sharing feelings, so if he asked I knew it was important. But I was not expecting it to be *his engagement*.

"So are you ever going to find a nice girl and let her tie you down?"

I nearly spit out my beer laughing. "Ok, bro. Very funny. You know I'm not *the get all emotional and attached type*. But I'd let one tie me up," I add with a wink.

Sure. It would be amazing to have someone in my life. But that sounds like opening myself up to a level of hurt, of vulnerability that scares the living shit out of me. "For real though, I can't believe you finally did it. You've only been in love with her since..." I put my fingers to my lips, pausing for emphasis. "Oh, I don't know. Since before I could even walk?"

He snorts and punches me in the shoulder. I look over at Collin, sitting across the hot tub from me and next to Tanner. He's just palming his face and shaking his head. I haven't seen him in ages either. He's always been like an older brother to me because of the time Tanner and him spent together. With all the holiday breaks and summers that the Perry twins would spend at their grandparents' condo in Wyoming when we were growing up, it felt like they were always around.

"And you." I point at him. "How on earth did you not see this for *decades?*"

Collin shrugs his shoulders, humming an *I don't know* under his breath. "I guess I was just oblivious. Chap's never really been one to pour his feelings out."

I take a sip of my beer and let out a huff of laughter. "Speaking of your *fiancée* though, where are the girls?"

Collin reaches out of the tub, grabbing a couple more beers from the mound of snow he was using as a makeshift cooler. "Oh, they're upstairs getting some snacks and probably cracking a second bottle of Champagne. They've been non-stop giddy today since Chap popped the question."

"Yeah, I bet. So it's Grace, V, and her friend whose condo you're all staying at?" I ask, noting that there are only three open spots left in the hot tub.

"Yep. Should be a chill night." Tanner turns to face Collin, grabbing his fresh beer.

Looking around the hot tub on the snow covered patio outside the Aspen Grove Club, I can't help but relax a bit watching the steam rise off the rippling water. The hot tub is doing wonders for my sore body after working all day. It feels good to be with my brother, seeing him so happy. He lives almost five hours away and I don't get to see him enough since we're both busy with work. I take a deep breath, relaxing back into the jets and it's almost enough to shake the thought of my mystery girl from last night.

She isn't the distraction I need right now in my life.

I have two job sites to manage. I've got condo renovations and expansions in the exact condo complex I'm at right now and then the project over at the Grand Lodge. Thankfully, that is wrapping up soon, but this one here is demanding. And ever since I got promoted, it feels like I have even more pressure on me. This is why I don't obsess over random girls I'll never see again. Tourists like her come and go. And I don't do girlfriends. I don't get attached.

Normally that's perfect because it never ends well for me when I get attached to anyone, to anything. But how is that prissy little blonde already under my skin so much? We talked for maybe five minutes and we made out. Somehow though, I haven't been able to stop thinking about her. Her smell. The taste of bourbon on those red lips.

I'm pulled from my thoughts by a pair of familiar laughs. I look over to the patio door, seeing Grace and V come out in fluffy white robes with plastic wine glasses of Champagne in hand.

"Hey ladies!" I shout. "You two finally ready to be real sisters?"

Grace is almost six feet tall and V isn't far behind. They even have the same long, brown hair, minus Grace's streaks of purple, pink, and orange. She's always felt like family. It's going to be awesome having her around more, especially if it means my brother isn't moping around like a lovesick puppy and she makes him visit more often.

"You came!" V's eyes go wide and she grins. It's been a long time since I've seen her, just like Collin.

She steps towards me, away from Grace. And that's when I make out the golden blonde pony tail of the shorter girl behind them. When V gets further from Grace and I can see all of her, my lungs stop functioning and I can feel my heart pound into my rib cage.

Fuck.

Her big, blue eyes meet mine and I freeze.

This must be Lizzy. My future sister-in-law's best friend.

And my mystery girl.

EVERYONE'S HUGGING and joking and bullshiting. But I can't focus. I can't hear what they're even saying. I'm pretty sure my brain has short circuited. The girl I've been obsessing over for the last twenty-four hours is here, in the hot tub with me, in an absurdly tiny pink bikini. I knew she was a smokeshow last night, but fuck, this is too much.

My mind is a tangled mess. She ran out of the bar, looking like a deer caught in the headlights. After obsessively playing last night out in my head all day, I remembered it was after I tucked her hair back that she froze. I realize now she must have seen the tattoo on my wrist. So I take it she's seen that tattoo before, a pretty specific one. We all have it: Tanner, Collin, and now I realize V has it with that bikini. It was our badge of honor, a little inside joke, after skiing Corbett's at Jackson Hole.

So she recognized me and freaked out?

But she didn't even try to talk to me. She just ran and left me feeling like an asshole. And now, she's sitting across from me looking anywhere but at me. Like I don't even exist.

So I didn't do anything wrong after all. But also, this is *definitely* not what I need. She's Veronica's best friend. This can't happen.

Two can play this game I guess. I'm just going to pretend she doesn't exist either. I need to keep distance between us.

CHAPTER 5
LIZZY
JAGGED LINES

I KNEW this was eventually going to happen. I was going to have to see *him*. And now he's going to be my best friend's brother-in-law. Of course, my *Tour de Lizzy* would come back and bite me.

But that doesn't make it any easier, especially when he's shirtless on the other side of the hot tub from me. I knew he was fit at the bar, but holy shit, this is just unfair. Clay has boulder shoulders and pecs covered in a thin smattering of dark chest hair that would make a Hemsworth brother jealous. The tattoos I saw on his neck continue down his shoulders in an intricate, flowing mix of roses and vines. There's a growling bear's head on one side of his chest, mirrored by a snarling wolf's head on the other. He is a piece of art, and not just the tattoos.

That's not why it's so hard though. He clearly remembers me. And it's painful. He's barely said a word since I walked out with Grace and Veronica and just quietly nursed his beer while either wearing a muted scowl or just staring out towards the ski slopes.

And I'm not the only one to notice.

"Who pissed in your beer?" Tanner leans across the hot tub, shoving his brother. "Come on, let loose a little. You don't have to have a stick up your ass all the time."

Clay shakes his head and looks back at everyone in the hot tub, his glare briefly lingering on me, clearly shaking himself out of some kind of trance. Or maybe he's just pissed at me? His expression is so cold, borderline indifferent.

"Sorry." Clay mutters before taking another sip of his beer. "Been a long day."

He looks at Tanner and then Veronica and for the tiniest moment, I can see one side of his lips quirk up and his jaw relax. I can almost make out one of his dimples popping through his five o'clock shadow, giving me a glimpse of the playful man I saw last night. He takes a deep breath and his broad chest fills out. "I'm happy for you guys. V, glad you're *officially* joining the Chapman family." He tilts his head over towards Grace. "Maybe you can keep this feral granola girl in check."

Grace huffs and glares back at Clay, then gives him the middle finger.

"Thanks. But that sounds like a challenge. We know she's the free spirit of your family." Veronica's been sitting in Tanner's lap, wrapped in his arms all night. She's glowing and I can't blame her. Who doesn't want a hunky 6'4" tattooed mountain man that's completely obsessed with you for a fiancé? I mean, sign me up. She smirks back at Clay.

"And I hope you're ready to get close with Lizzy."

Our gazes snap to each other and Clay has an equally startled expression.

"Um. What?" I give her a puzzled look, holding my glass out and tipped towards her, asking for a refill.

Tanner wraps her in his arms tighter, planting a kiss on her neck before looking Clay then me. "Yeah. We obviously want you two as our best man and maid of honor."

Shit. Shit. Double shit. *Tour de Lizzy* is definitely biting me in the ass now.

I put on my best cheery smile, even though I'm terrified about the idea of having to be next to this man for all the wedding stuff. I can probably manage small doses of Clay - that would spare me from my embarrassment. But spending lots of time together? When he clearly is less than thrilled to see me based on his scowls and glares? That might be hard.

"Of course! You know I'm your girl." I clink my fresh glass of champagne against hers.

I look at Clay, whose face looks like he's forcing it into some kind of contorted, painful smile. Is he serious? That face better not be about me. I am not that bad. I can be a bit much, sure. And I did run off last night without any explanation. But he won't have to spend that much time with me. I'm sure V will make all the plans and itineraries and we'll barely have to work together. We'll just have to show up and smile.

"Just let me know what you need. But hey, I'm going to call it a night. Have to be at the job site at seven tomorrow morning."

I watch as he stands up, the water beading off his abs with the faint trail of hair running to his waistline. You have to be kidding. I didn't even know you could have that many abs. And the way they taper into that V right where his trunks hang off his hips. It takes every ounce of self control to not bite my lower lip and moan thinking about touching him again.

He's built like a young David Beckham. But not the weird, blonde one. No, more like if you took tattooed, fit, mature Daddy Beckham, and just made him twenty-eight years old.

And...

And yeah. I have to tear my eyes away from the way his swimsuit clings to him. I'm starting to see why he was that cocky last night.

I'm about to begrudgingly look away when he stands completely up. There are tattoos on both of his defined thighs peeking out of his mid-thigh shorts, but it's his knees I can't look away from. Each knee has a brutal looking scar. The jagged line on his right knee stretches from the top to the bottom and his left knee has a similar, but smaller scar. A small part of me winces at the thought of what caused those.

He gets out of the hot tub and walks towards the door. I'm glad he's walking away otherwise he'd probably smirk knowing how I'm staring at his muscular back and ass. This guy should seriously take up underwear modeling or something.

I don't know why, but against my better judgement I find myself calling out to him. "Do you know your way out? I can show you." The rest of the group is busy talking and aren't paying attention. Maybe I want a moment alone with him to talk about last night or to apologize for running off. Maybe I want to make sure we can be cool with the whole wedding thing. Either way, I feel like we need to talk.

He looks back at me, standing by the door of the patio with a towel wrapped around his shoulders. He flashes that same sinful grin he gave me last night at the bar, this time without a hint of the playfulness underneath it.

"Thanks, princess. I'm good," he says before smirking at me. "I know the way out."

The way he says it is almost a taunt, like he's baiting me to ask so he can deliver the punchline to an inside joke. And against my better judgment, I give in.

"Oh, so you've been here before?" I lean over the side of the hot tub, folding my arms and resting my chin on them, waiting for his answer.

He lets out a low laugh. "Yeah. I work in construction. I'm the first one at the job site every morning."

Holy. Shit. Clay is the ape that's been stomping around the floor above me. Not only did I not sleep at all last night because I was thinking about him, but he is literally waking me up in the morning. "Oh. So that was you loudly banging around up there this morning? Can you like, tone it down a notch? I'm trying to sleep in the unit under you."

He shrugs. "It's a construction site. Kinda hard to be quiet. If I'm too loud, you could just *run off* though." He looks back at the rest of the group before turning to open the door and disappears inside.

CHAPTER 6
LIZZY
NEW BEGINNINGS

SPAS WERE NEVER MY THING. That was always Meredith Frank's thing to do while I'd be out skiing growing up. But I'm almost thirty-five years old and I understand it now. After a few days of skiing, everything hurts. Like literally everything. Even muscles I didn't know I had.

I really need to get back to yoga or something if I want to keep skiing. V and I used to do boot camp and yoga classes together, but I haven't been great about keeping up with it after she moved out to Wyoming. I need someone that could stay on top of me to be disciplined about it. An accountability buddy or personal trainer would be great.

The massages this morning were amazing, but these pedicures are otherworldly after wearing ski boots the last few days. And there's even a mimosa cart, which I will *never* complain about. Plus the snowy views from the second floor spa on Main Street only make it that much more relaxing and cozy.

I'm glad I'm here with Veronica and Grace today. The last few days on the mountain and out in Park City have been just what I needed. Having friends out on the mountain has been a welcome change, unlike skiing solo or with ski school when I was a kid. I never get to play tour guide, so it's been surprisingly fun showing Tanner, Collin, and Veronica around the mountain. Grace knows it well enough, having lived here since she was in high school.

"Seriously, V," Grace says with a laugh, sitting back in the massage chair on the other side of Veronica while I enjoy watching the tourists walking around on the snow lined street below us. "I don't know how you never knew he was in love with you. I swear Clay and I were taking bets on if he'd ever man up." She takes a sip of her mimosa before turning back to V.

I watch my best friend, admiring her reaction. She turns a bit pink, but she hasn't stopped beaming this entire trip. I just can't get over how happy Veronica is. If anyone deserves it, it's her.

I remember it wasn't that long ago that I thought I had my shit together. I thought I was in love with Johnathan. We were living together, making plans for the future. A house, maybe a family. I don't know why I wasn't enough for that cheating asshole.

"I'm just happy we're together now." She air tips her mimosa at mine and then Grace's. "Even work has been great too." She sets her glass down for a second, pulling out her phone.

"Please tell me your new boss isn't messaging you on another vacation." I look at her, remembering how shitty her last boss, Jeff, was.

She laughs and shakes her head while scrolling on her phone. "Actually no, quite the opposite. Cindy is literally the best. Like Jessica level amazing. That's what I wanted to bring up. What are you ladies doing the first week of May?"

Grace shrugs. "Nothing I can't cancel or rearrange."

"Same. Why, what's up?" I ask, leaning out of my chair to top off my drink.

"I have to go to the Earth SnaX headquarters for a couple days. Meet with my new team again, get some face time with Cindy, and meet a couple vendors. But Tanner and I were going to make a week of it, rent an Airbnb or something, and get some spring skiing in at Mount Bachelor since Jackson will be closed for the season by then."

She looks back and forth between Grace and me grinning. "Would you want to stay with us? We should have extra room."

"Sounds perfect. I'm in." I pull my phone out, immediately marking my calendar.

"V, you have no idea. I've literally been looking for excuses to get out of my apartment and the office. After everything with Johnathan and then you not being at the office, everything at home is a drag. Even if working for Jessica is awesome." I sigh, sinking back into my comfy chair. Lately, I've dreaded being alone at my apartment. It just reminds me of my ex. I know I could move, but my lease isn't up yet and it just feels like a lot to handle.

So this trip could be another good thing to look forward to that might help me get out of the rut that I've been in. Things are looking up.

I relax into my chair and start thinking about a ski trip with my friends. I think about what I've learned about Grace. The first being that she's cool as shit. Not that I need another ride or die with Veronica and Collin as friends, but I could see her joining that club. The second, is that she is anything but *Grace*. This girl is intense. She is energetic and talkative, always wanting to be on the move. She doesn't take shit from her brothers or Collin from what I've seen. But just like her brothers, she also seems so calm and steady.

And the more I relax, the more Clay starts to drift back into my mind. The thought of that massage earlier and what it would have felt like if those were his rough, strong hands.

"Really, Grace, your brothers are *a lot*," I find myself saying. What the hell is wrong with me? Why did I bring that up. I'm trying *not* to think about Clay. Clearly my subconscious hates me today. I try to think of the best, least awkward thing to say. "It had to be insane growing up with them."

She laughs and it is infectious as ever. Veronica just shakes her head.

"Girl, you have no idea." Grace looks at me before palming her face. "Always trying to keep up with them on the mountain. You get a thick skin real fast around those two. And don't even ask about dating. Boys were terrified of dating me because of them."

"Oh my god. They were terrified of you too." Veronica almost shouts, sitting up in her chair, startling the nail tech. "I still remember when I heard that you punched that one boy in high school because he made fun of the tie-dye shirt you made."

"Holy shit," I blurt out. "You really are a badass. And maybe even a little terrifying."

She looks down at her hands in her lap, going quiet for a second like she's deep in thought. "Yeah. I've been told that. But it wasn't Tanner and Clay that taught me that. It was our mom. She always wanted us to be happy and free spirited."

I sip my drink, not really knowing what to say. I remember that their mom was killed in a car accident while Grace and Clay were still in high school after they moved from Wyoming. That had to be so hard. My mom and I aren't super close, but I still couldn't imagine losing her at that age.

"Why am I not surprised? Lilly was amazing. I definitely can see where Tanner gets the free spirited side from," Veronica says with a muted chuckle.

"Yeah she was." Grace smiles warmly back at her. "If she could see you and Tanner finally together, she'd be so happy for you two. Seriously. So happy for you guys."

V raises her glass and we bring ours to meet hers. "To family and new beginnings."

New beginnings. Now that is something I can relate to.

"Cheers," we say in unison.

CHAPTER 7
CLAY
IMPECCABLE TIMING

"YOU'RE A HUNGRY BOY TONIGHT." I watch while Ani scarfs down his food. On one hand, it's probably terrible that he always eats like this. I should really look into one of those slow feeder bowls for him. It cannot be healthy to eat that fast. On the other hand, I need to get going if I'm going to be ready when my Uber gets here so I can meet Collin and Tanner at Wasatch Whiskey Distillery.

He would have to pry the words out of me, but I do love my brother. And Collin, well, he is basically a brother too. I know I should be glad they're in town, but I'm beat. Work's been hell. I only like to be two places when I'm not working: at home or at Roxy's for a beer. At least it's just going to be the three of us. Tanner said the girls were doing something at the spa. Still, I could just pour a whiskey at home, sit in my office, and crack open a book. That would be an awesome night in and I'd enjoy every second of it.

If I bundled up enough, I could even hang on the deck and just enjoy the view of the mountains by the fire pit. I loved that idea *so much* in fact that I tried to get them to come over here instead, but no. They wanted to go out on the town so I'm being the good little brother and tagging along with them. Namely because if I didn't go,

I'd never hear the end of how I'm being a grumpy, antisocial asshole from my brother and sister.

Sometimes I wish I could just lay it all out there. I don't enjoy being this way, but I don't do well around people. It's not that I don't want to be around people, especially the ones close to me. But outside of my *very* small circle of friends and family, people suck. They drive me nuts. They let you down and hurt you. Or worse, you let them down. And I don't need more of that in my life than I've already been through.

IF I WAS GOING to be dragged out of my house against my will tonight, I guess Wasatch Whiskey isn't the worst place. It's a local distillery with a tasting room and restaurant right off Main Street. The outside blends in perfectly with the old mining town façades of Park City and they do make pretty solid bourbon and rye.

Walking in, I immediately spot Collin and my brother at the corner of the bar.

"Hey, what's up, asshole?" Tanner calls to me with a raised hand already holding a glass of whiskey.

"Seriously, Tanner. You know, when I greet people like that, it's just normal, *me being me.*" I sit down at the stool next to him, but not after punching him in the shoulder probably harder than I should have. "But when *you* do it, it just sounds like you hate me."

That gets a laugh out of Collin. "Okay, *boys,*" he says in a mocking tone. "If I knew you were going to come in hot like this, I'd have gone to the spa with the girls."

I cock my head to the side, casting Collin a sidelong glare.

Tanner wraps an arm around, trying to pull me into a hug from our bar stools. "Come on. Lighten up." He takes a sip of his drink before ruffling my perfect hair, only deepening my scowl. "So, you ready to be my best man? That's a lot of responsibility, *little bro.*"

"Remind me how I got chosen for this again? And you know I

practically run a construction company, right?" I glare at both of them. "How come you didn't pick him?" I tip my head to Collin.

Tanner turns and smirks at Collin, who's already grinning ear to ear. It's always been like this with them. Given how much time he's been around our family since before I was even born, it was like I had two big brothers every time the Perry twins visited their grandparents. "I have plenty of other duties. Perks of being the bisexual brother of the bride and best friend of the groom. I get to do bride *and* groom shit."

I groan in exasperation and mutter to myself under my breath before placing my order.

After a couple minutes of catching up with them, the bartender comes by, bringing my twelve year old bourbon, served neat - my normal drink here. I'm going to need it to deal with these two tonight.

I grab the crystal rocks glass and notice a table of girls across the bar. They're all dressed in fancy shit like fur lined jackets and silly boots. They'd probably slip and fall in them the first time they step on the ice outside. Their table is covered in girly cocktails. I know the type. The obnoxious tourists that come in thinking it's cute to have a wild night and make some waiters night a living hell with over the top, particular orders. They remind me of Lizzy.

I roll my eyes and take a swig of my bourbon. The second it hits my lips, it immediately brings back the memory of that kiss that's been haunting me.

Ok. Maybe Lizzy is a little different than *those* girls. At least she can throw back some bourbon.

AFTER BULLSHITTING with Tanner and Collin over another round, I feel my phone buzz. I check it and smile seeing that it's Kayleigh.

> Kayleigh: Hey. What are you doing later?
> Can I come over?

Perfect. I needed an excuse to get out of here and Kayleigh is exactly who I need to see tonight. I need to vent and I'd much rather hang out with her at my place.

> Me: You have impeccable timing as always.

> Kayleigh: Let me guess. You were just going to ask me to save you from being social. Is Lizzy there?

I shake my head and laugh. God I love that she knows me. She's been my best friend for years for a reason.

> Me: Yes. And no, she's not here. I'll be home in half an hour. See you there.

I tuck my phone back into my pocket and pat my brother on the back. "As fun as this has been, I need to get home. I'll see you guys tomorrow for dinner. The Aspen Grove Club, right?"

"Yep. We're in unit 601." Tanner stands and gives me a bear hug before Collin fist bumps me.

I know 601 is the Frank unit, Lizzy's family's condo. Great. The last thing I want to do is be forced to spend more time with her. Unless...

"Hey. Would it be cool if Kayleigh came along tomorrow?" I ask, knowing Tanner and Collin both know her and the Jensens.

They look at each other and both shrug. "Sure, why not? Been forever since we've seen her. The more the merrier."

"She'll be excited to see everyone. See you tomorrow." I nod and grab my jacket before heading to the door.

This should be fun.

※

I'M LOOKING DOWN at my phone to check where my Uber is when a familiar voice gets my attention.

"Hello, Clay." I look up to see Mr. Jensen. My boss, the founder of JSC Construction, and also Kayleigh's dad. "What are you up to tonight?"

I've known Mr. Jensen since I was in high school. I still remember meeting him when I trained and skied with Kayleigh. He's practically been like a second father to me. He helped me at my lowest point. He hired me, and trained me to practically run part of his company over the last eight years. But he's also *very old school* and traditional and has given me a bit of an uneasy feeling that I can't place. Drinking is on his long list of things he does not approve of. So it would be just my luck that I run into him outside of a distillery waiting for my ride. Ever since he promoted me to be his lead project manager, it seems like he's been extra focused on everything I'm up to, both at work and outside.

"Oh. I was hanging out with Tanner and one of our friends that's in town." I offer a smile, but I really just want this conversation to end so I can get home to meet Kayleigh.

"That must be nice. I know you don't see them too often. You can never spend enough time with family. That's just so important." He looks at me with his usual casual, but always somewhat judgmental look I've become accustomed to over the years. "Calling it an early night though?"

"Yeah. I'm actually heading out to meet Kayleigh. Just waiting on my Uber." I look down at my phone again, seeing that my ride is about a minute away.

That answer gets an immediate smile and the judgmental look is gone. "Oh good. I'm glad you two are still spending time together. I still don't know how it never worked out between you two. You were such a great couple." He nods at me before he looks down at his watch. I'll always be grateful for how he took me under his wing, but this is one of those things about him that has always rubbed me the wrong way. I know he's wanted to take on a partner for the company so he can take a step back and eventually retire - and that day can't come soon enough.

He's always had this delusional dream that Kayleigh and I would end up being a thing, ever since we were teenagers on ski teams together. But we only *dated* for months, a silly high school thing, holding hands and watching movies with parental supervision. Neither of us want to tell him why it's never going to happen for a long list of reasons. She's my best friend though and nothing will ever change that.

"Well, don't let me keep you. Tell Kayleigh I said hello. I'll see you at the Aspen Grove Club next Thursday to get your update on that and the Grand Lodge project."

He pats me on the shoulder before continuing down the side-walk. It would be just my luck that I would run into him tonight.

CHAPTER 8
LIZZY
CLAYTON

THE LAST TWO days on the slopes with everyone have been perfect. Friday was a bluebird day with crystal clear skies. Then a storm rolled in Friday night and we got to ski fresh powder Saturday morning.

Watching Tanner and V ski after each other like lovesick puppies has been adorable, if not nauseatingly cute. Grace is a wild child, dropping off into trees and popping back on the slopes out of nowhere. And I can't get enough of catching up with Collin and talking about his dates with the hot cowboy, Walker.

We've had dinner out on the town the last two days, but it's Sunday night now and President's Day is tomorrow. Tanner, V, and Collin are heading back to Jackson tomorrow night after we squeeze in another day of skiing. Then I'll fly home Tuesday afternoon. All good things eventually come to an end.

So to cap off the trip, I thought it would be nice to play host and do dinner at the condo. I say *host,* but only in the loosest of terms. I told V she has to cook because I'm terrible at it. Thanks again, Mother, for the lack of cooking lessons growing up. Whatever though, V loves to cook, and her food is incredible. She's obsessed with gourmet kitchens like the one in our renovated condo, and probably would have insisted on it anyways. So, this is really a win-win for everyone.

I've also managed to avoid seeing Clay the last two days. I know I sort of brought this on myself by panicking and running out of the bar.

I think I was embarrassed about the whole thing. I usually own it, so this is a new one for me.

On our last ski trip, Veronica caught Walker sneaking out of my room after her brother and I shared that cowboy for a night. That was one way to ring in the New Year and I didn't bat an eye about that.

Or maybe it's the idea of lusting after someone I'm so attracted to. Someone I can't easily walk away from, even without really knowing them was absolutely terrifying. We didn't even hook up and I can't stop thinking about him.

He was so damn cold that night out in the hot tub. I get it though - I'd be a bit annoyed at me too.

But now, the scowl that I'm met with from across the table is so harsh. I'm sitting face to face with him at the end of the dinner table. No more hiding from him or the way his intense stare makes me feel. Another thing that's coming to an end I guess.

Oh. And he brought a date. Tanner asked if Clay could bring a family friend to dinner. But when he showed up with a date, that wasn't something I was expecting. Apparently she's also friends with Tanner and Grace, and Tanner hasn't seen her in a long time. So they've all been excited to catch up.

But there's something familiar about her, like I've seen her before. Maybe it's her smile? The way her perfect white teeth stand out against her red lipstick, and long, wavy black hair. I swear I've seen her before.

And why am I fixated on her? I should be glad someone is getting Clay's glowering eyes off of me. I really didn't think much of it when Tanner asked, but now I'm unusually curious about her.

But I'm also tormented by the idea that he could be just like my ex. Some dirtbag looking to cheat with someone from out of town.

Was I almost the *other woman* for him that night?

My blood almost boils thinking about that possibility. I take a deep breath, remembering that from everything I know about the Chapmans they are insanely loyal people. But it still doesn't sit right with me.

I look down the table at Tanner, V, and Collin. "What time do you guys need to hit the road tomorrow?" I tilt my head, squinting with one eye in thought. "It's like a five hour drive back to Jackson, right?"

Tanner sets his beer down and wraps his arm around Veronica, who rests her head on his shoulder with an impossibly sweet smile, almost as if it was a natural reflex to his touch. "Yeah. About five hours. There might be more snow coming in tomorrow night, so ideally we should hit the road a little after lunch."

I take a sip of my wine, nodding. "Great. Then we should still be able to get in a full morning of skiing."

"You guys lucked out on conditions this week." I look back at Kayleigh, almost startled by her. She's been mostly quiet, sharing little whispers and giggles with Clay after catching up with Tanner earlier on. "I'll be out on the slopes tomorrow training."

"Training?" I ask, leaning forward on my elbows. "Do you work at the mountain or something?"

Clay snorts a laugh and brings his fist to his mouth trying to hide it. "You could say that."

"Clayton Michael Chapman!" Kayleigh chides him playfully, slapping his hands, bringing my attention to them. I can finally make out the letters on his other hand. Together, his knuckles spell out OVERCOME.

Maybe it has something to do about their mom? Veronica told me how hard it was on Tanner. I can only imagine it was hard on all of them. Clay and Grace still lived with their parents here in Park City when it happened. I remember Tanner was out of school and living in Jackson Hole since he was the eldest.

Clay's head snaps up and his cheeks show the slightest hint of pink. For the first time, he looks his age, young and playful.

"Awww. Your name's Clayton?" I use my best baby talk voice and rest my head on my fists, making a pouty face. "That's so cute."

Immediately the playful look is gone and he's back to glaring at me. I swear I can hear his teeth grinding from here. "Clay. Not Clayton." He turns his glare to Kayleigh. Veronica said he could be a grumpy asshole and she wasn't kidding. This is something else. "She's called me that since high school because she thinks it's funny. And it's not."

High school? Ok. She really is an old family friend I guess. Still could be a girlfriend or something though.

"Be nice, *Clayton*." She runs a hand through his hair, ruffling it until he swats her away. "But yeah, he's not wrong. I guess you could say I work at the mountain."

I look around the table, realizing I'm missing something when I see Tanner and Grace grinning as well.

"The Jensens *work on* the mountain. Normally you'll find them on the racecourse," Grace says, huffing a laugh before turning to Kayleigh. "Your speciality is still giant slalom, right?"

Suddenly it clicks and I can feel my jaw drop. Giant Slalom? Jensen?

Kayleigh Jensen. That smile. I've seen it dozens of times on posters all over Aspen Valley resort. She's always wearing goggles in her promotional posters, but she's always flashing that signature smile. She's the middle Jensen kid - a two time Olympian, training to qualify for her third Olympics three years from now.

The Golden Jensen Family. They're all Team USA ski legends. Her grandfather was an Olympian. Her father was a multiple world champion professional before retiring. Then he got into real estate and development. And now the three kids are all Olympians. They're practically Park City royalty. I'm pretty sure my dad even has a vintage poster of some of them in the other room.

Veronica laughs. "You should be proud, Kayleigh. It's almost impossible to make Lizzy speechless and you did it the first time meeting her." That prompts another chorus of laughter from Collin and Tanner.

I lower my eyes at Veronica. "Very funny." And that's when I can just hear Clay mumble something to himself at the end of the table, almost inaudible. From the corner of my eye, I can see Kayleigh punch Clay in the leg, not so playfully this time.

"Seriously." Tanner's deep voice gets my attention. "Kayleigh's the best skier here. Hands down. It's not even close."

She rolls her eyes at him. "You're a pretty epic skier, Chap. You just don't like cameras or crowds."

He shrugs and smiles. "You're not wrong."

I notice Clay, looking out towards the windows at the lit ski slopes beyond.

"What's wrong, *Clayton*?" I tease. "Cat got your tongue? Aren't you a great skier too?"

He turns to me slowly, but doesn't say anything. His glares don't scare me though. He can be as much of an asshole as he wants, but I can play that game too. I don't back down. That's one lesson from Dad I took to heart.

I continue. "Why don't you come out with us tomorrow? Or are you scared the girls will show you up?" I say again, using my teasing baby talk voice.

And that's when I realize I've done *something*. Something bad. Something *very* bad.

"I don't need this shit. Fuck right off," Clay snarls before he practically jumps out of his chair. Kayleigh tries to grab his arm, but he shakes free and storms across the room. Before I can even try to say something, he slams the door behind him.

I look around the table, painfully aware that everyone is now staring at me with a mix of pained expressions ranging from *What's wrong with you* to *sorry we should have warned you.*

I bury my face in my hands and groan. "You guys mind telling me what the fuck that was? I was just joking. Clearly I don't know something that I should."

To my surprise, Kayleigh is the first one to speak up to defend her friend. "He *used* to ski." She looks at Tanner, almost pleading for him to explain.

"He was better than me. Probably would have been better than Kayleigh." His voice is nowhere near the, fun playful one I expect from him. Veronica, Collin, and Grace are eerily silent.

"*But...*" Kayleigh says, wincing and looking away, as if reliving a horrible memory, "he's had a brutal history of injuries."

My stomach sinks and I feel like I'm going to throw up. I remember the scars I saw on his knees the other night when he got out of the hot tub. Those horrible, jagged lines that look painful.

His knuckles.

Overcome.

Shit. I really fucking stepped in it.

"It's not your fault, Lizzy." Kayleigh's voice is soft when she looks at me. "I'll go talk to him."

And that's when I hear stomping around in the penthouse above us.

A small smile forms on my face and I look back at her. "I know exactly where he is."

"IT'S FINE. You can go talk to him." Kayleigh walks out of the penthouse construction site door.

"Thanks," I say quietly, walking past her into the penthouse that's stripped down to the studs. Even in the winter with below freezing temperatures outside, it's still warm. They must be using some kind of job site heaters. I walk through the sprawling condo and see Clay, standing in the corner by the French doors leading out onto the wraparound balcony that overlooks the ski resort. The only lights out on the mountain are from the snowcats out grooming the slopes for tomorrow. He sees me before turning back to looking outside.

"So you finally want to talk to me now? Color me surprised." His voice is low, with that same sense of playful irritation when he accused me of taking his seat at the bar.

"Clay, I'm sorry. I didn't -" He turns and faces me, catching me off guard. He looks at me with such intensity I can't even finish my sentence. What the hell is wrong with me tonight? I've been speechless twice in the last hour. That's a first.

"Do *not* apologize to me. I don't want your pity." His jaw is clenched and I can see the muscles of his tattooed neck straining.

"I didn't know about your injuries. I would have never said that if I had." I inch closer to him, not knowing what I'm doing. I want to apologize. I was out of line. I *should* apologize. But he's also so damn prickly, like a wounded animal. I don't want to scare him off, even though the last time we were this close, I was the one that ran.

He looks at me curiously before letting out a short, low laugh. "Maybe if you had stuck around at the bar and told me you recognized me instead of running off, we could have talked and actually gotten to know each other. It's not like I bite." He pauses and looks down at his hands, before looking back at me, grinning with a playful wink. "Unless you're into that, princess."

My breath hitches just a teeny bit, seeing and hearing that cocky attitude return. The one that I was into before and still would be if he wasn't such an asshole or about to be my best friend's brother-in-law. I groan and roll my eyes, pretending to be unfazed by him. "Ah, there he is. I was wondering where cocky ass Clay Chapman was. This storm cloud, emo version of you is pretty lame." He turns away, letting out another low huff of a laugh and looking back outside. I step up next to him, looking out the other French door to watch the groomers running up and down the slopes.

"Good. Now that you're laughing..." He turns to face me with an amused, curious look on his face, shaking his head. And that's when I punch him in the shoulder, which only knocks me back. I huff in frustration before getting what's been on my mind all night off my chest. "So, who is Kayleigh?"

His brows furrow and the questioning look on his face intensifies. "What do you mean?"

"I mean, is she your girlfriend? Are you two dating? Were you trying to cheat on her with me? I would love to know *now* if you're a douche like my cheating ex." The words spew out of me. I'm finally releasing some of my pent up anger over Johnathan, and directing it all at him.

The confused expression there seconds ago morphs into something dark. I watch his jaw tense and I swear I can hear his molars grind. The anger in his eyes is nearly palpable. "She is my best friend. My oldest friend." He grabs the railing of the balcony and his tattooed knuckles are nearly white from clenching it so hard. He looks away from me when he growls, "I'm not some piece of shit. Are we done here?"

The immediate shift in emotion and the intensity of his reaction catch me off guard. It's like he's physically pained by what I said.

"Ok. Good." That's the only response I can get out, thrown off that I clearly triggered him again. "Hey. I'm sorry about what I said at dinner. I don't care if you don't want my apology. Can we please start with a clean slate and just be friends?"

I turn to face him. He's still staring outside and I try to follow his line of sight, but he's just staring at an empty spot on the mountain. It's hard to make out on the dimly lit mountain, but I know it's the mogul course. The look in his eyes is distant, like he's dwelling on an old memory. Silhouetted by the dark sky and few lights outside on the other condo buildings, the features of his face are so defined. From the square line of his jaw, to his full lips to the neck tattoos that look like shadows creeping up from the collar of his shirt.

"Start over?" His voice is gruff as he nods his head. "Yeah. We can start over. I can be civil, I guess. We're going to have to be if we're going to be in this wedding together."

A sigh of relief escapes me and I can feel my shoulders relax.

"But let me be very fucking clear, we aren't friends. Friends don't just waltz in and assume I'm a piece of shit." He glares at me and any hint of playfulness is gone. His eyes almost look dead, like a pale gray in this light. "We can start over as strangers, because that's what we are. Strangers that will do what we need to so we can get along for my brother and your best friend. That's it. Nothing more. That should be easy between now and the wedding. It's not like we have to see each other every day."

Well that's not what I expected. But he's right, we shouldn't have to see each other very much between now and the wedding.

AFTER AN UNEXPECTEDLY NICE night of sleep, courtesy of Clay's crew not working on the holiday, the morning on the slopes was pleasant with everyone. We even stopped by the race course and watched one of Kayleigh's practice runs. After saying goodbye to the Jackson Hole crew at lunch, I make my way back to the condo for the night to pack and enjoy a quiet evening alone. Just me, a bottle of wine, and the book I plan to read.

As I walk into the condo, I feel my phone buzz in my pocket. Pulling it out, I see it's my boss. Not what I expected on a holiday.

"Hey, Jessica. What's up, girl?" I'm lucky to have a relationship like this with my boss. I *really* love having a great female boss.

"Sorry to call on your trip. I assume you're having a good time?" I can hear her rummaging around and I'm pretty sure I even hear a toilet flush. We clearly have no boundaries between us.

"Yeah, it's been great. Honestly, I wish I was out here more. But looking forward to catching up with you. We need to talk about my next project."

"See? This is why you're my favorite, Lizzy. You make things so easy." I hear a door open and shut in the background.

"I know I'm pretty good at reading your mind, but you're going to need to elaborate a bit more," I say, taking off my jacket and setting my keys down on the kitchen island.

"Well, since you're having such a great time, how would you like to stay out there?" I stop, standing up straight in the kitchen.

"What do you mean? You better not be firing me!" I meant it to come out jokingly, but she is being a bit weird, even for her, and it might have come out a bit genuinely startled.

"No. I'm not firing you. You know they'd have to fire me with you. And not like *literally* stay there right now, I assume you need to come back and pack. But our plant in Salt Lake, it's only like half an hour from Park City. They've been struggling." I exhale the breath I was holding in, getting an idea of where she's going with this. "We've been looking at everything. Overhead costs, labor rates, optimal shift schedules, and scrap rates. We're going to do a deep dive project on their financials. Since your current project is wrapping up, I thought you might be interested."

I pause, thinking about it. Normally I'd want to think about something like this, but it just seems like perfect timing. I've been desperate to get away from my apartment at home. I already planned on moving out as soon as my lease was up this summer. But it would be nice to get away, even if just for a bit and feel like I'm moving on from that mess finally.

"*Hellooooo?* You still there, Lizzy?" Jessica's voice in my ear snaps me out of my head.

"I'll do it." I blurt out the words so fast, catching myself off guard. "Send me the details, but I'm in."

I can hear Jessica already clapping in the background. "That's great! I was hoping you'd say yes. It'll be a great opportunity and I know you'll kick ass. It's totally fine if you want to work remote the next week or two so you can pack, prep, whatever you need to do to be ready to get back out to Utah. They want you to kick off this project two weeks from now."

"Sounds good to me."

"Perfect. And we'll give you a stipend for a short term rental. But I know your family has a place out there, so if you just want to stay there, by all means, pocket that stipend or go out for extra happy hours and buy all the books you want. Whatever suits you best."

Now that I can get behind.

After getting off the phone with her, I look around the condo again. This place is free from memories of Johnathan. I love being out here. This could be the fresh start I need to move on.

CHAPTER 9

CLAY

"WHERE IS THAT DUMBASS PLUMBER?" I glare at Luke. He's the best guy on my crew, one of the few I actually trust to do things right besides myself. And he's also one of the few friends I have besides Kayleigh.

He lowers his head and lets out a muffled grunt before looking back at me, already knowing I'm in a mood. "He said he'd be here this morning. I'll call him."

"Yeah, you better fucking call him back. We need him here if we're going to stay on track." I take a deep breath and sigh. "I'm sorry, it's not your fault. I've just been-"

He laughs and cuts me off. "An even bigger asshole than normal? Yeah. Why do you think the guys have had me do all the talking with you?"

I lower my eyes at him. "Have I been that bad? Jesus fuck, dude."

He shakes his head and chuckles, patting me on the back. I hate not being in control and do everything in my power to make sure things go smooth. It's taken me years in this job to finally accept that some people are just flakes. That's not why I'm a particularly grumpy asshole today though. I've been on edge the last two weeks, ever since Lizzy stormed into and then right back out of my life in a matter of days. Thankfully, I've been getting closer to keeping her out of my thoughts and focus more on work, my usual distraction in life.

I look back at Luke, who already has his phone out, and pat him back on the shoulder. "Still, it's less than an hour 'til lunch, so there's not much morning left if he's going to show up. We need him here today to get the plumbing turned back on so we can have it leak tested and inspected before we blow in the insulation and move on with the job."

Thankfully, this job has gone smooth so far. Tomorrow is March first and we're getting closer to spring. Originally, I wasn't thrilled about gutting this place down to the studs and completely redoing it in the middle of winter. But so far, the temporary job site heaters have worked fine, we've had no major issues, and we're on track to start insulating and drywalling in a few weeks once all the major mechanicals are installed, tested, and inspected.

While Luke's on the phone with the plumber, I walk over towards the balcony where I stood that night with Lizzy. I can still remember the look in her sparkling blue eyes. Marco, Luke's main helper, and one of the other guys are already having lunch out on the balcony. But all I can think about is talking with Lizzy at the French doors. Part of me regrets being so harsh with her, lying to her, and if I'm being honest, lying to myself and telling her we could be *strangers*.

What the actual fuck is wrong with me?

I told myself that I needed to keep distance from her. I was only around her for three short nights, at the bar, in the hot tub, and at dinner that last night and I could already feel myself becoming fixated on her and vulnerable in a way I don't ever want to feel.

I look out at the slopes, trying to clear my head. Skiing used to do that for me. It used to be the safe place for me to drown everything around me out and just feel free. I lean against the railing and watch the Carpenter Express chairlift take skiers up over the main mogul course. I blew up at dinner when she teased me about not skiing, but looking at the mogul course still brings just a hint of joy even now. I watch one of the mogul skiers, likely out training for a competition, violently attack the course.

My head bobs watching them bounce cleanly through each mogul, left right, left right, left right, up until the jump in the middle of the course. That was always my favorite part. Simultaneously in control but spinning wildly in the air.

And then he bites it. His skis come off, and fly through the air when he tumbles into a yard sale.

I cringe and shudder, instinctively grabbing for my right knee, feeling that pain like it was yesterday. I feel my held breath escape when he finally stops tumbling, gets up on his knees, and taps his helmet signaling he's ok.

I watch the next two skiers take the course, relieved that they make it through uneventfully. I do miss *it*, that *free* feeling - the one Mom taught us to chase and enjoy.

I'm snapped out of my trip down memory lane by something truly fucking ridiculous six stories below me. Coming up the drive to the valet circle outside of the Aspen Grove Club is a shiny white Bronco. To top it off, it has pink fucking rims. This is exactly the kind of prissy little tourist that would have a place here. I yell back inside, "Luke, come check this shit out."

He walks over, leaning against the railing at my side. "Jesus, dude." He leans out over the railing and spits. "It never ends with these people."

I scoff, "At least they have 4x4 for the snow."

He chuckles while we both watch. The Bronco pulls into the covered valet entrance to the building. Seriously, who the fuck would drive that thing?

A short, smoking little blonde hops out of the driver seat, tossing her keys at the valet guy who has barely made it to the side of the Bronco.

And I get my answer.

Fuck. My. Life.

I know that ponytail anywhere. I don't even have to wait for her to turn to realize it's Lizzy.

I thought she went home two weeks ago. I was supposed to have a break from seeing her for months until the next wedding thing for Tanner and V.

I palm my face. At least she has 4x4 and good tires and is safe. I guess she drove here all the way from Ohio in that. I hear one of the guys on the job site let out a long low whistle and I have the sudden urge to punch one of my employees.

I look back outside and watch as she walks to the main entrance of the building. God, she's beautiful. The way her leggings are molded to her sculpted ass is unreal. I could watch her walk away from me for hours and never get tired of that sight.

I'm snapped back to reality when I hear a crash behind me and Marco yelling at someone on the other end of the penthouse. I turn and walk towards the source of the noise, already irritated that I'm going to have a new mess to clean up.

Seriously, I can't focus around this woman. Add this to the list of reasons I need to stay away from Lizzy Frank.

CHAPTER 10
LIZZY
THIS WAS A BAD IDEA

"JEEZ, GIRL. YOU LOOK ROUGH." Jessica scrunches her face and pulls back in mock disgust.

"Wow." I drag the word out and raise my eyebrows. "That's exactly what I want to hear from my boss on a Monday morning to start my week."

Jessica shrugs and fiddles with something on her desk. These weekly Monday morning video check ins have been nice. I've been back in Utah for two weeks and so far it's been smooth sailing in the office. I work a few days in the office, like today. Then I take advantage of Dad's nice office at the condo a couple days a week and work from there.

Life at the condo though? It's been *alright*. I've avoided running into Clay, the *stranger* working upstairs every day, but that doesn't mean he hasn't been a pain in my ass.

"Just telling it like it is, Lizzy." She leans on her desk, propping herself up on her fists, looking into the camera and waiting for my answer.

I roll my eyes and groan. As much as I like Jessica, I don't want to give her all the details about Clay. "It would be just my luck that the contractor working upstairs hates me and likes to stomp around every morning, waking me up."

She laughs and shakes her head. "I never thought I'd see the day that someone would get under your skin. It's been two weeks of early mornings and you haven't gone full Lizzy on them?"

I squint at her through the video chat, thinking about what she just said. Ignoring the fact that I know the loud, grumpy jerk upstairs, she's got a point.

"You know I'm right," she continues. "If this was a vendor or plant manager, you'd have already gone off on them and gotten them in line. Come on, work that Lizzy magic."

BY THE TIME I get back to the condo after the day in the office, I'm beat. After my call with Jessica, I had non-stop meetings with the plant management and accounting teams. Throw on getting stuck in traffic and all I want to do is get into bed to take a quick power nap to make up for my lack of sleep at night.

I change into a pair of sweats and an oversized t-shirt and hop into my bed. It feels like heaven after the long day. I really need to start getting to bed earlier so I can get a full eight hours of sleep. But somehow, a glass of wine and a good book just seems so much more appealing most nights.

My eyes are just fluttering shut for my power nap when I hear a loud bang on the ceiling above me, followed by shouting.

You've got to be kidding me. I try burying my head under the pillow, but the noise only continues. I hear Jessica's voice in the back of my head fueling my rage. She's right. I don't put up with this shit.

I grab the pillow and throw it across the room before hopping out of bed.

I slide on my slippers and head out of the condo towards the elevator.

This is bullshit and I'm going to give Clay a piece of my mind.

He's going to get a full dose of the bad bitch energy I bring at work every day.

Do I expect it to fix anything? Probably not.

Am I going to feel better for doing it? One thousand percent yes.

I ride the elevator up one floor, my arms crossed and my foot tapping, already looking forward to the confrontation. Who does he think he is?

When the elevator pings and the door opens, I stomp as dramatically as one can across the hall in fuzzy slippers and bang my fist against the door to the penthouse.

"Clay Chapman!" I shout. "Get your ass out here."

The sound of power tools come to a stop and I hear some mumbling followed by laughter. My blood is boiling now. They're really laughing about this? Or at me? The nerve of these assholes. I guess it makes sense if they are anything like Clay.

I hear the door unlatch and watch as the door opens.

Ok.

This was a bad idea.

CHAPTER 11
CLAY
OH THIS IS TOO GOOD

"HOW MUCH LONGER ARE YOU going to be here? I'll stay and make sure the place is cleaned up and closed tonight." I tip my head to Marco on the other side of the penthouse before taking a sip of my iced coffee. I probably shouldn't mainline these the way I do, but it's the only way I make it through the second half of the day. "He can't be too much longer right?"

Luke puts his hand on his hip, surveying the penthouse. "No, not too much longer. Probably half an hour or so?"

I nod, taking another sip when we're startled by loud banging at the door. I jump, spilling my coffee down my shirt.

"Son of a bitch." I set the coffee down and glare at Luke who's already wearing a shit eating grin and laughing at me.

"Would you go grab my bag? I have another shirt in there." I point across the penthouse foyer towards my gym bag in the corner and pull my shirt off.

"Clay Chapman!" We both jerk our heads towards the door when I hear her voice coming from the other side of it.

Oh, this is too good.

I walk to the door, running my fingers through my close cropped hair, already knowing who's waiting on the other side.

I swing it open with my best fuckboy grin. If she wants to start shit with me, I can play this game with her. I'm Tanner Chapman's little brother after all. I love to start shit. I was born for it.

Standing in front of me is all five foot three inches of blonde, pink fury. She looks pissed. Smoking hot as always, but fuming mad. She's wearing baggy sweats and oversized cropped t-shirt and I have to practically pry my eyes away because she's not wearing a bra. The way she's crossing her arms is just propping her tits up more, making me almost forget that I'm pissed as hell at her and she thinks I'm some kind of cheating prick.

I look away from her chest and clear my throat, smirking at her. "Can I help you with something?" I lean into the doorway, stretching my arm out to grip the doorframe over my head. "This is a job site and we're on a schedule."

She's still stone cold angry with me and her jaw is tight, but I don't miss the way her eyes quickly dart from my outstretched, flexed arm and all the way down to where my tool belt is hanging off my hips. Clearly she wasn't expecting me to be standing here shirtless when she barged in. Her eyes come back up and go wide when she see's that I caught her eyefucking me, again. I click my tongue in my cheek. "You can keep window shopping if you want."

She huffs out a breath. "I told you the other day, Clay. Can you *try* to be quiet on off hours? I get it that most of the building is only seasonally occupied by people on vacation and empty most of the time. But not my unit. Not for the foreseeable future. Some people actually live in this building and try to sleep occasionally." Her deep, sapphire blue eyes stare right back into mine, but there's zero playfulness there. Just cold, icy blue gems trying to cut through me. "You guys stomp around and make so much noise I swear my ceiling is going to cave in or one of you is going to come crashing through it."

Yep. She's definitely pissed.

"I remember what you said before." I wink at her. "And I told you, *princess*, it's a construction site. Kind of hard to be quiet." I keep grinning at her and clearly that was the *wrong* thing to do. Well, the right thing if I wanted to really get under skin.

She uncrosses her arms and steps toe to toe with me, digging her finger right into my sternum. Her face is now only inches from mine and I'm swimming in that coconut and citrus scent that's been haunting me for weeks.

"I don't care. I'd like to actually get a solid night of sleep or take a nap after work. Maybe you'll appreciate that when you're not a twenty-something-year-old fuck boy and you're in your mid-thirties. So can you just be a good boy and please do what I ask?" Her nostrils flare and I watch as her chest rises and falls. It takes all my will power not to stare down at her chest, put my hand on her hip, or lean into kiss her. *This* is the fiery little blonde I saw that night in the bar. The one that wasn't going to put up with my shit then, or right now apparently.

My self-preservation instincts kick in. I know when to pick my battles and this isn't one I'm going to win.

I clear my throat and put my hands up in front of me. "I'm sorry. I will *try* harder," I say softly. Her lips part like she's confused that I'm giving in. It really is killing me not to fist that ponytail and pull her in for a kiss. I've been dying to find out what that snarky little mouth tastes like when she hasn't been drinking bourbon.

I take a step back and she squints at me. "What? That's it? No witty comeback? You're just going to rollover and do what I want?"

"I can be a *good boy*, sometimes." I wink before shrugging and turning my palms up. "And I didn't make any promises. I just said I'd try."

She rolls her eyes, but finally lets out a long sigh and relaxes. "Thank you. Please *try* hard. I don't like to miss out on my beauty sleep."

"Why? You don't need it." I blurt the words out before I even realize it. Her lips part again and her cheeks go a shade of pink matching her t-shirt. I look down and wring my hands, trying to spare both of us the awkwardness of more eye contact.

After a moment, I lift my eyes but she's looking down at my hands. I trace her gaze to the tattoo on my wrist.

"It was this tattoo, wasn't it?" I ask, getting her attention.

Her voice is softer than I've heard it before and almost catches me off guard. "Yeah. I've seen Tanner's, Veronica's, and Collin's. Plus you have Tanner's eyes. What is it with you Chapmans and your freakishly perfect green eyes?"

I grin back at her and flick my eyebrows. "Perfect?" I point one finger at my eyes, running my hand back and forth. "You think my eyes are perfect?"

I swear her eyes roll into the back of her head as she sighs in exasperation.

"Alright. Fine. What time do you wake up?" She looks up, bobbing her head side to side like she's counting.

"If you're asking what time loud noises would be ok in the morning, how about after quarter till eight? I don't have to be in the office until nine, so that would be amazing." She looks almost relieved at the idea.

"Alright, I'll see what I can do."

"Whatever, Clay. Just *try* to keep it down. I don't have the energy for this tonight." She laughs, but with no real enthusiasm. I take her in again, she does look tired and worn out.

WALKING INTO FINCH, I always feel out of place until I talk to the staff. The woman owned coffee shop and independent bookseller just off Main Street is a welcoming store. Still, I'm pretty sure grumpy tattooed contractors aren't their main clientele. But they have the books I like, they have good coffee, and it's on my main route between Kimball Junction and Aspen Valley, where most of the job sites I work are at.

After walking the rows of shelves, I grab a book I've been waiting for the release of and head to the counter to place my order.

"Morning, Hannah." I lean against the butcher block countertop and smile at my favorite barista and fellow book enthusiast.

"The usual?" she asks and I nod. She sees my book and shakes her head with a quiet laugh.

"Yeah, you know me. Creature of habit." I watch while she heads back towards the nitro tap to get my cold brew. I'm on track to get to the Aspen Grove Club on time as usual. But today, I will *try* to be quieter. Not sure if my idea will work, but Lizzy asked last night and I can't quite shake how worn out she looked. I'm all for tormenting her, but I don't want to be an *actual* asshole.

"Hey, Hannah." She looks back over her shoulder at me, topping off my nitro cold brew. "I know this is a long shot, but have you seen a fancy little blonde thing coming in?"

She looks away from me at my drink again, shaking her head before coming to the counter. "You're going to need to be a bit more specific. This is a bougie tourist ski town, there are lots of fancy little blondes."

This time I'm the one laughing. "Fair enough. Let's see." I tap my finger against my lips looking up at the ceiling. "She's been in town a couple weeks. She's pint sized, probably gets something absurdly girly. From Ohio, always has a ponytail, striking blue eyes." I hum to myself for a second before piling on with this ridiculous description. "Drives a white Bronco with pink wheels. Oh, and the name's Lizzy. Is that specific enough?"

She quirks an eyebrow and cocks her head, grinning at me. "Oh yeah, she has been in. Friend of yours?"

Friend. I wouldn't go that far. "Family friend. I was going to grab a coffee for her. What's her order?"

"She's been getting nitros like you for the last week." After a second, she laughs to herself.

"Oh out with it. What's so funny?" I prod Hannah.

"You two don't just have the same coffee order, you have the same taste in books." She points down at the book on the counter. "She picked that one up yesterday."

Now that gets my attention. Oh, this is too good.

"Hannah, you literally just made my day." I can't help the shit eating grin that's spread across my face. I'm going to have too much fun with that little bit of info. I look at the chalkboard menu on the back wall. "Add a chocolate croissant, and I think I need two more drinks."

CHAPTER 12
LIZZY
CLOCKWORK

TUESDAY MORNING ROLLS around and much to my *very* pleasant surprise, it's eight o'clock before I hear even the slightest sound from upstairs. Either Clay isn't here yet, which seems highly unlikely because he seems to be a robot or he's magically learned to walk around like a ballerina. Either way, I'm not complaining. Working from the condo today means I get an extra hour of sleep and my body is in heaven.

I roll out of bed in my same oversized t-shirt and sweats from last night and head to the kitchen. There's a good half hour before my first call, so I start making a pot of coffee and sit on the kitchen counter, reading my new book. I get a few pages in before I practically jump out of my skin at the sound of banging on the front door.

What the hell?

I head to the door and open it, groaning in exasperation. I flop against the doorframe, dropping my head to my chest.

No one is here. There's just a small brown bag from Finch and a drink.

If you can even call that a drink. I was interrupted from my relaxing morning for this?

I grab the cup and bag and head right to the elevator. Just when I thought Clay could be civilized, he does something like *this*.

When the elevator doors open, I'm not even surprised that Clay is already there, leaning against the door to the penthouse grinning like the Cheshire Cat, sipping what appears to be a nitro cold brew. My current drink.

I would almost think this is funny if it were anyone else.

But no.

Not today, Clay *Fucking* Chapman.

I stomp towards him, holding out the cup.

"Seriously, what the hell is this?" I hold out the abomination in front of me. Honestly, I'm not even sure if you could call it *coffee*. It's practically white, except for the string of red peppermint and caramel swirls around the inside of the clear cup. Then there's the overly generous serving of whipped cream on top with pink sprinkles and cinnamon.

He shrugs and his grin doesn't even waver. "Morning to you too."

I roll my shoulders before looking back at him. "I appreciate you being quiet today, but I don't want to play your games. Especially if you aren't going to even get my order right."

He crosses his arms and his chest rises with a low chuckle. "Did you even look at it? That's not yours."

I furrow my brows and look back at the cup and see *LUKE* sharpied inside of a big heart.

"Luke!" Clay's voice nearly catches me off guard when he shouts into the penthouse. I hear footsteps when a man, maybe about Clay's height, but bigger and broader with shaggy auburn hair walks through the door.

"What's up, boss?" He eyes Clay and then looks at me curiously. I'm wondering if Clay has mentioned me to him or something until he sees the *coffee* in my outstretched hand and his eyes go wide. "Oh shit. You got my sugar fix?" He grabs the drink and takes a giant gulp. "They only have these like one month a year." He punches Clay on the shoulder and walks back inside.

"That was *his* drink?" I look at Clay and point back towards the door way. Another low chuckle rumbles from his chest before he sighs and stands tall. We're back in this doorway again with him towering over me and his scent is everywhere, making the hair on my neck stand and my empty stomach do a weird thing.

"Yeah. He's kind of a big softie." His lips press into a line and he shrugs. And then I remember that I'm still mad at him.

"So, let me get this straight, this was just a game to fuck with me?"

He grins back at me, uncrossing his arms. My eyes don't miss the way his biceps stretch out, highlighting the veins running down them to his tattooed forearms. "I like seeing you all fiery like this. It's not every day I get to see a brat throw a temper tantrum. Makes the rest of the day seem a lot less dull." He tilts his head down towards the bag. "And I did get you a chocolate croissant."

Brat? Temper tantrum?

"That's rich coming from Mr. Dark and Broody, running off in the middle of dinner." His brows knit together and his nostrils flare, but he still just keeps smirking at me. "Next time, just leave that at my door, OK?"

He shrugs and extends a finger towards me. "If I did *that,* then I wouldn't get to see *you* like *this.*" I watch him motion his finger in a circle around my face.

I know he's toying with me, but I can still see the lust in his eyes. And there's something almost refreshing about it. I'm used to being told to *tone it down* or *be less.* But I think he likes me like this and that's new for me.

I pack that idea into the back of my mind and focus on the moment and roll my eyes at him. "Well, thanks for the croissant, I guess. And for being quiet this morning."

Then I grin at him, take his drink, take a giant gulp, and turn back towards the elevator. I make it a few steps when I hear him call back to me.

"Lizzy, wait."

I look back and see him reaching down towards the floor and notice the coffee carrier at his feet.

And then I notice his feet. Or more accurately, the oversized, fluffy shoe shaped slippers that he's wearing over his work boots. They're the kind you'd buy as a kid and wear to sleepovers or in your college dorm. Was he wearing those over his boots all morning just to be quiet?

While I stand there gaping at him like an idiot, he reaches down and grabs the cup from the carrier and hands it to me. It's a nitro cold brew, just what I've been drinking lately, with *PRINCESS* sharpied on it.

"Here you go." He holds the drink and winks. "You have good taste."

"Oh." I stand there, awkwardly still gaping at him like a fish gasping for air. What the hell is this game? I shake my head, bringing myself back to the moment. "Do you want this one back or...?" I hold out his drink that I just took a big gulp out of like the temper tantrum throwing brat he already called me.

He grabs his cup back from me and hands me the new drink, smirking. "Not the first time I've had your spit in my mouth."

Before I can even process anything, he's gone back inside, closing the door behind him.

He went out of his way to be quiet in possibly the most comical way I could imagine. He got me a pastry and my coffee. Is this a giant game to him? Is he just fucking with me?

I WAKE UP FRIDAY, pleasantly surprised when I get up right before my 7:45AM alarm. Since Tuesday, I haven't heard a peep from the construction site upstairs before eight in the morning. Clay might be a bit prickly and obnoxiously cocky, but he did what he said he would do. It's been quiet and I've gotten to sleep as late as I prefer.

But he's also done a bit *more* than he said he would. Each of the last three mornings, he's left a drink and a pastry at my door after knocking loudly. Each time, it's some over the top, sugar filled monstrosity with Luke written on it. And each time, I go upstairs, play his little game, and leave with my actual drink. I'm still not sure if he just enjoys tormenting me or if it's a genuine gesture of goodwill, but I'll take it. And today, I find myself oddly let down when 8:05 comes and goes without a knock at my door. A couple minutes go by and curiosity gets the better of me and I open the door.

To my pleasant surprise, there's my coffee and a bag with a pastry.

No crazy, sugar filled cavity maker. Just my coffee and a pastry. Seeing it weirdly gives me butterflies in my stomach. Even without the knock, like clockwork, my little treat to start the day has shown up. I reach down to grab and notice another bag from Finch under the pastry bag.

I walk back inside my condo and set the drink and pastry on the counter. The mystery bag is heavy and about the size of a book. It's from Finch, so I assume that's what it is. Dipping my hand into the bag, I pull out a book. That's not a surprise. But what would Clay buy me?

My jaw hangs when I get my answer. This isn't just a book. This is *smut*. Like the smuttiest, why choose, hockey smut. Sure, it has a discreet illustrated cover. Does he even know what he just bought me?

My cheeks heat, but it's equal parts embarrassment and equal parts giddiness. I love good books and this series has been on my TBR list. I drum my pink fingernails across the cover before I start flipping through the pages, enjoying the smell of a new book. When I get towards the end, a note falls out.

Settle a bet for me. Me and the girls at the

coffee shop said this would be right up your alley.
I would have pegged you as more of a faerie girl.

I GRAB the book and my coffee and head to the elevator. While my little coffee and pastry deliveries are great, the smut might be a bit much, even given our history, namely us having our tongues down each other's throats. I feel like we'll need to establish boundaries at some point. But in the mean time, I'll play his game.

Walking off the elevator, I'm not the least bit surprised that Clay is waiting there, fluffy pink slippers over his work boots and a knowing grin plastered on his face. The jokes on him though.

"Cowboys and werewolves," I say, calmly, smirking back at him.

He looks puzzled and eyes me cautiously. I'm already so pleased that I've thrown him off for once.

"What are you talking about?"

"Your bet. You and the girls are both wrong." I hold out the note. "I like westerns and werewolf books. Don't get me wrong, I like other stuff too, but those are my favorite."

He huffs out a laugh. "I'll keep that in mind for next time."

I raise my finger to him. "No. I would appreciate it if there wasn't a next time."

He coos at me. "That's no fun."

I glower back at him. "Clay, I'm serious. I feel like we're starting to get to a better place and I would like that to continue if we're going to be doing wedding stuff together. The last thing I need is you probing around in my sex life trying to figure out what I'm in to."

He takes two long, predatory strides towards me, closing the distance between us.

"It's alright, princess." His voice drops low and he lingers on that nickname. "We're adults. No kink shaming here." His lips quirk up into a smirk.

I try to ignore that comment and not let my mind race through what kinks he might have. "First, stop calling me *princess*. It was fun at the bar, but we're trying to be friendly and I'm pretty sure friends don't call each other that."

"Who said we're friends yet?" He eyes me and I feel my cheeks heat under his stare. It's unnerving how he always makes me feel this way just by looking at me. "Friends don't assume friends are cheating pricks. Remember?"

I stare right back at him, not giving an inch and his eyes soften. "I don't have to justify myself to you. You tried to take me home, then you show up later with a date or whatever."

His chest fills as he takes a deep breath, but he doesn't say a word. He just glares back at me and crosses his arms.

"But..." I sigh and wobble my head.

He turns and holds his cupped ear. "But what?" he says, dragging out the words.

"But you're right. I'm sorry. My last relationship was a mess. My ex was a cheating asshole. I didn't need to take that out on you."

He doesn't even hesitate to respond. "He sounds like an idiot. It was his loss." He doesn't flinch and his gaze holds mine.

I look away, not wanting to maintain this intense eye contact or talk about that more than I have to. "It's fine. I don't exactly go around broadcasting that."

He studies me and looks at me softly. Not with pity, not sadness, but understanding. His lips pull to one side and he nods. "Yeah, I get it. No one likes to talk about being hurt." He lets out a long breath and rubs his stubble. "We can be friends, Lizzy. We are friends."

He extends a hand out to me and I take it. The feeling of his warm, rough hands instantly brings back all the sensations from that night at Roxy's. I watch his eyes drift down to our hands before he pulls it back, almost like it pains him.

Does he feel it too? Or does he just dislike me that much even though he says we're friends now?

SATURDAY MORNING COMES and I find myself pleased that I got to sleep in. I stayed in last night and started my new book from Clay. It's definitely living up to the hype.

Girl, I get it.

Why choose?

I got to bed at a responsible time. But when I check my phone and 8:05 comes and goes and my coffee and pastry aren't there, I feel the slightest bit of disappointment.

I know Clay isn't working today.

I know I shouldn't expect it.

But I was starting to enjoy our morning sparring matches. Even Luke is sort of adorable with how excited he gets about his sugar-coma-inducing drinks.

On the bright side, I get to spend my morning with a different, much more pleasant Chapman. I'm meeting Grace for brunch at the cafe overlooking downtown, just across the street from Finch.

She's the closest thing I have to a real friend out here, even if Clay says we're friends or friendly or whatever now. We've done brunch two weekends in a row and gone out for drinks a couple times in between. Collin was right. She's fun and we've hit it off. I'm glad I'm sitting across the table from her for brunch today and she brought Kayleigh this time.

"You're really going to have to tell me more about this cowboy sandwich." Grace flicks her eyebrows at Kayleigh before grinning at me. "I mean I get it. The whole rugged Wyoming cowboy thing. But sharing with Collin?" She looks back down at her food and shakes her head. "I told you, Kayleigh, Lizzy's a wild one."

I cover my mouth and snort a very unladylike laugh. "You could say that. But yeah, it was definitely something. A story for another day. My *Tour de Lizzy* is starting to catch up with me."

She quirks an eyebrow at me and stabs a strawberry with her fork, and points it back at me. "Yeah, you've told me about Johnathan.

Now you're living for yourself. I get it. I mean, I have no idea what I want either. I want to travel. I want to see the world. I want to know myself. And I don't know how that fits into dating."

I look at her with a new appreciation. I'm sure growing up with two domineering brothers and losing your mom so young meant maturing in a different way. When I was in my mid-twenties, I was growing my career but also already dating and looking for a husband that my mom would approve of. I was on a mission and found Johnathan in my late twenties. So I'm glad she's living for herself and not rushing.

"Yeah. That's sort of where I'm at now, just eight or nine years ahead of you." I look towards the ceiling and roll my shoulders. "I think I'm fine living by myself and not settling. It's not that I don't want someone. I just want a man that's going to be a *partner* with me, an equal."

The truth is, I'm not sure I really know what I want. I feel like I have a second chance after dodging a bullet with Johnathan. An equal would be amazing. Someone that lights a spark in me and sees me for me. But do I want to try to settle down again?

Grace smiles and chuckles. "Girl, good luck. Dating sucks. The dating pool isn't exactly filled with great options. Too many boys, no men."

"You can say that again." I couldn't think of anything truer right now. The lack of decent, dateable men in the world is truly horrifying. And they don't just grow Tanner Chapmans on a tree in Wyoming. I notice that Kayleigh has been quiet all brunch except for the occasional laugh here and there. "What about you, Kayleigh? How's the dating world treating you?"

Grace's eyes dart to Kayleigh's, who smiles half-heartedly. "My career choice and training schedule don't exactly make dating easy. But Charlie is pretty easy going and the long distance thing has worked for us for the most part." She takes a sip of her drink and smiles back at me. "But Grace tells me you're liking full time life in

Park City? I loved growing up here. It's a great place to live if you like the outdoors and skiing."

"So far, so good." Taking a second to actually think about it, I'm glad I chose to come out here, however long this assignment might take. It's already looking like I'll be here long enough for my lease back home to be up by the time I go back. "It's been a good change. I needed a fresh start, or at least a reset from life back in Ohio. And besides, now I have Grace as a friend. And maybe you eventually." I smile warmly back at them both.

She beams back at me before Grace chimes in.

"Same, girl. Met anyone else out here besides your coworkers?"

"Not really. I've seen your brother around though. Almost every day. He's actually grown on me a bit after he started bringing me coffee every morning." I know it's been sort of a weird game with us each morning, but I do find myself looking forward to it, as obnoxious as he can be.

Grace stops mid bite and puts her fork down, looking at me like I have two heads. Even Kayleigh gives me a curious look before Grace talks. "My brother, Clay Chapman? He's being nice?"

I look back at her, nodding. "I think it started as a joke, but he's actually been nice, well *nicer*, lately."

They're both still staring at me like I'm crazy. "Again. My brother, Clay. Not Tanner, the nice one. Are we talking about the same person? Tall, tattoos everywhere, shit eating grin, stupid constant scowl?"

Kayleigh snorts a laugh and I shrug. "Yeah. That one. He even did what I asked and he's been quieter in the mornings so I can sleep in."

"Huh. That's... interesting." She shakes her head, looking at Kayleigh and then back at her plate. "He hates practically everyone except family, the Perrys, and Kayleigh here. If I didn't know any better, I'd say he likes you."

She looks up at me with a smug smirk and glint in her eyes. I huff a laugh. I haven't told anyone about that night at the bar and I would definitely prefer for that secret to stay between Clay and me.

I turn to find that Kayleigh is looking at me with an almost knowing smile. "As an expert on all things Clay, I have to agree with her here."

I toss my head back with another short, dismissive laugh. "Don't be crazy. I'm still pretty sure I annoy the hell out of him."

Grace rolls her eyes at me. "Ok, Lizzy. Let me know when he starts being a grumpy ass again so I don't have to worry that he's been replaced by a robot or something."

"You got it." I smile back, but for the rest of brunch only one thing is on my mind. Does he actually like me? The grouchy guy that seemingly hates everyone might like me?

While that thought bounces around in the back of my mind, we finish lunch and hang outside by our cars, planning our next meetup.

"So I know brunch is a Saturday thing, but how about a girls' ski day?" Kayleigh asks. "One of the next Sundays. Why don't you ladies come out to the slopes? It's an off week competition, so I'll be training. Check out a session then we can ski a few runs together."

Grace and I both nod. "Yeah, I'd love that."

Utah is already starting to feel more and more like home.

CHAPTER 13

CLAY
SLIP AND SLIDE - NEXT WEEK

I LOOK DOWN at my watch, checking the time. It's almost five o'clock. The work day is almost over and I really just want to get home. This week has been brutally busy, but it's Thursday night and that means Mr. Jensen is meeting me at the Aspen Grove job site. The job is going smooth enough, but he still likes his weekly updates and the Aspen Grove site is the closest one to his house.

It's been unseasonably warm the last few days for March and I'm enjoying the weather out on the balcony while it's here. I'm sure it'll cool down soon enough and we'll get some more snow, but I'll take all the nights like these I can get.

"Evening, Clay." I look up and see Mr. Jensen standing at the French doors back to the penthouse. "So, how's it going here? Are we still on track?"

I stand with my legs crossed, propping myself up on my elbow on the balcony railing. Pointing back inside, I nod. "Yeah. The plumber finished up at the start of the week. It was leak tested and inspected yesterday." I rasp my fist against the railing. "Knock on wood, the spray foam guys show up tomorrow and we can insulate the whole place and start up the HVAC systems. Honestly, it's going smooth

Mr. Jensen. And the Grand Lodge job should finish next week. Under budget too."

"Good, Clay, very good. You should be getting the final invoices for the lodge project soon." He looks back inside and nods before looking back at me. "And again for the thousandth time, call me Randall. You've practically been family for a decade."

This is one of the little areas where I've tried to keep a wall up. I know he's done so much for me, but I like it being professional. Sure, his daughter and I are best friends. But it feels like if I ever want him to understand that's all we'll be, keeping things formal and calling him Mr. Jensen is an easy starting point.

And these invoices. This is part of the promotion I wasn't looking forward to. I can manage arguments between contractors and architects, subcontractor timing, planning, quality checks, but I hate dealing with the finances of these projects. And it always seems like there's a flood of invoices at the end of the project.

"Hey, boss." Marco walks up behind Mr. Jensen towards me and stops when he realizes *my boss* is also here. "Oh, hi, Mr. Jensen." He looks back to me nervously. "Clay, that propane tank for the heater is about empty, you want me to swap it out?"

I wave him off. "Nah. You're good. I'll take care of it. Get going. I'll see you tomorrow morning." He dips his chin and heads back inside.

We chat for a bit before Mr. Jensen finally leaves. I take another minute on the balcony to enjoy the weather, looking out over the slopes and the Aspen Valley condo village below us. With the warmer weather, I can hear the steady sound of water dripping off the roof from melting snow. It'll probably freeze back up soon when cooler weather rolls back in, but it almost feels like full on spring skiing weather right now.

Looking down at the village, even six stories up, a flash of golden hair catches my eye. I see Lizzy leaving the building heading out towards the valet circle.

Fuck me. She's dressed girly as hell, but she looks so good. She's got pink yoga pants on, some white sneakers and a black cropped hoodie showing off some of her stomach. Not practical, but definitely hot. Her hair is still pulled back into what I now know is her trademark ponytail, bouncing along with each step. I watch shamelessly from here, half tempted to whistle and cat call her like a cliché construction worker, but settle for admiring from a distance. I already fucked with her enough this morning with our silly coffee routine, even if I gave her the right order today.

I'm leaning against the railing when I notice Grace's van pull into the valet circle. Grace hops out and pulls Lizzy into a hug before they both get back in the van.

Ok. That's terrifying. Those two together would be *a lot*. God help anyone that tries to talk to them at a bar. They're either going to catch one of Grace's fists or Lizzy's words.

From what Veronica and Tanner have told me, she's loyal and fierce - two things I admire. I mostly called Tanner to get tips on how to tease her and instead he gave me a lecture and told me to stop being a dick and be nice. So I told him Veronica really has him whipped and he told me to fuck off.

But still, he's not totally wrong. She did assume I'm some shit bag cheater, which is still bullshit. But I'm being just as bad. I need to stop punishing her for making assumptions about me when I was doing the same thing. Maybe *friends* won't be that bad I guess. I can still keep my walls up and be nice.

I STAND on my front porch in the cold winter air, waiting to make sure Ani has had enough outside time for his potty break. Being here, my mind keeps going back to seeing Lizzy and Grace together. Maybe she's not as bad as I was thinking originally. Yes, she's definitely extra. But she isn't some self-absorbed little tourist. Not like the one that upended my life - my entire family's lives - nearly ten years ago.

"Come," I bark at Ani , looking out into the front yard. It got cold tonight, fast, and it definitely doesn't feel like it did only a few hours ago. I cross my arms across my chest to stay warm when I finally hear Ani's collar jingle as he comes running back towards the house.

I've been bad lately keeping up with his training, but he still came on the first call. Sure, I might seem even more controlling than usual with as much as I spent training him as a puppy and every week since. But he's bombproof and always there when I need him. And with as cold as it is tonight, I just want to get back inside and I'm glad his recall is so good right now.

IT'S Friday morning and I made the extra stop into the office before going to Finch and heading to the job site. Sure enough, there's a stack of invoices on my desk. There's one that catches my eye. *GJF Inc.* I don't remember working with them, but this is the third time we've gotten a large invoice from them at the end of a project. I mentioned it to Mr. Jensen before and he said it's a consulting firm that helps with permits and approvals. Whatever, I'll deal with them later.

I already made up my mind that today, I'll keep being a little nicer and leave Lizzy another nitro at her door with her pastry and save her the trip up. If Grace likes her and wants to hang out with her, then she's definitely not as bad as I originally thought.

I step off the elevator towards the penthouse with the coffee carrier and my bag on my shoulder. I just need today to be easy so I can get to the weekend. All I'm doing is cleaning up the site and getting it ready for insulation on Monday. Then I can relax all weekend.

After unlocking and opening the door, I'm hit with a rush of cold air. I guess it really was cold last night. I step inside the dark entry way and drop my bag off my shoulder. I step towards the wall to turn on the lights.

Except I don't make it there. My foot hits the floor and I slip and slide across the tile entry way. I hit the ground and a second later, two coffees land and spill on my chest.

"What the fuck?" I mutter to myself, grabbing the back of my head. I put my hands on the ground to steady myself and stand, but the floor is wet. That's not good.

I finally get to my feet and flip on the lights.

Oh fuck. Fuck fuck fuck.

There is water everywhere. Why in the hell is there water everywhere?

I rush over to the utility closet and then bathroom. I see the bare copper pipes in the walls and at least a few of them are cracked. They must have frozen last night, ruptured, and then started leaking everywhere when it warmed up this morning.

But we have heaters. It shouldn't have gotten this cold in here last night.

I remember two things in this moment.

That blast of cold air when I walked in, meaning the heat hadn't been running for a while.

And last night... Marco's words.

I was talking to Mr. Jensen and then I got distracted watching Lizzy. I *never* let myself get distracted like that. But last night, I did and I forgot to swap over the gas tanks.

CHAPTER 14
LIZZY
FML

THE LAST WEEK has been nice. The grumpy asshat upstairs has learned to walk like he isn't trying to put his feet through the floor every day. I assume he's still wearing those ridiculous slippers until a quarter 'til eight every morning. I will begrudgingly admit that I do appreciate that, so far, when Clay says he's going to do something, he does it. I know something as little as trusting someone to not be loud every morning until a reasonable hour shouldn't matter so much, but it does to me.

It's been nice waking up on my own every morning and then getting my coffee treat and pastry from him is an added bonus. So far there haven't been any more book deliveries, but I have plenty to read. And on this particular morning, I roll over in the plush sheets of the king size bed, enjoying the rays of sunshine peaking in through the gaps in the blackout blinds.

However, I'm still *restless*. Not because I didn't sleep. No. And not because I was out late last night. I met Grace for a drink at Roxy's and was home at a responsible hour.

No. I'm restless because I've been dreaming about *mother fucking Clay Chapman* every night. Why is he in my dreams? Why am I thinking about him at all? Ok. I know why. It's the abs. It's those dimples. That fucking smirk he gives me like he knows what's going on in my head. Those intense green eyes that feel like a flame on my skin. All I've thought about for weeks is that asshole upstairs. For all I know, he's probably wandering around up there shirtless again because that sugar addict Luke spilled coffee on him.

Before I drove out from Ohio weeks ago, I had just started a werewolf smut reading binge. So I packed my new knotted werewolf dildo. Have I been picturing Clay when I've been using it? Yes.

Add that to the list of things he can never know. He's already so cocky, I don't know how big his head would get if he learned I was pleasuring myself thinking about him. I'm probably going to need to unpack why I'm obsessed with the guy who's driving me crazy later, but it's doing it for me right now. And that's exactly what I'm going to do with my extra time this morning.

I reach into my nightstand, pulling out the black silk bag with the toy in it. Did I splurge and get it with the ultra premium, sparkling purple soft silicone? Yes. I wasn't convinced the smooth and veiny toy with the knot just above the base would be fun, but I have been *pleasantly* surprised. Thank you for the inspiration, smutty books.

After taking my toy out of the bag and setting it on the nightstand, I dip my fingers under the waistband of my shorts, reaching for my swollen clit. I'm already so wet. Clay can definitely never know he gets to me like this. The bar was one thing. He knows about that. But he would never let me live it down if he knew I was this into him. Well, his body anyways. His cocky, prickly attitude could use an adjustment.

I stretch across the bed towards the other nightstand to grab the remote for the blinds. I'd like a little more light in here to see what I'm doing. My arm is draped across the pillow when I can feel that it's wet.

I mean I drool in my sleep sometimes, but I didn't sleep on that pillow. I press the remote to open the blinds, looking around the room.

And that's when I see it. The giant spot on the ceiling. You can't be serious. Looking up at the ceiling, there's a giant wet spot over one side of the bed stretching towards the hallway and en suite bathroom. The drywall is sagging and there's a trail of little wet spots in the carpet the whole way.

I rush out of bed, reaching for my phone. I need to call maintenance? I don't know. Maybe Dad? It's his fucking condo. The contractors upstairs? Fuck. That's Clay.

No. No. No. This cannot be happening.

I hear a large tearing sound and a crash. I look behind me.

Oh. My. God.

The fucking ceiling collapsed in half the bedroom. There's a trail of drywall running from one side of the bed to the bathroom and the hallway.

Fuck. My. Life.

I just got settled in and now I have to deal with this mess? I still need to get to work today and it looks like at least one of the bathrooms is out of commission.

Before I can get too far with that train of thought, a whole new concern is emerging. I can hear shouting upstairs, presumably the dipshit guys working for Clay responsible for this. And then I hear it. My condo door opening and shutting and stomping down my hallway.

"Lizzy, are you ok?" Clay rushes into my bedroom. He looks terrified and panicked until our eyes meet and he sees that I'm out of the bed and in one piece.

"Jesus fuck, Clay. I could have been naked." Why is the first thought I have when Clay is in my room about me being naked? "And how did you get in here? Did you break my door down?" I snarl at him, arms outstretched and flailing pointing at the mess in every direction.

He chuckles. He fucking chuckles at me. "I have a master key."

I put my hands on my hips, glaring at him. "Why the fuck would you have a master key?"

He looks side to side with a puzzled look and shrugs his shoulders. "For exactly this reason? It's a job site. Things happen."

I tilt my head back and I just want to scream but instead a muffled groan comes out. I watch as he scans the room, taking inventory of the damage.

"Lizzy, I'm so sorry." He shakes his head, gripping the back of his neck beneath the brim of his hat that's flipped around backwards. He keeps scanning the room until his eyes stop on something. I turn to see what has his attention and that's when I see it.

Ok.

Really. Fuck my life.

I watch as the corner of his lips quirk up into a wide shit eating grin.

"Is that a werewolf...?" He points at the toy still sitting on my nightstand and gives me the most knowing grin but he still looks like it's taking every ounce of self-control he has to not burst out laughing.

I didn't think my cheeks could get any redder between how flustered and angry I am, but I can feel the blood rushing to them.

"Shut up, Clay. Not a word. You're the one that just destroyed my ceiling." I step towards him, jabbing him in the chest with a finger. "But also, how the hell do you even know what a werewolf dick looks like?"

His knowing grin only grows when he shrugs, looking down at me. "I read a lot of smut. Utah has shitty porn laws. Bold choice though." He looks back at the toy and then back at me slowly. "I like the sparkly purple."

That is not the answer I was expecting. My mouth opens and shuts and opens again like a gasping fish because I don't know how to respond to that. Before I can say or do anything with that unexpected tidbit, he walks beneath the gaping hole in the ceiling and pulls out his phone. He paces around the room, like only men do, waiting for someone on the other end to answer.

"Luke. Get down here. Right now. Bring Marco and the cleaning supplies," he shouts into the phone. I watch as he rolls his eyes and nods. He presses his hand to his face, groaning. "It's Unit 601. The fucking unit you can see through the goddamn hole in the floor, you fuck stick."

He hangs up, looking back at the ceiling. If I wasn't so furious at him and frazzled right now, I would almost think the way he's in control and taking charge is hot. Ok. Who am I kidding? It is hot.

CLAY IS LEANING on his elbows with his face buried in his hands as we sit at the island in the kitchen. His crew left after getting the water shut off and the debris cleaned. Now it's just us sitting in awkward silence processing this shit show of a Friday morning.

"I'm sorry, Lizzy. I'm so fucking sorry." He doesn't lift his head or his eyes and there's no sign of the brash, cocky man I've seen almost everyday for the last month.

"Yeah, you've said that a bunch." I look around the condo. With all the debris gone and the water shut off, I can see just how much of a mess this place is. There are gaping holes in both bedrooms, in the hallway, and main bathroom.

"We'll get this fixed, but it might take a while." He sighs and looks up at me and I'm almost shocked by his eyes. There's remorse and the normally piercing, green eyes are soft and shy. "But this place is going to be almost uninhabitable for a few weeks while we dry it out, fix the ceiling, and floors."

"I'll call Grace. Maybe I can stay with her." He frowns and shakes his head side to side.

"She doesn't have a room. She literally lives in a studio apartment with a pullout sofa."

I close my eyes and take a deep breath. "Fine. I'll start looking at hotels or an airbnb or something. Don't worry. I'll send JSC a bill."

He rolls his eyes at me, but then cocks his head to the side like an idea just hit him. "Or you could stay with me. I have a spare guest suite."

Ok. He did just have an idea. A completely laughable one. Is he insane? Did he even hear what he just said? I burst out laughing, covering my mouth.

"Are you crazy, Clay? That's a terrible idea. You must be some kind of sadomasochistic psycho to think we could exist under the same roof." I glare back at him but he just grins and his gaze hardens.

"Are you into that?" Yep. There's the Clay I know.

I palm my face. "Seriously, I'll find a place."

He looks back at me, but his eyes are pleading.

"Look. First, this is my fault. I should fix this for you." He looks down at his hands for a second before looking back at me. "Second, my place is in Kimball Junction. It's closer to your office in Salt Lake City. I know you won't complain about the extra sleep."

Oh my god. He's serious about this.

"Third, maybe it would be good for us to actually be friendly since my brother and your best friend are getting married." He looks at me, his eyes still pleading.

I let out a long sigh. I don't have the energy to deal with this today. "You know what, screw it." I can't believe I'm agreeing to this, but at least for tonight, I'll give it a shot. Crashing there for a night while I sort this mess out should be alright. What's the worst that could happen? "Fine, I'll stay tonight and then figure out what I'm doing next while you fix this mess."

He looks back at me with a gentle smile and those stupid perfect dimples that make it hard to stay focused on being mad at him. I'd probably say yes to anything he asked if he was flashing those all the time.

"Ok. Good. I'll text you my address. Just come by later today. I'll make sure the guest suite is ready for you. And Lizzy, I'll make this right. *I promise.*" He looks at me with eyes taking on a familiar seriousness.

I swallow hard. For some reason, a sense of relief floods me as he walks out the door, my mind going back to what he said at the bar about promises.

CHAPTER 15
LIZZY
I FEEL LIKE BELLE

DRIVING up the hill along the long, snow covered gravel driveway to Clay's house is picturesque. I'm glad I have the Bronco because otherwise this would be rough to get in and out of. And he's right, his house is fifteen minutes closer to my office. I will give him that.

I spent the rest of the morning packing up a few things while also calling my dad to let him know about the condo. I gave him a piece of my mind about not telling me about the construction upstairs in the first place. Surprisingly, he wasn't that worried about the condo and just asked if I was alright. I told him that fortunately, none of my things were damaged but the condo is going to be out of commission for a few weeks. He told me to keep him posted on how the repairs are going and that he'd be out in a few weeks to check in on some of his new investments and entertain some business partner.

No surprise. Nothing new there. He'll come out for his business, but not even a *hey, let's get together and get lunch or hey, I would love to see you and catch up, Lizzy. Let's have dinner.*

I'm stewing on that conversation until I pull up through the trees to the end of the driveway and reach Clay's house.

I don't know what I was expecting, but this wasn't it. Clay's a bachelor in his late twenties and a rough and tumble contractor at that. I turn down my radio and take off my sunglasses to fully appreciate it.

But *this?*

The sleek, but somehow rustic modern house is set back in the trees on the edge of a hill looking back towards Park City and the mountains. In the center, there's an A-Frame roofline with floor to ceiling windows on the front and back, giving a clear view straight from the driveway to the view of the mountains and ski slopes off in the distance. On the right of the A-Frame is a three car garage with black metal and frosted glass doors and on the left the house continues in a low, single floor wing. The whole house is rough, exposed timbers, raw steel, glass and concrete, like a beautiful mid-century modern design was fused with a rustic mountain home.

It's almost so striking and stunning that I would doubt it was Clay's, until the garage door on the end opens to reveal him, leaning against a covered car, shaking his head at me. I pull the Bronco into the open third spot in the garage, curiously taking note of the covered car in the center spot that he's leaning against.

I park and almost jump when Clay is at my door, already opening it.

"Um, hi." I look at him skeptically. "You're opening doors for me now?"

He lets out a hushed laugh as he leans against the car door. "Well, this Bronco is ridiculous and I had to see for myself how your short ass hops out of it."

I glower back at him. "I'm surprisingly athletic I'll have you know." I turn and hang my legs over the side of the seat and hop down. Suddenly, I'm now eye level with the open neck line of his black henley and trapped between him and the door of my car. How is it that I'm always so up close with him like this? He must sense it because he stands to the side and shrugs one shoulder.

"And besides, you're a guest. Manners matter. Come on, let me get your bag." He takes another step back and holds the door open, gesturing towards the door into the house. *Manners matter.* That's refreshing, but not something that jumps to mind when you look at Clay.

He leads me into the kitchen from the garage, setting my bag down on the bench just inside the door. He stops and points back towards the wall next to me. "Shoes in the tray there on the floor and keys on the hook up there."

I look to my left and see the wall hooks with keys, coats, hats and then the tray on the floor with his shoes and boots. I huff a laugh and look back at him. "Didn't have you pegged for the neat and tidy type." He just stares back at me.

"Please. I just like to keep the place organized."

I roll my eyes and sigh. "Ok, ok." I put my things where he asked and then look around the kitchen. Or more like the whole main living area. The center of the A-frame portion of the house is a modern, open floor-plan space. The living area along the back main wall with floor to ceiling windows looks out over the ski resorts and mountains in the distance.

But that's not what catches my eye. Everything is so meticulously laid out. The place is spotless but not sterile. It's decorated in a sort of cozy meets modern ski lodge with beautiful polished floors. There's a big leather couch with square arms and a southwestern patterned wool blanket folded neatly across the back. A fireplace is in the center of the windowed wall, framed by exposed wood beams coming down from the ceiling. There are two leather chairs on either side of it, facing the couch. The table in the dining area is a warm, live oak edged table big enough to seat ten people.

And then the kitchen. Wow, Veronica would lose her mind if she hasn't seen this already. It's all clean lines, but still homey and warm with flat fronted, walnut cabinets and a white marble waterfall island. But like everything else I can see around me, it's methodically organized and clean with everything in its place.

This is definitely not what I expected from Clay Chapman, the rugged fuckboy from Roxy's. This isn't a bachelor pad or even a small rustic cabin like Tanner's place in Jackson. This is stunning.

It's not huge, but it's so thoughtful and cozy and beautifully designed.

Clay clears his throat, getting my attention. "Something wrong?" I look at him and there's a contemplative, almost concerned look on his face.

I huff another laugh and smile back at him. "Nothing's wrong. But are you sure this is *your* house?" I gesture my hand around the room, admiring the place.

He looks back at me with a proud smile I haven't seen before, letting his dimples peek out. "Yep. Lived here since the day I finished building it a few years ago."

My eyes go wide. "You built this place?"

He grins back at me, the smile from earlier replaced by the cocky, smug one I'm much more familiar with. "What? You thought I was just some eye candy construction worker you could eyefuck at the bar and again at the penthouse door?"

I palm my face and shake my head. "Fair point." I look over at the fireplace and windows and gesture around again. "But this? It's beautiful. Did you work with a local designer?"

I look back at him and notice his cheeks are almost pink. "No. I designed it," he says softly.

"*You* designed and built *this*?" I say, pointing my finger towards the ceiling.

One side of his mouth pulls together and he shrugs while looking down at the ground.

"Yeah. My parents had the land and always meant to build their own place here. But after mom. My dad didn't have the heart to build on the lot." His voice trails off for a second before he clears his throat. "It took me a couple years working on it in my spare time, salvaging material from other jobs, and calling in favors with other construction guys I know. But I got it done eventually."

This side of Clay is so different than the other ones I'm used to seeing. The softness is so jarring that if I hadn't met him before, I'd think he's a big teddy bear like his brother.

My thoughts are pulled away when a sound coming from the hallway catches my attention. I look up and I'm instantly terrified by the monster running at me.

"Jesus Christ. What is that?" I practically scream, leaping behind Clay and grabbing him.

I'm holding him so tightly that I can feel his chest rumble when he laughs. "That's little orphan Ani," he says, casually and mater-of-factly.

Clay kneels down, forcing me to let go of him. "That is a wolf, Clay." My voice is breathy and my heart is still pounding.

"What? You don't like dogs?" I watch as he ruffles the fur on the dog's head in both of his big hands.

I stay standing with Clay between *Ani* and me. "I like dogs. He just caught me off guard. Sorry, it's been a day and I'm just on edge."

"Bed!" Clay's voice is deep and cool. I watch as the dog turns, walks over to a dog bed on the floor in front of the fireplace and plops down on it with a huff before chewing on a toy. Ok, that was kind of hot. A man in command.

"Good boy," he says calmly before standing and turning to face me. Something about his commanding presence stirs up a funny feeling in my stomach. "Yeah. Again, sorry it's been a rough day. I still can't believe I fucked up like that. But you don't have to worry about Ani. He's harmless and will do whatever you say."

"*He?*" I look at the dog and back at Clay. "Isn't Annie a girl's name?"

He laughs and shakes his head. "He's named after Anakin-"

"Skywalker," I cut him off and smile back at him. "Let me guess. He's a rescue?"

He looks at me with wide eyes and his mouth slowly morphs into a smile. "You are full of surprises. I would never guess that you'd get that reference."

"Those movies are my dad's favorites. I can't tell you how many times I watched all of them. I swear he wishes I loved them as much as he does." I roll my eyes and scoff. "At least I have him to thank for understanding way too many pop cultural references now."

"Yeah. Our dad loves them too. Tanner, Collin, and I were obsessed and always made Veronica and Grace watch them with us." He looks toward the TV above the fireplace like he's thinking about a distant memory. "Anyways, let's get you to your room."

He leads me down the hallway that Ani originally came running out of. I notice an open door on the right and stop for a second to look in the room. There are floor to ceiling bookshelves on two sides of the space, another leather and walnut chair in the corner, and a large sit-stand desk in the other corner, facing me.

Clay stops and turns, noticing that I'm not right behind him any more. "That's my office. If you need a space to work, you're welcome to use that desk." I'm still only planning to just stay tonight and look for another place until the condo is fixed, but it's still nice of him to offer.

"Thanks. You weren't kidding - you read a lot." I wave my hand at the books on both walls.

His brows furrow and he shrugs, looking back into the office. "I don't have much of a social life. I prefer books over people."

Now that I can relate to. A book boyfriend has never let me down. And books are always an escape from reality. Sometimes a much needed one. But still, there's something oddly amusing about picturing this rugged, tattooed, works-with-his-hands man sitting in a chair by the fire, reading a book. Honestly it's kind of hot.

"Hey." Clay clicks his tongue, getting my attention back from my thoughts. He cocks his head back towards the shelves in the office. "You're welcome to read any of them. If you're here, my house is your house."

He turns and walks down the hall, stopping at the second to last door on the right. "My room is at the end of the hall. Both our rooms have en-suites, so you'll have a bathroom to yourself. It should be stocked, but if you need anything just ask." He opens the door and extends an arm inside, gesturing for me to walk in. "But this is you."

I walk in, not surprised at all to see a room as meticulously decorated and thought out as the rest of the house. Large windows look out over the mountains in the distance. There's a chair in the corner with an end table and reading lamp, a dresser, and a king sized bed with a gray upholstered headboard.

And the pillows! This bed looks incredibly cozy. I always think of men as having one, maybe two pillows and worn bedding. But this guest bed has shams, pillows, accent pillows - all the bells and whistles. It looks like someone got turned loose with a credit card at a home goods store.

I turn back to look at him. He looks amused but nervous, watching me take in the room. "This is nice, but again you really didn't have to let me stay here. I'll look for a place over the weekend. But I appreciate this for tonight."

He swallows and his jaw tightens. "Yes, I did." He rolls his back and stands tall in the doorway. "I told you. It was my fault. You're welcome to stay here as long as you want."

I hear Ani come down the hall and stop behind Clay. He turns and looks down, patting him on the head. "As for him, he might try to come in the room and sleep with you. He's kind of clingy. If you don't want him in here, just lock the door. Otherwise he'll flip the handle. Not sure how he learned that."

I let out a laugh and look at the dog. "Well, that's slightly terrifying, but thanks for the heads up."

Clay just nods. "Anyways, if you need something, just let me know. I need to take him outside."

He turns and walks down the hall. I lean against the door and listen as I hear the front door open and close. I set my bags in front of the dresser and plop down on the foot of the bed.

Ok. This bed is soft and comfy. I need to ask him where he got this bedding.

I lay back further, sinking into the cozy bed and finally exhaling after the shit show of a day I've had.

This won't be that bad. I can stay here tonight, maybe the week-end, and find a new place for next week while they fix the condo.

Clay promised he'd make things right and there's something almost comforting about the way he said it.

I WAKE UP, almost in shock. Not because I'm in Clay's house, but because I slept better than I have in ages. Maybe it was the stress of everything happening yesterday, but I slept like a rock. Or maybe it was the insanely comfortable bed and not having a noisy upstairs neighbor.

But either way, I slept great. Maybe I should consider staying here after all. But now, my grumbling stomach is screaming at me for food and coffee.

I begrudgingly pry myself out of the warm, cozy bed, put on some socks, and quietly open the door to head to the kitchen.

I don't know why I'm being so quiet. I remember that Clay gets up at the crack of dawn and has already been at the job site for an hour before I'm even awake.

I walk down the hall, stopping at the office when something catches my eye. When I saw it last night, I was tired and groggy and the books were the only thing I noticed.

So many books.

Fiction novels, books on the history of skiing and racing, books on architecture.

But now, I see the other wall. It's covered in old skis, framed pictures, and floating shelves with trophies and medals. I step towards it in awe. There are so many medals and trophies from Clay's juniors and early pro career. So many golds. Still, I feel like Belle, as if you could call Clay a *beast*, wandering around his home and peering into his life.

There are pictures of him and his ski teams, him on the slopes skiing, and on the podium. But two photos jump out at me. The first is a late teenage Clay with a taller, brown haired woman with an infectious smile. It's impossible to not see that it's his mom. They're in the trees near a black rocky outcropping in typical ski gear, not racing gear, both smiling ear to ear. It's a smile I have never seen on Clay or could even imagine on him from my interactions with him.

In the second picture, it looks like he's in his late teens or early twenties. His eyes have already started to take on that hardened look I know. He's smiling, if you could call it that, with his lips closed and pressed together. More like a grimace. Kayleigh is next to him and her dad is standing behind them. Something doesn't sit right with me about it. Her dad looks possessive and neither Clay nor Kayleigh look genuinely happy, especially compared to the picture of him with his mom.

I keep walking along the wall, looking at all the pictures. That is until my stomach growls again.

OK, you win stomach. Coffee and food it is.

CHAPTER 16

CLAY

TIGHT

I'M INSANE. I've seriously lost my damn mind.

I jog down the long driveway, enjoying the crisp, cool morning air against my skin and the sound of snow crunching under my running shoes. Ani runs steadily, heeling by my side with his snow boots keeping his paws warm.

We reach the end of the driveway and turn back towards the house, jogging back up the hill. Sure, our morning routine of running laps up and down the long driveway, even in the snow, might seem crazy. And yes, I'm wearing shorts because I like the feeling of the cold air on my achy joints. But that's hardly crazy compared to what I did yesterday.

No. I've spent years building routine on top of routine, craving control over my life. I enjoy the *very* limited number of relationships I have to maintain and manage. Plus I love my space and having my privacy and solitude.

So yes, I must be crazy or maybe I suffered from a temporary moment of insanity.

I needed to make things right with Lizzy. It's my fault she can't stay in her condo.

But inviting her to stay here as long as it takes, to be in my space, is fucking crazy. Masochistically crazy.

She gets under my skin so damn easily when I see her in small doses. And I go and invite her to stay with me?

I need to stay focused with work because I'm clearly dropping the ball lately. I don't need distractions.

"What the hell is wrong with me?" I mutter out loud between breaths. Ani quirks his head up at me and I snort a laugh.

After a couple more laps of thinking about that question, we head inside. I take Ani's snow boots and my shoes off, putting them onto the tray next to the door. I flip on the lights and look around the kitchen and living room. I'm startled by the sound of pots and pans clattering on the floor.

Yep, I'm definitely a masochist.

On the floor, on her knees across the kitchen from me is Lizzy. She's rummaging through one of the lower cabinets like a feral raccoon, whose contents are now scattered around her on the floor. She's wearing some plaid sleep shorts and I can make out the curve of her ass and can't look away from her toned legs.

Fuck. Me.

I can feel my blood pulsing through my body, but I don't know if it's from seeing her in this position or catching my breath from running. I clear my throat. "Can I help you?"

The clattering and clanging stops and she freezes in place. "Coffee." Her voice is irritated but muffled because she's still neck deep in the cabinet.

I stand there, looking around the kitchen, noticing all my other cabinets open. I can feel the vein in my forehead throbbing. This is the kind of shit that drives me mad. I can't stand clutter and my things being out of order.

"There isn't any," I say, trying to hide my irritation. She shuffles away from the cabinet and looks over her shoulder at me. Her blue eyes stare at me like I have two heads.

"You don't have coffee in this house or food for a sane person that doesn't eat like a robot?"

I roll my eyes and snort a laugh, amused at the sight in front of me. I'll give her this. She's a wildcard.

"I feel like the answer to that is pretty obvious."

She stares back at, raising her eyebrows and shaking her head at me, prompting me to explain.

"You've seen me almost every morning for the last few weeks *buying* coffee." I gesture around the kitchen. "Clearly, I go out to get it."

She sighs and hangs her head. "Of course, this house is too good to be true." She stands and leans against the counter, crossing her arms just at the hem of her cropped t-shirt. I can't stop staring at her. She's wearing shorts with the waistband folded over showing off those hip bones. I suddenly want to reach out and grab her. With the way her arms prop her tits up, I have to look away before blood starts rushing to my cock. My running shorts definitely won't do me any favors hiding that.

Masochist definitely sounds accurate right now. I'm into my brother's fiancée's best friend. She's very off limits, but man she makes it hard when she's in my damn house wearing *that*.

I walk over to the kitchen, slowly shutting cabinets and putting things away. "Next time, can you please wait for me to get back before you throw all my stuff around the kitchen?" My tone is rough and clipped. I don't want to be mean, but I hate when my stuff is out of order and not where I expect it to be.

"Fine," she groans. I reach her and lean against the counter next to her.

I look into those blue eyes, forcing her to crane her neck to meet mine. "Come on. Put some clothes on and I'll take you for coffee and groceries."

She rolls her eyes and tosses her head back and forth. "What's wrong with my clothes?" Her lips curl into a smirk and points a finger at me, running it up and down. "You're wearing basically the same thing."

I groan and scowl at her. "Because my shorts don't have half my ass hanging out and my shirt isn't showing off my abs in the freezing cold."

She huffs a laugh. "Shame." She turns away from me and flicks her ponytail, hitting me in the face with it. I watch, open mouthed as she saunters towards the hall to the bedrooms. "I'll be right back."

"Hurry up, *princess.*" I call back in a growl, glad she's looking away as I watch her hips sway.

"YOU'RE RIDICULOUS. You know that, right?" I stand next to my truck, holding open the door and watch Lizzy practically have to jump out of the truck, kicking up a puff of snow when she hits the ground. "What? You said put on clothes and I did."

When I said to change out of her pajamas, this isn't what I had in mind. Pink leggings, a matching pink cropped sports top, a cropped hoodie, fluffy white earmuffs, and furry boots hardly seem practical with today's weather.

"Seriously? Do you own any tops that cover your stomach? You realize this is a ski town right and it's still cold as hell?"

"Whatever. Don't be such a baby. You were the one out running in shorts this morning. Come on, let's go inside."

She's got me there.

When I walk into Finch, still in my running outfit, I see Hannah behind the counter. She cocks her head and gives me a curious smile, looking up at the clock and then back at me.

"I must be seeing things because you never break your routine," she teases.

I grab the back of my neck. "Yeah, today isn't routine." Hannah laughs until Lizzy walks in the door and comes out from behind me, finding a seat at the counter against the window. Hannah's eyes go wide and she grins.

"I think you already know Lizzy," I say, my voice awkwardly ticking up a notch.

Lizzy waves from her seat to Hannah before turning to me. "I'll take my usual."

I nod and walk to the counter where Hannah is still sheepishly grinning at me. "What?"

"I don't think I've seen you here with someone besides your sister or Kayleigh." I palm my face and groan in frustration.

"No. It's not like *that*." It's too late and I can feel my cheeks start to heat with embarrassment, like I'm being caught redhanded by my sister or something.

"Ok, Clay." She props herself up on the counter, still grinning. "So two nitros and her chocolate croissant?"

I nod and tap my card on the reader.

After grabbing our order, I walk over to Lizzy and sit next to her. She lifts her eyes from her phone and smiles wide when I set the coffee and food in front of her.

"Thank you!" She beams, grabbing the cold coffee and taking a way too eager gulp. She closes her eyes and exhales deeply. "Sorry about before. I am *not* a morning person. I definitely get hangry and snarky when I haven't had coffee or food."

"Really?" I prop myself up on one elbow and quirk an eyebrow at her. "I thought snarky was your thing twenty-four-seven."

She rolls her eyes before taking a bite of her croissant, letting out the quietest whimper that sends blood straight below my waist again.

Jesus. What is it with her?

"These are *so* good," she says, wiping a crumb off her lips. She eyes me again, but with curiosity this time. "So. Books. Romance books. Smutty romance books." She looks like she's about to burst from excitement, clearly ready to continue my misery.

"Yeah, and?" I answer, my tone shorter than I wanted it to be.

She holds a hand out, gesturing up and down at me again. "You,

Mr. Tall, Gruff, and Grumpy, come in here, buy, read and collect smutty romance books?" She props herself up on her elbow, matching my pose, but tapping one very pink fingernail against those pouty lips, looking right back at me.

I groan. "Can we please not? I already told you."

A soft giggle escapes her lips. "Nope, I feel like torturing you today after you flooded my condo. So, tell me more."

I grab my coffee and take a long drink. "Well first, I already told you that I don't like people. Books are fun and don't let you down." I take a deep breath, looking out the window at Main Street before turning back to Lizzy. "And second, like I said before, Utah has shitty porn laws and smutty novels are so much better. And lastly, I don't really date."

"You don't seem like the type to have a problem finding a date, even with your scowls and charming disposition," she says, smiling softly before looking back down at the counter. "You definitely had no issue picking me up at the bar."

"You were an exception." Her eyes meet mine, contemplating that statement before I chuckle.

"Seriously, how are you single? Employed, knows how to decorate, a sense of style, *this*." She eyes me up and down.

I feel my jaw tense and my forehead crease. "I don't need people. I'm fine by myself."

She looks at me like she wants to pry more, but thankfully doesn't.

"So, you were serious yesterday? I can stay with you as long as it takes to fix the condo?"

I slide my hand over, grabbing her drink and the croissant, getting her attention. She glares at my hand and then back at me. "I told you before. I promised I would make things right. I don't take that lightly. So yes, you're welcome as long as you need to stay." I study her deep blue eyes, driving home my point.

"Fine," she huffs before taking her drink and food back, carefully plucking them from my hands. "I'll stay, even with your *charming disposition.* But I have one condition." She taps her finger on her lip again, clearly pondering something. Oh my god, those pouty fucking lips. "Make that two conditions."

"HOW ARE YOU SO DAMN TIGHT?" I chide, trying in vain to push her straight legs back towards her chest, stretching her hamstrings.

"I'm not tight. You're just not strong enough," she groans. Seriously, how did I get here today?

Dumb question. I know exactly how. I should have asked Lizzy for more details. Instead, I blindly agreed to her conditions.

Would I still have agreed knowing what I know now? Yes, but at least I would have tried to negotiate a better deal for myself.

Condition one: a coffee maker. Easy.

Condition two: helping her do her yoga on weeknights and weekend mornings. Not so easy.

As soon as we got back from the coffee shop, she wanted to dive right into it. And it's definitely not easy, especially when it turned into me being pressed against her in every single suggestive way possible.

"You know, for someone that always wears matching yoga outfits, you suck at stretching." I hold her legs there, watching as she folds her arms around the back of her thighs to hold the position.

"Very funny. I'm sure you're as stiff as a board, Clay. I'd like to see you stretch." That hit a little too close to home considering the situation in my shorts right now. But the joke's on her.

"Move over." I kneel on the ground next to her, gesturing for her to get off the yoga mat.

Now, this should be fun.

CHAPTER 17
LIZZY
ARE YOU SERIOUS?

I ROLL off the yoga mat, sitting crosslegged on the rug in front of the fireplace after Clay gruffly told me to move. I will give it to him. This is definitely a scenic, cozy place to do yoga. A fireplace on one side and floor to ceiling windows looking out over the mountains.

But *this* view.

Clay, kneeling on the yoga mat in shorts and a tight, sleeveless workout shirt. He's stretching his arms behind his back and rolling his neck. I mean it's downright pornographic. He's a masterpiece of sinewy muscles flexing under a rippling painting of tattoos. If he was facing me, he'd see a shade of crimson crawling across my skin.

Somehow, my idea of Clay being my accountability buddy seems incredibly indulgent right now. A true *treat yourself* moment on my *Tour de Lizzy*.

Clay slowly goes through a short routine alternating back and forth between downward dog and cobra poses.

I sit here, crossing my arms in amusement. He's good at it, but that's nothing crazy. "Clay, you don't have to do this."

He stays quiet and pulls himself up into a cobra. I'm about to say something when he flawlessly shifts into a crow pose and holds it.

I sit in stunned silence while he transitions from that into a shoulder stand, balancing his entire weight on his hands.

"Were you saying something about stiff as a board?" he says gruffly, turning to look at me over his shoulder, smirking.

Are you serious?

"How on earth are you doing that?"

He gracefully lowers himself back to the floor and sits facing me, looking at me sheepishly. "You do know I qualified for the Olympics, right?"

I think back to the pictures on the walls last night, thinking about some of the medals for international competitions. But the Olympics? I didn't know that. The idea that this gruff construction worker, being a former world class athlete, is a stark contrast. I mean he certainly has the body for it. But how did he really get here besides the injuries?

"I didn't know that," I say in a whisper. "I thought with your knees and not being able to ski, you'd be a little less flexible than this." A half-hearted nervous laugh leaves my mouth as I gesture at him on the mat.

"I can still ski." His voice is ice, clearly not amused.

The abruptness of his comment almost startles me.

"Oh, well then when did you stop skiing?"

He shifts uncomfortably and runs his hand back and forth over the smaller scar on his left knee. "After this one." He stands and walks over to the window, looking out at the mountains in the distance. "Can we talk about literally anything else?"

He turns back to me, still sporting a scowl.

"Seriously, Clay. You should scowl less. You're going to get wrinkles," I joke, trying to change the topic and lighten the mood.

He continues to stand there like a statue, seemingly unamused. With the morning light coming in, his imposing silhouette is quite a sight.

"Actually, on second thought, you're already too pretty. Maybe you can keep scowling." I pinch my fingers together in front of my face. "Just a little."

His lip twitches flashing a dimple on his cheek that's quickly turning red.

"Clay Chapman," I say with a playful tone.

"What?" He looks concerned, like I've caught him doing something he's not supposed to.

"You're trying not to laugh, aren't you?"

He groans and strides back across the floor, settling down on the ground in front of me. "You're something else, Lizzy."

Again, there's something about that phrase, *something else*, that sticks with me and hits me in my heart.

Not too much.

Not tone it down.

I'm so used to hearing that I'm *not enough* or *too much*, that I should be anything other than my authentic self. So hearing just *something else* feels good, like he sees me for who I am.

"So... are we friends now or what?"

He shakes his head before reaching a hand out across the mat to me. "Friends."

I reach out and grab his hand, shaking it once. The feeling of his skin against mine sends a snap of electricity and heat through me, remembering the feeling of his touch at Roxy's. My voice trembles. "Yeah, friends." I quickly pull my hand away with a sheepish laugh.

"So, yoga then?" I ask, patting the mat between us.

He cocks his head. "I started doing it after my first ACL tear." He pats his right knee. "I also tore my meniscus and MCL and it was such a mess. Yoga became part of my rehab and stretching routine. I kept up with it. I do a little before my morning runs and a little afterwards or before bed."

I find myself thinking that the world is missing out on the sight of Clay Chapman doing morning yoga after a hot and sweaty run.

Lucky me.

No, Lizzy. No.

He's your best friend's soon-to-be-brother-in-law.

He's your temporary roommate and the one fixing your family's condo.

He's *your* friend.

Albeit, an insanely hot one with a dangerously irresistible dark and brooding side. But still a genuine friend, which I can never have enough of.

MONDAY MORNING COMES and I feel quite pleased with myself. Sunday went off without a hitch. I had fresh coffee. My new roommate, friend, and accountability buddy did yoga and a light workout with me again. I also noticed that Clay went and stocked the kitchen with the groceries we couldn't find Saturday at the small local store. And I even got some reading done.

Now it's back to the workweek, but at least I'm working from Clay's living room. He lit a fire before he left, and I have to say, a girl could get used to this. The house, the hot man servant - even Ani is actually pretty cool and has hung out with me all day.

It's lunch time here, but late afternoon in Ohio when Jessica calls me for our Monday check-in. I cozy up on the couch with my laptop on the coffee table when I see Jessica's face pop on the screen.

"How's my favorite subordinate today?" her familiar voice asks.

"Nice to see you too," I say, taking a sip of my second cup of coffee for the day.

"Oh, Lizzy, what would I do without you to brighten my soulless days in the office at Fischer?"

"Geez. Really selling the company hard there. Good thing I already work for you." I take another sip of my coffee while she starts to share something on her screen. My attention drifts when Ani's ears perk up and he walks excitedly over to the door behind me in the kitchen.

"Hey, boy. Good to see you." I hear Clay's deep voice in the kitchen.

"So, Lizzy, the numbers you sent last week." Jessica starts when I hear foot steps behind me going back and forth from the kitchen to the dining area.

I watch as Jessica's eyes go wide and her mouth hangs open on the screen. "Did you freeze or is something wrong?" I ask.

"Woah. What is *that*?" She points at the screen. "Or *who* is that?"

I turn around and see Clay, shirtless walking around the kitchen, tidying up my mess from making coffee.

Are you serious?

"Oh my god. Shit." I blurt out, frantically turning the laptop away from that view. "Sorry. That's my temporary roommate. You remember Veronica? It's her fiancé's brother. I'm staying with him until the condo gets fixed." I emailed her about it Friday, so this shouldn't be a surprise minus the whole shirtless eye candy she just saw.

"Sure." She drags out the word, grinning at me. "*Roommate*. Well, hopefully he's not too much of a distraction." I sigh and palm my face in embarrassment.

After my call is over, I walk over to Clay in the kitchen, who's standing there, still very shirtless, now eating a bowl of yogurt at the kitchen island.

"What the hell was that?" I stand right next to him, pushing him in the shoulder, which of course does nothing to him.

"What?" he says, still eating, like nothing is wrong.

"I mean, what the hell are you doing here in the middle of the day, parading around shirtless in the background of my video call."

He sets his spoon down in the bowl. "I come home at lunch every day. Normally let Ani out, eat, and do a chore or flip the laundry over. And today, I had an extra chore because you didn't clean up after yourself, princess."

I glare back at him. "And this needs to be done shirtless why?"

He shrugs. "I run hot. I don't like getting all sweaty running around the house doing chores and having to change. Normally I'm here *alone* so I just take off my shirt and put it back on before heading back out."

Ok. Maybe a little excessive, but I guess that's reasonable knowing Mr. Control-Freak-Hyper-Productivity here.

I take a deep breath and calmly exhale. "Ok. I guess that's fine. But condition number three." I hold up three fingers and wave them in his face. "Next time, can you just stay out of my camera's view?"

"Or you could just use my office for video calls," he says, pointing out the obvious answer. "Or better yet, you can use my office for anything you want. Oh, and speaking of..." he pauses for a second and shakes his head. "No, never mind. But yes, please use my office as much as you need to."

"OK, thanks. But what were you going to say?"

"It's nothing. Just, Tanner and V said you work in finance and accounting. I've been dealing with these invoices after I took on more responsibility at work and some of them just seem off to me." His brow furrows and his lips quirk together on one side. "If you have some time, I'd love a second set of eyes."

That's certainly not what I was expecting him to ask. "Sure. Of course. I'd be happy to."

"Thanks. Seriously." He nods appreciatively before finishing his yogurt.

I LEFT the house before Clay was home from work to meet Grace for happy hour. It was nice, but I'm beat, and thanks to my new account-ability buddy, I plan on being home and in bed at a reasonable hour. Ok. Maybe reasonable for me but late for most people, especially on a Monday night.

I put my keys on the hook, just like Clay asked and hang my purse and jacket on the coat rack. It's quiet except for the crackling of the fire, which seems odd because it's late, I assumed he would be in bed, and he doesn't seem like the type to leave a fire going all night.

I step around the corner quietly into the living room and to my surprise, Clay is there. I pull my hand to my chest, startled to see him. And boy, do I see him. He's sitting in the leather chair next to the fire with Ani curled up on the dog bed at his feet. My eyes move up from Ani, across Clay's bare legs, one crossed over the other, his scars and his thigh tattoos peeking out from under his gym shorts. He's holding a book, his tattooed hands delicately flipping the pages, his green eyes framed by black heavy rimmed glasses, and the fire is flickering against his short, dark, inky hair.

I stand there, hoping he won't notice and watch him for a second. A line in the book must be funny, because he laughs, a real laugh - not like the little chuckles or snorts I hear from him. His dimples pop and he actually looks like the twenty-eight year old he should be, not the hardened man that he is.

Seriously, where is the tree in Wyoming that the Chapman men grow on?

A giggle escapes my lips and I rush to cover my mouth. Ani's ears tilt to me but he doesn't move from his bed. Clay looks over and the content look on his face morphs into his usual scowl.

"Were you just standing there watching me?" he asks, turning his attention back to his book. "Fucking creepy."

I'm glad to see we're back to this Clay, moody and broody.

"I had to see it for myself. The dark and mysterious Clay Chapman, sitting by the fire and reading smutty romance books alone at night." I sit down in the other chair, on the opposite side of the fireplace. "And what's with the glasses? Aren't you too young for reading glasses? I didn't have you pegged for being the glamorous, fake lenses type."

He glares at me over the book and I have to admit, the glasses look good on him. "I wear contacts. It started with racing and moguls because glasses never work well with ski goggles. Then when I got into construction, it was easier with the safety glasses. It just became a routine. I take them out at night and to read to give my eyes a break."

I nod and settle into the chair, prompting a sigh of defeat from him. He dog ears a page and sets the book in his lap. "You're welcome to hang with me tonight. But if you're going to, I really want to finish this chapter. So read or yoga. Pick one."

I mock gasp at him. "Are you inviting me to spend time with you willingly? And did you just dog ear a page?" I clutch my hand to my chest. "How dare you assault a shelf trophy like that?"

He rolls his eyes and groans. "Don't ruin the moment."

"Fine. Yoga." I bounce out of the chair and head to the basket along the windows where we've been keeping our yoga mats. "You love giving me shit for my matching yoga outfits, but look who's already prepared."

I roll out the mat, take off my shoes, and settle into the start of my routine. I will begrudgingly admit that having Clay help me the last few days has been helpful. I can already feel a difference from three straight days of this routine.

And maybe it was the happy hour drinks, maybe it's the cute dog curled up on the dog bed, or maybe it's the warmth of the crackling fire, but I feel so relaxed here right now. I breathe deep, exhaling as I go into a downward dog.

My brief moment of bliss is interrupted by the sound of Clay clearing his throat. "You're loud." I glare at him, noticing he's doing the same over his book.

"Is that a complaint?"

"No, just an observation."

"I can go do it in my room if you'd prefer that." I start to stand, but he sets down his book.

"No. It's fine. Just never realized how loud yoga is when you're listening to someone do it."

My lips curve into a smile. "Well, no one has ever called me quiet." I wink back at him.

He rolls his eyes, but I don't miss that his cheeks go pink and his throat bobs. "I bet."

Ok. Maybe Grace was right. This isn't the rough, harsh man I expected.

"You know, you're not so bad, *Clayton* Chapman," I tease playfully.

"Please don't call me Clayton." His eyes are pleading, almost frighteningly soft compared to what I'm used to seeing. This look flat out catches me off guard.

"I'm sorry. I won't. I just thought-" he grabs his book and stands, with me still on the ground.

"It's fine." He steps over me and walks towards the hall to the bedrooms, stopping to turn back. I hear him let out a long, rough breath. "That's my full name, but only mom and Kayleigh would call me that. It's not your fault, you didn't know. I'm just tired. Good-night, Lizzy."

He turns again and heads to his room. My heart sinks at his admission while I watch his tall frame disappear from view. I feel like a jerk. I thought it was ok if Kayleigh was teasing him with it, but I didn't know that it was his mom's nickname for him. I guess they've known each other longer, since before that accident and he's ok with her calling him that.

CHAPTER 18
CLAY
ROOMMATE

"IF YOU WANT that nitro cold brew and croissant trip tomorrow morning, you're going to earn it," I challenge Lizzy from across living room floor on our opposing yoga mats.

"You're a sadistic asshole." She groans, trying to get deeper into her pose, stretching her hips. "Using my morning coffee to motivate me is pure evil. And am I quiet enough for you now?"

A deep chuckle rumbles in my chest. "You asked for an accountability buddy, here I am. And I never said you were too loud. It was just an observation."

There's something gratifying about her calling me sadistic when I've been calling myself a masochist for inviting her to stay here. But that said, I've actually enjoyed our workout sessions and coffee runs over the last week. This Friday evening is no different.

"Leave it to me to find someone that will actually take me seriously to hold me accountable and use my morning coffee against me along the way."

I pause, looking at her. She always seems so confident, but sometimes I notice these gaps where it feels like she doubts herself. "What do you mean take you seriously?"

I hear a frustrated breath escape her as she flops down on to her back, looking up at the ceiling. "I didn't realize I signed up for an accountability buddy *and* therapist."

If she only knew the shit I've had to unravel. I clear my throat, stride over to her and lay down on the floor beside her.

"Try me."

She rolls over, looking at me curiously with her ponytail draped over her shoulder, hanging between her breasts. I pull my eyes away to meet hers, which are already waiting with a knowing grin.

"The other day. You said I'm *something else*. And you said it at the bar too. But the way you said it stuck with me."

I roll to face her, propping myself up on my elbow, matching her.

"Yeah. I meant it. *You are* something else."

She scrubs her hand over her face before shoving me in the chest with a frustrated laugh. "That's what I mean, my whole life, I've been told I'm too much. *Tone it down, Lizzy. Inside voice, Lizzy.* But then with other people, - my ex, my dad - it feels like I'm not enough." Her eyes drop and I finally see a crack in that fierce facade. "I just want to be me and taken seriously for who I am."

Fuck me. This is the girl that dreams are made of. Everything about her is so genuine, so defiant, so real. Anyone that could make her doubt herself, much less one of her own parents, needs a sanity check or a fist to the face.

"Hey." I reach out and tilt her chin back up, forcing her to look at me. The feeling of her skin on my finger tips sends a jolt through me. "You're amazing. If you need a reminder of that, just remember the whole Chapman family, the Perry twins and even Kayleigh like you. I'd consider that pretty good company."

She nods and then pulls my hand away to the ground between us. "Alright, your turn."

"What?" I ask, sure that my face is expressing the right level of confusion.

A mischievous grin takes over her face. "I shared, now it's your turn. Tell me about..." she pauses and taps one of those pink nails against those fucking lips I keep thinking about tasting again. "The Jensens. How did you become so close with them?"

A shiver runs right down my spine. "You really don't pull punches." She shrugs and cocks her head, letting her smile do all the talking. "Fine. I met Kayleigh in my ski competitions during my last year of high school. I was in international qualifiers working up to the Olympic qualifiers at that point. And well, you know her dad and her family's history. He took an interest in me pretty earlier on."

She nods. "Did you and Kayleigh ever...?"

I snort a laugh. This is the question I was waiting for. "We dated in high school, if you could even call it that. We're entirely incompatible romantically. But we've been best friends ever since."

She hums curiously. "And when did you start working for him?"

"A couple years after Mom," I trail off, my voice strained. Even now the words still stick in my throat, not letting me finish the sentence. These are things I've buried in me, practically never talking about with anyone. "That's when I tore my other ACL. Up to that point, I was rehabbing and training to compete and in school for architecture. After my second ACL injury, I just needed to stop. My headspace was a giant mess. My dad had his hands full with Grace and his own grief. Mr. Jensen was there for me and mentored me. I took a break from school, started working for him, and never stopped."

The way her icy blue eyes cut into me with her soft smile makes me feel something I haven't felt in ages. She's not pitying me, she's not afraid of me - she's just here, feeling this with me. This time, she reaches out to me, cupping my jaw and running her thumb over my stubble. All of this just feels so charged. I can feel my heart pounding against my ribs. Everything about her makes me feel electric. She inches closer to me and I swear I can hear her heart beating.

And that's when I hear something else. Our eyes look to the same place, spotting Ani running towards us, his collar jingling. He's carrying something in his mouth. We're both laying on the ground, catching our breath when he reaches us.

You've got to be fucking kidding me.

"Someone has been a bad boy." I pat him on the head, already laughing to myself when I see what's in his mouth. "Drop it."

He immediately drops *it* on the floor between Lizzy and me.

Lizzy looks down and her eyes go wide and her cheeks turn bright pink when he drops the sparkly purple werewolf dildo between us.

She looks at me in abject horror, but all I can do is keep laughing.

"Oh my god! This isn't funny!" She punches me in my shoulder and Ani just sits there next to us, none the wiser at the hilarity of what he just did. "Why are you still laughing?"

Her eyes meet mine and that familiar icy blue is melting with embarrassment.

"Nothing. It's just..." I look at the toy, filled with teeth marks, and then back at her. "You called him a damn wolf when you first met him, and here he is, running through the house with that in his mouth."

She looks at me, her lips twitching and the muscles in her face straining to press her lips together.

"Oh my god, Lizzy Frank. Are you trying not to laugh?" I tease her with my best feminine voice. She rolls her eyes, but her willpower falters and a giggle escapes her parted lips. That giggle grows into outright laughter.

"OK, you're right. That's kind of hilarious." She grabs the toy and sits up, shaking her head, her cheeks still flushed. After a second, a frown spreads across her face.

"Hey, don't worry about it. I'll buy you a new one."

Another soft laughs escapes her lips. "Do friends buy each other sex toys?"

Now that is a great question. Lizzy Frank is anything but a normal friend.

She really is *something else.*

CHAPTER 19
LIZZY
NEVER AGAIN

I WALK DOWN the aisle at Finch, heading straight towards the back corner. I've always loved this shop. Something about the combination of an independent bookstore and a coffee shop is just right. Not to mention that they have a very well curated romance section. Seriously, whoever picks their books knows what's up.

And with my parents always busy when we were in town, I was always free to roam and buy whatever book I wanted on Dad's credit card. They'd either drop me off on Main Street after a day of skiing or let me take the condo's shuttle.

So it's only fitting that today, on my birthday, I stop in. I'm just glad it's Friday and I can wash away this feeling spending the weekend in bed with a new book. Go figure - my dad, yet again, has forgotten about my birthday. It shouldn't be hard to remember your firstborn's birthday. I just don't get it. Growing up I did everything my parents asked. My mom always remembers, but it's like my dad just forgot I existed at some point or didn't know how to talk to me. It would always be some excuse like getting caught up with work. It just never seemed like I was a priority for him as I got older.

So yeah, I'm treating myself today.

Do I *need* to find some faerie dragon smut today? Absolutely not.

Do I want it? Absolutely *yes*.

I hope they have the first book in that series Clay mentioned during our morning yoga the other day. I'd read his, but I'm not going to crease the bindings in his special edition hardbacks, even if he said *they're meant for reading, Lizzy.*

I browse the shelf, spotting the black jacketed book with gold lettering on the top row. *Scales of Fury.* I think it's supposed to be a pun on tipping the scales and dragons having scales? Either way, I've learned that Clay weirdly knows his books and I'm in the mood for some romantasy. His library and trophy room is the stuff of dreams. Who would have ever thought Mr. Dark and Broody was a book girlie under his all black wardrobe and constant scowls?

Grabbing the book, I head towards the counter to order my coffee and pay.

"Oh my gosh!" The girl behind the counter practically squeals when she grabs my book to ring me out. I think her name is Hannah? I can't remember what Clay said. "I *love* this series. The spice? Give me all of it."

I huff a laugh. "Yeah, that's what my friend who recommended it said. I think you know Clay, right?" He also said I should get a dragon dildo to go with it, but I'm not going to volunteer that tidbit.

She nods as she enters my coffee order and bags my book with the receipt. "Yep. Clay is here almost everyday, if not multiple times a day. He's our favorite customer, hands down." She laughs and then points back at my book. "We actually just had that author in for a signing. She was so sweet. She signed all the copies we had too." I flip to the title page and sure enough, it's signed.

"Wow. Very cool. Thanks!" I take my bag and find a comfy leather seat by the front window. I pull out my phone, opening my social media app. I haven't logged into my bookstagram account in ages, but some character art would be cool to see and get me in the mood to start the book.

I scroll through my feed. Books, more books, smutty memes. All the stuff I used to love seeing. But I freeze on one post. My thumb hovers over my phone screen.

"What the fuck?" I mumble under my breath.

That's a hand. A hand with a fucking engagement ring. On Johnathan's profile. I unfollowed and blocked him from all my accounts and feeds, but I must have forgotten about my bookstagram account since I haven't used it in forever.

I finally swipe to the next picture. They're sitting there, her hand out while she sits in his lap. It's barely been six months and they're engaged. He's engaged to the woman he cheated on me with.

I can feel my face start to scrunch together. I don't cry. But for once, I don't think I'm going to be able to stop it and I don't care.

Why am I not good enough? Why am I never fucking good enough?

I rush out of Finch, not bothering to wait for my coffee. I need to get home. Or at least back to Clay's house. I've had enough people for today.

No.

Screw that.

Enough people forever.

I suddenly get why Clay hates people.

Enough crap like this and I'd want to live in a cozy house, alone, up in the mountains too.

WHEN I PULL into Clay's driveway, I slam my car door shut and rush inside. Despite the shit show of emotions running through my head and tears running down my face, I still somehow remember to hang my jacket and put my shoes in their tray. Fucking Clay. It's only been two weeks and somehow he's got me remembering his control freak routine.

"Hey, princess. How was your day?" Clay's deep, playful voice rumbles from the living room into the kitchen. Shit. He must have come home from work early. I don't need him to see me like this. I never want him to see me like this. *No one* gets to see me like this.

I rush through the kitchen trying to cut through the living room towards the hall to the bedrooms. Clay must have been stretching because he's in his gray sweatpants and shirtless and just a bit sweaty. When he sees me, he jumps to his feet and rushes over, cutting me off from the hallway.

"I don't want to talk. I've had a shitty day. I just want to go lay down. I don't want to play games." I keep my eyes down, trying to hide my tears and get past him, but he stretches an arm out and catches me by my waist with his stupid and hot bear paw mitts he calls hands. My momentum carries me forward and I fall face first into his broad, muscular chest. The feeling of his warmth against my face and the sudden, unexpected skin to skin contact, is so over-whelming but soothing. I lean into him more, craving this level of comfort. My tears become sobs. I don't care that I'm sobbing into his chest. We've gotten past our initial bitterness since the misunder-standing at the bar. We're closer. We're friends even. But he didn't sign up for this. This isn't part of the *acquaintances that tolerate each other* playbook.

"Lizzy." His voice is deep, but the playful tone is long gone. "What happened? What the fuck is wrong?"

I sniffle into his chest, surprisingly enjoying his leathery cedar scent. How does he smell like this when he was just working out?

"It's nothing. It's not your problem. Can you just let me go? I just want to lay down." I try to side step him, but he matches my step, putting my face once again back into his chest.

I look up at him and his eyes are locked on to mine. There's a look in those beautiful emerald green eyes I haven't seen before. They're intense, like the night at the bar. But there's a softness to them too. It's like he's inspecting me for some kind of damage, where I might be hurt, trying to figure out why I'm crying like this.

His throat bobs but he doesn't look away. "Did someone fucking do this to you, princess?"

CHAPTER 20

CLAY
THE PRINCESS YOU ARE

I STARE DOWN AT LIZZY. It's taking every ounce of self-control I have to not interrogate her and find the fucking asshole that made her feel like this. That will have to wait because the defeated look in her tear filled, perfect sapphire eyes is tearing at heartstrings I thought I cut out years ago.

I tilt her chin up, not letting her look away from me. I can feel the column of her throat shift when she swallows. I run my thumb over her soft cheek, brushing away a stray tear.

"It's nothing." She twists her neck, pulling her face from my hand and burying it back into my chest. I feel her take a deep breath and hesitate before barely whispering against my skin. "I'm just never fucking good enough for anyone."

My blood is practically boiling with rage.

What the fuck? How could *she* think she's not enough? How could this woman not be *enough* for anyone? I might be younger than her. But I'm pretty confident that I know she's more than enough woman for me. My hands start to clench into fists at the thought of anyone ever hurting this little firecracker.

I cup the back of her head, putting my lips against her soft, blonde hair, drinking in the now familiar smell of coconut and citrus that's everywhere in my house and even my own bathroom because I've been buying her shampoo for myself. "Tell me what you need. Tell me how I can make you feel better. You just have to tell me."

She wraps her arms around me, running them up my back until she raises her eyes to look at me.

"Clay," she says, practically whispering between sobs. "I just want this feeling to go away. For once, I want to feel like I'm everything to someone."

The look in her eyes is pleading. Her lips part and she stands on her toes. It's almost adorable that she thinks she can reach me when I'm a foot taller than her. But fuck, *she* wants to kiss me. *I want to kiss her.* My body definitely agrees based on the amount of blood rushing to my cock.

This might be a bad idea. A fucking terrible idea.

But rejecting her right now? There's no way I can do that. I can try to hide my feelings tonight. I can do this for her. One more knife to my heart won't kill me.

I tilt her chin back up, pressing my thumb against her parted lips. "If that's what you need tonight, I will make you feel like you're the entire world. I'll make you forget about anyone that's ever made you feel like anything less than that, Lizzy." As soon as I say the words, I crane my neck down and close the distance between us.

Our lips meet in a hot, frenzied kiss. It feels electric. The way she opens her mouth, kissing me back furiously, lights a spark - fuck that - an entire fire in my cold, dark heart. The kiss at the bar was hot, but this is different. This is everything. My heart is thundering so goddamn hard in my chest.

I force myself to pull away just long enough for our eyes to meet again. "Lizzy. Are you sure you want this?"

She stares back at me. The defeated look replaced with the fiery one I remember from the first night we met. "Clay, shut up and make me forget everything."

I grin back at her. "God, you're such a fucking brat. I knew it the second I saw you in my stool at the bar in those pink boots. But I don't want to make you *just* forget. I'm going to remind you of everything you are."

I lean back down, pressing my lips into hers, cupping her ass in my hands and pulling her up to my waist. She wraps her legs around me and I carry her down the hall to her room.

"My room? Why not yours?" She breathes the words against my neck.

"Because you're a spoiled little brat and you have the nicer, comfier bed. And I'm going to remind you exactly how fucking special you are." I can't see her face, but I'm pretty sure she rolls her eyes and I even feel her giggle against my collarbone.

I reach the foot of the bed, letting go of her gently onto the thick comforter. I point to the headboard and tip my chin. "Now lay back against that absurd pile of pillows."

"I never pictured you as the fancy pillow type." She flicks her eyebrows, smirking at me.

"I'm not. I put them in here right before you moved in."

She looks almost startled and confused, turning between the pillows and me. "You mean you put all those here for me?"

I chuckle and kneel on the foot of the bed, grinning back at her. "I sleep with two fucking pillows and they definitely aren't pink. I knew you were extra and bought them before you brought your stuff over. And before you say it, I love that you're so fucking extra. Extra is good. You don't hide it. You're you - always you."

Her jaw drops and she smiles back at me. I'm glad she's enjoying this and her tears have stopped. That's all I want right now, for her to feel good.

I close the distance between us, kneeling in front of her. I drop my head to her neck, planting kiss after kiss. Behind her ear and on her delicate collar bone. She closes her eyes, tilting her head back and whimpering with each kiss. I can feel her nails dig into my back when she wraps her arms around me. I slide my hands down to her waist and pull her sweater over her head.

Holy fuck. She's wearing the hottest, lacy black bra and her hard pebbled nipples are showing through the sheer fabric. Her perky tits are unreal. The perfect size for her small frame.

"What?" she asks playfully. "See something you like?"

I'm pretty sure I'm drooling at this point. "You could say that. Now take it off and lay back in that ridiculous pillow nest." I keep staring shamelessly as she bares her fucking perfect tits to me. She pulls her arms together, pressing her breasts together and making my already rock hard cock twitch.

She looks at me, clearly noticing what she's doing to me, biting her lip and points at my erection which is now impossible to hide with my sweatpants. "Aren't you going to take those off?"

I look down at the bulge in my pants and shake my head with a smirk. It's going to fucking kill me to do this.

I lift my eyes to meet hers. She looks like a dream leaning back against the pillows and headboard. Her long, blonde hair is flowing over her shoulders and she's propping herself up on her elbows. "No. This isn't for me, Lizzy. This is all about *you*."

I move forward on my knees, settling myself between her legs. I slowly run my hands up her legs over the fabric of her tights and to the hem of her skirt. When I reach her waist, I drop my gaze back to hers. Her sparkling blue eyes melt the cold icy mess that's been my heart for nearly a fucking decade. "You're so goddamn beautiful." I drop my face to hers just long enough to softly kiss her. When I pull away, her head follows mine for the slightest moment, asking for more.

Sitting back, she unzips her skirt and slides it off with her tights. She's almost completely naked, spreading her legs in front of me. "Fuck me, Lizzy. You're perfect. So fucking perfect."

I lean down, bringing my mouth to hers. Her breasts are pressed against my chest and I can feel each one of her heavy, labored breaths. I stop kissing her and press my forehead to hers. "I mean it. You're fucking perfect. And I'm going to remind you just how perfect you are. You deserve to be worshipped. I'm going to savor every second, knowing I'm making you come like no one ever has."

Pulling away, I press a gentle kiss to her forehead. "You're so goddamn smart and determined. It's like you were made to press my buttons, you little fucking brat."

I kiss her just below the shell of her ear, prompting her to whimper and arch her back to press her body against mine. The way she's craving my touch is like a drug. "You listen to me like no one ever has. You're so fucking kind and caring. You make me want to tell you things that I've never told any one else."

I pull away again, looking into those deep sapphire pools. "You see right through me. Not the shitty, angry parts that everyone else sees or the broken parts people pity. But the real me."

"Clay," she calls out in a breathy whisper before I cut her off, leaning down to kiss her again on the lips, biting and tugging on her lower lip.

"You have the fucking sexiest, dirtiest, sassiest mouth. And you mean what you say. You never hold back." I lower myself further down, kissing the delicate skin between her breasts. Her chest rises and she reaches for me, running her fingers through my hair. "You have the biggest fucking heart. You care so much about everyone in your life." I linger there long enough to feel her heart pounding in her chest.

I run my hands over her ribs and down her waist, kissing each of her hip bones. She arches her back, pushing herself into me. "And you are so goddamn sexy, Lizzy. I mean it. You're perfect. Everything about you is perfect."

I plant one soft, teasing kiss on her swollen clit, rubbing my stubble against her inner thighs.

"Damnit, Clay. Please, stop being so sappy." She pulls my hair tighter, pulling my mouth against her. She's already so wet and she tastes so good.

"Don't worry. I'm going to take care of you. I'm going to make you remember you're a goddamn princess." Before she can say anything, I lap and lick her at her wet heat, flicking my tongue up and down, back and forth over her clit. I grip her hip with one hand, holding her against the bed as she bucks and writhes into me.

She moans my name and my cock throbs. If it were any other time, any other reason for doing this, I'd probably already be fucking that pretty little mouth of hers, loving the sight of those lips she's always tapping wrapped around my cock before burying myself in her. The best I can do is grind myself into the bed, enjoying the friction while I'm pleasing her.

With my other hand, I tease her pussy with a finger, lingering just at her opening.

"I need more," she whimpers, her nails digging into my hair.

I slide my finger in, curling it in a come hither motion while I keep sucking her clit and flicking my tongue across it.

"Holy fuck. You're so wet and tight," I groan against her clit. I add a second finger, pumping them deeper into her. She wraps her legs around me, pulling my face even harder against her.

I reward her, lapping with my tongue faster and more firmly over her clit, matching the pace with my curling fingers.

I knew being with her would be amazing, but this is an entirely different level.

CHAPTER 21
LIZZY
PRETTY DECENT

THE SIGHT of Clay's head wrapped between my legs with my fingers laced through his hair is not something I thought I'd see today. OK, maybe ever.

I've definitely imagined it, but he's every bit as good at this as I thought he'd be. I might literally combust. The way his tongue is flicking back and forth over my clit and his groans of approval reverberate through my pussy while his fingers stretch and fill me feels so good. He's like one of those sex toys that sucks your clit and hits your g-spot all at once.

And he's so eager - so fucking eager to please. I mean, yeah, he's younger... but he's also so much more man than I've ever been with. No one's ever teased me or worshipped me like he did with his trail of kisses and praises.

I'm getting so close, with a knot of tension low in my core, but I don't want this to end. It has never felt this good, this explosive and electric before. His words, his kisses, his presence. It's all-consuming.

My attention is drawn away from over processing and right back to him when he starts sucking on bundle of nerves while still lapping at me with his tongue.

"Holy shit," I whimper, tightening my grip on his short tousled hair. "Please, don't fucking stop. I'm going to come if you keep doing that."

He groans into me again, which only pushes me closer to the edge. "That's kind of the point."

I look back down at him, but I'm caught off guard when he takes one, broad, muscular forearm, loops it under my bent knees, and presses it against the backs of my thighs. He's pinning my legs down against my chest, leaving my aching wet pussy completely at his mercy. He devours me and that knot of tension breaks. I fall apart and his mouth stays on me. His fingers massage *that* spot deep in my core, wringing every last ounce of pleasure out of me.

"Oh my god." I pull his hair, desperate to be closer to him. He plants a kiss on my pussy before sucking my now hypersensitive clit and flicking his tongue over it, making me squeeze his head again between my thighs.

He sits back up on his knees, smirking back at me. I stare at him, melting into a puddle of pleasure on the pile of pillows I now have a *very different* appreciation for. I lay here, sated, happy, catching my breath, acutely aware of every nerve ending after the orgasm he just gave me. He just grins at me, clearly satisfied with his work. He's so cocky and I can't blame him, but I still feel the urge to push his buttons.

"That was pretty *decent,*" I tease.

His nostrils flare as he exhales and wipes my glistening arousal from his lips. "You're such a goddamn brat." I shouldn't be surprised that he's amused. "That was just my fingers and tongue."

He leans down, kissing the tops of both of my knees before grinning back at me. I give in, grinning at the sight of him, giving him some satisfaction. I know I can tease him, but he just rocked my world and he's right, that was *only* his fingers and tongue.

I watch as his deep emerald green eyes rake my body and his chest heaves, only making his muscular body look more defined. "I'm glad to see I can shut that sassy little mouth of yours up." He smiles back at me and leans forward, running his hands up and down my thighs. I'm still so overstimulated that the feeling of his worn, rough hands against my smooth skin sends a shiver through me.

I raise my eyebrows at him and reach for the waistband of his sweatpants. "I can think of another way you could shut me up."

For the slightest moment, his brows furrow and there's a look of doubt in his face. Whatever it was, it doesn't last long. That cocky, blazing intensity is back in his eyes and he grins at me so wickedly I'm almost afraid about what he has in mind. "I told you. This isn't for me, *Lizzy*. This is all about *you*. Now sit back." His voice is low and full of gravel. It's rough and commanding like that night in the bar.

He straightens up on his knees, shimmying his sweats down enough to let his cock spring free before sitting back again.

Oh. Shit.

I assumed he was *large* based on what I saw at the hot tub and the way he was straining against his sweats tonight. And he is. Thick, veiny, and lengthy. He would be a challenge, a fun *challenge,* to fit. And I don't back down from a challenge.

I reach towards him, eagerly wanting to grab him. I'm startled when one of his big hands bats mine away. "No." He growls at me. "Sit. Fucking. Back." He puts one hand squarely on my chest, flicking his wrist and pushing me back into the pillows with no effort.

I cross my arms and huff, glaring back at him. "You're no fun."

He lets out a low, mischievous laugh. "I never said I'd be fun." He rests one hand on his knee and grins down at me. "I told you you're so fucking special. Now I want you to *watch* what you do to me. I want you to *see* how you make me feel. You're going to remember that you're more than enough."

I watch as he grips his length with his other hand, slowly working it up and down. His eyes dart back and forth between my breasts, my still very wet and sensitive pussy, my lips, and my eyes.

Holy shit. This is... *intimate.*

My eyes do the same, struggling to decide where to look. His flexed abs, the forearm that's straining from stroking himself, his dimples, or his smoldering green eyes.

"I knew you were extra. I knew you were a brat." He grunts while he strokes his cock. His eyes stay fixed on mine, burning into me.

"I knew I wanted you to push my buttons to my limit and then I was going to enjoy shutting you up with my cock in that pretty little mouth when you finally made me snap." His other hand grips his knee harder and his tattooed knuckles whiten.

I nod and grin back. "What else did you want?"

He grins and bares his teeth while still stroking himself. "I've done this so many times thinking about fucking you so hard the only word coming out of your mouth would be my name."

His chest heaves faster and his breathing quickens. It's so hot seeing him start to unravel and let go like this. I know I've thought about him like this, but knowing he's done it too makes my throat go dry and my thighs clench.

"Oh yeah? And where did you want to come when you thought about me?"

His eyes flitter all over my body. "On your tits, buried in your tight cunt, in your mouth, wherever you want me to. You have no idea what it was doing to me knowing you were on the other side of my bedroom wall with that fucking toy."

My mind races, thinking that he might have been thinking about me the same time I was thinking about him, at night and alone in bed with only a wall between us.

"Then come on me. I want to watch." I pucker my lips and air kiss at him.

His eyes close for a second as he strokes faster. Then his eyes lock back on mine.

"Fuck, Lizzy." He leans forward, putting himself between my thighs. He strokes himself hard. His whole body is flexed and coiled like he's going to erupt in pleasure at any second. "Do you see what you do to me? I'm going to come so fucking hard."

I stretch my legs out and wrap them around his waist, pulling him closer to me. I want to see him let go. He's right. Knowing that he wants me this bad is so satisfying. But knowing that he wants me to watch is even better.

"Good. I want your cum on me. Show me." He strokes harder and I look down to watch as he grunts. He props himself over me with his free hand. His flexed and strained forearm, the veins in his abs and that muscular V running down to his cock, everything bringing my eyes back to him when he comes apart. He lets go of rope after rope of warm cum on my stomach and chest and I savor the view of his body letting go.

He leans down, his mouth craving mine. My tongue searches for his, but he pulls back, pressing his forehead to mine. Our bodies are pressed together and I realize there's something weirdly hot about a man not afraid to touch his own cum.

He pulls back further, making my body instantly crave his warmth again. "Come on. Let's clean up."

"What? No warm towel service?" I tease.

He shakes his head and grumbles something under his breath. Before I can say anything though, he scoops me into his arms and carries me out of bed. I can't help but giggle all the way to the en suite bathroom.

He starts the shower, waiting for the temperature to be just right before pulling us both in.

"Ok. This is better than towel service." I look into his eyes, but he doesn't seem amused. He just grabs my body wash and scrubs me. I take a dab of it and do the same to him.

"Hey, what's wrong?" I ask, stepping closer to him, continuing to run a hand over his thin, dark chest hair, leaving my hand over the wolf tattoo.

His concerned eyes study my face. "Nothing. Just don't let anyone ever tell you who you are, Lizzy." He keeps looking at me, but it's like he's haunted by a distant, sad memory. He shakes his head, realizing he's been staring and grabs my shampoo. "Turn around."

He doesn't give me the chance to follow his order and turns me around on his own. I'm realizing I like the way he manhandles me with his big strong hands. I thought it would be a fun change when I first saw him at Roxy's. Something to try on for size for a night. But now, it's comforting in a way I didn't know I wanted. Maybe even needed.

I lean back against him, feeling his cock against my lower back because he's so much taller than me. But when he starts to work the shampoo into my hair with those same, strong hands, dear god. I whimper at the heavenly touch. *Now this* I could get used to.

I hear him sigh behind me and press himself harder against my lower back. "Something wrong?" I ask.

His hands keep working and I really can't get enough of it. "This shampoo. This smell. I've been thinking about it every day since that night at Roxy's."

Something about that statement sends another jolt to my core.

"You're not what I expected that night." A low laugh rumbles in his chest and I can feel it against my back. He doesn't talk, but he keeps massaging my scalp, permission to keep going. "I knew you were hot. I assumed you knew what you were doing in bed. I thought you'd be a fun distraction. But Clay, you're so much more."

"Oh yeah?" Another laugh rumbles behind me. He pulls me under the warm shower and starts to rinse my hair. "What am I like? Tell me."

I tilt my head back, leaning into him more and enjoying the hot, steamy water running over me while his hands run through my wet hair. "I don't know. You look young, but you're somehow old and soulful. You're just different. You're not just a pretty face. You're more."

"That sounds an awful lot like *extra*. Very original." There's a playful, teasing tone to his voice.

I spin and lean against the cool shower wall, crossing my arms and playfully glaring at him. "Fuck off, Clay."

He laughs and turns off the water, stepping out and grabbing two towels. "Come on. I'll tuck you in, princess."

He grabs my hand, pulling me from the shower and drying me. After putting on my sleep shorts and oversized tee, I crawl into bed. To my surprise, he curls up behind me, draping a massive arm over me, pulling me in tightly. "I didn't think you'd be the cuddling type."

I hear a frustrated sigh behind me. "Shut up, Lizzy. You're ruining it."

And with that, I doze off in his arms. Completely, blissfully, not giving a shit about how my day started out. This is exactly how Clay said he'd make me feel. This is not what I expected.

Clay is not what I expected.

WHEN I WAKE, I reach behind me, suddenly missing the warmth that I enjoyed all night. I rollover, breathing in the scent of Clay.

Wait.

Oh my god.

My eyes fly open.

I hooked up with Clay last night. My best friend's soon-to-be-brother-in-law. He's my friend too. Also sort of my roommate. We didn't even talk about rules or anything.

My mind races. This could be a mess. I'm going to need to process this, but not right now.

Because all I can think about is the way he treated me last night. Like I was the only thing in the world that mattered. He did what he said he would do, make me feel like nothing else mattered and remind me who I am.

After my eyes adjust to the morning light peering in the window, I look over at the nightstand, noticing a small package wrapped in pink paper with a sparkly bow. I reach for it and carefully open it.

It's a novel. Of course, it's a smutty one. I feel my heart flutter when I open the book and see the note card in it.

Thought you'd like this. And no, I haven't dog eared any of your precious pages. Happy birthday, Princess.

I FEEL a stray tear run down my cheek onto the fluffy pillow. A tear, that for once, doesn't bother or upset me.

Clay Chapman is definitely not what I expected.

CHAPTER 22
CLAY
SHE'S EVERYWHERE

THE SOUND of the snow crunching under my feet and Ani's collar ring in my ears on our morning run. But it's not enough to block out the sounds of Lizzy flooding my thoughts, whimpering and moaning my name last night.

Fuck. She was amazing. Those eyes. That bratty mouth. I can still fucking taste her. I'm half tempted to run back to the house right now and get back in bed with her. The sight of her, sleeping so peacefully this morning, was nearly enough to keep me in bed if I wasn't so obsessed with keeping my routines. But that wasn't just some random hook up. That was someone I know, someone in my life. Someone I can't hide from. Someone with strings.

After another lap, I run back up the hill towards the house, still trying to clear my head. I was just being a good friend. I was there and she needed me. Is that what *friends* do? That didn't feel *friendly*. Jesus. I'm fucked up.

But that can't happen again. I can't let someone else get close to me and burn me.

When I walk inside, Lizzy is nowhere to be seen. Good. She must still be asleep. I walk through the kitchen, noticing her purse and keys are still on the counter. My hand twitches at the sight, but she did manage to hang her jacket and put her shoes away.

What is wrong with me? When did I really get this bad about being a neat and tidy control freak? Lizzy had an absolutely shitty day yesterday, was in tears when she came home, and all I can think about is that her keys and purse weren't put away.

See? This is why I don't let people in my space. This is why I'm alone. Me and people don't mix.

I grab her things and walk back towards the door, hanging them with her jacket.

I head back to my room to grab a shower. I need to get my shit together and a cold shower usually helps me process things. I stand under the water, finally catching my breath and clearing my head.

I'm right - that can't happen again with Lizzy. I've been losing my focus too much. The whole reason I'm in this mess is because I got distracted at work and forgot to change out the propane tanks. I'm letting my feelings and my own needs get in my way.

When I'm emotional, I lose focus and control.

When I lose control, I make mistakes.

And when I make mistakes, people get hurt. I get hurt.

WHEN I WALK BACK into the kitchen, I head to the coffee maker to turn it on for Lizzy.

"What the...?" I stop in front of it, noticing it's already on. I turn and look towards the living room and see Lizzy, already on her yoga mat, stretching with Ani lying next to her on his bed. She's glowing, all smiles, no traces of the distraught mess she was when she came in last night. And seeing Ani so calm and relaxed with her, tears at a place in my chest I'm not used to feeling anything in.

"Morning." She rolls over on her mat, facing me, propping herself up on her elbow, her hair already pulled back in that perfect ponytail.

"Hey," I manage to say gruffly. I don't know where to look. She's wearing another matching yoga outfit with a low cut cropped tank. Seeing her bare stomach and her tits propped up, the ones I painted in cum last night, makes my dick twitch in my sweats.

I make my way over to my chair, sitting next to her.

"Quiet and shy is a funny look for you." Her voice is light and playful as she flicks one eyebrow at me.

"Yeah." I grab the back of my neck. "So are we-"

She cuts me off me off before I can even ask the question. "Relax, Clay. We're cool. We're adults. We're allowed to fool around. Needs and urges, blah blah blah."

"But it can't happen again." I say, trying to look confident in my words, even if my dick and heart say otherwise.

She nods and rolls her eyes, sarcastically. "Yes. Even if it was good. Like *really* good." She winks before reaching out a hand towards me. "Still friends?"

A sigh of relief comes free from my chest followed by a light chuckle. I reach out, shaking her hand, doing my best to hide the way her touch lights a fire in me. "Yep. Friends."

"Good." She looks at me softly, still holding my hand. "And thank you for the book, for knowing it was my birthday."

I shrug. "It was nothing."

That tender smile weakens for a split second, but I saw it. I know it wasn't *nothing* to her.

Her lips curve into a mischievous smirk and before I realize it, she catches me off balance and yanks me out of my chair, pulling me onto the ground beside her.

"Now get down here and stretch me out, accountability buddy."

I groan internally. *Fuck my life.* This is going to be impossible.

SOMEHOW, I make it to Monday and I'm relieved to be back at the job site, even if I have to see Mr. Jensen while I'm here. Surviving yoga on Saturday and Sunday with her plus a coffee run tested every limit of my patience.

She's everywhere.

Her yoga mat in my living room. Her jacket and keys, even if they're neatly hung in the entryway, are still the first thing I notice when I walk in the door. Her stuff in my office. The smell of her shampoo on the throw blankets on my couch.

She's everywhere even if she's not physically there.

I stand out on the porch of the penthouse, drinking my morning coffee, which also conveniently reminds me of her. *Literally. Everywhere.*

"Morning, Clay." Mr. Jensen walks up next to me. I nod and take a sip of my coffee.

He leans against the railing, looking back inside through the French doors. "So are we getting back on track?"

"Yeah. It's starting to come back together. Plumbing is fixed and inspected. Soon we can put the drywall ceiling back in downstairs and then finally insulate and finish the floors and walls up here." I sigh and shake my head, looking around the job. "I still can't believe I fucked that up."

Mr. Jensen stands closer, putting a hand on my shoulder. "Just remember what I always taught you. Stay in control. *Get rid of distractions.*" I say the last part with him in unison. He's been telling me this for years.

"I know, I know," I say, trying not to remember the rest of the conversation the first time he told me to get rid of distractions. *You're broken. Look what happens when you get distracted.*

I blink, trying to erase that train of thought.

"Don't worry. We'll get that condo downstairs fixed up and get your little blonde friend out of your hair soon enough. You can't let her distract you." My eyes fly up and meet his. Did Kayleigh tell him that or maybe it was Luke? I'll have to talk to them about that. Not that either of them know about what happened the other night, but there are still some things, even with them, that I want to keep private. There's something about the way he said *little blonde friend* that doesn't sit right with me.

I'm not one to show emotions, but he still must catch my apprehension, because he laughs and pats me on the shoulder. "Oh relax, Clay. You think I don't know you after more than a decade? Boys will be boys. One of these days, you'll finally give up that bachelor title and settle down." He lets outs a laugh and grabs my shoulder and gives me a light shake. "But that girl, she's just a distraction. She'll go back home soon enough. Stay focused. Who knows? Maybe you and Kayleigh will get back together and you'll finally make an honest woman out of her. You'll need to if you're going to run this company for me one day."

My fist clenches behind me and my blood boils at the way he dismisses Lizzy and his daughter so easily. I can't hide the grimace that spreads across my face. This is exactly the kind of shit that hurt Lizzy the other night and it's shit my best friend has had to put up with for so long. I want to go off on him, but he helped me so much in the past when I needed it. Then there's the present issue of him being my boss, so all I can do is try to ignore him and change the subject.

"Yeah, that'll be the day," I say with a halfhearted laugh. I would actually love to run a company like this one day, just not the way he does. I have my own style, my own ideas about design and projects. I look back at him, the man that's been my mentor for so many years but also one I question more and more. "But you're right, I need to get her place fixed." That part is true. I promised her I would make it right and I need to make that happen.

"Another thing - you approved that invoice for GJF for the lodge job, right?" I nod, thinking it's odd though. He never asks about mundane invoices for vendors. That seems like something he'd be too busy for and have someone in the accounting department handle.

He smiles and rasps his knuckles twice against the wooden railing between us. "Good, I always know I can count on you." He stands up and walks towards the doors heading back inside.

He reaches the doorway and stops. "I'll still see you Thursday though for our normal check in. Oh, and don't forget, the annual company banquet is next month. Big announcement this year."

Maybe that means he's finally going to retire. Something I wouldn't mind. I nod politely. "Wouldn't miss it."

"That's the spirit," he says with that smile that still doesn't meet his eyes. "You know our customers love seeing you." There it is. He loves parading me around, the former ski prodigy, now his right hand man. I put up with it, partially out of a sense of obligation, but also because I've earned what I have. Sure, he took me under his wing. But I worked from the bottom up and probably do more for him than he even realizes.

I contain my irritation and match his fake smile, desperate for this conversation to be over. "Glad to help. Have a good night, Mr. Jensen."

He turns and leaves and I finally let my fist unclench behind me. I'm mad that he would just dismiss Lizzy like that.

But I'm mad that he's right.

I'm too distracted.

WHEN I WALK in my door, a flood of relief hits me. My house is empty. If I remember right, Lizzy is meeting Grace to go shopping. I'm genuinely glad they're becoming friends. After Mom, it was hard for Grace to make friends, going through a rough spot her last couple of years in high school. Sure, it's been a decade, but she's finally coming out of her shell the last couple of years.

But I'm equally, selfishly glad that Grace is sparing me some of the brunt of hurricane Lizzy. I put my jacket and boots away then hang my keys. Walking towards the living area, I grab a couple of logs and a handful of kindling to start a fire. If I have the house to myself tonight, I plan on stretching and taking Ani out, then ending my night with a glass of bourbon and a book in my chair.

Once the fire is going, I head to the laundry room. I strip down, throwing my work clothes right into the washer to start a load. When I look up, I'm already reminded again that Lizzy is everywhere in my life right now. Her tiny yoga outfits are hanging up to air dry and I try to ignore the thought of how her tight body looks in them. The memory of being pressed against her on the floor, folding her legs into a deep stretch. Or, when she wasn't wearing them, the feeling of her thighs wrapped around my head when she came with my tongue flicking her clit.

I shudder and grab a pair of clean, crisply folded dark gray sweats and a black t-shirt from my clean hamper and change into them. They do nothing to hide my growing erection, but I don't really care right now. I shift myself in my pants and start the laundry.

I head to my en suite bathroom, glad to have at least one room in my house that won't remind me of her, minus the smell of her shampoo. After taking out my contacts and putting on my glasses, I finally make it to my office. I start towards my bookshelves, but something on my desk catches my eye. Lizzy did a good job after I said to *try* and keep my desk clean, but there's one stray sheet of paper with some bubbly, girly handwriting on it.

I step over and read it. Most of it is lost on me, but two lines jump out. *GJF. Only under budget.*

Standing there, I stare at the note. Come to think of it, I only get GJF invoices when our projects are way under budget. Funny, I never caught that before. Lizzy really is good at this stuff and something about that warms my heart. I know what it's like to be doubted, thinking you only have your job because of connections or appearances. Still, I'll definitely have to talk to her about that.

I walk over to the shelves and grab the next book in the *Scales of Fury* series, the one I told Lizzy to start. I wonder how she's liking it. I laugh, shaking my head. That reminds me I owe her something. I grab my phone, placing a quick online order, laughing the entire time. I walk towards my chair in the living room, setting my book down.

"Come on, Ani. I just finished cleaning up your mess from the other day." He quirks at me curiously before hopping up and trotting over to me, mouth open and tongue hanging out like he's smiling. It's almost like he forgot he left a trail of chunks of silicone around the house. I pat him on the head, flopping his ears around, making him flick his head to get me to stop. A chuckle rumbles in my chest again. "Still can't believe you did that. Now come on, let's go outside."

Ani bolts out the door the second I open it, clearly needing to burn off of some pent up energy. I feel you, boy.

I stand on the edge of the front porch, grabbing a ball to throw for him after he looks back at me. We play toss for a bit and I finally start to feel like myself again, getting back into my normal routine.

THE LAST FEW hours of peace and quiet were exactly what I needed. I got my stretching in and read almost half of my book. I enjoyed a couple glasses of bourbon and a light dinner by the fire in my chair. This is my routine, what I like, what I thrive in.

I do better when I'm by myself.

Or maybe, at least that's what I've convinced myself for years. It's what I've let others convince me for years.

Could I actually be happy with someone in my space, in my life, all the time?

Could I still be focused and successful and not make terrible mistakes?

I think about that electric feeling, being so close to Lizzy on the floor stretching the other day. Could I have that feeling?

I pour another glass of bourbon, rubbing my thumb over the rim of the heavy rocks glass.

No, that's not how my life works.

My pityfest is interrupted by the sound of the garage door opening.

I sigh and mumble to myself. "Right on cue."

I hear keys rattling on the other side of the door from the kitchen to the garage, followed by it opening.

"Come on, Ani. Let's get to bed," I call to him from my chair, hoping to avoid Lizzy tonight and give myself a little bit of space to focus. To my surprise, he ignores me and runs to the kitchen door, just out of my sightline.

"Oh, who's a good boy?" Lizzy coos at him. "I found something for you today."

Little traitor.

I hear something thud on the floor and paper shopping bags rustling, followed by Ani's collar jingling.

Lizzy's gasp cuts through the room. "Oh my god, it's perfect. You're a stud, Ani."

At that, I stand up, walking her way with my glass. I'm stopped in my tracks when Ani runs up to me, wearing a sweater. He stands in front of me, mouth wide open and spinning in excitement. Surprisingly, it fits him perfectly. But when I look closer, I notice the pattern. It's the same southwestern wool pattern of the throw blankets in the living room and his dog bed.

My head whips over to Lizzy, whose smile is so warm and proud while she watches him run up to me.

"You dressed my dog?" I ask, my tone way less grateful than it should be, still shocked by the gesture. I fold my arms across over my chest, shaking my head and glaring at Ani. He looks happier, much happier than the mood I'm in right now.

She gets down on her knees, patting her thighs to get Ani to come back to her before looking back up at me.

Fuck me. Lizzy on her knees, those sparkling blue eyes looking up at me, is the stuff of dreams. I feel my throat bob and my mouth go dry. She smirks back up at me like she can read my mind. Hell, she probably can. It always seems like she's in my head.

"I saw it and it was cute." She rubs his shoulders, prompting him to roll on his back for belly rubs from her. Seriously. That little traitor. He is definitely not helping me keep distance. "Besides, he's growing on me now, even if he chewed up my favorite toy." She looks up and flicks her eyebrows with a knowing smirk before standing back up.

Yep. She can read my mind.

"Yeah, sorry about that." I rub the back of my neck, trying to block the mental image of her using that toy. "Anyways, I'm going to get to bed. It's been a long day." I take the last sip of my drink and set the glass on the island behind me.

Her eyes meet mine and her smile falters. "Oh." Her voice is almost a whisper. She rubs her hands before clapping them together once. "No problem. I should probably catch up on some work and get to bed too." Her halfhearted, plastered on smile digs a hole in my chest. Does she really like hanging out with me? Was she actually looking forward to being around *me*?

No. No one actually likes being around me.

This is for the best.

"Thanks for his sweater, Lizzy. Night," I say gruffly, not meeting her eyes. I turn towards the hallway, but I swear I hear another whisper behind me that hits me right in my heart.

Goodnight, Clay.

CHAPTER 23
LIZZY
YOU'RE EVERYWHERE

I PRY myself out of bed, thankful that I get to work from *home* - well, Clay's house - today. I'm tired and groggy after barely sleeping last night. I've slept great here every night until last night. Something about the way Clay was distant and just took off for bed didn't feel right. It seemed like we were starting to genuinely enjoy each other's company. Was it something I did?

No playful comebacks, no flirting, not even a scowl or an eye roll. Just *night* and walking off to bed.

We even talked about the other night. We said we could be adults and be friends. I like our friendship or whatever we're going to call it. He's one of the few people I've ever felt good about opening up to. It felt like I was being worshipped for being me for a change. And he takes it and runs with it, pushing back and playing with me. And those things he said in bed, I've never been praised like that.

But to just slink away like he did last night? He was so different last night. Not the moody, cocky, asshole Clay I first met. And not the fun, almost sweet one I've started to see. He wasn't him.

Whatever it was, I hope it was just him in a mood and not how he's going to be going forward. Because the one that *saw me* the other night, I want more of that Clay in my life.

After changing out of my pajamas into some yoga clothes for some morning stretching, I open the door, nearly tripping on a sleeping Ani, curled into a ball at the foot of my door.

"Oh! Hey, bud." He stirs and wags his tail, following me to the kitchen. "Let's go find your dad."

Heading down the hall, I peak into the office.

No Clay, but I see something sitting on the floor. I groan, irritated that Clay's already rubbing off on me this much. I walk over to the desk, grabbing the paper off the floor and putting it back on the desk.

See, Clay? I can be neat and tidy too.

I set it back down, noticing that it's my scribbled notes about the invoices he asked me to look into. He wasn't wrong to ask. It is weird. Which is funny, because that's what's written in his beautiful, cursive script underneath my note. *That's weird, right?*

It seems like they only get these consultant's invoices on projects that were completed under budget. You'd think they'd use them on all their projects and throughout the scheduled work, not just at the end. I'll definitely talk to him about this more later, but right now, I want coffee.

I set the note down, putting a paperweight on it so it doesn't end up on the floor again. You're welcome, Clay.

When I make it to the kitchen, there's no sign of him to be found, which is weird because this is when we'd normally start our yoga workout. I head to the coffee maker. I start a pot and grab my mug, noticing a note on the kitchen island.

No yoga today. Headed in early and staying late. Working on your condo. We'll get you back in ASAP.

SOMEHOW, that hurts a little. Is he already that tired and irritated with me and wants me gone? Or can he not handle being friends any more?

I crumple up the note, throwing it in the trash. I'm stronger than that. I don't need to worry about what he thinks. I'm not letting someone else define me anymore. That is the post *Tour de Lizzy* motto. I'm always me and no one is going to make me feel bad about that.

After finishing my coffee, I do my yoga with Ani next to me on his bed. "You can be my accountability buddy if your dad's going to be a jerk and avoid me."

He huffs and seems to sink deeper into his bed. Maybe it's just me, but I think he looks stylish and comfortable in his new sweater. I watch as he yawns and drifts back to sleep.

"You're lucky. I wish I could go back to bed."

Except I find myself thinking that I probably won't get much sleep if I keep thinking about a certain, tall, handsome, confusing man.

MY DRIVE HOME from work on Wednesday is a blur. The plant manager got in my face today, making a snide, condescending remark after I questioned him on a few issues with their shift schedules and vendor preferences. I've heard them all.

Doll, honey, sweetheart.

Just relax. Calm down. Smile more.

I've been doing this since you were in diapers.

Nothing they would ever say to a man. Never mind that I'm there to clean up their mess. Never mind that I'm right.

As Jessica would say, I went *Full Lizzy* and put him in his place.

But between that and the way my roommate and *friend* has been a ghost the last few days I'm already on edge. I couldn't get out of there fast enough at the end of the day.

When I walk into the house from the garage, to my surprise, Clay is sitting at the counter looking at something on his laptop. He's already wearing his glasses. I have to admit that the rough, muscular, tattooed man with the heavy, dark rimmed glasses is a *look*. If I wasn't so pissed off at him right now, I'd probably just stand here and enjoy the view. But not today.

As soon as he sees me, he starts to get up, presumably to go to his office and continue to pretend I don't exist.

"Oh no, no way, Clay!" I stomp towards him, not bothering to hang my keys or take off my shoes. I throw my purse on the counter and get right into his face. "You're not going to keep doing this."

He looks irritated. I still don't get it! I know he said it wouldn't happen again and that's fine. But we were being genuinely friendly before that. I enjoy being around him. I want that back. He owes me an answer on why we can't be like that again. I know *that* night was so intimate, so deep and sexual. But I still want that connection, even without the physical part.

"Doing what?" he says, looking equally confused and startled.

I step towards him, poking him in the chest, that hard, muscular chest. "Acting weird since the other night after we said we're good. Pretending that I don't exist. Ignoring me."

"You think I'm ignoring you?" His voice is a low growl. He steps towards me and towers over me, crowding my space. "You think I could *ever* ignore you, princess?"

My hand falls. I try to step away and give myself space, but I back up against the kitchen island.

"You've been acting like it ever since *that* night. You're almost acting like you did right after Roxy's." I stare into his eyes and they're so intense, so focused on me I can feel my skin heat and flush. My mouth goes dry and I lick my lower lip. His nostrils flare and his eyes track the movement.

"You're *everywhere*, Lizzy." He steps towards me and I have to put my elbows on the marble island to prop myself up. "You're in my house." He leans forward and puts a hand on the island next to mine. "You're in my thoughts. You're in my dreams." He takes his other hand and tilts my chin up towards him, forcing me to maintain this insane level of eye contact that I feel in my core. "I couldn't ignore you even if I wanted to. You're all I can think about. All the damn time."

I watch as his chest heaves and a muscle ticks in his jaw. "That's not how it feels. You're acting like you can't bear to be around me - like I'm such a burden to you and you want me back at my condo," I say, not flinching from his presence. I swear it looks like a vein in his neck under that beautiful rose tattoo is going to pop and I can hear his heart pounding. The look on his face is pure torment, like my words pained him.

"You're not a burden. You're anything but a burden. I thought I made it very clear what I think about you. I *showed* you." One side of his lips quirk into a hint of smile, showing off the dimple on that side. If I wasn't already so flushed and worked up, I can't imagine the shade of red my cheeks would turn from the thought of *that night*.

"You have an awfully funny way of showing someone they're not a burden. Maybe you could remind me what you think of me?" I say with a shaky, muted voice. I don't know what I'm doing. I don't know what I expected to happen by getting in his face and poking the bear, the *literal bear* I know is tattooed on his chest.

He exhales a long, frustrated sigh. "Can we not? I'm not used to having people in my space all the time. I'm not used to new people in my life. I don't handle distractions well."

Distractions? Am I a distraction to him? That thought washes away when I breathe in, his leather and cedar scent reminding me of falling asleep in his arms. I stand tall, looking right at him. He's not going to ignore me. He's going to tell me what's wrong, whether he wants to or not. I am not stepping down.

"Why don't you like people in your space?" I look towards my hand on the counter and see my keys and grin. "Because they'll do something like this?" I flick my wrist and bat the keys on to the floor. My grin grows watching him track the motion and flinch at the sound of them hitting the floor.

"You really do want to make me snap, don't you?" he snarls.

"Why? What would that look like?" I tease, pleased at the response I'm getting. He doesn't say a word. He just continues to stare into my soul with those eerily hardened emerald eyes. I look at my other hand and see my phone sitting there. I flick my wrist and watch him finally come undone when my phone hits the ground and slides across the floor.

He closes the final inches between us, pressing himself against me. I can feel the warmth of his muscular body as he leans over me, pushing my back against the island. "What the fuck do you want, Lizzy?"

I raise one hand, cupping his cheek, relishing the feeling of his stubble against my soft hand, remembering what it felt like between my thighs. I lean towards him, bringing my lips to his ear, feeling that stubble against my cheek, and whisper. *"You."* I run my finger over the open neckline of his henley and down his sternum and muscular chest.

The intense, focused look explodes into something different, something scorching and animalistic. It's like that evergreen forest in his eyes ignites into a raging wildfire I can feel like a brand on my skin.

"Fuck it." His voice is raw and gravelly.

He moves in a flurry, grabbing me by my hips and lifting me onto the counter like a rag doll, bringing me eye to eye with him. I wrap my hands around the back of his neck, startled by his strength. He cups the back of my neck and fists my ponytail, pulling my head back and baring my neck to him. His mouth crashes to mine and his other hand roams my body, pulling us closer.

I moan into his mouth, feeling my chest rise and fall. His mouth is taking, his tongue gliding along mine. He tugs my ponytail, sending a shiver through my scalp, pulling me back from him. He looks deep into my eyes. There's a question, a hesitation in his eyes to go with that hunger. "Is this what you want?"

If he only knew. Everything with us is always so charged, so heated, and moves so fast. But it feels so right, so easy. I wrap my legs around him pulling him between them. His eyes dart to the hemline of my sweater dress when it rides up my thighs. I can feel the bulge in his jeans pressed against my aching core through my tights. I look into those smoldering eyes. "Shut up and fuck me, Clay. *You're ruining it.*"

That wicked grin of his morphs into something feral and devious. "I have condoms in the bedroom."

"I'm clean and have an IUD." I squeeze my calves around his muscular ass, pulling him closer. "So if you're ok with it, I want to feel you inside me."

He leans forward, bringing his lips to my ear and I relish in the feeling of his stubble against my cheek. "Good, I'm clean too." His voice is low and raspy, building anticipation in me. "I know how wet you get for me. I haven't been able to stop thinking about how good you taste, so I want to feel your tight pussy on my cock." He nips my ear and I arch into him. I feel his rough hands run up my tights, pulling them down one leg at a time. He pushes up the hemline of my sweater dress, looking down between us.

"Goddamn, this fucking pussy." He licks his lips and puts one hand on my chest, pushing me back onto the island. "Lay back."

"You know I'm already wet enough for you." I tease, playfully tapping his ass with my feet, loving the sight of this imposing man standing over me, between my legs.

He runs one finger over my wet core, bringing it to his lips. "Just wanted to make sure I wasn't dreaming about how good you taste."

He closes his eyes, licking his finger, humming a low moan. When he opens his eyes, that devious grin is back. I watch as he pulls a bar stool over and sits, right between my legs. "What happened to world class athlete?" I pout.

"Shut up, Lizzy." He grabs my thighs and spreads them, kissing down each one before his mouth stops at the apex of my thighs. His eyes look up at me through his ruffled hair. I didn't think I'd be seeing this again so soon. All I know is I definitely would never be tired of seeing this man between my legs. "Just a taste before I fuck you hard enough that you can't walk straight. Don't think I've forgotten that first night we met and you know how I feel about keeping promises."

This time it's my turn to grin back. "I've been meaning to remind you about that." He rolls his eyes and buries his face in me. I'm instantly sure of one thing. Clay Chapman knows how to use his mouth. Talking, kissing, and eating me like I'm the last meal on earth on his kitchen island. His tongue has barely touched me and he already has me so worked up. Each lick, swirl, and nip, all start to build that coil of tension I can feel at the base of my spine. He slides one finger into me, pumping in motion with his tongue. "Fuck. Clay." My words are a needy prayer and I feel myself clench around his finger. He groans in approval, only heightening the sensation.

"Don't worry, I'll fuck you soon enough." He licks and sucks my clit and I feel myself barrel to that edge. I lay back, savoring every second of this. Until he stops and I hear the barstool slide back against the floor. I open my eyes and look up, only to see Clay look down at me with what I can only describe as animalistic intent. "Come here." His voice is commanding and before I can even move, he grabs me by my hips and slides me off the counter, bringing me into his chest.

He cranes his neck, bringing his mouth down to mine, his tongue finding the back of my mouth. I moan into his, tasting my own arousal. "Why did you stop?"

"Because I know you're ready to take this dick now." He kisses me one more time before grabbing my hips, manhandling me with his big strong hands and spinning me around, splaying and pinning my hands out on the island in front of me in one motion. I hear him unzip his jeans and let them fall to the floor. He steps out of them and I push against that counter top, backing my ass into him, grinding against the bulge in his briefs. I'm so desperate for the friction, aching with want. I think deep down, I've wanted this every second since that night we met.

He must feel the same way because he grabs my hips, pulling me against him and I can feel him shudder. "Goddamnit. We're really doing this?" he asks, excitement lacing his low voice.

"If you don't hurry up, I'm going to start playing with myself. Now, shut up and fuck me." I back my ass into him again.

I feel him drop his briefs before rubbing and tapping the head of his cock against my swollen clit.

"You're something else." His voice is rough and strained, but those words still hit me the same. I love hearing that from him, whether he knows it or not. I look down between my legs, just in time to watch him stroke his length before notching it at my entrance. I push back, wanting to feel him in me. But he stops me, grabbing my hips tight. "I'll go slow. Let you get used to me."

I look over my shoulder at him, rolling my eyes. "I swear if you don't put that dick in me right now, I'll-"

He cuts me off. "You'll what? Do something bratty?" He gives my ass a light slap and I whimper.

"Yes. Exactly. Like remember that I was pissed off at you five minutes ago." With that, he eases into me, slowly, but surely in one devastating thrust, forcing me to look forward. He's thick and long, stretching and filling me, pain and pleasure rush through me. I bite my lip so hard I swear I can taste blood before moaning his name.

"Jesus, fuck, Lizzy," Clay growls through gritted teeth. I look back over my shoulder and take in the sight of him behind me, digging his hands into my hips. "You're so fucking tight. Your pussy looks so good stretched around my cock." His eyes lock on to mine and the ravenous, desperate look of him finally letting go unleashes something in me. I arch my back and push my ass back into him again and again. I smirk when he shudders and I whimper at the sensation of him bottoming out in me.

The way he stretches and fills me is so overwhelming, so sinfully painful. I want to feel him for days afterwards. He digs his fingers in harder and I know it's going to leave a bruise. He starts thrusting. Slow, but hard and punishing. I drop my head onto the cold marble counter and whimper. "Tell me how good I feel." My voice is a breathy, teasing plea. I want him to let go. I want to see him, this side of him.

"Is that what you need?" His voice is raspy and husky in a way that sends shivers of want through me. "You need me to tell you how perfect this pussy is, how perfect you are? That's going to get you off?" He thrusts hard into me again and I moan into the crook of my elbow, savoring the sensation of him.

I look back at him, grinning and nodding. "Yes. Tell me."

He thrusts harder and faster, flicking his eyebrows at me with a lust filled smile, baring his teeth. "You already know it's perfect, princess."

I always knew I had a praise kink, but hearing things like that from him confirms it. I want to hear it from him. *Always.*

The way I don't have to tone myself down or hide from him is so freeing. I turn and bury my face back into my elbow, enjoying him pounding into me relentlessly.

"Spread them," he growls at me, stopping for a moment. Before I can even ask what he means, he kicks my feet apart, spreading my legs. "Now play with your clit, princess."

I look over my shoulder at him, intoxicated by the lust in his eyes, loving the sight of his tattooed hands on my hips. I see my purse next to me on the counter and smile back at him. He arches a questioning eyebrow and tracks my arm when I stretch it out and knock my purse onto the floor, spilling the contents. *"Make me."*

His nostrils flare and he pulls me *hard* by my hips into him. He grabs my hand that I knocked the purse off with and laces his fingers through mine before bringing it between my legs. "Brat," he snarls, before teasing my clit with our woven fingers.

My eyes roll back into my head. I love the way he manhandles me. I look between my legs at our fingers, watching them push me closer and closer to the edge. A giggle escapes my lips between whimpers when I see the letters tattooed on his knuckles.

"Did you pick that hand on purpose?"

He doesn't stop fucking me, but I watch as he looks at his other hand on my hip. The grin that takes over his face is perfect, showing those dimples.

CHAPTER 24
CLAY
RUBBING

I'M A WEAK MAN. I tried to avoid her. I did try to create some space. But now I'm buried in her and I never want it to stop.

The sound of my name on her lips is music to my ears. The sight of her tight cunt taking every inch of me over and over is unreal. And the mouth on her is perfectly filthy.

I've spent most of my life feeling like people have to tip toe around me. Either they know me and my history and are afraid to bring up the wrong thing, or they don't know me, just see the constant scowl, and stay away.

But fucking Lizzy. We're like magnets, drawn to each other. She sees right through me and doesn't back down. She just comes back for more and more and I want it.

I want all of her.

I look down at my hand on her hip, seeing the letters *OVER* spelled out on my knuckles. I let out a rough laugh, realizing which hand is rubbing her clit. "Does that mean you're about to *come* on my cock and our fingers?"

"Yes, I want to come with you buried in me so bad." Fuck that mouth of hers.

I thrust harder and faster, loving every second of being in her. It's like she was made for me the way our bodies fit together. I hold her hand tighter, rubbing her clit with our fingers and I can feel her pussy start to tighten around me. "Come for me, Lizzy."

"Don't stop." I can feel her fingers work faster and harder between mine.

"Did you forget your manners?"

She glares at me over her shoulder. Her eyes are lazy and hooded with lust, but that fiery defiance is still there. "Please."

I purse my lips back at her. "As you wish." I thrust hard, burying myself in her to the hilt, working our fingers relentlessly. I feel her pussy flutter when she shatters on my cock. I can feel her knees buckle as she collapses onto the counter.

"Oh, don't quit on me now. What was the point of all those workouts?" I quip, thrusting into her again, bottoming out and forcing another moan from her. Despite every part of my body telling me to stay in her tight, wet heat, I ease out of her. I grab her by the hips and spin her around to face me. She looks up at me with those beautiful baby blues, now clouded and glazed over with a sultry fog.

She smirks and grabs my cock, stroking it. "I know you didn't come yet. I said I wanted you to come in me."

I cup her ass and lift her off the ground. She instinctively wraps her legs around me and I can feel her slick, wet pussy pressed against me.

I hold her with one hand and cup the back of her neck with the other, bringing her ear to my lips. "We're both still half dressed. And I want to see you, all of you, and look in those beautiful eyes when I come in you." I can hear her small moan over my own heavy breathing, the friction of my cock rubbing against her sensitive clit driving us both wild. I carry her like that, grinding against me, down the hall to her room.

When I open the door, I can't help but notice her bed is perfectly made and not a thing is out of a place. "Have I been rubbing off on you?"

I feel her cute puff of a laugh against my neck. "You were definitely rubbing me off just a minute ago."

"No. I mean this." I gesture to the room, and spin around with her still in my arms.

"Oh," she says, acting surprised. She presses her lips to my neck before grazing her cheek against my stubble. "Maybe a little. Now put me on the fucking bed, Clay."

I lower her to her feet in front of the foot of the bed, reaching down to pull her dress over her head. Seeing her with nothing on except a tiny, thin little gray bralette with her peaked nipples showing through sends blood rushing right back to my cock. She steps towards me, running her hands down my side to the hem of my shirt and slides it over my head. Something about her touch feels like fire on my skin.

She kisses my chest, then my stomach, humming breathy moans as she lowers herself to her knees. She looks up at me with those sultry eyes, making my breath stick in my chest. "I've thought about this since you told me *no* the other night and made me watch you."

"Thought about what exactly?"

She fists the base of my cock, squeezing and making me buck into her hand. "That I don't like being told *no*."

I watch as she licks me from the base to the tip and takes the head in her mouth. Finally seeing those pouty lips around my cock is almost too much. She moans, taking more of me in her mouth and my lips hang open.

"Fuck, princess. Your mouth is so good." She hums and starts to bob her head up and down. "Too fucking good."

She laughs - she fucking laughs - with my cock down her throat. The vibration of her laugh makes my cock ache. I can see tears welling at the corners of her eyes as she takes all of me in. "Holy shit, Lizzy."

She hums again, going faster and hollowing her cheeks. I grab her ponytail, loving every second of this, but this isn't how I want to come tonight. I fist her ponytail and pull her off of me, my cock leaving her mouth with a pop.

I tilt her head back and she looks up at me, her eyes blazing a trail along my body. "I wanted my turn to make you come. You're no fun *again*."

"I told you I want to look in your eyes when I come in you. Now get in the fucking bed on your big pillow pile." I point to her head-board. "*Now*."

I watch her crawl across the bed, enjoying the site of her curvy ass and puffy, well-fucked pussy before she lays on her back. I follow her, lowering myself between her open thighs, notching myself at her entrance. I lean down, kissing her collarbone, then her neck, until my lips stop just under her ear. "I made you a promise and I'm going to keep it." I thrust hard, burying myself in her, my cock already feeling like this is its new home. I feel the rush of air against my neck when she gasps and the pang of her digging her nails into my back.

"Fuck me harder then," she breathes against my ear.

My heart pounds in my chest. This woman never stops amazing me. I grab her thighs, pushing them back, letting myself get even deeper in her. I pull back just enough to meet her eyes before we both look to where we're joined. "See how fucking good we look?"

I rock my hips harder, enjoying how deep I'm getting. "You take me so fucking good."

"Less talking, more fucking," she chides playfully. I know that's a lie. She loves hearing me praise her.

I reach down between us, pumping myself in harder and teasing her clit with my thumb.

"That's it, don't stop," she cries into my shoulder and her teeth dig into my collarbone.

And that's what I do.

I fuck her hard and senselessly, circling and flicking her clit. I can feel her walls tighten, bringing me closer to completely falling apart, as if I already wasn't every time I'm close to her.

I feel her dig her nails into me deeper, her hard buds rubbing against my chest through her bralette. She wraps her legs around my ass, pulling me in deeper and I can feel her pussy flutter against my cock when she comes undone again. And this time, I barrel over the edge with her, losing myself inside her. The edges of my vision blur, but not enough to keep me from staring right into the icy blue eyes looking right back at me - into me.

I wrap my arms under her, flipping us over with her on top of me, cradled in my arms with us still joined together.

She burrows her head into my neck and I plant a kiss on top of her head, noticing her ponytail is now a flowing, beautiful mess of blonde hair.

"You're really something else," I say softly against the top of her head.

She hums contentedly against my chest. "Shut up, Clay. You're ruining it."

I laugh and roll my eyes. "I'll be right back." I pry myself loose from her grip and get out of bed, gathering our clothes from the floor and setting them neatly in the corner chair. She watches me curiously as I head to the en suite bathroom. I cock my head towards the door. "Warm towel service." She smiles so brightly at me before I head in and grab a towel, her robe, and a couple hair ties from the counter.

I come back to bed, laying beside her while she cleans up and puts on the robe.

"Here. Sit up." I pat the bed beside me. She gives me a questioning glance but doesn't push back. I sit up behind her, rubbing her shoulders under the robe, cleaning up what's left of her disheveled ponytail, my hands working absentmindedly. She leans back into me and I love this level of intimacy, like the other night, something I haven't experienced in years - maybe ever. I enjoy the comfortable silence between us. It feels like an entire, unspoken conversation happens between us.

"I want to know something about you. Something new." Her

voice is soft and curious. Maybe I spoke too soon about enjoying the silence. But I think I might actually *like* talking to her.

I sigh. "Then pick something."

She hums thoughtfully. "Why don't you ski anymore?"

That is not the question I was hoping for and not one I even know where to start with. There's so much to unpack there. My mom, my injuries, Kayleigh, all the pain and memories. I think about it for a minute, my hands still mindlessly playing with her hair, and I come up with the best answer I'm willing to give right now.

"I've lost enough things in life that matter. It hurts saying goodbye." I swallow hard, so many memories running through my mind. "After I tore up my right knee, it was almost a year of rehab and physical therapy. But I came back stronger than before, physically anyways. I still wanted to try."

She nods, still facing away from me, but doesn't say anything.

I let out a deep breath. "But a few years later, after I'd already been through it once, after we lost Mom, that's when I tore my left knee. And I just... I couldn't do it again. I couldn't put myself through that. Getting so keyed up to get back to it, only to have it ripped away again. Sure, I'm physically capable. But mentally, my heart - I just can't. I don't want to have to say goodbye to it again."

"Oh, Clay. I can't imagine." Her voice is a soft whisper and I can feel her shoulders sag. "Thank you for telling me."

Hearing the soft, compassionate side of her is something that tears at my heart. It's so starkly different than the fiery, fierce side I see all the time. I roll my shoulders, exhaling again. "Don't be. It's in the past."

A moment passes where we sit here, just enjoying the silence again.

"Clay?" Her voice is skeptical.

My name on her lips pulls me out of my trance. "What?"

"Did you just braid my hair?" I look down at my hands, realizing that I did in fact just give her two long, nearly perfect braids.

"Um... yes?"

She stands up and walks gingerly over towards the mirror, twirling around in her robe.

She looks back at me. "Mind telling me why you know how to do a perfect dutch braid?"

I wring my hands together. "Grace. It was after Mom. She was still in high school. She could do it on her own, but she taught me and I think it was good for both of us. I like routine, repetition, working with my hands. She just wanted to be close to someone. Tanner was living in Jackson and Dad was so busy. It was just our thing back then."

She turns and looks back into the mirror, running each braid through her hands. We make eye contact in the mirror, smiling. "I like them."

She saunters back towards the bed, still walking gingerly, before climbing on top of me, straddling me with her open robe. The feeling of her naked body against mine sends blood rushing right back to my cock.

She grins and traces her finger over the tattoo on my neck. This time she's the one to bring her lips to my ear and whisper. "Also, I can still walk straight. So fuck me again."

My sense of calm is immediately erased by the desire to be close to her again, to let go.

A new feeling burns in my chest. When it comes to Lizzy Frank, I might just have to accept that I'm not in control. And maybe I like that.

WHEN I WAKE UP, I find myself sprawled out on Lizzy's bed, enjoying just how soft her pillow nest is. I will *never* admit it to her, but fuck, it's so comfy and I'm buying the same set for my room as soon as I can. I breathe in the pillows, loving the smell of her shampoo. I reach across the bed, opening my eyes when I realize Lizzy isn't here.

Now that's odd. It's normally a chore for her to get up early. I climb out of her bed and walk to my room, throwing on a pair of sweats and head to the kitchen. When I walk in, I find Lizzy, cleaning up the mess from last night when she acted like a cat, batting everything off the kitchen island. She's wearing a cropped sweatshirt and those sexy little sleep shorts I love. She meets my eyes and smiles, lighting the room and my heart.

"Now *this* I could get used to." I smirk at her before closing the distance, grabbing her by the hips and pulling her in for a kiss.

"I'm not going to wear a maid outfit." She makes a kissy face at me and slaps my ass. "Don't even ask."

I laugh, leaning down to kiss her again. "I wasn't going to." I slide my hand up the back of her thigh and cup the curve of her ass. "Because this is so much better."

She purrs and nuzzles into my bare chest. I hold her tight, savoring every second of her closeness. A moment passes before she breathes into my chest. "What are we doing, Clay?"

I run my hand up her back, cupping the nape of her neck, running one of her mussed braids through my fingers. "I have no idea." I sigh and plant a kiss on top of her head. "I just know we're drawn together. There's something here and I can't ignore it anymore."

She hums contentedly into my chest, wrapping her arms around me. "I feel it too."

I lower my head, rubbing my cheek against her hair. "So now what?"

She hums and wobbles her head. "We could skip yoga and you could take me back to bed and fuck me again." She looks back up at me with her eyes sparkling with desire. "*Lots* of cardio."

Yes, when it comes to Lizzy Frank, I am a weak man.

CHAPTER 25
LIZZY
BUDDY

"OH MY GOD, you're so slow," Clay says, standing by the door to the garage, visibly irritated, waiting on me to get ready. "We're going to be late."

"Calm down, we won't be late," I scoff, glaring back at him. I look back into the entryway mirror, humming to myself and fixing my ponytail. I check my lip stain, popping them before turning and walking past Clay in the doorway.

He grabs me, peering down at me. Every second we haven't been at work the last few days, we've been together in bed. And on the counter. And on the couch. And the floor. Everywhere. Still, the way his emerald green eyes make me feel seen stops my heart every time.

"You sure you want to go? Still have time to cancel." He looks at me, his eyes darting from my eyes to my lips, his hand trailing up my back before tugging lightly on my ponytail. "Could go back to bed."

A shocked gasp escapes my lips. "You're bad. You practically invite yourself to Saturday brunch and now you want to cancel?" I give him a light tap on the cheek before turning and walking into the garage. "Nope. Come on, Chapman."

He rushes ahead, opening the passenger door of my Bronco for me. "Thanks." I smile back at him. "Besides, we can go back to bed after brunch." I shimmy in my seat and clap my hands on my thighs.

"Deal." He smirks, flashing his dimples before closing the door and walking around to the driver side.

I love my Bronco. Is it extra? Yes. But what I love more is watching Clay drive it. Something about the big, tattooed, brawny man driving my white, lifted SUV with pink wheels makes me laugh. And he *insists* on driving every time.

I get the sense there's a reason, but there are still some things I don't feel like he wants to share. He still wears a scowl most of the time, but some of them are softer and more playful.

SITTING at the window table in the charming little Main Street Cafe with Clay and Grace feels surprisingly natural. I love how her and I have already become friends during my time in Utah, two weeks of which I've been living with her brother.

But now, I'm slightly terrified at the way she's been smirking at us all morning. After Clay finishes telling Grace about how his new stretching routine has helped with the stiffness in his knees, she raises her fork, pointing it between us while chewing a bite.

"So who made the first move?" I look at her, feeling the air rush out of my lungs. She's looking back down at her breakfast, forking another bite. I look at Clay, who's looking back at me with raised eyebrows, mouthing *what the fuck?*

"Um, what?" I ask, hoping she doesn't know anything about us.

She takes another bite and mumbles while chewing. "How long have you two been fucking?"

Ok. Cool. This was not how I thought brunch would go today.

Clay nearly chokes on part of his biscuit sandwich and grabs his glass of water coughing. "Fuck, Grace." I watch as his cheeks turn a shade that probably matches mine. "Why would you even ask that?" he scoffs.

She laughs before looking back up at us and taking a sip of her mimosa. I sit here, jaw still gaping open, half in horror and half in amusement at what's unfolding. Clay is blushing and it's almost adorable seeing him this flustered at the hand of his little sister.

I collect myself and reach over to Clay, who's now choking on the water he drank too fast, patting him on the back, and coo. "Aw, did it go in the wrong hole?"

Clay coughs again and gives me a one fingered gesture before taking another, more careful sip of water. "Brat."

I look over at Grace and feel a sense of accomplishment, seeing that now she's the one with a stunned look on her face. "I can't believe it. You two are like..." she waggles a finger between us. "Cute."

Clay puts his elbows up on the table and buries his face in his palms, muttering to himself. "Great. Just great."

Grace holds a finger to her lips, hiding a grin. "First off, thank you for making Clay like almost moderately not grumpy." She smirks before looking at Clay. "And second, Clay, seriously? I've invited you to brunch like every weekend for the last year. How many times have you showed?"

She puts her fork down, holding up both hands in the shapes of zeroes and even I can't help but laugh. "Zero, big bro. Zero. But suddenly, I check that Lizzy and I are still on for brunch today, she says yes, and not even ten minutes later you text me saying you're coming to brunch too." She rolls her eyes and looks back at her food with a laugh. "This was so predictable. I called it when he brought Kayleigh to dinner that night at your condo."

"Excuse me?" Clay chimes in, sounding slightly annoyed with his sister.

"Oh, don't give me that." She grabs her fork and spears another bite of food. "You call her into social settings when you're absolutely terrified of having to talk to someone." She grins back at me and winks. "When I saw Lizzy and how you reacted to her that night in the hot tub, I knew you were into her and needed your Kayleigh buffer to protect you."

I put one finger up, getting her attention. "I will neither confirm nor deny anything you're saying." I wink at her and she chuckles. "Because on the gondola the day I met you, you were pretty adamant about not wanting to know about your brothers' sex lives."

"Well that was before I thought it was possible Clay was capable of," she waggles her finger between us, "whatever it is he's doing with someone as cool you." She rolls her eyes and sighs. "But fair enough, I won't ask for any more details."

A defeated groan catches my attention and we snap our eyes to Clay. "There aren't enough mimosas in the world for this," he mumbles into his palms. We glare back at him.

"Shut up and be a good boy," I say, sharing a glance with Grace.

"Oh." She beams at me with that infectious Chapman smile and giggle. "I like this."

Clay groans again and mutters something under his breath.

"So, you ready for the Bend trip?" I ask, already excited to see Tanner and V again. "I already talked to V. She has a *light and loose suggested* itinerary for us."

She laughs. "Of course she would. But yeah, I'm excited for the trip."

I roll my eyes. "Yeah. Some things never change with her," I say, remembering that not that long ago, V was obsessed with planning every little detail.

"When are you guys going?" Clay's low voice breaks up the light hearted talk. I look at him, noticing the look in his eyes is different. The look isn't the *please make my little sister stop asking about my sex life look*. No, it's a different, disappointed look.

"First week of May. Going to do some spring skiing and explore town a bit," Grace replies, shrugging. "Do you want to come? Tanner's got a house for the week, right on the Deschutes River."

He takes a sip of his drink and nods, a small smile crossing his face. "Yeah, I think I can do that. Finally back on track and even a little ahead of schedule at work."

"Cool. I know Tanner would love to have you there too." Grace smiles at him before turning back to me. "You still free for happy hour on Tuesday?"

"Yep. Roxy's?"

She nods and takes a bite of food.

We continue talking about the trip, I'm definitely looking forward to seeing V and Tanner. Grace rambles on, talking a mile a minute about all the things she wants to check out in Bend. Apparently, there's a great river park, lots of breweries, and some great Western bars.

Her excitement is in stark contrast to her brother. I can't help but notice that Clay is quiet the rest of the time. Not the brooding quiet I'm used to, but a quiet that gnaws at me.

WHEN WE GET BACK to Clay's house, he opens the passenger door for me like normal and heads inside to let Ani out. He was quiet the whole ride back, more so than normal. He heads in and opens the front door, standing on the porch watching Ani bolt out into the yard. Seeing him run and play in the spring snow in his sweater still brings a bit of warm pride to me.

Clay leans against the railing of the porch, watching Ani. I lean next to him, enjoying the warmth of being so close.

"You want to tell me what's got you all quiet for most of brunch and the ride back?" I bump my hip into him, trying to get his attention.

He looks down at me with a smile that doesn't quite meet his eyes. "Not really." I lean further into him, nuzzling my head into his shoulder, humming to myself. "But I know you're not going to drop it."

"Nope." I grin and give him two quick pats on his very firm, delicious ass. "You're a fast learner."

He sighs and I can feel his big, burly body deflate next to me. "It hurt my feelings." Now that isn't what I expected. A giggle bursts out of me and I reach to cover my mouth. He looks down at me, glaring. "Do you want me to keep talking or not?"

I smile back up at him, one hand on my chest and one still covering my mouth. "I'm sorry. You're right, that was mean." I shake my head, putting my hands on my hips. "I'm just shocked that something got under your skin like that."

He hangs his head again and something about it is both sweet and endearing, but also heart wrenching. "You all have had this trip planned for over a month and no one ever even thought to ask me if I'd want to go."

I take a second to think about that. He's right. I mean, I get it. He was grumpy and moody and I'm sure his family knows that better than I do. He still is prickly with almost everyone I've seen him around. But that has to hurt to not even be asked by your own family to go on a trip with them.

"Did they ever ask in the past if you wanted to do things together like that?" I ask, wondering if this is a new thing.

His lips pull to one side and he rocks his head side to side. "Years ago. But at some point, I don't know what happened. Either I kept saying no or they stopped asking." He lets out a long sigh. "It's been so long, it's hard to remember who stopped first. I don't like being like this. I don't like feeling like this."

I reach up, rubbing his back between his shoulders and an idea comes to me.

"You need a buddy."

He looks back down at me, quirking a brow.

"A what?"

I lean against the railing, crossing my arms and grin back up at him. "You're my accountability buddy." I reach toward him and boop him on the nose. "A very pretty one."

He snorts a laugh. "OK, and?"

"You need a..." I hum to myself and tap my finger to my lips, not missing the way his eyes follow that motion. "A disposition improvement buddy."

His lips press together into a line. "How's that supposed to work exactly?"

"I'm going to help you socialize with people."

"That's what Kayleigh is for," he says gruffly.

Rolling my eyes, I grab him by the hands. "No. Apparently, she's your buffer." I pull his hands apart, leaving space between his palms. "See? Buffer. You need to learn to socialize, without a buffer." I press his large, rough palms back together.

"This sounds miserable." I glare back at him, not putting up with his attitude and his expression softens. "But what else do I have to lose?"

"Good." I clap my hands together, bringing them to my lips. "I am going to coach you on being more social and nice to people." I poke him in each of his shoulders. "Who knows, maybe they'll even like you?"

He snorts another laugh. "Let's not get ahead of ourselves."

I lean into him, putting my hands in the back pockets of his jeans. "Well, people like me if you haven't noticed and I like you. So there's no one better to teach you."

He hums playfully to himself, cupping my ass with his big hands and bringing me closer to him. "I can't argue with that. So, when do we start this *disposition improvement?*"

"We start today."

CHAPTER 26

CLAY
HOW DID I GET HERE?

"REMIND me why I agreed to this?" I look at Lizzy, standing in the middle of the fancy athleisure-wear store on Main Street. I'm holding more pink stuff than I've ever seen in my life. How did I get here? How is this my Saturday afternoon?

She rubs her fingertip over her lip, both of which are also very pink. She hums, biting her lip. Her eyes meet mine with that look that makes me forget I'm irritated. "Because I want to get some new yoga outfits *and* I want to torture you."

I drop my head and mumble an expletive to myself before looking back at her. "No, that's why *you* agreed to this." I shift the fistful of clothing I'm holding in one hand into my other one, freeing it one up to jab myself in the chest. "But this helps *me* how?"

She shakes her head, flicking her ponytail over her shoulder in a distracting flurry of golden blonde. "Because you're going to go see if they have each one of these in a different size and make small talk with the girl at the counter."

Fuck my life. What level of hell is the pink one that involves talking to strangers? "There has to be an easier way. Come on."

She shrugs and hums. "Maybe, but I like this one." She steps towards me, running a finger down my chest. Even with a hoodie on, the feeling sends blood rushing south. "Now be a good boy, smile, and go get my clothes for me to try on. If you do a good job, maybe I'll send you some pics from the dressing room."

Newly motivated to talk to a stranger, I head to the counter with my armfuls of pink. I make small talk with the girl, remembering each of the sizes Lizzy asked for, all the while looking over my shoulder, plastering on a smile and checking in with Lizzy.

She looks back at me, hovering nearby, pretending to sift through a rack of men's clothing. Or at least I hope she's pretending. I walk back to her, carrying the requested sports bras, cropped tanks, and leggings in the right sizes. She smiles and I point at her, noticing what's in her hand. "No."

She smiles and nods her head frantically. "Oh yes, please." She bounces up and down, holding a pink athletic shirt up in front of her.

"I don't wear pink." I hold her clothing, pointing at the dressing room doors and smirk at her. "Now, go. I believe you have a photo-shoot to get to."

She sighs, grabbing the hangers from my hand and casts me a sidelong glance. "Too bad. You'd look great in pink." She walks past me, running a fingernail along my jaw, sending a shiver down my spine. "But a deal's a deal, I guess."

I stand in the store, feeling like every other idiot wondering what to do while they wait on their girlfriend to try on clothes. Well, not girlfriend. What are we?

I've never felt like boyfriend material and I don't know if that's what she wants. I know she still has trust issues and I've got all my own baggage. I just know I've never felt like this with anyone. No one's ever made me want to try or feel like there could be more for me.

I'm pulled from my thoughts when my phone buzzes in my pocket. I swipe to unlock my phone and feel instant heat crawl up the back of my neck.

Holy shit. There are two topless photos of Lizzy, her hand placement strategically hiding her nipples. I'm so distracted by them that I don't even see the text message that follows at first.

> Princess: Which do you like more?

I look back at the pictures, taking a good minute to realize she has on different leggings in each one.

> Me: Both. Get out here. I'll buy both, but we're going home. NOW.

I watch as three dots appear.

> Princess:

Ok, I definitely see myself wanting more of Lizzy Frank in my life - whatever that looks like, but I'm assuming it will be very pink.

❄

ENJOYING A BOOK BY THE FIRE, I look around the house. It's quiet except for the crackling fire. It's been a few days since Lizzy's improvement plan has started and I haven't lost my mind yet. Our last lesson involved calling Tanner on speaker phone and asking "how are you doing" and if he had anything he wanted to do together in Bend. She sat there, watching me, egging me on to keep talking.

And it felt good, even if a little forced.

Sitting here now, while she's at happy hour with Grace, I sort of miss the chaos of her being around. But Kayleigh texted earlier and said she needed to vent, something I'm happy to let her do. She's been there so many times for me over the years. It's just what we do. So it works out that Lizzy is out with Grace.

An hour goes by and I finish a couple more chapters in my book. I see Ani's ears perk up and he runs to the door, wagging his tail. I head to the door and open it, letting him out when I see Kayleigh getting out of her SUV.

He runs up to her and I laugh when I notice her cock her head and give him a curious look when she rubs his sweater. She walks up the stairs to the porch, shaking her head laughing. "Let me guess, Lizzy's handiwork?"

My lips quirk up and I nod. "Nailed it. Have to say though, he seems pretty happy about it."

"He's not the only one that seems happy." She winks at me before closing the distance and giving me a hug.

I look down at Kayleigh. Her eyes are red, like she's been crying. I swallow, never wanting to see anyone I care about hurting. "So it's not going well with Charlie?"

She shakes her head. "I don't know how much longer we can keep up the long distance thing. It just feels like we've drifted apart." I watch as a tear streaks down her cheek.

I pull her in, pressing a kiss to her forehead. "You're going to be fine, one way or another." I hold her close, hoping my best friend knows I'm always here for her, like she's always been for me.

The sound of Ani's collar jingling and his paws kicking up snow catch my attention. I lift my eyes just in time to see him sprinting down the driveway. I look to where he's heading and see Lizzy's Bronco stopped.

Even this far away, I can see the look in her eyes. I know that look. It's the one filled with panic and self doubt, the one she had right before she ran out of Roxy's that night. I watch as she looks behind her and starts backing down the driveway.

"Fuck." I let go of Kayleigh and she turns to see the Bronco drifting out of sight.

"Oh shit. I'm sorry." I meet Kayleigh's eyes.

"Don't be. You did nothing wrong." I rub her shoulders, trying to reassure her. "But I have to go. Will you be ok?"

She nods. "Yeah, I'll be fine. Go find her."

I run to my truck, thinking to myself about that night at the bar. I kicked myself over and over for not following Lizzy to find out why she left. I'm not going to let that happen again.

I QUIETLY OPEN the door to the Frank's unit at the Aspen Grove Club. I look across the kitchen to the living area and see Lizzy, standing by the French doors to their balcony. It's almost the same layout as the penthouse upstairs, so the view outside is nearly identical.

I slowly walk over, watching as her head tilts towards me, but not enough to see her eyes.

"How'd you know I was here?" I reach her, standing by her side. I look at her and the expression on her face is cold and icy. She keeps staring ahead, not looking back at me.

"As soon as we started working on repairs, I put temporary sensors in. If the doors open or there's a temperature change, water hits the floor - you name it, I get a notification." I look at her, but her gaze doesn't waver as she looks out at the ski run in the distance. The sun is setting and the lights are just now coming on, bathing it a blueish hue. "I didn't want to take any chances on more mistakes."

She nods and finally looks at me. "Can you please tell me what your deal is with Kayleigh?"

I knew this was coming but I still hate that she could think this about me. But I also get her past. "I told you, Lizzy. We're old friends, best friends. We've been through a lot together. I don't want to talk about this anymore." I feel my molars grind with how tight my jaw is. "And I told you that night in the penthouse after dinner that I don't like being thought of as a cheating piece of shit." My tone is harsher and voice louder than I wanted, but I can't hide my agitation.

Her head snaps to me. "I want to trust you. But you need to give me more."

"I know your ex was horrible, but that's not me. It never has been, never will be. Please can you just drop this? You're overreacting. It's just in your head." I regret it the second I say it, watching as her blue eyes turn to fire. Fire that I just doused in gasoline by telling her that her feelings aren't valid.

"I'm not overreacting, Clay. Don't fucking tell me that, ever." She starts to step away, but I put an arm out blocking her. "You don't know how it feels to be constantly told that someone else knows what's in your own head better than you do. Please, just let me go."

"No," I say, holding my arm steady as she pushes against it. "You're not running away from me again. Not like at Roxy's. Tonight, we're going to talk this out. I'll start: I'm sorry."

She grunts in frustration before turning to look at me, the fire in her eyes softening to a dull glow before she rolls them. "For what?"

"I'm sorry I said you're overreacting. I'm sorry I questioned how you feel. You're right, only you truly know that." I meet her gaze, wishing for some better way to put her at ease. "But I meant it. I will never be that person. It hurts when you've thought I could do that to someone more than once now."

Her shoulders sag and she sighs, looking back outside for a moment. I stand firm, my arm still outstretched, watching the way the light dances in her eyes.

"I saw you two. That looked-" she frowns and her nose scrunches, "intimate. Like more than friends."

I sigh and step towards her, noticing that she doesn't back away from me. "I don't know what else to say. Kayleigh and I are friends. She's had a rough few days. That's all."

She turns toward me, cocking one hip out, and folding her arms across her chest. She gnaws on her lip, pulling my eyes down to them. "I'm never going to let what happened with my ex happen to me again. I don't want to feel like you're hiding something from me."

I reach out, grabbing her by the hips, holding her firmly in front of me. I look into her eyes, my heart warming when she looks right back into mine, searching for reassurance. "I'm not hiding anything. In fact, she knows all about us."

She quirks an eyebrow at me. "She knows about *us*?"

I huff a laugh. "Yeah, I told her after that first night at Roxy's. There isn't much we don't share. For the record, she really likes you."

She gnaws on her lip again, her eyes looking away before she nods. "Okay."

"Okay?" Her eyes meet mine again.

"Yes." I take a chance, pulling her in for a hug. She nuzzles into my chest, letting me finally exhale the breath I've been holding since I got here. "How'd you two get so close?"

I rub her back before turning her towards the view of the mogul course. "That's where I tore my right knee, on that course." She pulls away just enough to look up at me. I look away, back out towards the mountain. I hate reliving those days, but with her, it's almost like they don't even matter, like they're truly in the past. "She was there. She was competing on the giant slalom course, but had time to watch. This was long after our high school *dates*. By then, we knew we didn't like each other like that."

"Romantically incompatible?" I look back down at her, holding her closely, nodding.

"Yeah, exactly. But we still had so much in common. She was going through some things at home, in her life, at the same time. After my surgery, she spent the little free time she had outside of school and training with me. She helped me with my rehab routines." I swallow hard, not wanting to go much further. As relaxed as she makes me feel, I know there's so much here, so much pain, things that aren't my story to tell. "And that's right around the time when Mom's car accident happened."

Her eyes meet mine with that look, the one that makes me feel safe. The one that isn't pity, just understanding. She rubs her cheek into my chest and I rest my chin on top of her head. "What'd you tell her about us?"

A laugh rumbles up in my chest as my stomach finally calms down, knowing that she's not going to run off on me again. "That you drive me crazy. That you push my buttons." I feel her try to pull out of my hug.

"Not a good start, Chapman."

I squeeze her tight. "And that you make me feel better about myself than I have in ages. That you make me feel seen. That you're the only person I've wanted to seriously date and you're the only person in my life."

"Clay," she says, her voice hesitant, "I don't know if I'm ready for something serious yet. I can't tell you what I can give you right now, where this can go." She turns, her sapphire eyes meeting mine with a soft smile. "But I like you, a lot. I want you to be the only person in my life too. I know that much."

"I can live with that." Her words feel like a weight lifted off my chest.

"No secrets, no hiding?"

"No secrets, no hiding and no more running," I say. "Promise. Now stay still for a second."

She looks confused, but stands there and humors me while I open my phone to the settings and security page. I hold my phone between us, letting the camera take her picture, programming her in.

Her eyes look down at the phone and then back at me, still confused.

"There. I'm not going to hide anything from you. I mean it. You want to use my phone, look at it, whatever. It's there for you now. But I'll tell you, it's pretty boring except for my kindle app."

She looks back down at my phone and then me, now with an understanding expression. "Thank you." She gets up on her toes to kiss me. "Now can we go back to your place?" She smirks back up at me and I feel more at ease.

"Let's go home, princess."

CHAPTER 27

LIZZY
DISCREET PACKAGING

I HAVE to admit that living in Clay's house over the last month has been a pleasant surprise. It might have started out like a weird version of Beauty and the Beast, except he was already smoking hot and fucking him has only made him hotter. I mean I know it's not a giant French mansion in the countryside. But I also would never have expected the rough, tattooed cocky man in Roxy's that night to be the type to buy a giant pile of plush pillows and stock the house for me. The kind of man that worships me in a way I've never experienced.

He even set up my docking station and an extra monitor in his office for me so I can work from here on the days I don't need to be at the plant, like today.

And Jessica was right. The plant here is a giant mess and I really, really need to go through some of this data and honestly it will be easier here away from the distractions of my office.

Well, not zero distractions. Even though Clay is at the site at the Aspen Grove Club fixing the condo's entire ceiling and half the floors, he still left me some house chores because *I'm a brat and it would be good for me.*

Sitting at the desk with my coffee, I look down on the floor beside me. "Ani, your daddy called you a chore. How do you feel about that?"

I was sort of terrified of Ani at first, but now I love him being around. He feels like an extension of Clay. I watch as he grunts and sighs before rolling over on his back with his tongue hanging out. I roll my eyes. "Your dad is way more of a gentleman than you, sir." That thought brings a little welcome warmth to my heart. Clay really is a gentleman at heart. I know that is true.

Still, seeing him the other night with Kayleigh spooked me. They looked so close and so intimate that it felt like there's more to them. I know he says they're just friends, but it still got to me. I don't want to feel like Johnathan made me feel again. I don't want to doubt myself or be told to be something other than myself.

And I do feel like Clay is trustworthy. I feel like I believe him about Kayleigh. They have shared baggage. But I still get this feeling that there's something hiding there and I'm not getting the full story.

I do feel better knowing that Clay already told Kayleigh about us. The way Clay was so calm put me at ease. Grace might have figured it out on her own, but the fact that he told her and that I'm not some hidden other woman, counts for something. And being on the same page, explicitly saying we're the only ones in each others' lives, feels good. I meant what I told him, I don't know if I'm ready for more. But with him, I feel like I could be, like I want to be.

While I dwell on that, Ani gets my attention when he rolls over and jumps to his feet, looking around before running out of the room. Before I'm even out of my chair, I hear a knock on the door which makes Ani bark. I definitely feel safe with him around.

By the time I get to the door and open it with Ani sitting by my side, as Clay said he's trained to do, I watch the delivery driver pull down the long, snow covered driveway. At my feet, on the doormat, is a brown box. "Ani, that was a lot of excitement for nothing."

I reach down and grab the box, noticing the plain packaging. But it's addressed to me, which is odd because I have uncharacteristically avoided online shopping since I've been out here. Walking back in and closing the door behind me, I set the box on the counter and grab a knife to cut the packaging tape. I hold a finger over my lips when I look at Ani. "Your dad doesn't need to know I'm using the fancy knives to open it." To my surprise, Ani steps closer to me nudging me with his snoot. "Damn, ok. But I'm telling you, I didn't order you treats or another sweater."

I open the box, pulling away the black and gold tissue paper when my jaw drops.

It's a dildo.

Not just any dildo.

No, it's a big, veiny, knobby, ridged, dragon fantasy dildo. I pull it out, half admiring it, half terrified of the soft, smooth silicone toy. It's pretty. A shimmery pink and orange ombré. I set it on the counter to root through the rest of the box when I find a note.

I shake my head, wishing he was here to see my eye roll before I read it.

I saw you got the book I suggested and you're reading it. Chapter Thirty-Three. Enjoy slaying those dragons.

I BRING my hand to my still gaping mouth, giggling. I grab the toy and head over to the kitchen sink. Clay says he won't counter surf, but I'm still skeptical after he grabbed my other toy off my nightstand. After rinsing it, I set the toy on top of its silk storage bag to dry, still shaking my head.

It never ends with him. It really doesn't. He's a unicorn. He reads smut. He opens my car door for me. He's secure in himself and he's not intimidated by some sex toy. He really is something. How has he never been locked down by someone like Kayleigh?

That's when my phone buzzes, distracting me from that unwelcome thought, and I see Jessica's name flash across the screen.

Shit. I completely forgot it's time for our one on one. I head back to sit down at the desk, with Ani following me.

I will always be grateful that I like my job at Fischer and work for Jessica. I feel like if I didn't actually work for her, we'd be friends.

Sure, we're both bright, bubbly, and outgoing blondes. But I don't think that's why we get along so well. We both know we got to where we are because we worked our asses off to get there.

And the second that someone doubts us and treats us like something less, that's when we pounce. I can't count the number of times I've seen someone doubt Jessica, rolling their eyes at her or saying something patronizing only for her to come back and catch them off guard with a half dozen detailed reasons.

I sign on and turn on the video when her familiar voice comes through my headset. "What's up, girl?"

"Not much. Just crunching these numbers. You weren't kidding. This place is a hot mess, but we can get them where we want."

She laughs. "I knew you were the right one for the job. Also, no video today. I'm heading out of the office early and I'm out on vacation tomorrow. Heading to Red River Gorge for the weekend with the husband."

"Nice, enjoy it. We're leaving for Bend next Thursday. Looking forward to the time off."

I switch off my camera and relax, leaning back in the desk chair. Knowing Jessica, this will be a pretty casual call with her if she's distracted in the car with her husband.

After a couple minutes of chatting, Ani gets up and trots excitedly to the kitchen, which is when I hear the front door open and close. Seconds later, Clay stops in the office door, grinning from ear to ear. Of course, he's shirtless, part of his normal lunch routine to come home, do house chores, eat and let Ani out.

Is it distracting? Yes.

Do I mind it? No, definitely not.

I'm glad I'm not on video though because I turn fire engine red, knowing that he's grinning because he saw the toy on the counter. His dimples and his muscles immediately disarm me. It's criminally unfair to look like that.

He continues to stand there, grinning at me. I roll my eyes at him and mouth *thank you,* cocking my head side to side, trying to show I'm being sarcastic.

He crosses his arms and chuckles, which only makes his muscular chest puff out more. He mimes in question *video,* one side of his lips quirk up into a smirk.

I give him a puzzled look shaking my head no and shrugging my shoulders. He grins and disappears, leaving me to my call.

"So, what's your timeline looking like for next steps?" Jessica asks. I reply, but my attention is only half there because Clay has reappeared in the doorway. Still shirtless, which is distracting enough, but now with a flat-out sinful grin. His smoldering green eyes lock on me and I can feel my skin heat under his gaze.

He walks towards me, practically like a wolf stalking his prey. He leans forward on the other side of the desk, looking down at me and mouths *no video?*

I nod, almost unable to form words in his presence and unsure of what he's thinking about it. Until he pulls his hand from behind his back and sets *it* on the desk. The big, sparkly fucking dildo and a bottle of lube.

My eyes go wide and I click mute, hearing Jessica in the background arguing with her husband about the GPS. "Clay, what the actual fuck? I'm not playing with that right now. Are you batshit crazy?"

He laughs, smug as ever and grins back at me with a smile that makes me ache between my legs. His deep, gravelly voice only heightens how much I want him. "*You* are not going to play with it. You are just going to scoot that pretty little ass to the edge of the seat, lean back, and let me have the meal I've been thinking about all morning so I can focus when I go back to work."

Holy shit. The balls on him. Like literally, I've seen them. But also figuratively. Not wanting to let him enjoy getting to me, I collect myself and flick my ponytail over my shoulder, and thank god I'm still on mute. "Aw, did you get that because you knew you couldn't please a real woman?" I know very well that he can, but I'm not letting him have the satisfaction of knowing that I've been thinking about him all morning too.

He snorts a laugh before grabbing the dildo, dropping to his knees and crawling under the desk. His desk. It's almost as comical as it is hot. He's 6'3", but this man is on his knees now, barely fitting under the desk. He rests his head on my thigh and is looking up at me with nothing but playful lust in his deep emerald eyes. I drop my hand to him, running it over the stubble on his jaw.

"So, Lizzy, do you think you can send over your initial findings?" Jessica's voice makes my eyes go wide for the second time in minutes.

Shit. I click unmute. "Yeah, that's doable." I click mute again, looking down at Clay. "Are you serious?" I don't even know why I asked. I know he is. Everything about him is always so serious.

He nods, which only drags his stubble along my leggings, making the ache in my core that much more intense. "Fine, but you have to be quiet."

I grab the bottle of lube from the desk, tapping it against his forehead while I raise my eyebrows at him. "And don't you need this?"

He snorts a laugh, reaching both of his big hands around me and looping his calloused fingers into the waistband of my leggings. Even with them on, I still can feel the warmth of his breath, making me squirm. "I'm not the one who should worry about being quiet. And that-" He snatches the bottle from my hand. "That was more of a courtesy. I know you're already fucking soaked for me." He takes one finger, running it down from my waist over the fabric to my clit. I watch him grin as I squirm when his finger traces over the wet fabric.

"Oh, fuck you, Clay." His lips quirk up and he takes both hands, tugging my leggings down slowly to my ankles.

"Careful what you wish for." The sensation of his warm breath and stubble between my now very bare legs is almost too much already.

I roll my eyes until he looks away and starts to plant a trail of kisses up my legs until he reaches my clit. He wraps his big hands around me and pulls me closer to the edge of the seat, spreading my legs wider and propping them on his shoulders. I'm completely exposed to him, but I trust him completely right now.

"So, let's put some time on the calendar next week before you're out. We can go over your notes and next steps." The tip of Clay's tongue traces from the wetness pulling at my opening up to my throbbing clit.

I click unmute. "Yes, perfect, that works."

I click mute again, just in time for a whimper to escape my lips.

Clay's muffled laugh against my clit makes my thighs squeeze his head. Except the burn of his stubble only drives me more insane because it feels so good against my skin. "Careful now, you almost let that one slip out and I'm just getting started."

Holy shit. This is hot. This is wild.

I run my fingers through his hair looking down at him. The sight of this man with no shirt between my legs working my body is pornographic. This is the stuff I read about. Men like him don't exist in real life.

He lowers his lips back to my swollen clit, sucking and flicking his tongue. I can hear the sound of just how wet I am as he works my body. "You taste so fucking good, Lizzy. This pussy is so perfect."

"Cool." Jessica's voice is almost a distant whisper in my headset. "I will put something on the calendar for Monday or Tuesday. How does that sound?"

I click unmute again. "Sounds perfect." My voice is breathy, but hopefully masked out by the background noise from her car ride.

"Yeah, that sounds great." Clay's tongue moves faster and I feel him dip a finger in right before I click mute again, digging my finger nails further into his tousled hair.

"Don't you have somewhere to be? Like fixing my condo?" I don't know why exactly I'm still so insistent on playing with him like this when he already has me so close to coming apart on his face. Maybe I'm crazy. That thought is immediately erased when he plunges one thick finger into me, curling deep inside me.

"So fucking wet." He pulls his finger out and licks it before plunging it back in. "And there's literally fucking nowhere I'd rather be, princess." Before I can even register that or look down at him, he slides his finger back out, trailing it down my thigh leaving a trail of my own wetness behind and leaving me feeling suddenly empty.

His mouth is already back to work on me when I hear Jessica fumbling with her phone, probably trying to juggle speaker phone and looking at our calendars. "Is the morning or afternoon better? Looks like you're wide open, girl." You have no idea.

I look down, catching a glint in Clay's eye while he still works wonders on me with his tongue. He winks and I eye him suspiciously until I realize he's reaching down to grab the toy.

I unmute my headset again. "Yep. Wide open. Just put it in there. The sooner, the better." I mute right when Clay notches the head of the toy at my entrance and I moan so desperately, ready for that full feeling again. "You sure you're bigger? That's a lot."

His deep laugh reverberates through my clit, through the toy, through all of me. He slides the toy further in and the knobby ribs sends shivers through me. "You're such a fucking brat. You and I both know the answer to that question."

Almost in defiance, he pumps the toy in harder and faster, all while still working his tongue on my clit. Watching this is so damn hot and it's bringing me closer and closer to the edge. It feels so good, too good. The tension grows and I curl my hands into fists.

"Such a pretty, good boy." The words escape my mouth as a playful whisper.

I hear a questioning hum on my headset. "What was that?"

Oh my fucking god. I squeezed the mouse. I made a fist and I squeezed the mouse.

If I wasn't on cloud nine with Clay between my legs about to combust from pleasure, I'd combust from embarrassment at what I just did.

"Oh! Sorry. I was talking to my roommate's dog. He's sitting under the desk." I look down at Clay and stick my tongue out at him. "He's being such a *good boy* today."

Jessica snorts in what I hope was amusement. "Anyways, I'm going to be coming out to touch base with the team at the plant in a couple weeks. Who knows, we could even talk about this being a more permanent thing for you, over dinner, if you're enjoying being out there. The team there has nothing but glowing reviews of you. My husband is also going to join so he can hopefully get some skiing in too. If I find a good place for dinner, would you join us?"

"Yeah." I practically mutter and whimper through heavy breaths. "Yeah. I'll definitely come."

I can feel Clay laugh against me as he bottoms out the toy. His tongue, the fullness, the vibration of his laugh all send me completely over the edge. The knot of tension deep in me explodes as I come apart. I dig my nails into his scalp while my other hand covers my mouth, trying not to scream.

"Awesome," Jessica says, "Speaking of my husband, he says it's time to hangup. I'll catch up with you next week. Bye, bye!"

"Sounds good. Talk soon." I barely get the words out and hang up.

"Oh my god." My chest heaves. "You." I grab him by the hair. "You're fucking crazy."

He looks up at me, his jaw propped on the edge of the desk chair between my thighs. He looks up at me and licks my own arousal from his lips, which suddenly makes me want more. "Yeah, crazy good at making you come on my face."

He grins and pulls the toy out and a sudden gasp leaves me at the empty feeling. He eyes the toy and flicks his eyebrows at me. "Glad you like it."

I palm my face, smiling and laughing before looking back down at him. That toy isn't the only thing I find myself liking right now.

No, I definitely like being around Clay Chapman more and more.

CHAPTER 28
LIZZY
FAMILIAR

"NO," Clay says, drawing out the word. "I do not jerk off in the shower." I huff and cross my arms as he glares at me from the driver side of my Bronco before rolling his eyes and getting out. I glare right back at him, holding eye contact as he walks around the hood, watching him still mouth *no* the entire time until he reaches my door.

He opens it for me and somehow the simple gesture still makes my heart flutter each time. But I'm not going to give him the satisfaction of knowing that. I turn, sitting in the passenger seat with my arms crossed, my legs dangling out. "Don't ruin this fantasy for me. This is my Roman Empire."

He snorts a laugh and rolls his eyes again, setting his coffee on the roof of the car. "Hate to burn Rome down for you, but I don't jerk off in the shower. I don't know why romance authors always do this. But I will die on this hill. It's not happening."

We debated this for the last hour of the drive from Salt Lake to Bend after listening to an audiobook the whole way. But he insists this trope is wrong. I don't know why he won't let me have this. It would be so hot to watch him in the shower. Just picturing his tattooed forearm working, his veins popping, his tattooed hand gripping his thick length, and his muscular form glistening in hot, steamy water is enough to get me worked up. I feel my thighs clench as my body reacts to my thoughts and him being so close to me.

But this is exactly what I don't need since we'll be staying in a house with his sister, brother, and Veronica for the next few nights. Grace knows about us, but we didn't want to tell Veronica or Tanner yet. And after sharing a bed with him for the last two weeks, the idea of not sleeping with him every night, falling asleep in his giant arms, is almost unbearable. I'd be lying if I didn't think about him sneaking into my room in the middle of the night.

Sitting here, I'm eye level with him. I watch as he holds his hand out to me and I eye it skeptically. I huff and grab it, hopping out and looking back up at him. "You're no fun."

He looks down at me, smirking and shrugs. "Already told you, I never said I'd be fun."

"Yes. You keep reminding me." I give him a light punch and a huff of laughter rumbles from his chest. "So, you're still good with pretending like nothing's happening in front of everyone, right? I'm just not ready to take that step."

"Whatever you want. I'll do whatever you need." He sighs and shakes his head. "Besides, Tanner would give me so much shit if he found out and I don't know if I have the patience for that yet."

I let out a laugh. "That's probably true, but thank you." I place a hand on his chest, feeling his muscles through his black t-shirt. His gaze lingers on me and I feel my heart flutter. I inch closer to him, wanting to hug him and feel his warmth. I'm about to bury my head in his chest when a shrieking voice interrupts me.

"Oh my god! You guys are here!" We pull apart and I look to the front door of the beautiful, gargantuan house. It's stunning but somehow so familiar. I don't have time to place it when Veronica runs out towards us. She bolts up and hugs us both. "I have so much to tell you guys."

"V, one sec." I clear my throat and look at Clay, raising my eyebrows.

"Thanks for inviting me, V. Seriously, I'm happy to be here with everyone."

"Good job." I pat him on the back like praising a puppy that just sat down on command. "See? That wasn't hard."

She pauses, her lips parting, and her eyes darting between us. "Thanks? Glad you're here too," she says, almost like a question. She hums to herself, looking back at me. "What was that?"

Clay drops his head, sighing, and I grin back at her. "We made a deal. Since I don't have you around everyday anymore, I've been bad about working out. So Clay, my new roomie, is my accountability buddy. And I'm helping him..." I wave a hand at him, prompting him to glare back at me. "Do less of that."

She eyes us both for a second before continuing. "Yeah. Good luck with that, both of you. Anyways, like I was saying, *big* news."

"Is it about how awesome this house is? Because Tanner really came through with the hook up on this place."

V grins back at me. "Yeah. You're right. This place is awesome." She looks over at Clay. "You already knew that though."

I give him a puzzled look and he turns a little pink before V grabs my shoulders and shakes me. "Anyways, TJ's in the house. Like literally *in the house*."

Suddenly, it clicks. Tommy Jacob - TJ - is the lead singer for the band Teal Tigers. Tanner befriended him while managing his property in Jackson Hole and I guess that's how we ended up getting this place for the week. V and I hung out there with Tanner and Collin one night there in Jackson while TJ was out of town. Now I know why this place looks so familiar. It looks so much like his house in Jackson. More importantly though, V has had a rockstar crush on TJ since before I knew her. Looking back at her, I can't help but laugh at how excited she is.

"You're literally losing it, aren't you? But also, are we sure it's still ok for us all to stay here?"

She nods eagerly. "Yeah, I might be fangirling hard. He wasn't clear on why he's here, but I'm *really* not complaining. And he was more than happy to have us." She looks back to Clay, tilting her head. "But that does leave us a bedroom short."

"It's fine. I'll take a couch," Clay says in his gruff deep voice, before forcing a smile. He turns back to grab our bags before adding, "Princess needs the last bedroom for her beauty sleep anyways. Make sure it has *plenty* of pillows."

"There he is." Veronica looks at me, raising her eyebrows. "Seems like you still have some work to do with him. I don't know how you've managed to live with him for weeks."

I feign a laugh, but deep inside I feel for him. I've loved almost every second I've been around this very misunderstood man. Suddenly I feel possessive, protective of him, remembering how being dismissed hurt him, something I can relate to all too well.

I LOOK DOWN at the hand held out in front of me, noticing the musical notes tattooed around the ring finger and the leather bracelet around the wrist. Then I take in the tall, fit man it's attached to. All of it, from his shaggy unkempt hair to the silver and leather necklace to the cut off sleeves of his plaid flannel shirt showcasing his biceps and muscular forearms. It all screams grungy rockstar.

Tommy Jacob is here in the flesh, holding his hand out for me to shake, in the entryway of his house. I've seen pictures of him before, but they don't do him justice. On camera, he always looked lean and slender, but in person, he's *built* with well tanned skin and muscles everywhere I can see. The hair that always looked light and blonde in videos and pictures is more of a light auburn. It's trimmed down to a medium length now instead of the shoulder length I remember from the poster Veronica had in our apartment in college. Instead of the beard I remember from that poster, he has a light stubble covering his square jaw with a few distinguished grays.

I mean he's no Clay Chapman, but I get why Veronica fangirled over him for years.

"Hey, it's good to meet you," he says in a raspy yet silky, well worn deep voice. He smiles and huffs a laugh. "But I feel like I know you already with how much Veronica has told me."

He takes my hand, kissing the back of it before shaking it in both of his. I laugh, feeling my cheeks go a little pink with his playful tone and gesture. "Thank you *so* much for letting us stay for the week."

He scoffs and waves me off. "Nah, it's nothing. Anything for the Chapman brothers." He leans in closer to me, holding a cupped hand in front of his mouth. "But seriously, Veronica hasn't stopped talking. Is she always like this?"

A giggle escapes me and I cover my mouth and whisper. "Actually, between you and me, normally she's the quiet one."

My attention is pulled away when I see Grace and Tanner walking in from a hallway and over to Clay. He drops our bags, bumping his fist with his brother before bringing his sister in for a hug. I look back at TJ who's also tracking their movement. He clears his throat and steps over to Clay.

"Long time, no see man," TJ says, before Clay holds out a hand.

Wait. Do they know each other?

TJ scoffs and shakes his head, making his shaggy blonde hair sway. "Oh no, friends don't shake hands in this house."

I watch, half in horror for Clay, half laughing to myself as he wraps his arms around him, pulling him in tight for a hug.

Clay lets out a muffled groan, patting TJ on the back. There's something amusing about seeing a Chapman caught off guard by an even bigger bear hug. "Good to see you too."

I make eye contact with Clay, making an exaggerated smile at him. He rolls his eyes at me. "Thanks for having us."

I make an OK gesture at Clay, who just rolls his eyes again as TJ lets him go. "Are you serious? It's the least I can do. Look at how this place turned out man." TJ turns and waves one hand towards the rest of the house.

I take a second to look at the rest of it. Beautiful polished concrete floors and a mix of exposed wood and steel beams. Floor to ceiling windows with views of Mount Bachelor, the evergreen forest around us, and the Deschutes River. A beautiful fireplace sits right in the center of the main wall of windows. All of it feels familiar. Too familiar.

I look back at Clay when the realization sets in that he designed this house. His eyes meet mine and his cheeks turn that boyish pink before he looks away, giving his attention back to TJ. Somehow this cocky, grumpy man is capable of adorable, admirable humility too.

"Glad you love it, TJ. But really, thanks for having us. Looking forward to seeing how you decorated the place." I mouth *there you go* to him, mockingly clapping my hands together, prompting a playful scowl.

"For sure. I'll catch up with you later." TJ pats him on the back before heading down the hall, leaving us with Grace, Tanner, and Veronica.

I step towards the three of them, one hand on my hip.

"Alright. Can we skip the rest of the greetings and figure out dinner? I missed you guys, but that was a long drive from Utah and Clay apparently doesn't like to stop unless it's for gas or a bathroom break." I look to Tanner and V, raising my eyebrows. "And I don't know about you guys, but I'm getting a little hangry and I know you don't want to deal with that."

Clay lowers his brows and glares at me. "I offered to get you chicken tenders at the gas station. They're the perfect passenger princess snack, easy to eat on the road."

I glare back at him, turning up a hand. "Do I look like a child? No. I wanted *real food*."

He grins back. "Well you're about as tall as a child and wear a lot of pink."

Tanner laughs and turns to Veronica. She wraps an arm around him and leans against his shoulder. "I can't imagine how that ten hour car ride was. Surprised you two survived."

The jokes on her because we listened to a book the whole way and it was great. I stare her down, bringing my hands to my face like

I'm eating a sandwich. "Enough chit chat, V. Food. Think about *food*."

AS ALWAYS, V's food suggestions are on point. We're sitting on the patio and it's perfect after the long drive. Plus we have a prime view of the Deschutes River and the surf park in the center of town, able to watch the wetsuit clad surfers ride the man-made rapids. I will never complain about food with a side of eye candy.

"Alright. These aren't quite Frisky Fox spicy margs, but they're a very close second." I put my drink down and grab a taco and take a bite. My eyes roll back in my head at how good the al pastor is. Ok. I was definitely hungry.

I dab the corner of my mouth with a napkin and look at V and Tanner. "So skiing tomorrow then dinner out?"

V takes a drink of her margarita and nods, setting it down. "Yeah, get up early and get out for first chair. We'll probably call it an early day though and come back a little bit after lunch when the temperatures warm up and the snow gets a little slushy."

"Sounds good to me."

She quirks an eyebrow at me. "Really? That easy? It's normally impossible to pry you out of bed that early."

I give her a healthy dose of side eye before tipping my chin to Clay. "My *accountability buddy* here has been making sure I'm up early for our morning workouts."

Veronica lets out an amused hum as her eyes go back and forth between me and Clay.

Tanner shakes his head and grabs his brother's shoulder. "Are you still doing your crazy crack of dawn runs in the snow?"

Clay huffs a laugh and nods. "You know me."

"Yoga's one thing. But I'm not crazy enough to join him and Ani on those runs." I lift my drink and take a sip. I will probably never want to go on a run like that, but that doesn't mean I wouldn't mind watching. The way his shorts show off his thighs is criminal.

"OK, cool," V says, snapping my mind back to the conversation. "So, we could come back to the house, get ready, and go out for happy hour before dinner."

"Perfect." I nod and lick the salt off the rim of my glass. I catch Clay's eyes watching me. I grin back at him, but he frowns and grabs his phone.

> Grumpy Roommate: You should have said something if you were that hungry. I'm sorry.

I read the text again, getting a warm and fuzzy feeling knowing that he's still worried after I complained about being hangry.

> Me: It's fine. Just laid it on a little extra to sell it to them. But yes, future reference, I will never turn down real food.

> Grumpy Roommate: Noted. For the record, you're the perfect passenger princess.

I put my phone away and look across the table at him. I spent all day in the car with him and still, I already miss being close to him. His eyes meet mine again, his frown gone. I watch him lift his drink, admiring the way the muscles tick and shift under his tattoos. I feel my cheeks heat, wishing his hands were on me right now.

I shift my eyes to Grace sitting next to me, her eyes are already on me. She grins at me knowingly and winks before turning to Clay.

"So what are you going to do tomorrow while we're out at the mountain?" she asks.

He reaches an arm across the table, scooping some salsa onto a chip. "Probably just hang around the house. TJ said he was going to fly fish in the morning." He nudges his brother in the side with an elbow. "So I might join him after one of my *crazy crack of dawn runs.*

And I'm definitely going to check out the rest of the house to see how it turned out, since I never actually got to see it in person."

I feel fingers graze my elbow before Grace leans in, whispering to me. "I honestly can't remember the last time he's smiled this much."

She squeezes my arm before letting go, turning her attention back to the conversation. Something about what she said is both heartwarming and heartbreaking all at once. There's so much I don't know about their family dynamic, but I do know from V that they all used to be so close. And seeing Clay now, smiling and laughing with his siblings, all I can think about is how much he had to have been hurting when he felt left out. I'm glad he's here.

And I'm glad I have him in my life.

CHAPTER 29
CLAY
ALONE

LYING on the pullout sofa in the upstairs loft, I stare up at the ceiling trying to sleep. *Trying* being the keyword, because I can't sleep at all knowing that Lizzy is on the other side of the wall. As much as she drove me crazy the first couple of weeks with chaos, from her stuff all over my house to her constantly pushing my buttons, suddenly I want nothing more than to have her wrapped in my arms so I can breathe her in.

I have never felt this way about someone. She consumes my thoughts. She's not just some distraction like I originally thought. She's so much more.

I've never thought about *more* before. *More* means opening myself up to getting hurt because it's something I could lose. And the thought of losing anything I care about, something I might even love, if I'm even capable of that, makes me feel like I'm going to lose control and fall apart.

My thoughts are interrupted when a dim glow catches my eye on the end table. I lean over, checking the notification on my phone.

> Princess: Come in here? Everyone's asleep.
> It'll be fine.

I LOOK at the message and smile, glad that I'm not the only one awake with this feeling.

> Me: Miss me already?

I WATCH three dots pop up, disappear, and reappear before her message comes through.

> Princess: I could tell you... Or you could
> just come here and see how much I
> miss you.

MY COCK TWITCHES and I throw the covers off in a flurry.

Yep, when it comes to Lizzy Frank, I'm a weak man.

I walk across the loft, taking careful steps to avoid hitting anything in the dark, quietly making my way to Lizzy's room. I open the door to see her curled up in bed, the glow of her phone bathing her face in light. She smiles and I stride over to her, getting under the covers beside her.

She rolls onto her side and I pull her into me. I hear her let out a contented sigh and she wriggles her ass up against my hard cock. Even through my sweats and her flannel sleep shorts, the curve of her ass against my body sends shivers through me.

She lets out another low hum, pushing her ass against me harder. "I see you missed me too."

"Definitely." I rock my hips into her, suddenly wanting there to be less layers of clothing between us. I bring my mouth to her ear, breathing in that citrusy shampoo scent from her freshly washed hair. "But I'm not fucking you tonight, princess."

She lets out an adorable, pouty huff. "Now *you're* being a brat."

I run a finger over her lips, feeling them part. "Don't give me that. You know if I fuck you, I'll lose control and I'll pound you so hard into that headboard, everyone in the house will wake up and hear you calling my name."

She whimpers in frustration and a low laugh rumbles from my chest. I run my hand down her chest, my fingertips grazing her pebbled nipples over her shirt. She pants as I reach the waistband of her shorts.

"Don't worry. I'm still going to take care of you."

"Clay." My name is a whisper on her lips. I dip my fingers under the front of her shorts, cupping her. I can feel just how much she missed me, making my throbbing cock twitch again.

"Fuck," I rasp. "You're so goddamn wet for me already."

I part her wet heat with my fingers and slowly run one up and down her swollen, aching clit. This time she writhes at my touch, rocking her hips and pushing herself into my hand.

"You're so needy for me." I put more pressure on her clit and work my finger slower on her bundle of nerves. "If I didn't come in here, you were going to play with yourself while thinking about me. I bet you packed a toy, didn't you?"

"Why-" her voice is cut off by her moan when I slide in one finger and keep teasing her clit. "Why would I pack a toy when I packed you?"

I plunge my finger into her deeper and add a second, rewarding her for that compliment. I feel her walls clench on my fingers and flick my thumb back and forth over her clit. Feeling her so worked up is driving me crazy and I grind myself against her ass, desperate to feel friction on my cock.

"You're already so close for me." I lean down, kissing her neck, nipping under her ear. I can feel her pulse pounding on my lips and her breathy moans and whimpers drive me wild. "Let go."

My words undo her and I feel her buck into my hand, her pussy clenching on my fingers. Knowing that I can make this sassy, snarky woman let go and lose her mind at my touch, with my words, is so damn satisfying. I dip my fingers into her, wringing every last bit of pleasure out of her, coating them in her slick wetness.

I slide my fingers out, prompting another whimper from her. She turns and nuzzles her head into my chest. Every time she does that, I feel my chest fill with pride that being that close to my heart brings her comfort. I wrap one arm around her, holding her tight against me. I take my other hand, still covered in her arousal and start stroking my cock inside my sweats.

Her eyes meet mine, hooded and lazy in her post-orgasm bliss and she kisses me. I moan into her mouth. "I can't get enough of you."

I'm so fucking worked up from feeling her come on my fingers that I'm almost ready to let go myself. Each stroke in my tight fist brings me that much closer.

Her eyes drop to my hand working in my sweats and she grins back at me before kissing me again, biting and tugging on my lower lip. "Good thing I can't get enough of you either."

I watch as she plants kiss after kiss down my stomach, trailing her fingernails between my abs sending a shiver through me. I love the way her unkept waves of blonde, not in their normal ponytail, hang over her shoulders and drag along my stomach. When she reaches my waistband, she pulls them down, freeing my hardened length. She gently grabs my wrist, humming in amusement and rubbing the back of my hand with her thumb. She brings her mouth just above my throbbing cock and swirls her tongue over the head, licking off a drop of precum.

The feeling of her wet, hot tongue unravels me.

"Fuck. I'm going to come."

She hums and grabs my wrist, pulling my hand off my cock before she lowers her mouth onto me. I fall apart, bucking into her mouth, grabbing and fisting her hair out of the way into a ponytail, wanting to watch. She looks so good when she takes me to the base. I come hard, spilling into the back of her throat and she moans in approval, making me buck again. She slowly pulls herself off me, letting the tip of her tongue drag along my shaft before kissing the head.

She looks over her shoulder, swallowing and smirking at me before she lays her head on my chest. I tilt her chin up with my thumb, bringing her lips to mine, claiming her mouth. The fucking mouth that barely touched me and got me off. The mouth that I can't look away from when she licks the salt off the rim of her glass or she taps one of her pink fingernails against those full, pouty lips.

I pull away, breaking the kiss to the sound of a small gasp leaving her lips. "I couldn't sleep. I was wide awake thinking about you when you texted me." Having to be so close to her all day without being able to touch her has driven me crazy.

"I couldn't sleep either." She hums thoughtfully, gnawing on her lip and tracing her fingertips through my thin chest hair. Her touch feels like fire on my skin. She drapes a leg over my waist, curling herself completely into me. "Will you stay with me?"

I know she's asking about staying in bed tonight, but part of me wishes she was asking for something else, something more, something that I find myself thinking about with her for the first time in my life.

I reach down, pulling the comforter over us.

"Of course."

I pull her into me, rubbing the back of her neck. She yawns and her eyes flutter shut. I savor the feeling of her soft even breath on my chest as she falls asleep.

❄

WHEN I WAKE UP, I take in the beautiful woman that's upended what I thought was my simple, carefully planned life. Her blonde hair flows over the pillows around her. Her eyes open, revealing that icy shade of blue that lights me on fire. She rubs the back of her hand across them.

"What time is it?" Her voice is groggy as she yawns.

I kiss her forehead, running my thumb over her cheek. She grabs my wrist, bringing my hand to her lips and kisses my knuckles.

"It's early. No one's up yet. I'm going to go for my run. Go back to bed."

She sticks out her lower lip, pouting. "Stay a bit longer?"

I hum and run my thumb over her bottom lip, pulling on it. "As much as I'd like that, I need to get out of here and make my bed before anyone else gets up."

She huffs and bites softly on my thumb.

I laugh and lightly slap her ass. "Brat. Get your beauty sleep."

I stand and tuck her back in. I walk around the bed, still wearing just my sweats, and I don't miss the way her eyes follow me.

"You're shameless," I tease, puckering my lips blowing her a kiss. "Take a picture if you need it."

She rolls her sleepy eyes and pulls one hand out from under the covers to flip me the bird.

I shake my head and laugh quietly. "See you later."

I WIND down my run along the Deschutes River trail, heading north back towards town and TJ's house. I've been enjoying the just right spring air of the Eastern Cascade Mountains. It might be snowing up at Mount Bachelor where everyone is skiing today since it's a few thousand feet higher in elevation, but here near town and along the river, it's a comfortable spring day.

I think back to the last time I was in Bend, running this very trail. It was earlier in the same season that I first tore my ACL. I came here with Mom for one of my competitions. Mount Bachelor has always been known for some epic powder days and we caught one while we were here on our extra day in town. We skied lap after lap in deep powder on the backside of the mountain, loving every second of it. Thinking back on it, those laps with Mom might have been the last time I really, truly remember just skiing for the joy of skiing, not competing.

I run along the trail, thinking about that day as I see TJ's house in the distance. I designed it after Tanner first saw my house in Utah. He introduced us on a video call and then I was hired. While I might have come up with the design, his builder did an amazing job of bringing it to life the way I hoped it would turn out.

When I get to the part of the trail that goes between his house and the river, I chuckle to myself when I see TJ already out in the water in waders, fly fishing. He might be a rockstar, but he's got some pretty normal hobbies.

I take the side trail that heads back to his house, stopping when I see Grace in a robe walking towards me.

"Morning, big bro." She stops and looks me up and down.

"What the hell are you doing out here in a robe at the crack of dawn?" My voice is gruff from running and still catching my breath, it probably sounds harsher than I meant it to.

She scoffs and waves me off. "Going for a cold plunge in the river."

"You're crazy. It might be warm out here, but that's still fed with cold snow melt from the mountains. You know that right?"

She raises her eyebrows at me. "Duh. That's kind of the point. *Cold* plunge."

I roll my eyes at her. "Whatever. I'll see you inside for breakfast. Don't get pneumonia." I start to walk past her, but she grabs my arm and stops me.

"Hey, I'm really glad you came."

I nod. "Yeah, me too."

She gives me a knowing grin. "She's good for you. You look happy."

I glare back at her and she snorts a laugh. "Don't get mushy on me. Have fun with your cold plunge."

I turn and head up the side trail to the house, trying not to obsess over what my sister just said. It's the same thing that I've been thinking, that I might want this thing with Lizzy to be something bigger.

I slide open the doors from the back patio and walk towards the kitchen.

I turn the corner and pause for a second, startled to find V sitting alone at the kitchen island, with an iced coffee in a plastic to-go cup.

"Jesus, V. Wasn't expecting anyone to be up yet."

She takes a sip of her coffee and shrugs a shoulder. "Could say the same thing about you. Not used to having someone up and around as early as me."

I walk past her at the island to the fridge, grabbing the two cans of nitro cold brew I picked up at the store yesterday and set them out on the counter.

V gives me a curious look and I realize what I've just done.

"Figured she'd need her coffee if she's going to get first chair with you guys today. Kind of forgot how militant you are about that." I grab two pint glasses from the open shelves and pour our coffees. I tilt my chin and point to her drink. "Speaking of coffee, did you already go out and get one from Dutch Sisters up the street?"

She nods and takes another sip of her coffee. "You know me. It's not quite as good as a Cowgirl Coffee Honey Badger, but it's pretty close."

"I haven't had one of those in forever. Finch in Park City is pretty good though."

I grab the two cold brews and head to the island, sitting down next to V. With as much time as we spent with the Perry twins growing up in Jackson, she's always kind of been like a sibling the same way Collin is. But knowing Lizzy now, I can see why they're such good friends.

"So what are you getting up to today?"

"Going to take Lizzy her coffee first, then head out and fish with TJ." I take a sip of my drink. My mind drifts off when I remember what Lizzy's lips taste like after she's had her morning coffee. I shake my head, trying to get my mind back on track sitting here with V. "But I'll be around when you guys get back. I'll definitely hang with you tonight."

"YOUR SISTER'S NUTS, DUDE." TJ's voice cuts across the sound of the rippling water in the river.

A laugh rumbles from my chest and I cast my line out into the water. "Tell me something I don't know. She's always trying new health trends."

"I about leapt out of my skin when she jumped off that rock over there into that swimming hole." He tilts his head towards a large boulder and deep pool along the bank behind me.

A few minutes pass and I enjoy the sound of the water, thinking about how Tanner and I would do this with our grandpa in Jackson on the Snake River. It ran right behind the cabin that Tanner lives in now and we spent so many spring and summer days fishing.

"Glad it worked out that I was here when all of you came to town. Looking forward to showing you how the rest of the house turned out." I turn to see him looking at me and I nod.

"Looking forward to it." I remember what we originally talked about when we first started working on the plans. It's a bigger version of my house with an upstairs loft plus two more bedrooms on the first floor. One of the garage bays was repurposed into a soundproof studio. I know he has other places too, like his house in Jackson.

I find myself thinking that these are massive houses for just one person, even one as wealthy as him. I think back to my house and how it just feels different with Lizzy there. I've loved my space, my peace, and quiet and order for so long. But the last month with Lizzy there, it just feels warmer, more like home than it ever has. From her yoga mats in the basket by the fireplace to her used coffee cup collection on my counter to her notes on my desk in my office. It all just feels right.

No, I definitely don't think this is where I want to be ten years from now. I don't want to be alone. For once, I don't mind that someone is there. For once, I want someone to be there. I want her there.

CHAPTER 30
LIZZY
WHAT DID I DO WRONG?

AFTER V DRAGGED us out of the house this morning, we managed to get first chair just like she wanted. I say *us*, but Tanner and Grace were already awake and eating with V by the time I got down to the kitchen this morning. So it was just me holding things up, as usual.

Sorry, not sorry. She knew what she signed up for asking me to come.

Having Clay bring up my morning coffee definitely helped though. I don't know what came over me last night, but I felt restless without him in bed. It was about to be the first time in weeks we didn't fall asleep in each other's arms. And as we got to the slopes and skied our first runs of the day, all I could think about was how much better I slept with him holding me last night, in those big, muscular arms I can't look away from. I remember the comfort I get when he holds my hands in his rough, callused ones.

Now I'm sitting next to V, Tanner, and Grace on the chairlift. We're going up for one last run before lunch when I look down at my gloved hand and remember what that comfort feels like - what he feels like. I'm thinking about the spark, that tingle of electricity I felt when he handed me my coffee this morning when our fingers grazed each others. The feeling I get every time I see him, every time he touches me.

Watching V and Tanner, I see the way they laugh and bicker and make each other smile. It wasn't that long ago that she was a burnt out mess. Now I watch the way she nuzzles into him and rests her head on his shoulder. Is that what I look like when I'm with Clay and it's just the two of us? Because it feels like I'm in my own little world with him where I can just let my guard down and just be me.

I don't know what this is yet. But I'm glad I have him and only him in my life. I know I want to see where this could go, even if I'm not sure I'm ready for more.

While I try not to spiral about that revelation, I hear the sound of the chairlift reach the top terminal, bringing me back to the moment. The safety bar raises, I pull my goggles down and I slide my poles out from under my thigh before we ski off the lift, heading towards the trail map at the top.

V stops in front of the big map and props her goggles on top of her helmet while the rest of us circle around her.

"Alright. How does a nice easy groomer run sound to get us back to the main lodge for lunch?"

As much as my workouts with Clay have been helping, I rarely ski as many days in a season as I have this year. Between the Jackson trip, Aspen Valley trip, and the few spring days in Utah, my legs are beat at this point in the day.

I chime in first, thinking about my sore legs. "That sounds perfect to me. Nice and mellow."

She pulls her goggles down and grins. "Last one down buys the first shotski."

I laugh as Tanner and Grace follow closely behind her. I'm not even going to try to keep up with them. I already know they're going to beat me down to the lodge.

I enjoy the run, thinking about the beauty of the Eastern Cascade Mountains. I've never been here before and Grace was right, this place is stunning. To the East are high plaines deserts. In all the other directions are little dormant volcanic peaks, dotting the horizon, just like Mount Bachelor that we're skiing on. All of them are still capped in snow, even in early May. On a bluebird day like this, it's breathtaking.

I admire the view on my way down, eventually getting to the lodge. They're already there waiting on me, skis off and resting in the racks outside. Grace looks at the patio and then back at me. I spot the bar immediately. With it being spring, it looks inviting and we can take in the views from here. "Outdoor dining today? Looks like you can buy us that round out here," she says with a wry grin.

I look at V who shrugs back with her palms up. I turn to Grace, nodding. "Sounds good to me."

AFTER LUNCH, I head to the bathroom before heading to join the others back on the patio. Just when I reach the door heading out to the patio, my phone buzzes in my pocket. I'm instantly annoyed at the thought of having to take off my gloves and unzip at least one of the layers I just put back on to get my phone out.

It might be spring skiing, but it's still chilly out for me, and I bundled up.

Groaning, I take off my gloves, pull down my neck warmer, and unzip my jacket to get to the inner pocket where my phone is. I'm about ready to rip whoever's calling from my office on my Friday off a new one when I look down at my phone.

It's my dad.

I'm so caught off guard that I realize I've been staring at my phone long enough that it'll go to voicemail any second. I swipe my finger across the phone.

"Hello," I say. My voice is shaky. Why is he calling me right now? He almost never calls.

"Hi, Lizzy. Did I catch you at a bad time?"

I walk towards the edge of the patio and sit back against the railing.

"No. I can talk."

"Oh good. Are you at the condo?"

I realize I never told him I'm going to be out of town this weekend.

"No. I'm up in Oregon with V and my friends."

I hear a muffled huff come from his side of the call.

"Got it. So I assume the condo is not ready yet. Do you know if it will be ready by next week? I need to come out and visit with some business partners for the company we just bought."

My eyes start to water, but I hold back the tears. There it is. It's never about me with him.

"Yeah. Clay said it should be finished by Tuesday."

"Perfect. Anyways, didn't mean to keep you from your friends. Love you. Talk later."

I start to say *bye Dad*, but he hangs up before I can get the words out.

What did I do wrong for him to always be like this? Sure, he said *love you.*

But he never asks about *me.* He never has the time to talk. It's just this transactional relationship, not a father-daughter relationship.

I just don't know what I did wrong. It hasn't always been like this. We were close once. He used to show interest in my life. Was it something I did?

CHAPTER 31
CLAY
KARAOKE

AFTER SPENDING the day around the house with TJ and catching up on some project planning work, we meet everyone else in town. TJ and I grabbed an early dinner after he insisted he has nothing important to do when he wanted to tag along. I figured he would have less free time on his hands than he seems to. Or maybe he's just lonely, like I'm slowly realizing I was back home.

Either way, I see why he likes towns like Bend and Jackson. Everyone seems to leave him alone. And when he wanted to tag along tonight, I was more than happy to let him join since he's hosting us after all.

I texted Lizzy to see if everyone else wanted to get dinner. She sent back a jumbled text. All I could make out was that they already grabbed a bite to eat, so it looks like it's a night out on the town - not that I plan on getting too wild. I'm driving Lizzy's Bronco and just want to enjoy my time away with everyone *without* a hangover.

When I walk into Cascade East with TJ, an old locals' après ski bar, I immediately realize that Lizzy clearly has other plans tonight. She's up on stage with Grace, singing karaoke. Fittingly, she's singing a song about a certain pink clad doll and her boy-toy. I smile to myself, knowing my girl doesn't want a pretty, clean cut blond city boy. She likes it real and rough.

We walk through the dimly lit, wood-paneled bar looking for Tanner and V. The place immediately reminds me of the Silver Dollar Cowboy Bar back in Jackson, mixed with the locals crowd of Roxy's in Park City.

I spot them close to the stage, sitting around an indoor gas fire pit made out of stones and timbers. I feel the soles of my boots stick to the floor with each step as I walk towards them.

Yep, this is definitely a locals' dive bar.

TJ and I walk around the fire pit with me grabbing the chair next to Tanner.

V sees me first and smiles softly, tipping her drink to me. I tilt my head, gesturing for her to look behind her. She turns and I chuckle when her jaw drops as TJ pulls out a chair and sits down beside her.

"Looks like you're going to have to win back your fiancée." I give Tanner a brotherly punch in the shoulder, prompting him to snort a laugh. V pulls her attention away from TJ, just long enough to glare at me.

"Ha. Ha. Ha." V mockingly laughs at me. She hops out of her chair and into Tanner's lap, grabbing his face and kissing him, much to his surprise. "Very funny."

I laugh and tilt my head towards the stage where Grace and Lizzy are flipping through a list of song options. "So what's up with them? It looks like they really got after it early."

Tanner grins back at me as TJ and V both look up at the stage, hollering song suggestions to Grace and Lizzy.

"Looks like you need to push her a little harder on her workouts. She got tired early in the afternoon and went to the lodge." He looks back up at the stage and shakes his head. "Grace joined her and it looks like they had their own little *pre-game happy hour.*"

"Sounds about right," I say, looking back up at my sister and the woman I'm falling for. She hops off the stage and heads towards the bar.

I look to everyone around the fire pit. "Anyone need a drink? I'm going to grab a beer."

They wave me off and I make my way up to the bar beside Lizzy and order my beer.

She hears me and turns, smiling so wildly. She claps her hands to her face. "Oh my god, I've been waiting all day to see you."

She practically leaps at me, pulling me into a hug and rubbing her face into my chest. I look back to the stage and fire pit area, seeing that no one is looking our way. I lean down, kissing the top of her head, inhaling the smell I've become completely addicted to.

"Missed you too, princess." My voice is low and the sounds of the bar are loud, but I know she hears me by the way she hums into my chest. She holds me tight and doesn't let go.

I pull her back just enough for her to look into my eyes.

"Looks like you and my sister are having quite the afternoon." I look down at my watch, smirking. "And evening."

She rolls her eyes and slaps my chest. "Don't be a party pooper." She smiles again, but it doesn't quite meet her eyes or have the unrestrained brightness that melts my heart.

I lower my gaze to meet hers, noticing a frown appearing.

I tilt her chin up, running my thumb over the indent between her lower lip and chin.

"Hey, everything ok?"

Her lips pull together in a line and her brows knit together.

"It's nothing. My dad called today. Just threw me off." She looks up at me, smiling softly now. "Can we just have fun tonight and talk about anything else?"

I nod. "Anything you want."

She stands on her toes and plants a kiss on my cheek. "Thank you."

I grab my beer, now the only one I plan to have tonight, and watch as she practically skips off back towards the stage to join Grace.

It looks like my night just got a whole lot more interesting.

❄

I WATCH as Lizzy points at the song list, jumping up and down, smirking devilishly at Grace who's grinning right back at her. She pats Grace on the back before walking off the stage towards the bar.

They have done at least four or five songs over the last hour, each a bit sloppier than the last.

I head to meet her at the end of the bar, standing next to her, but she doesn't notice me. I watch as she leans over the bar, standing on her toes to stretch out to flag down a bartender. Seeing her stretched out, her ass up like that, makes my dick twitch.

I stand next to her, shaking my head when she turns and notices me standing there. "You're drunk."

She stands straight and steps toward me. "Am not."

I arch an eyebrow at her, clearly not believing her. "We should get you home before you do something stupid."

She leans into me and hooks a finger into one of my belt loops, pulling me closer. "Like this?"

I look again towards the stage making sure our friends can't see us. I pause when I see Grace pointing two fingers at her eyes and then at TJ, gesturing for him to join her up there. I raise my eyebrows and look down at her. "Yes, exactly like that. You're lucky no one can see us right here. Now come on, I'll take you back to the house."

I step away and she stumbles forward, her face landing in my chest. "Ok. Fine. Maybe you're right," she says, "but you've been drinking too," emphasizing it in a singsongy tease, poking my chest with each word.

I clench my jaw and exhale through my teeth. If she wasn't so adorable like this, I doubt my patience would last this long. "I'm twice your size and I've been nursing the same beer since we got here. Now come on, let's go."

I hook my arm around her and she begrudgingly follows at my side.

I walk past the table where Tanner and V are sitting, stopping on our way out. I hear Grace and TJ singing another round of karaoke and notice they have a crowd gathered around them now.

"Hey, I'm heading back early. Just a little tired. But I think she's had a little too much fun tonight and is going to call it a night too. I'll take her back to the house with me."

V looks at Lizzy and frowns. Lizzy tosses her hand back with a sigh. "I'll be fine, V. Grumpy McGrumperson here is just being his usual *no fun* self, convincing me to be responsible too." She flicks her eyebrows at me and I glare back at her. She might be tipsy, but she knows what she's doing and she's definitely starting to test my patience now.

"Yeah, right. That's exactly it." I look at V and Tanner, cocking my head at Lizzy. "Good luck getting this one up in the morning for first chair."

Tanner and V both laugh and I tip my chin before gesturing for Lizzy to lead the way out of the bar.

When we get to her Bronco, I open the door for her. I watch as she steadies herself on the grab handle, still a little off balance. I grab her by her hips and help her up. She turns and glares at me, fire in her eyes. "I can do it myself, Mr. No Fun."

I scowl back at her. "I don't care. I'm helping you anyways."

My eyes stay locked on hers as I pull her seatbelt across her chest, my knuckles grazing the soft fabric of her sweater when I feel her hard nipple pressing through. Fuck me. She's not wearing a bra tonight.

She grins at me, knowing what I just felt. "See? One of us knows how to have fun."

Now she's testing my patience in a different way.

I buckle her in, close the door, and walk to the driver's side. When I get to the door, I reach for the handle and hear a sound.

No. She didn't.

I reach for the handle and yep, it's locked.

My eyes meet hers and she blows a kiss at me. I look down at her hands and see the one resting on the lock button.

I mouth *brat* before pulling out her car keys, the ones she must of forgotten I had since I drove her SUV from the house. I jingle them in front of the window and I watch as she relents and unlocks the doors.

I get in and get situated before starting the car and driving off.

After we leave the parking lot, I feel her finger tips run up and down my thigh. Even through my jeans, it sends a shiver up my spine.

"You need to lighten up." She stops her hand when she reaches the bulge in my pants from just learning she's not wearing a bra right now. She hums and runs her finger over my crotch, making me squirm in my seat.

"Not now. The roads are bad and I need to focus." As much as I would love to feel her touch, I'm not going to be distracted and put us or others on the road at risk. I grab her wrist with one hand and set it back in her lap.

"You know you're cute when you're mad."

I glance over at her and I see her biting her lip, looking at me.

OK, she's definitely buzzed.

"We'll get you tucked in bed with a glass of water and some ibuprofen soon enough."

I look over again to see her press a finger to her lips as her eyes roam my body. "I bet you would have looked really hot in your ski gear."

I roll my eyes. "Yeah, sure. If you say so."

I turn at the roundabout, heading down the road to TJ's house when I hear her slap her hands to her thighs.

"Oh my god, yes. You should totally come out and ski with us. You said it yourself, you *can* still ski."

I feel my grip on the steering wheel tighten. I know she doesn't realize what she's doing right now, but it still hurts, bringing back so many memories.

I swallow, keeping my eyes on the road. "Appreciate your enthusiasm, but it's not going to happen. You know that."

We pull into the driveway and I park the car.

"Oh come on, don't be a party pooper. Come out with us tomorrow." She clasps her hands together like a prayer. "Please."

My jaw clenches and I practically hear my molars grind. I turn, snarling at her. "Lizzy. Drop it. Now."

I look away, shut off the SUV and get out. I walk over to her side and open the door. I offer her a hand to help her down, unable to look at her.

She knows not to push this button. And right now, it doesn't matter if she knows what she's doing or not. I don't want to deal with this.

She takes my hand, her warm, soft skin easing some of the tension coursing through me. I look down, seeing that the bratty, playful look on her face is gone. Her blue eyes are soft but dead sober and locked on mine.

"I'm sorry. I forgot. I didn't reali-"

I bring my hand to her cheek before cupping the nape of her neck.

"Please. Just drop it and move on."

She nods and I help her down, shutting the door behind her and leading her inside the house.

I walk her up to her room, not saying a word when we stand at the door. She stops and turns to look at me.

"I mean it. I'm sorry. I shouldn't have asked you that." Her voice is hushed and filled with remorse. I might be pissed but there's no way I can stay mad at her.

I reach out and tilt her chin up to me, looking her right in the eyes. Her eyes might be soft and understanding, but she holds my gaze as always, never backing down from me.

"Just please never push that with me." I close my eyes and take a deep breath. "A few people, like my doctors and physical therapists, like Grace and Kayleigh, they know I'm physically fine. After my rehab and recovery from the injuries, everyone kept asking why I wouldn't ski again. *Just get over it, move on. You know you can do it.*"

She reaches out to me, running the backs of her fingers over my stubble. I lean into her touch, reaching up to hold her hand against my face.

"I hate that. I hated having to talk to people about it. I hated having to relive everything and explain it."

She stands on her toes, placing a soft kiss on my other cheek. "You don't have to tell me anything else. I won't ever push you on trying to ski again. I'm sorry I got carried away."

"Thank you." I lift her hand off my cheek, kissing her palm. "Your turn now."

She gives me a questioning look. "Um, what?"

"Do you want to talk about your dad calling and why you spiraled?" I cross my arms and lean against the door, raising my eyebrows. "You called it an early day on the slopes and went a little wild with my sister. Any other day, I'd just say that's you being you, but you seemed off."

She reaches her hand out and takes mine, her eyes pleading.

"Can we talk about it in bed?"

I look back down the stairs from the loft to the main living area. "Everyone else is still out. I should stay out here so I'm on the sofa when they get back."

She pats me twice on my cheek. "Relax. Not a single one of them has come up to the loft at night. No one's going to notice." She pulls my hand and leads me into her room. I shut the door behind us and follow her to bed.

I strip down to my boxers and get under the covers. My eyes follow every movement as she walks to the dresser and peels off her jeans and sweater before changing into her pajamas. I could watch this every night for the rest of my life and never get tired of it.

She climbs into her side of the bed. I drape the covers over her, pulling her in to be my little spoon.

I reach behind me to turn off the light on the nightstand. She sighs and her head slumps into the pillow.

I run my palm over her hair, stroking it and tucking the loose strands of her ponytail behind her ear. It's soothing me as much as it is her. With her body pressed against mine and my arm wrapped around her, I can feel her chest rise and fall with each breath.

"Whenever he calls, whenever we do talk, it just feels like it's never about me." Her voice is a shell of itself, not the normal fierce, defiant one that drives me wild. I keep stroking her hair and holding her tight.

"It feels like I've never been enough for him. No matter how hard I try, it's not enough. I'm not enough."

I run the backs of my fingers over the pulse point on her neck and she reaches up to grab my hand, holding it there. "I know it's not the same, but I'll tell you every time I can. You're more than enough. You're so, so much more than enough."

"Am I being childish for wanting more from him?"

I huff a laugh. "Sorry, I know it's not funny. But it's far from childish." I sigh. "But if it bothers you that much, have you ever talked to him about it? Told him how he makes you feel?"

She rolls over and looks at me, confusion lacing her expression.

"Because if there's one thing I've never seen you be afraid of, it's challenging someone. You challenge me, you call me out on my shit. You don't put up with BS at work. You don't let people talk down to you."

She hums thoughtfully before resting her head on my shoulder. "I might just do that someday. I don't know when, but someday."

"Good, because from everything you've ever told me about him, it sounds like he does love you. He sent you to private prep school, he sent you to a damn good college, he took you traveling, and taught you to ski. To me those sound like things someone who loves you would do."

I bite my tongue, holding back what my heart wants me to pour out.

"Maybe he's just bad at actually saying how he really feels. Maybe he's not much for talking, like me."

She tilts her head up, looking up at me, her eyes a sky blue in this dim light. "There's no one like you. You're one of a kind." She kisses my chest and I feel her eyes flutter shut as she breathes against my skin.

For the second night in a row, I watch her fall asleep in my arms, exactly where I want her.

And for the first night in my life, I fall asleep *knowing* that I'm in love.

CHAPTER 32
LIZZY
SURF'S UP

"COME ON. GET UP." I straddle Clay and pat him on the cheek, watching his eyes slowly open.

Clay looks at me with a bewildered expression and looks around the room. "Shit, did I sleep in?"

He tries to get up but I push him back down in bed with both hands against his firm pecs.

"Nope. You didn't."

He squints at me, clearly still groggy. "Then why are you up and so damn perky already?" I glare at him, arching an eyebrow.

He's right. I'm definitely perky. I felt so bad about pushing him about skiing last night that when I got up to get more water in the middle of the night, an idea hit me. One that I'm super excited about.

"Just because I don't like getting up early doesn't mean I can't. Now come on, I want you to come out and try something with me today." He eyes me skeptically and I drop my head back, groaning. "And I promise it's not skiing."

"Fine." He reaches up, grabbing my hips and running his thumbs under the waistband of my shorts, caressing my hip bones. "But if you want me to get up, you're going to have to get off of me."

He pushes his hips up into me and I can feel his hard length through his boxers and my shorts. A quiet gasp escapes my lips. I hop off of him, and grab his hand, pulling him out of bed. "Save that thought for later. Now come on, we need to get started."

He wipes his face with his other hand and swings his legs over the side of the bed to sit up. "I'm going to regret this, aren't I?"

I smirk back at him. "Nope, because it's my idea. So you're going to love it."

CLAY CHAPMAN in a wetsuit is sinfully unfair to look at. He only has it pulled up to his waist and his bare, chiseled abs and chest are on full display. My eyes shameless run from his shoulders to his tattooed pecs, following the thin trail of hair down his abs to the V just above the waist of the wetsuit.

This early in the morning, it's a private display just for me on the sandy bank of the Deschutes River. We got out of the house before everyone else was up. I texted V that I was still hungover and was going to stay in for the day. She said no problem and they'll see me at dinner. I'm just hoping she didn't come up to my room to check on me after we left. And Clay, well, everyone already knows he wasn't skiing and they would probably just assume he went out for a longer run this morning.

"Where the hell did you get wetsuits?" he asks, his deep voice still somewhere between irritated and confused about what we're doing here.

"Jeez, I thought you were a morning person," I tease, "and they're TJ's. He said we could use any of the gear when we got here, remember?"

He shakes his head and pulls the sleeves on before shimmying the rest of the way in. Already in my wetsuit, I walk over to him, and help him with this zipper.

"You look good in this."

He glowers at me. "And why do I need this again?"

I smile back playfully and point over his shoulder. "Because we're doing that."

He looks over his shoulder, palming his face when he sees the surf park and the two rental surfboards already propped up against a boulder by the river's edge.

"You're kidding, right?"

I press my lips together, trying to hide my grin and the giggles welling up inside. I shake my head. "Nope. Not kidding at all. We're both going to get out of our comfort zone today."

He runs his fingers through his dark, inky hair before turning back to look at the river again. I walk up beside him, leaning my head against his bicep.

"I'm sorry I asked you to ski yesterday. I get that there's baggage there. But I want to see you have fun on this trip. I want to see you give up a little control." I grab his hand and start walking towards the river, pulling him with me. "Besides, you're a world class athlete, right? Should be easy for you."

His frown morphs into a wicked, almost boyish grin at my tease. "Want to make a bet?"

I ALMOST IMMEDIATELY REGRET MY decision when it's Clay's turn. Did I think I actually had a chance to beat him in any sort of competition involving athleticism? No.

But I did want to see him enjoy himself and let go for once. That's worth losing any bet, even if it involves naked morning yoga for a week. I'm pretty sure that's a win for both of us anyway.

My first attempt, if I could even call it that, was to surf the manmade waves in the sectioned off channel of the river. It did not end well. I instantly fell off the board, backwards into the cold water. Clay sprinted into the shallow water to make sure I was ok.

Now, I'm starting my second attempt, getting ready to stand up on the board.

"Come on, princess." I look over at Clay sitting on a boulder at the edge of the water. He's smirking and laughing at me, clearly enjoying watching me struggle. "Think about your prize when you win." I'd be pissed at him if I wasn't so glad to see this side of him, laughing and joking.

I toss my head back and groan, prompting another laugh from him. I try again, laying on the board before hopping up. A second passes and then another. I start to gain my footing and I even make a turn. Alright. For my first day trying this, I'm pleased with myself. This is sort of fun. I might want warmer water on the beach instead of central Oregon's cold river water, but I would definitely try this again.

"There you go," Clay says from his perch on the boulder.

I turn my head to smile at him, reaching up to wave back.

And there it is. I lose my balance, bite it, and fall into the water again.

He takes his time to swim out to me, grabbing the board, and checking on me again.

"That was better," he teases, tucking my hair back over my shoulder. He reaches for my hand, pulling me to my feet in the shallow water.

"Let's see you try," I scoff playfully, shoving him in the chest, almost losing my balance again. He catches me and pulls me into him. Even through these wetsuits, I can feel his warmth.

He grins and gestures with his head towards the boulder he was sitting on. "Alright then. My turn."

I wade over to the boulder, prop up my board, and hop up onto it to watch him.

I watch as he wades into the water. He looks focused as he lays on the board before he pops up into a standing crouch in one smooth motion.

He makes short, smooth graceful turns, left and right before losing his balance and falling into the water.

He pulls the board back to him, shakes his head in frustration and slaps his hands, sending beads of water flying. He lays back on the board, ready to try again.

"Not bad, Chapman," I shout.

He looks at me and gives me a small smile before turning back to the waves, clearly focused. I can see that competitive side in him now.

He takes a second before popping back up into a low crouch. But this time, he doesn't fall. He makes turn after turn, riding the wave.

Of course.

Of course, he'd be instantly good at this.

I stay silent watching him. The longer he does it, the more natural he looks. The intensity, the harsh scowls I'm used to, all of it fades away.

He keeps reacting to the waves, not trying to control them. He looks relaxed, calm, and confident. He looks like his brother, Tanner.

I hold my hands to my lips, trying to contain the smile spreading across my face. This is what I wanted.

And then I see it. The harsh man, the one who's given up so much, slowly fades away, revealing what should have always been there. He smiles and laughs with each turn he makes.

I watch in pure glee. I'm in awe at the happy, beautiful, twenty-eight year old, enjoying life to the fullest. The smile on his face, with his dimples popping, is so warm and infectious that it would melt glaciers the same way it melts my heart.

Finally, he hops off his board, grabs it, and wades over to me.

He props the board up next to mine and stands between my legs facing me. I cross my arms and look up at him, trying to look annoyed but I can't hide my excitement.

"Did you get bored or do you just want to rub it in that you're better?"

He shrugs. "Maybe a little of both." He winks before leaning down to kiss me. I loop my arms over his shoulders, pulling him to me. My mouth opens and his tongue grazes mine before he pulls away. He presses his forehead to mine.

"Thank you." His raspy voice is softer than I'm used to as he still catches his breath.

"For what?"

He lets out a long, ragged sigh. The rush of warm air across my cheek sends goosebumps over my damp, cool skin.

"For everything."

WE WALK into the garage at TJ's house, still in our damp wetsuits. Clay opens the door heading into the mudroom.

"Anyone home?" His voice booms through the house.

He waits a second and shrugs. "Guess no one's here."

"You sure?" I ask, hoping to have a moment, maybe a few moments, alone with him in the middle of the day.

He waves his hand and looks around the garage. "TJ's car is gone and Tanner's Sprinter isn't in the driveway. I'm pretty sure it's just us."

He grins at me, clearly thinking the same thing judging by how fast he strides towards me. His hands find my hips, and his lips crash down, meeting mine. His mouth is taking and hungry. I'm just as wound up as him, wrapping a leg around his and pulling him tight against me.

"Now can we get these damn wetsuits off?" I pant.

"Yes, thank god." His hands move from my hips to my zipper, pulling it down in a swift motion. He peels the wetsuit down my shoulders and off my arms. He freezes, his stare feral when he looks down at me. "That fucking bikini. I've thought about it so many damn times."

I lean up to him, whispering against his cheek. "I thought you'd like that." I remember the way his jaw dropped when I wore this bikini in the hot tub that first night at the condo.

He steps back, unzips his wetsuit and peels it off. His eyes never stop raking over me, leaving a trail of scorching flesh behind. But when he gets his wetsuit below his waist, it's my turn to stare at the bulge in his board shorts that are straining to keep his length inside.

I bite my lip, already desperately aching between my thighs. I want him inside me. He grabs our wetsuits from the floor and hangs them along the drying hooks on the wall before striding back to me.

His mouth crashes down to mine again in a hot, messy, frantic kiss. His full lips are overpowering mine. His tongue slides over mine. He pulls back, staring at me with that emerald wildfire intensity that makes me clench my thighs in anticipation.

"Your room." His voice is a command, not a question or suggestion. A command that I'm all too eager to follow, for now at least. Because I have one more surprise for him today.

CHAPTER 33
CLAY
DEAD WRONG

I PRACTICALLY SPRINT up the stairs behind Lizzy, pinching her ass that's barely covered by the tiny bikini she was hiding under her wetsuit. We get to her room and I shut the door behind me, turning to see her standing between me and the bed. She's giving me a wry smirk with one hand on her hip cocked out to the side.

I step towards her and she raises up one finger, gesturing for me to stop. I tilt my head, giving her a curious, amused look. She brings that finger to her lips and taps them. She looks at me and then points to the bed.

"Sit your ass there, against the headboard."

My heart is pounding and I want to be all over her, against her, in her. I don't know what she has in mind, but I'll play along. I walk past her, getting on the bed and resting against the headboard.

She watches me, still with that same smirk plastered on. She steps towards the nightstand, opening the drawer and pulling out a familiar black silk bag.

"You little liar." I look at her, shaking my head when a short laugh rumbles from my chest.

She shrugs and flicks her eyebrows. "I never said I *didn't* pack it."

Fair point.

She steps towards the foot of the bed, her bag in hand, and climbs on, kneeling across from me. Her knees are spread wide and that bikini leaves nothing to the imagination.

She bites her finger tip before pointing at my shorts. "Take those off."

"You're awfully bossy today." I smile before sliding them off, letting my throbbing cock spring free. Her lips part, watching it before bringing her eyes back to mine.

That fiery, defiant look in her eyes, the one I've loved since she first stared me down in the shitty dive bar months ago, is practically blazing now.

"I loved watching you have fun on the river." She holds my gaze, but I watch her take her hands behind her neck, playing with the tie of her bikini top. Fuck. She's driving me insane going this slow and I can practically feel my cock twitch with each beat of my heart. "But I want to show you how much fun you can have if you really give up control."

With one flick of her wrists, her bikini top falls, exposing her breasts, each one a perfect handful I can't resist. Her tiny pink nipples are already hard and I just want to nip and suck them.

"Princess," I practically moan, sitting up on my knees to reach for her. I stretch out, dying to grab her and pull her into me.

She puts her finger back up between us, glaring at me. "Nope. Sit back down." She curls her finger, pointing behind me towards the headboard. I feel my chest rise and fall with each breath.

I slowly sit back down, wondering how long she's going to play this game. She drops one hand to her hip, slowly untying her bikini on one side while her other drops below the thin triangle of fabric covering the place between her thighs.

My jaw drops when she starts to swirl her fingers over her clit, whimpering. I reach for my cock, wanting to enjoy the show. When I grab the base of my shaft, she grins at me. "No, not yet. Just watch."

I grunt through gritted teeth. "You're going to drive me crazy."

I let go of myself and feel my balls tighten and ache. I'm equal parts insanely turned on watching her and frustrated from playing her game and not touching her.

I need to fuck her. I need to have my hands roaming her body. I need my tongue down her throat and feel her whimper into my mouth.

She smiles and rewards me when I put my hands at my sides. She drops her hand and unties the other side of her skimpy bottoms, letting them fall away and giving me full view. My mouth waters as I watch her hand continue to rub circles on her clit. I lick my lips, seeing just how wet she is already. I instinctively reach for my cock again, stopping when she shakes her head.

"Do you think I'm ready?" My eyes search hers and she smirks before tilting her head towards the bag next to her on the bed.

I nod hungrily and she reaches for the bag, pulling out the fantasy dildo I bought her. I never thought I'd be watching *this* when I ordered it. I need to go back and shake three-weeks-ago-Clay's hand.

She holds the toy in front of her, looking at it in amusement, tilting it side to side. I arch an eyebrow when she looks back at me with a mischievous grin and extends the toy for me.

"I did pack *this*, but I didn't pack the *lube*."

I look down at her hand, her fingers still sliding up and down her clit, glistening with her arousal. I smirk back at her. "I don't think you need it, princess."

She shrugs with an unamused hum. "Probably not. But where would the fun in that be?" Her eyes dart from the toy then back to me. "Now be a good boy, open your mouth and get it wet for me."

This is definitely not what I expected today. But she's in luck since I've been practically drooling since the second I peeled off her wetsuit. I sit up on my knees again and she tilts the sparkly pink and orange dragon cock towards my face.

Her lips part and she nods eagerly, practically giddy watching when I take it into my mouth. I keep my eyes on hers, lowering my mouth on to it, feeling the ridges and veins of it against my tongue. I stop when it hits the back of my throat, holding it there in my mouth, swirling my spit around to coat it for her.

Whatever she wants, she gets.

She starts to swirl her finger over her clit faster and her blue eyes light up as she watches me intently. I wink back at her and her lips curl to the side before her teeth dig into her lower lip. She licks her lips and pants. She is so damn sexy. I hold her toy there for another second, before slowly pulling my mouth off, coating the tip in saliva when I let it go.

"Wet enough for you?" I grin back at her and swipe the back of my hand across my mouth, wiping off the spit that ran down the corner.

She nods and sits up on her knees, bringing the toy between her legs and notching it at her entrance. I can't take my eyes off her when she slowly lowers herself down on to it. She gasps and throws her head back, swiveling her hips on it. I look away for just a second to see a drop of precum already on the head of my cock. I'm not even touching myself and she has me so ready to be buried in her and come harder than I ever have. She looks at me, following my eyes to my cock, licking her lips.

"Don't worry. We'll get there."

This is torture, but the best kind. "I can't wait."

She smirks. "I can see. Now, hold your cock."

"Thank god." I grab it, finally able to give my aching length some much needed friction. I start to work it slowly and she smirks back at me. I'm so worked up I need something, anything.

"I said hold it, not stroke it." She makes a kissy face at me and starts bouncing up and down on her toy faster, circling her fingers in a matching pace. My breathing quickens in frustration. I give in, holding my dick in my clenched fist, feeling my pounding pulse from the blood rushing to it.

The look on her face tells me everything. She's enjoying this so fucking much. She looks at me, smiling and tugging at her bottom lip with her teeth. She curls a finger at me and I inch closer to her, kneeling just in front of her, close enough that I can hear just how wet she is riding her toy. Between gasping breaths, she barely gets the words out, giving me something I've been craving. "Hold your cock and play with my tits."

I take my free hand, cupping one of her breasts, massaging it and rolling her stiff bud between my thumb and fingers, teasing and tugging. Craning my neck, I bring my mouth to her other breast, sucking and licking. She drops her head, panting and moaning against the back of my neck with each lick and nip. Her fingers run through my hair, holding me against her.

My grip on my cock tightens to an almost painful level, just so I can feel something. This woman tests all my limits.

I crave control. I crave being in charge. But for her, I'm willing to let all that go and come undone as fast as she undid the ties of that fucking bikini.

"Good boy. You can stroke that big fucking cock now. Get it ready to fuck me." Her words are breathy against the back of my neck.

"It's more than ready, princess. You just have to say when." The relief, the feeling of finally stroking myself when I'm so goddamn hard, is almost instant. I stroke slow, trying not to come already even though I've barely done anything.

She looks down between us, watching the toy go in and out of her drenched pussy and watching my hand work, the veins in my cock throbbing from gripping myself so tight.

"Tell me how crazy I drive you." Her voice is fraying and her cheeks are so flushed. I look up, taking my lips off her breast. I'm still holding one in my other hand, tweaking and tugging her hard nipple, loving the cute little whimpers she makes each time. I slowly stroke my cock in the other.

She thinks I'm *finally* not in control. She might be right in a way. I did let go this morning. I tried something totally new to me and took a risk. But she's dead wrong when it comes to her. I lost control of myself the first time I saw her that night at Roxy's.

I watch her drop her head, still riding her toy and fingering her clit. Her eyes are hooded, barely able to stay open and hold my gaze. I tilt her chin up, forcing her to look at me. I know she's close, ready to ignite. I lean in, giving her exactly what she says she needs, exactly what I *know* she needs.

"I've never been in control with you, princess. I can never get enough of you. You're *my everything.*"

She finally comes undone, shattering on her toy, my *teammate,* moaning my name. I reach down and circle my fingers over her sensitive bundle of nerves one last time, getting her to buck into my palm before she collapses into my arms.

I hold her, lifting her off of my chest just enough to look into her glassy eyes. A thousand unspoken words pass between us. But there's one thing we both know.

Neither of us are in control anymore.

CHAPTER 34
LIZZY
WANTED

CLAY MOVES in a frantic blur after I come. In a flash, he's picked me up in one of his toned arms and flipped me on to my back. Now I'm back against the headboard with him in between my thighs.

I'm still riding my post-orgasm high, but the way he looks down at me, hungry and possessive, lights a new fire in my core.

"Now, can I take this out and fuck that wet pussy properly?"

He looks down at the toy still inside me. Then his eyes meet mine, his chest puffing out with each breath.

I nod. "Yes, please." My words come out as a faint breath.

He reaches down, easing the toy out, dragging it against my clit as he does it. I savor the feeling of each ridge, each vein, and knob against my sensitive clit. When it's out, I gasp and feel my walls clench, instantly missing the fullness.

I look at him, my eyelids still heavy. His eyes are blazing, with no trace of hesitation or question in them now. He notches himself at my entrance before caging my head in with his elbows.

His full lips meet mine in a powerful, consuming kiss as he thrusts himself in to the hilt. I gasp into his mouth as he moans into mine. The almost painful sting of him filling and stretching me is sheer ecstasy. It's like he was made for me. I hear a hiss through his gritted teeth.

"You're so goddamn tight, princess. You still needed me to fill this pussy, didn't you?"

I wrap my arms around him, feeling his warmth against me and his muscular back under my palms.

I whimper into the crook of his neck against the rose tattoo. "Mmhmm."

"Good." He rocks his hips into me, pushing himself in deeper.

I wrap my legs around his waist, bringing him in further, prompting a guttural moan from deep in his chest.

He starts thrusting harder and faster, grinding his length against my clit and hitting that spot deep inside me. My lips part and I feel my own breathing quicken. He pulls his head back just enough for our eyes to meet.

He pounds into me, but his eyes never leave mine. And the look he's giving me now sends a fire down to my core. I feel that knot of tension low in my stomach building again. Just minutes ago, he played my game with no pushback or judgement. He gave me everything I wanted and just watched me in awe. Anyone else would have made me feel ashamed, but Clay, he made me feel perfect just the way I am.

And now, the look in his eyes is one of almost feral need. He breathes me in like I'm his air and drinks me in like I'm his water in the desert. This feels like so much more than I've ever felt in my life with anyone. It feels like that other four letter word that I keep buried in the back of my thoughts, never to see the light of day again. That word I don't know if I'm ready for.

He leans down, pressing a kiss to my forehead. My thoughts instantly come back to the way he consumes me and works my body. When I look back at him now, I can see the fiery lust in his eyes. His breath is ragged and uneven, and I know he has to be getting close. Just seeing that drip of precum on his cock when he wasn't even touching himself yet was almost enough to make me unravel on the spot.

I tease him between panted breaths. "Surprised you lasted this long."

He grins back at me, baring his teeth, his wicked grin only slightly softened by his boyish dimples. He pulls himself almost completely out, leaving me gasping before he seats himself back in again, bottoming out in one fell push. I cry out into his shoulder.

"You and I both know we're so fucking close. Now I'm going to fuck you until you remember this pussy is mine. Your orgasms are mine." He picks up his pace again, erratic but still grazing my clit with each thrust. "All of them. I want you coming on my face, on my fingers, on this cock. I want my name on your lips each time, because you're *mine*."

Those words on his lips, that look in his eyes, all of it undoes me. That knot of tension unravels and I feel myself come apart and clench him buried deep inside me.

"Fuck, Lizzy." He grits out. "Yes, just like that." I feel his cock throb and twitch as he spills himself into me. We stare at each other, our breathing the only sound in the room. But I feel it, I know it. This *is* more.

I reach up to him, my hand running through his tousled inky hair. "What are we doing, Clay?"

"I have no damn clue," he says softly, still catching his breath.

"But I know I'm craving every second I can get with you."

I smile softly back at him. "Or in me?"

He snorts a laugh that I can feel to my core with his hard cock still in me. "Yeah, and that."

His eyes search my face and that soft smile, the one I saw on the river today, is there. I can practically feel the words on the tip of his tongue before he speaks.

"But I know one other thing." He runs the calloused pad of his thumb over my flushed cheek. I reach up to hold his hand there. "I know that I'm madly in love with you, Lizzy."

My lips part and I know he can see it in my eyes. I might feel it too, but I'm not ready to admit it to myself, much less say it.

As if he can read my thoughts, he puts a finger to my lips, making me focus back on him. "I know you might not be there yet. I know you might not be ready." He brings his lips to mine for a tender, short kiss. "But when I said you're my everything, I meant it. I can never get enough of you and I will spend every waking minute waiting for you to get there with me."

I swallow hard and nod. "OK."

"OK? So we're doing this for real?" he asks, that boyish excitement from earlier is back on his face. The one that makes my stomach feel warm and fuzzy.

I roll my eyes before smiling back at him. "Yes. We can give this a real shot. I'm pretty much able to work in Utah at the plant or remotely indefinitely. So yes, let's try this."

His infectious, giddy smile hardens and his thumb traces my cheek again. "I mean it though. You know I don't open myself up to heartbreak, but I trust you. I'm trusting you with my heart." He swallows hard and I can feel the tension build in him. "And I'm going to be here in this with you, waiting for you to catch up. I'm not going to run from this because I know you feel it too."

I reach up to him, running the back of my fingers over his stubble, a feeling I've come to crave.

"I know. Thank you. I'm not going to run from it either. I think I'm just a few steps behind you."

A thought hum rumbles from his chest while I think about what just happened. "So now what?"

I wrap my hands around his head, pulling him down to kiss me. "We could go again."

He cocks his head, looking away in mock thought. "I think we'd actually have to have stopped to be able to go again."

We both look down between us, again realizing he's still deep inside me. Laughing, we fall into each other's arms, one thought running through my mind.

Maybe I can do this. If there's anyone I'd want to try with, it would be this man that makes me feel ok to be me.

No. Not just ok. He makes me feel good about being me.

Both of our heads snap up when we hear the double chime of the alarm system for the garage door.

"Shit," he says, getting up and sliding out from me, leaving me feeling unexpectedly empty. He gets out of bed and grabs his sweats in the corner of the room he left the other night. "Stay there. I'll go see who's here."

Before he can even reach the door, there's a knock and we both freeze.

"Relax you two, it's just me." Grace's voice calls from the other room. I look at Clay, the same sense of relief washing over his face as the one flooding me. "I tried texting you, but I'm assuming you two were too busy to check your phones. We called it an early day on the slopes. You've probably got about five minutes before the other love-birds finish putting their gear away in the garage."

Clay palms his face, sighing. "Thanks, sis. See you in a bit."

A laugh echos from the other side of the door. "God, I love being right."

Clay throws his head back groaning before walking back to the edge of the bed. He looks down at me, my head propped up on my elbow, while I admire the way his sweats hang off his hips and his still mostly hard erection strains against them. I look up to meet his eyes, practically melting under the heat of his stare.

"You still want to hold off on telling them?" he asks, a concerned look taking over his face.

I shrug. "I honestly don't know yet." Part of me is aching to. I don't know the last time I felt so completely happy and at peace. I want nothing more than to share this with my best friend. And I want him to be able to share this with his brother. Part of me is still scared to open my blissful little bubble to everyone else and bring in the expectations that come with a relationship. I take in his soft smile, seeing no worry or hesitation there. "I still need a minute. But soon. Ok? We'll know when it's the right time."

He nods. "Whatever you need, princess." He turns and leaves the room, leaving me watching the man of my dreams walk out. The man that minutes ago told me he would wait his whole life for me to feel the same way as him. In this moment, I know it will be sooner than either of us think.

I WAKE up the next morning, a mix of blissed out from another night with Clay and groggy knowing that I need to get up and stick to Veronica's first chair schedule. Clay's already gone for his run and I check my phone. There's a message waiting from him.

> Grumpy Roommate: Out early. I'll see you later today, princess.

> Me: Can't wait. 😘

I add the emoji for good measure. For some reason, waking up already knowing he was thinking about me makes my stomach flutter. I pry myself out of the comfy bed, and get dressed in all my base layers for the day of skiing. I head downstairs to meet everyone else for breakfast.

They're already around the dining room table with TJ. There's a plate ready for me, I'm sure courtesy of V. I sit down next to Grace who gives me a knowing smirk after nearly catching us yesterday.

"Did you guys see Clay this morning before he went for his run?" I ask, taking a sip of my store bought nitro cold brew that Clay restocked for me. If he could put a nitro tap in his house, I'd truly be in heaven.

Tanner and V shake their heads before TJ chuckles at the end of the table. He looks down smiling at his coffee, like he knows something we don't. "He was up even earlier today. I swear I never thought I'd meet someone who's more of a morning person than me."

Grace scoffs at him. "Yeah. What time do I need to get up so I can get a cold plunge in before you're out there fishing?"

TJ rolls his eyes. "I just want to fish in the morning without having someone scare all the fish away."

I hold my coffee to my lips, instantly intrigued by this exchange.

Grace glares back at him, flicking her hair over her shoulder in a wave of bright colors. "Did I scare the fish or are you just saying that because I nearly made you jump out of your waders?"

"Whatever, Rainbow," TJ groans before taking his plate to the sink. "I'll see you guys around later. Have fun out at the mountain."

TANNER AND V lead the way back to the lodge for lunch. A late season storm rolled in last night and brought more snow this morning, so we had an unexpectedly nice powder day.

In Aspen Valley they go out of their way to groom as many runs as possible. It seems like the locals here in Oregon really like untouched powder though. It's only been half a day of skiing and my quads are *burning*. I make a mental note to tell my accountability buddy, and now boyfriend, that he's going to have to step up my workouts. We definitely need to hit quads more.

Wait. *Boyfriend?* Is that what he is now?

I think about that the whole way down the mountain, catching up with V, Tanner, and Grace who already have their skis in the racks outside the lodge. I ski up next to them and I click out of my own skis. I rest my goggles on top of my helmet when I hear Grace shout something at Tanner.

"Hey. Is that..." Her voice trails off and I look up to see her pointing up the slope, both of them watching something. V joins them and I follow their gaze until my eyes spot it.

There's one skier, clad in black gear, effortlessly, methodically, beautifully working their way down the ski run towards where we're standing. He makes his way down and hits the shallow run out of the slope, skiing up to the others and clicking out of his skis. The only thing visible from under his gear, helmet, and goggles is his proud, square jaw.

But from where he is, I recognize that figure, that posture, that presence.

No.

There's no way.

Tanner and Grace stand there in disbelief as he brushes past them and strides right to me. I look up, noticing the mirrored goggles, tinted a brilliant green, one that I know matches the eyes underneath them that are boring into me.

I stand there in disbelief, my jaw hanging open, watching until he's standing inches from me. My arms hang down at my side help-lessly and I'm pretty sure I look like a deer caught in headlights.

He takes off his helmet and goggles, throwing them to the ground and looks right down at me.

It's him. I still can't believe it.

He looks at me in such an intense, longing way that makes my heart flutter. He reaches down to tuck one of my slut strands out of my face, his finger grazing my exposed skin, which sends a spark through me.

His voice is low and gravelly when he leans down for just me to hear. "Is now the right time?"

CHAPTER 35
CLAY
SPARK

I LOOK DOWN AT LIZZY, into the blue eyes that melt my cold dark heart. I look at the smile that makes me want to do whatever it takes to keep it on her beautiful face. I look at the woman I'd give up every bit of control I have to make happy. I look at the woman I love.

"Is now the right time?" I ask, tucking one of those little strands of blonde hair I'm obsessed with out of the way.

Last night, she said we'd know when the right time was. And when I woke up this morning, suddenly I didn't have the urge to go out and run. I didn't care about my routine. I just wanted to enjoy the way Lizzy makes me feel, like nothing else matters. I just wanted to enjoy the things I love for once, consequences be damned.

I look back down at her, watching her smile grow wide and bright before she jumps up, wrapping her arms around my neck and her legs around my waist.

"I'll take that as a yes, princess?" I chuckle.

"Shut up and kiss me," she says, pulling on my neck, bringing her mouth to mine. Her soft lips meet mine and the kiss feels like an eternity. In this moment, it's just me and her. I couldn't care less about anything around us. The only thing that matters is how she makes me feel, how we make each other feel.

Eventually, we pull apart just enough for me to look into her eyes, still sparkling and brimming with joy. "Thank you," I whisper, feeling her warm breath on my cheek.

Curiosity crosses her face. "For what?"

I hold her against me, her legs still wrapped around my waist like she's a little koala. "Making me realize that I'd rather enjoy the things I love, even if for a day, than spend my life being afraid to lose them."

She hums and presses her forehead into my neck. "Good. You're welcome."

And at that point, I realize we are in fact not the only people in the world.

"So, we might have an audience, Princess." I set Lizzy down carefully and she turns to look at Tanner and V, staring at us.

Lizzy cocks her head to one side, groaning and looking right back at V.

"What? You can't be the only one allowed to have a Chapman boy-toy. Don't act surprised."

My brother snorts a laugh, prompting V to shove him. "Really?" she asks, glaring at him.

He shrugs. "Good for them. I can't wait to watch this."

Lizzy smirks and nods at Tanner then looks back to V. "Don't be jealous I got the newer model."

V finally laughs and shakes her head before palming her face.

I toss Lizzy a wink for the unexpected compliment from *my girl* and she air kisses back at me.

I watch V look around until she spots Grace, who's looking off in the distance at the surrounding mountains.

"Did you know about this?"

Grace turns, a knowing grin on her face. "About what?"

V gestures towards us with an outstretched hand.

Grace looks at us and scoffs. "Oh! Those two? Yeah, I've known for weeks. That's old news."

V continues to shake her head. "I've got like a thousand questions." I step towards her, putting myself between her and Lizzy.

"As long as you're not upset, cool."

She throws her head back and laughs. "Upset, no. Shocked, yes."

I step back towards Lizzy, draping an arm around her.

"Well, good. In that case, so can we go inside for lunch now? I'm sure princess here is about to get hangry."

I look down at Lizzy, her smile hardening into a playful glare. "Are you going to try and feed me chicken tenders again?"

I chuckle. "Nope. Already learned that lesson."

"Good." She stands on her toes to kiss my cheek before turning to look at everyone else. "Ok. Ask all the questions you want, but after we go inside and after I get my food."

AFTER LUNCH, we stand outside the lodge by the gear racks. Surprisingly, everyone was actually very cool with us. Tanner was happy for me and V kept saying she should have seen this coming and that this is such a Lizzy thing to do.

But now, I want some alone time with her.

I turn to face my siblings and V. "Hey, guys. Can I borrow her for the afternoon? I promise you can ask the rest of your questions later at happy hour. But I want to go show her some of the mountain."

I look back at Lizzy, her beautiful smile that hasn't stopped since she saw me walking towards her, still plastered to her face before she gives me a curious look. "Do you have another surprise up your sleeve?"

I shrug. "Maybe. You'll just have to wait."

"You know I hate waiting," she huffs.

"I know."

I turn to look back at V, who's smiling and watching in amusement. "I'm starting to see how this happened," she says with a laugh. "And of course. We'll see you guys back at the house."

I tip my chin to her. "Thanks, V." Tanner nods and Grace smirks before I turn to Lizzy, grabbing her hand.

A few minutes later, we're riding up the lift together, just the two of us. Looking at her next to me, this is all so surreal. Here I am, back on skis, sitting on a chairlift next to the woman I'm in love with, two things I never thought would happen in my life. All thanks to a random stop for a beer three months ago.

I scoot closer to her, grabbing her hand. "I'm sorry."

She whips her head to mine, concern on her face. "For what?"

I sigh, wrapping my arm around her shoulders. "I hope that wasn't too fast to tell everyone. But you said we'd know when the right time was and this morning, it just felt right."

She smiles and looks back up at me. "It was the right time. I thought about it this morning when you were already gone." She takes a second, looking me up and down. "And I was right."

I quirk a brow at her. "About what?"

"You do look hot in ski gear." She flicks her eyebrows at me and grins. "Speaking of, where did you get all of that?"

I smirk back at her. "Well, instead of going for a run this morning, I went down to the river to find TJ, and ask if I could borrow some of his ski gear. It's a little snug, but good enough for today."

She nods and I continue. "Then I borrowed his SUV and went into town to rent the other gear I needed."

She shakes her head. "Now that I think about it, he was pretty smug at breakfast when he said he was sure we'd see you around today." She pauses. "But wait, you've been out here all morning just skiing by yourself? And how'd you find us?"

I nod. "I got out here for first chair at the other base lodge. I needed a few runs by myself to just think about things, enjoy the mountain again. Reconnect with skiing." I look at her as she gives me an understanding look. "Then after a while, I texted Tanner and asked when and where you guys were getting lunch, just said I wanted to stop by and see you guys. I didn't tell him I was skiing."

She hums to herself, bringing a glove to her chin. "So what are you going to show me now that you have me to yourself?"

"Just a run I haven't skied in a really long time."

I feel her hand squeeze mine tight. "You've skied here before?"

I look back at her and nod. "Yeah. My last season of racing while Mom was still with us." I pause, thinking about that trip. "We had an off day between heats and it happened to be an epic Mt. Bachelor powder day. Terrible for racing, but amazing for just hitting the slopes. Dad was always the big racer and taught me. But Mom, she taught us all to just love the mountain, ski the terrain, and enjoy it."

Lizzy's eyes meet mine and it's that look I've come to welcome. The one that isn't judging or pitying me. She's just listening. "I can't wait to see it then."

She leans her head, with her big clunky helmet on, against my shoulder for the rest of the lift ride. I hold her gloved hands in my lap, enjoying the ride in comfortable silence. At least for a moment anyway.

"Some more big news happened this morning before you got here."

I tilt my head to her. "Oh yeah?"

She nods, but doesn't lift her head from my shoulder. "TJ offered to let V and Tanner have their wedding at his house in Jackson in December." She lets out an adorable giggle. "They already wanted a small ceremony in the winter, but it sounds perfect for them. They can use his guesthouse to set up and everything. But I know V is losing it, getting to know her idol *and* getting married at one of his houses."

I chuckle. "That sounds perfect for them. And if I know Tanner, a winter wedding in Jackson is exactly what he wants."

When we reach the top, I guide Lizzy along the cat track towards the top of the run, a long black diamond with some of the best tree skiing and wide open, ungroomed powder stashes on the Northwest side of mountain.

I stop and wait for her to reach me. "So, I probably should have asked this before. You're a good skier, right?"

Even with her goggles on, I can feel her eye roll. "Don't let the pink fool you. I can keep up with Tanner and V." She brings a finger to her lips in thought. "Most of the time anyways. They're kind of extreme."

I huff a laugh. "Alright, princess. Just stay close to me, especially in the trees."

She skis right up next to me, tapping my ass with one of her poles. "Look at you. Always the perfect gentleman."

I grin back at her, baring my teeth. "I'll see if I can make you reconsider that later." I pucker my lips together, sending her an air kiss before taking off down the run.

The upper part is a long, open area, lined with thick trees on either side, still holding untracked powder even this late in the day. We cruise through the upper part before getting to an area of trees that's more open and suited for tree skiing. It's this area that I was looking for.

I check back behind me to make sure Lizzy is close by before going into the trees. To my pleasant surprise, she's holding her own, right on my tail, which somehow makes me feel pride. The woman I thought was a prissy little, firecracker can *definitely ski*.

I get to a small clearing in the trees. I stop and let her catch up to me. I prop my goggles up on my helmet and watch her ski up next to me. "You doing alright?"

She nods and takes a few deep breaths. "Yeah. But seriously, maybe less yoga and more quads. This powder is tough."

I shake my head at her. "I think we can do that." I point ahead of us through the trees towards a ridge top. "We're heading over there. Just a view I wanted to check out."

She gestures ahead with her ski pole. "After you." This time she air kisses to me before I pull my goggles back down and ski ahead.

After a few turns through the powdery snow in the trees, I reach it, the spot I've been wanting to see. It's a ridge littered with black, volcanic rocky outcroppings, the kind all over Mount Bachelor. But the view of the lake in the distance is breathtaking.

Lizzy skis up to me a few seconds later, stopping to enjoy the view with me. "I can see why you wanted to come here."

I nod, not saying a word. I feel a smile creep across my face. Being here, in this spot, with her, just feels right. She looks back at me, pausing and studying me.

"What is it?" I ask.

She furrows her brow, lifting a gloved hand to her chin. "I feel like I've been here before, seen you here before." She looks around us, at the trees, the rocks, and the view and then looks back to me. I see the moment something clicks in her head and her eyes go wide with excitement.

"That picture in your office. The one of you and your mom. That was here, wasn't it?"

I nod, smiling back at her, with no need for words. She leans into my body, resting her head against my shoulder and wrapping her arms around me.

"Thank you for bringing me here."

I rub my gloved hand up and down her back. "Thank you for making me want to." I tilt her chin up and pull her goggles off, forcing her to look at me. "You remind me everyday that I can't control someone's heart and that terrifies the shit out of me, Lizzy. You make me want to lose control though. You make me want to accept I can't control everything. To just take on whatever life gives me. It threw you right into my path and I've loved every second of it."

BACK AT THE house after dinner, finally not hiding from everyone else, Lizzy and I pack up our room so we can get an early start on the eleven hour drive tomorrow.

"I don't know why we have to leave so early in the morning," Lizzy whines from her perch on the bed, already in her pajamas.

I glare back at her from the dresser. "Well, I have to budget an extra hour so we can stop for *real food*," I say, making an air quotes gesture.

She groans. "Fine. I guess that's ok."

"Good. Not like you really have an option anyways, passenger princess." I wink at her, prompting her to roll her eyes and flop back into the pillows.

I open the middle drawer, noticing all of her stuff in a chaotic mess of pink and pastels.

I sigh and start grabbing each piece of clothing, folding it and packing it into her bag.

"You don't have to pack my stuff." I hear her over my shoulder.

I shrug. "It's fine. I don't mind. Just relax. Tomorrow's going to be a long day."

I look back at her, propped up on her elbow watching me from the bed in amusement. "You *really* like being neat and tidy, don't you?"

Turning to face her, I cross my legs and lean against the dresser, folding a tiny t-shirt that feels like it should belong to a child in my hands. "Some habits are hard to break."

She hums thoughtfully to herself. "When did that habit start? All the cleaning and hyper organization?"

I shift uncomfortably against the dresser, tightly folding the shirt and grabbing some leggings to fold. "Right after I tore my knee the first time."

She sits up in the bed, looking at me more intently. "Why would that make you do *that*?" she asks, pointing to the perfect little squares of folded clothes in her bag in front of me on the floor.

Taking a deep breath, I go back to that time, those months.

"Because I was being young and stupid. I wasn't disciplined in my training back then. I wasn't studying the conditions for each competition like I should have been. I was always distracted, not focused. I was just being careless."

"Sounds like you were just being a teenager. Mistakes happen,

Clay. I mean, you flooded my condo after all. I don't hold it against you. Look where that got us," she says with a wink.

I roll my eyes. "That was actually because I was too busy staring at your ass from the balcony and I forgot to swap out the propane tanks."

Her eyes go wide and she laughs, briefly washing away my tension.

"We are definitely going to revisit that later." She shakes her head in disbelief. "But seriously, mistakes happen. You were a kid. Don't keep beating yourself up."

I frown, feeling irritated and anxious like I do every time I think about this. "Yeah, well. My teenage mistakes had horrible consequences. Mr. Jensen helped me a lot after that first injury. Taught me how to stay focused, cut out distractions."

A cute, amused laugh escapes her. "It sounds like he taught you to be a robot when you were just a kid."

I scrub my hand over my face. "A kid whose mistakes got my mom killed."

Any amusement in her expression is gone, instantly replace by disbelief. The shocked look in her eyes is one I know I never want to see again. "What are you talking about? She died in a car accident. You weren't even in the car."

A shaky, ragged breath leaves my chest. I look down at my hands, my knuckles whitening as I grip the leggings I was folding. "It was my fault she was even driving that day. She was on her way to pick me up from my physical therapy appointment after getting Grace from practice, because I couldn't drive." I look back up at her, those blue eyes searching mine. "She should have never been there. Instead, we lost her and almost lost Grace. I was there waiting to get picked up outside and saw her car get t-boned by someone that was too busy to look up from their phone."

I've never said this part out loud. "So yeah, I blame myself for my mom. I'd rather be a robot than make mistakes and hurt the people I love, or worse, lose them."

She looks at me, pure confusion and anger in her eyes. "Clay, that's horrible. I had no idea that you were there. But also, that's bullshit." She stands and walks towards me with that defiant, confident stride I admire. "I mean it, that's complete bullshit. That was not your fault, period. You can't control everything. Some shit just happens, but that's life." She grabs my hands, pries my fists open and takes the leggings from me. She sets them on the dresser before holding my hands in hers.

I freeze, looking into her eyes. A moment passes where I'm lost in them and I forget everything I was tense about.

A nervous, booming laugh rumbles from my chest, catching her off guard. She looks at me like I'm crazy. "What's so funny?"

"I just poured myself out. I relived the worst day of my life and you called *bullshit* on me," I say between laughs. "Only you would do that with me. This is why I love you."

She takes my hands, bringing them to her hips before letting go and hugging me. She breathes against my chest. "Please, don't ever blame yourself for that again. That's so messed up and unfair to you."

I drop my head to hers, resting my chin on her soft hair. "You're right. I won't."

Her eyes come back to meet mine, that defiant anger there. "You have nothing to apologize for. Remind me that if I ever meet Mr. Jensen, I'm going to give him a piece of my mind for turning you into a robot. He was your mentor, your idol, and that's just so messed up to put all that on you."

I shake my head, laughing at the idea of her getting in his face. But my heart also burns at the idea of someone sticking up for me, something I'm not used to. "Speaking of that, you might get your chance to do that sooner than later."

She quirks an eyebrow at me. "Care to elaborate?"

I grab my phone, showing her the calendar reminder for the company banquet. "Would you come to this dinner with me as my date? I know it's short notice with it being next Saturday, but it's hosted by JSC. Kayleigh should be there too. It's a black tie thing, the whole nine yards. It's mostly just for important customers and some investors, but-"

She cuts me off. "I'd love to be your date." She pulls my head down, bringing her lips to mine. "Because I bet you in a tux is downright criminal and now I have another excuse to go shopping."

CHAPTER 36
LIZZY
BLISSFUL BUBBLE

WE'VE ONLY BEEN BACK from Bend for a few days, but it already feels like we've fallen into such a blissful little bubble together. The last few nights, we've either made dinner or ordered in food. I love that he already knows better than to ask me to cook. We've spent the nights reading together by the fire or working out or just enjoying being snuggled up on his couch.

And the sex.

I knew there were perks to dating a man a few years younger than me, but he's relentless. He gives me everything I want and even some things I didn't know I needed. All of it without judgement or questioning, just that always present look of love and need that he shows me.

It just feels like everything has gotten better now that we're actually dating. Which makes dinner with Jessica tonight bittersweet. It's one of the first nights in weeks I've been away from Clay, but I was looking forward to seeing her and now it's just the two of us.

"So your husband didn't come with you after all?" I look at Jessica from across the table.

She shrugs, taking another sip of her wine. "Nope. Trip got

pushed back. It's too warm in Park City now, so no spring skiing. He decided to stay home and save his vacation time."

I take a deep breath before taking a long sip of my wine.

"Good, because I wanted to talk to you about actual work related things."

She flicks her eyebrows, telling me to go on.

"Well, just one big thing."

She props an elbow on the table, holding her chin between her thumb and forefinger. "You're really building up the anticipation here, girl." She smirks back at me, taking another drink.

"I'm taking the plant up on their offer. I'm going to be here full time." I start rambling a mile a minute, nervous to tell my closest work friend, my mentor, that I won't be working for her anymore. "Obviously, we'll still work together on projects and things here and there. And I'm always going to be grateful-"

She reaches a hand across the table, grabbing mine. "Lizzy, it's fine. I was hoping this is what you wanted to tell me."

I look back at her, remembering how she recruited me to Fischer and how much I've grown under her. But I've been in Utah nearly two months now and I feel like I've grown so much personally by removing myself from my life back in Ohio.

I squeeze her hand. "It just feels right. I want another new challenge. This has been the fresh start I needed. Thank you for understanding and thank you for suggesting this in the first place."

She shrugs and winks. "I had a feeling it would be a good fit, especially after how much you raved about your Wyoming trip and how happy Veronica is now." She lets go of my hand, grabbing her wine glass and swirling it around before grinning back at me. "Now, would that *roommate* of yours have anything to do with this too?"

I feel my cheeks flush and a nervous laugh escape me. I peer at her over the rim of my wine glass. "Boyfriend now, not roommate. He certainly made the choice easier, but this is still for me. He doesn't even know I've made up my mind yet."

"I never thought I'd see the day that Lizzy Frank would get tied down by another man."

I laugh, this time out of pure amusement. "You wouldn't say that if you met him." I smile to myself, thinking about Clay is the exact opposite of that. He's the only person I've known that's completely accepted all of me and wants more. "He knows I'm going to do whatever I want and he's more than ok with that."

She shakes her head in approval. "Good for you, girl. I'm happy for you."

WHEN I GET BACK to Clay's house, what might be *our* home sooner than later, I'm more than excited when I find him reading by the fire with Ani. He's shirtless, wearing just a pair of gray sweats and his glasses with a glass of whiskey on the end table. This is the sight I dream of coming home to.

And now, knowing that I'm going to be living in Utah full time, giving us a real chance, it doesn't feel like such a crazy dream.

I walk in from the kitchen and Ani gets up from his bed, coming over to me. "Who's my *good boy*?" I lean down to scratch him behind his ears, which I learned is his absolute favorite spot. I look over to see Clay smiling and rolling his eyes over his glasses at me. "Jealous?" I give him a playful look.

He scoffs. "We'll see what you're calling me later, but I doubt it will be *good boy*."

I hum thoughtfully, walking towards his chair. When he sees me in my black sweater dress, the one I had on that night at Roxy's, he sets down his book and watches me stride up next to him.

"What were you reading?" I ask, standing behind him, between the chair and the fire, looping my arms around his neck.

He grabs my hands, kisses my wrists and splays my fingers out over his broad, warm chest. "Nothing too exciting. Mostly just killing time waiting for you to get back."

He leans his head back enough for me to look into his eyes. His fierce green eyes that always have that hungry look and take my breath away each time. It's almost enough to make me want to tell him I'm taking the job here, right now. But I want to take care of some things in the office first and make it official with HR tomorrow.

I drop my head, bringing our lips together, palming the sides of his face in a short kiss. "Good, because I would be pissed if you were reading something fun without me." I stand, slowly walking around the chair, tracing my finger down his shoulder, until I'm in front of him. "And I'm glad you're up, I wanted to spend some time with you tonight."

I step forward, bringing my knees onto the chair on either side of his broad thighs, settling myself down into his lap. He groans as I put my weight down against his stiff length. He's already so hard I can feel him even through his thick sweatpants. I give him a playful smirk. "Looks like you wanted to spend some time with me too."

His teeth dig into his bottom lip as his eyes run up from my bare legs to the hem of my dress and over my breasts. "I'd spend every second of every day with you if I could." He leans forward, pressing kiss after kiss to my neck, his big, rough hands running up my thighs sending shivers up my spine and heat to my already aching core.

His hands run higher up my thighs and his lips meet mine. I open my mouth for him and his tongue finds mine. I feel his hands stop when he reaches my hips. He pulls away from the kiss just enough to whisper. "Did you forget to wear panties to dinner, princess?"

"I'm not *that* wild." I nip playfully at his bottom lip. "I took them off before I came inside - told you I wanted to spend some time with you tonight."

"Fuck me," he says through a strangled breath.

I grind myself down onto his lap, making him groan through his gritted teeth. "Take my dress off already."

He wastes no time in running his hands further up my hips, under my dress, along my ribs and over my bra until the dress is lying on the floor. His eyes snag on my breasts, covered in my favorite lacy bra. "Were you planning this?"

His eyes rake over my body again. Between the heat from the fireplace and his scorching gaze, I feel emboldened. He never fails to make me feel special, like I'm the only thing in his world. Like he wants me, exactly how I am.

I bite my lip and nod back at him, leaning forward to loop my arms around his neck. "Now what are we going to do about these pants?" I flick my eyes down to where I'm grinding against his erection.

"You're so damn wet, princess." He brings his lips to mine for a brief kiss. "I can already feel you even with these damn pants on. So do you want me to fuck you here or in bed? Because I know you're ready for me."

I lean forward, bringing my lips to his ear, savoring the feeling of his stubble against my heated cheeks. "Take the pants off and find out."

He lifts me up off of his lap with one burly arm, sliding his pants down with the other and kicking them away. I sit back down, instantly feeling his hard, throbbing length against my wet heat. Instinctively, I grind myself up and down along his shaft, loving every second of the feeling against my swollen clit. I feel that knot of tension low in my stomach, the one it seems like he's always tying and untying.

He leans toward me, pressing our chests together. "You're already close and I'm not even inside you." His low, husky voice only builds every sensations even higher. He just pushes my buttons so easily, so quickly and I'm already needy for him. He must sense it because he rocks his hips into me, giving me that friction I'm desperate for.

"Fuck. Yes. I'm so close." I pant against his neck, holding him tighter.

"Good," he praises softly into my ear. "My cock is your toy tonight. However you need it. Grind on it, ride it, sit on it. However you need me, because I'm all yours, Lizzy."

I'm so close, so ready to give in. His praises fill that spot in me that no one ever has.

But then again, I'm me.

I bring my lips to his ear. "But does it vibrate?"

I hear a low laugh rumble from his chest when he grips my hips tightly. He pulls me against his length while thrusting his hips up into me. In an instant, I feel the pressure and the friction I need, grinding myself against him. I feel each pulsing vein of his cock dragging along my clit and the warmth of his body against mine. All of the blissfully overwhelming sensations unleash that knot of tension into a wave of pleasure as I fall apart in his lap, coming so hard I see stars.

I collapse into his chest when he whispers into my ear. "No. But it does that." He kisses me just under the shell of my ear, sending a shiver through my body. "Brat."

"Fuck you, Clay." I whimper into his neck, not meaning the words while I nuzzle his collar bone.

My head stays pressed against his warm neck while his big hands cup my ass, lifting me off his lap. I suddenly miss the warmth of his body against mine, the friction, the closeness to him.

He breathes against my neck. "It does this too." I feel him notch himself at my entrance. Before I can prepare myself, he quickly lowers me back down on to his length, impaling me with his cock still soaked with my wetness. In a second, I feel every sweet, delicious inch of him invade me, fill me, and stretch me.

I gasp into his neck, still sensitive from my own orgasm.

"You didn't think you could sit in my lap without panties and not get this dick now, did you?" His voice is low and raspy against my neck. A whimper of a laugh escapes my lips between panted breaths. "That's what I thought."

He grips my ass harder, guiding me up and down on him, stretching and making me feel full like only he can.

"God, you're so ready for me. You're doing so good, riding this cock, taking all of me."

I rock up and down in his lap in sync with his thrusts, swiveling my hips to take every bit of him. The way he palms my ass, guiding me and manhandling my body makes me feel so uninhibited, so free.

My eyes meet his and I can see the passion, the joy, the intensity in them. I feel *that* word on the tip of my tongue again. I feel that word in my heart, in my body.

"What can I do to make you come again?" He grins at me as his voice brings my attention back to the pleasure rocking my body.

I drop a hand from his neck, reaching behind me to pull one of his hands off my ass and bring it between us. "This," I pant.

He looks down where I placed his hand, the one that says COME across the knuckles, and traces my hip bone with his fingertips. He brings his thumb to my clit. "Did you mean to pick that hand?" He smirks, but I can see from his flushed cheeks and the way his chest rises and falls faster and faster that he's getting just as close as me.

"I'm getting pretty attached to it."

"Good, because it's yours too, just like the rest of me." He circles my clit faster, matching his relentless thrusts. I hear his breathing fray as he bucks into me wildly and increases the pressure with his thumb.

I hold him tightly in my arms, feeling my orgasm coming, my walls starting to clench when I whisper into his ear. "I think I might be yours too."

He grunts and buries himself in me in a powerful, harsh thrust. I feel his cock throb and twitch as he drains himself inside me, the sensation making me let go, my vision blurring and my body melting into his again.

It feels like an eternity passes where we sit there, our bodies molded together perfectly into one, our chests rising and falling in unison. I was so close to saying *it*. I want to say *it* so badly.

As if he can read my thoughts, he cups the back of my neck, playing with my ponytail in his hand, bringing me to look at him. "It's ok if you're not ready to say it. I feel it enough for both of us."

He brings his lips to my forehead, gently kissing me.

"Thank you," I say, still catching my breath.

He nods and in a swift move, stands from the chair with me still wrapped around him, impaled on his cock.

I hum in confusion, grabbing him and holding myself against his warm, rugged body tighter.

"Where are we going?"

He laughs and I can feel it through my whole body the way we're still connected. "It's funny you think you're only coming twice tonight. Now let's take this show to your pillow nest."

An uncontrolled giggle escapes me. "So bossy tonight."

He growls against my neck. "You can call me whatever the fuck you want as long as you remember this pussy is mine, princess."

He carries me like that to my room and the whole way I think that I could get used to his stamina. A younger man, especially a *former world class athlete*, definitely has some perks. But I know that I could get used to everything about him because I am definitely in love with him.

CHAPTER 37
LIZZY
VACATION'S OVER

I'VE BEEN LOOKING FORWARD to tonight all day. I could barely focus at the office. I know after last night, I want to tell Clay how I feel about him. And now that things are finalized with HR, I want to tell him I'm going to be here full time. I know I'm not doing it just for him, but he's a very real, very big reason why too. He's opened up so much to me these last months that I want to reward that trust.

So tonight is our first real date and it feels like such a big step. It feels like the perfect time to tell him everything. And when I get home from the office and see him, already dressed to go out, I practically can't contain my excitement.

"Sure you can be ready in time? Reservation's in an hour." He smirks at me and taps his watch. "I seem to remember you're pretty slow at getting ready."

I hang my bags and jacket on the coat rack by the door before setting my shoes in the tray. Surprisingly, that routine has become so normal for me, even if he doesn't seem to care about it as much now.

"I think you'll like tonight's outfit." I walk towards him, reaching up on my toes to kiss him, breathing in his woodsy scent. I run a finger down the open neckline of his shirt before playfully grabbing his firm ass. "Now, get out of my way so I can get ready and, if you're lucky, maybe I'll *forget* part of my outfit so we can repeat last night."

I walk past him toward the bedrooms, looking over my shoulder to see him frozen where I left him. His hungry eyes are locked on me, watching every step. He doesn't know it, but that hungry stare makes my heart flutter and my breathing hitch every time.

"ALRIGHT. I STAND CORRECTED." Clay watches me walk down the hall, dressed for date night. I wore a cute red dress, a color he's never seen me in, and I already like the effect it's having. "You got ready in time *and* you look like that. Remind me never to doubt you."

He steps towards me, backing me into the kitchen island. I smirk up at him when his hands run up and down the skin tight fabric of my dress that matches the color of my lip stain. He cranes his neck to bring his lips to mine for a long, lingering kiss.

"If you keep doing that, then you'll be the reason we're late for dinner." I tap him on the nose.

He flashes me a wicked, wanting grin and brings his lips to my ear. "Maybe we should just skip dinner and I can peel that dress off of you right here."

He nips my ear and I suck in a short breath, thinking for a second that staying in with him would always be a good choice. But I collect myself, remembering that tonight I have plans with him that I've been excited about all day.

I grab him by the hand, leading him towards the door to go out to my Bronco. "Come on, let's go. But save that energy for later." I wink at him before heading out the door.

"Don't worry. I'll be thinking about ripping that off of you all night." He walks in front of me, stepping down off the porch and opening the passenger door for me. He holds my hand while I climb up, slapping my ass before I sit down. I glare back at him playfully and he chuckles before shutting my door and walking around to the driver seat, plugging his phone in for the GPS.

Looking in the mirror to check my makeup before we leave, I realize my handsy boyfriend smudged it. I reach down for my purse to get my lip stain and realize I left it inside, probably distracted by said handsy boyfriend.

"I'm going to run in to grab my purse. I'll be right back."

He reaches over, putting his hand on my bare thigh, tracing his thumb over the sensitive skin. "Stay here. I'll get it."

He smiles at me softly before opening the door and walking inside.

I sit there, practically giddy about tonight when my car's touch-screen lights up with ping after ping. I look at the notifications, seeing Kayleigh, Kayleigh, Kayleigh. New Message. New Message. New Message.

I grab his phone to silence the notifications and it opens.

Shit. I forgot he programmed my face in it.

In an instant, his messages are opened.

> Kayleigh: Are you busy? I need to see you.
>
> Kayleigh: Are you home? Can I come over?
>
> Kayleigh: Is Lizzy there? You can come over here if it's easier. I need you right now.

My heart pounds and my ears ring while I stare at the messages.

No. No. This can't be happening again. I grab the phone and swing open the passenger door, not even sure where I'm going or what's happening.

There's no way. Clay isn't Johnathan.

I take two steps from the car back toward the house when Clay walks out with my purse. The smile on his face, that boyish, carefree one I've fallen in love with, disappears in an instant when he sees my face.

"What's wrong?" he asks, his voice filled with concern as he steps toward me.

I hold out the phone, saying nothing, trying to hold myself together. He grabs it, confusion on his face before he scrolls through the text messages.

"Shit," he says gruffly, combing his fingers through his inky hair before pulling it in a fist. "Did you scroll up?"

"No, I didn't." I look at him almost dumfounded. "And that's all you're going to say? Shit?"

He looks back at me, eerily calm but still tense. "I told you. We're just friends. She needs me for something."

My breathing quickens and my apprehension overwhelms me. "That doesn't sound like she needs just anything, Clay. I want to trust you, I want to believe you." I hear my frantic breaths through my nose as my jaw clenches. "But I need *more*."

He stares back at me, but the look on his face is something else, something I've never seen before. There's doubt. There's conflict. He looks tortured.

He lower's his eyes to the ground and his voice is a faint, broken whisper. "I've told you everything I can. Nothing is happening between us. That's it. I need you to trust me."

"I don't know if that's good enough for me anymore. Not right now."

I turn away and start walking to the driver side of the car when he cries out. "Lizzy, please. Don't go." I turn to see him taking a step towards me and I hold up a finger between us, stopping him in his tracks.

"I can't do this right now. I need to leave."

"I'm telling you the truth. Please, don't." His voice is still the quiet, eerie whisper that shakes me to my bones. And the desperate look in his eyes is one I can't reconcile with the cocky, playful man I know.

"I'm sorry. I just need to take a beat." I start to turn back to my car when he drops to his knees between me and the house. "I am begging you, please stay."

The sight is jarring. This is the proudest, most stubborn, determined man I've met. Seeing him kneeling before me, on the verge of breaking down, is nearly my undoing.

I step back toward him and kneel down in front of him. I reach out, holding the sides of his face, rubbing a stray tear away from his cheek. Those beautiful green eyes, the ones that make me feel so seen, so wanted, look so distraught. The way his chest heaves from labored breathing, the veins pulsing in his neck, all tear at my heart. This isn't the look of a man who would lie to me or hurt me. He's not defensive or angry. He's not lashing out.

No. This is the look of a man terrified of losing something he needs to live, like he's running out of air to breathe. This is a man grasping and clawing for purchase, for any semblance of control, desperate to fix something he thinks is broken. This is a man trying his best not to fall apart in this moment. This is the man that I've fallen for when I didn't think I could truly feel love again.

I run my hand through his hair, watching his throat bob and his pulse quicken while he leans into my touch. I want so desperately to trust him. In my heart, *I do trust him.*

But something in the back of my mind is telling me I need more from him, more than he's willing to give me right now in this moment. My brain is telling me I deserve to feel good about this. I need space to make sure I'm right. I said I wouldn't let myself be defined by another man and I don't want to make a mistake in the heat of the moment. Looking into his eyes, I know if I stay here right now, I won't be able to stay away from him and think clearly.

"Clay," I whisper, trying to keep my voice from fraying.

Stay calm, Lizzy. Be strong.

"I'm not leaving you. I'm not ending this between us. But I need space. I need to clear my head. And I need you to realize this isn't something you can control or fix, as badly as you want to." I take a deep breath, steadying myself. "I'm not something you can control."

His eyes lock on mine, but he doesn't move. The only sounds are his labored breaths. "I could never tame you, Lizzy." Something about that tears right at my heart again because I know he means it. "And I wouldn't want to."

"And that's why I love you, Clay Chapman. That's why I fucking love you, against every self-preservation instinct I have." This time, I wipe a stray tear from my eye. "You think everyone sees you as left-overs from all your tragedies like it's some weakness or flaw. But to me, that's the most beautiful thing about you. What you see as the broken shards of yourself, I see as special, perfect little pieces that come together to make the beautiful mosaic you are. The unique person that sees me and makes me feel special. That's why I'm so helplessly in love with you."

I raise my eyes to meet his and there's the slightest bit of hope there. "Then please. Don't go."

I rub his cheek again, the feeling of his stubble still sending shivers through me even right now. "I'm sorry, Clay. I need some time for myself tonight. But I'm not running from you." I look back into his eyes, trying to remind him of that night we talked at the condo. "I'm going back to my family's place. I'm not leaving you, but I need space. Please respect that."

I plant one, soft kiss to his forehead, breathing in his soothing scent. Then I gather all the strength I have to stand, turn away, and walk to my Bronco, already fighting every fiber of my being telling me to turn back and go to him right now.

BY THE TIME I get back to the Aspen Grove Club and get in the elevator, I'm a frantic mess. I almost feel like I did that day last summer when I showed up on Veronica's porch, for an entirely different list of reasons.

I just walked away from the man I love. Three months ago when we first met, I didn't even think I was capable of that. I didn't even know what I wanted in my life after I was given a second chance to start over. And now I'm reeling because I found him, I found what I want, who I want.

I don't want safe. I know I want Clay, the man that lights a fire in me just by looking at me with those eyes that see me like no one else. I want him and all of his broken shards that fit into mine. I want him and that heart that's seen so much loss and still pours out more for the people he loves.

And if I'm reeling, I know he has to be heartbroken right now. He's poured so much of his soul out to me. But I need to be sure that I'm ready for this, because there's no recovering from this kind of love.

My heart pounds as I step off the elevator and head into the condo. At this moment, I'm glad Clay is the obsessive, reliable person he is because everything was fixed on time and I have a familiar place to take a night and think by myself.

When I walk in, I'm completely caught off guard when I see my dad sitting at the kitchen island on his laptop.

He briefly peeks over the screen, barely noticing me, before turning back to his work. "Oh hey, Lizzy. How was your day?"

I stand there with my purse still clenched in my hand, in complete disbelief. He just asked me how my day was. Did he even look at me? Can he not hear how hard I'm breathing?

"It was shitty, Dad." I can't hide my irritation, my anger, my sniffling.

He doesn't look up, but he points to a bottle of wine on the counter.

"Welcome to grab yourself a glass. Just opened it." I stride around the island, grabbing a glass from the cabinet before standing next to him and pouring myself a very generous amount.

I glare back at him, taking a sip. He still hasn't even looked up from his laptop again. This is how it always is with him, like I'm a ghost.

"That's it? Nothing else to say? When did you even get here?"

He finally stops typing and looks up, taking his glasses off.

His eyes search my face, seeing my smeared makeup and my puffy red eyes. "I got here a couple days ago. I told you I was coming to town to check on a new investment, a company we just became the majority owner of. Is everything alright?"

My rage boils over. "You've been here for days and you haven't even called me or messaged me? You haven't even noticed that I haven't been here at the condo and I've been staying at my boyfriend's house the whole time?"

I look into his eyes again and think about what Clay asked. Have I ever told him how he makes me feel?

"And no, everything isn't alright. My boyfriend is - I don't know - it's complicated. And then there's *you*." His eyes are softer now, fixed on me. "Why do you always make me feel like I'm not good enough for you? Why does it feel like I'm an afterthought all the time?"

I take a long sip from my glass, sitting down at the island next to him, and bury my face into my palms as the tears fall.

A moment passes before I feel him wrap his arm around me, his hand rubbing my shoulder. His voice is almost like wind in the tree-tops, distant and faint. "I'm sorry, honey. I'm so sorry I ever made you feel that way. Tell me how I can help."

I drop my head to his shoulder, not remembering the last time I ever felt close or safe like this with him.

"Just be my dad, please. Talk to me, remember my birthday, find time for me." I look up at him and I see the second set of broken eyes in a man today. "Show me that you love me."

He lifts his hand, wiping away a stray tear before it reaches his cheek.

"I'll try, Lizzy. You grew up so damn fast. You became so inde-pendent and so strong. It felt like overnight you became this fierce woman that didn't need her dad anymore." He chokes back another tear. "Charlotte was never like that. Then when she got sick and was in and out of the hospital, she needed us so much."

"I needed you too, Dad." I feel my lips quiver, remembering what it was like for all of us then. I know she was sick, but I still felt so cast aside.

"I know, sweetie, I know. It was so easy to take it for granted because you were so brave. I'll always be sorry for that, but that doesn't mean I ever stopped loving you. I always wanted the best for you. Schools, family trips, internships, everything. Somewhere along the way I just didn't know how to talk to you anymore. But I love you, exactly the way you are."

I drop my head back to his shoulder, suddenly glad that he's here and that I'm not alone tonight. "Ok, Dad. I love you, too."

He hums against my head, holding me tightly. "Now tell me about this boyfriend."

This time I'm the one that rubs a tear from my eye. "I don't know. Like I said, it's complicated. But he's special. He makes me feel special like no one else ever has."

He hums softly in thought. "And do you love him?"

I groan and say it out loud for the second time today. "Yes. Yes, I do."

"Then I'd love to learn more about him and meet him. If anyone can work their way into your heart, they have to be something special."

I laugh between my slowing tears. "Yeah, he's something else."

Minutes pass and I just enjoy the unexpected but welcome closeness of my dad. Today's been a rollercoaster and this was definitely not how I expected it to end.

"What about you? What company did you buy now?"

A laugh rumbles from his chest behind me. "You really want to talk about my business? You never showed interest before when I offered to hire you."

"Well, if I expect you to try harder, so should I."

He lets out another short laugh. "Alright. We bought a local real estate developer. We've wanted to grow our footprint out West, especially with resort and leisure travel in ski towns. Their founder was looking to take a step back and it seemed like a good company. And he's a local icon, which should help with marketing. They're profitable, but could be doing better. I'm sure we'll make something out of them."

I nod, my tears and sniffling finally ending. "Sounds like a good fit."

He hums in agreement. "I'm actually going to their annual banquet tomorrow. The Golden Jensen Family night at the Grand Lodge's event hall."

Golden Jensen Family. My head jerks up. "Say that again."

I look at him and he shrugs. "Golden Jensen Family. What about it?"

Golden Jensen Family. GJF, Inc.

"Did you buy JSC?" I ask, a wave of realization hitting me.

"Yep. Sounds like you know them pretty well?"

I nod. "You could say that." I don't know where to start with this. There's a lot to go over. I point towards the bottle of wine. "Is there another one of those around? We might need it."

CHAPTER 38

CLAY
OLD TIMES SAKE

IT TOOK every ounce of self-control I've built over the last decade not to run after Lizzy. She said to give her space and I will, even if it's killing me now. I'm a mess, pacing around my house, surrounded by reminders of how good things were just an hour ago.

I don't know how to fix this. I wanted to spill my heart to her, to tell her everything, but that's not an option. I can't do that.

I'm desperate.

I know I'm desperate because after twenty minutes of pacing around the house and pulling my hair out, I do the last thing I want to do.

I call for help.

I'M SITTING in my chair, rubbing Ani's head when Kayleigh and Grace arrive minutes apart. I get up, following him to the door when they come inside.

I grab Kayleigh, hugging her, only breaking to look into her eyes. They're red from crying and I remember why she probably messaged me in the first place.

"Are you alright?" I ask, rubbing her shoulders.

"I'm fine."

"You sure? What's wrong with Charlie?"

She glares at me and lets out a long breath through her nose. "Clay, we don't need to talk about Charlie right now. We broke up, but deep down, I knew it was coming."

She reaches out and cups my jaw as Grace stands next to us. "Seriously, tell us what happened so we can help."

I gesture to the couch and chairs in the living room.

I sit down with them and I do just that, tell them everything. Some of it they know, some of it they don't, some of it they're apart of.

After I pour my guts out, Kayleigh looks to Grace then back to me.

"You trust her, right?"

I swallow hard, nodding. "Of course."

"Good, I'll go talk to her." Kayleigh stands and heads toward the coat rack.

I jump to my feet and stride towards her. "No, you don't have to do that."

She shakes her head with an amused smirk on her face.

"What did Lizzy just tell you before we showed up you big, sweet, dumb idiot?" I think back, my shoulders sagging when I realize what she's saying. "Accept that you can't control everything. Whether you like it or not, I'm going to talk to her. Don't do anything stupid until you've heard back from me, ok?"

I nod and run my fingers through my hair.

"Fine, but you don't have to do this though."

She laughs and pats me on the cheek. "See? You're still doing it."

I groan and roll my eyes.

She looks at me, cocking an eyebrow. "Try to relax. Think about what you *can* actually do." She looks over to Grace who's watching with an amused look on her face. "I'll see you two at the banquet tomorrow night, right?"

Grace smiles. "Well, I wasn't invited but sure, I'd like to go."

Kayleigh looks to me, smirking. "Take your sister as your plus one. Let me worry about Lizzy."

"Alright, sure."

"Good," she says, grabbing her jacket to go.

I step in front of her, putting myself between her and the door. "You really don't have to-"

She glares at me, stopping me mid sentence. "It's what best friends are for." She tilts her head towards Grace and whispers to me. "Now go enjoy a night with your sister. When was the last time just the two of you really hung out?"

I pull her in tight for a hug. "Thank you."

"No. Thank you, Clay." She pats me on the back before breaking our hug, heading out the door.

I watch her pull down the driveway before heading back to the living room. Slumping into my chair, I try to wrap my head around how I got here. A moment passes before Grace breaks the silence from the kitchen. She walks into the living area, with two glasses of bourbon in hand.

She takes a sip and grimaces. "Surprised there's no open wine. I see Lizzy really made herself at home." She smirks, handing me the other glass. "But I didn't come over for the pity party, big brother. Of course, the first time you call me to *talk* in years is because of a girl. Who would have thought my big brothers were both such hopeless romantics?"

I glare at Grace. "You're already reminding me why I don't ask for help."

She sits down on the floor in front of me and crosses her legs, facing the windows and staring out at the mountains. I watch her shoulders rise and fall as she takes a deep breath. "*She* would have loved Lizzy." With the soft tone of her voice, I already know who she means. I feel a lump stick in my throat, partly thinking about our mom and partly because Grace is right. She is exactly the kind of confident spirit that mom would have been instant friends with.

I watch Grace pull two hair ties from her wrist, handing them to me over her shoulder. "For old times' sake." Like a reflex, I take the ties from her hand, already feeling more at ease as my heart beat slows down, back to its normal rhythm.

We sit there in front of the fire for hours. I unload everything else on her. How bad my need for control has gotten. How I've grown to resent the person I thought was my mentor, someone I could look up to. How Lizzy makes me feel.

We even talk about how Lizzy, even when she isn't here, has brought Grace right back to me. Sure, we've always seen each other around and done some family things together. But we haven't talked like this in years.

Talking with her, I'm reminded of how easy it is to forget that she's the youngest sibling.

As the night winds on and our bottle of whiskey is drained, I look at her, yawning by the fire, remembering all the times we'd stay up late as kids over the holidays at our grandparents' condo in Jackson.

"Alright. You're staying here tonight."

She checks the time on her phone. "Sheesh. Yeah, it's late."

I stand up, holding out a hand to her. "Come on. You can have Lizzy's room tonight."

She reaches out and I tug her up off the floor. She smirks back at me with mischief in her eyes.

"Besides, this works perfectly for our plans tomorrow."

I quirk an eyebrow at her. "What are you planning?"

She hums with childish enthusiasm, practically bouncing down the hallway past my office to the bedrooms.

She stops at the door and turns to me. "We're going shopping for your black tie dinner."

I look down at her, my brows scrunching together. She's so tall it's in stark contrast to looking down to meet Lizzy's eyes, which I have to crane my neck to do. "I already have an outfit for that."

She shrugs. "Maybe. But not the right one for tomorrow."

"What do you mean?" I grumble, already tired from the long day and not in the mood for a game, even if I'm enjoying my unexpected night with my sister.

"You're like really slow at picking up on this. What part of let go and accept you're not in control did you not get?" She teases, patting my cheek.

I throw my head back and groan. "I already hate this."

She laughs and heads into the bedroom, stopping a step inside the door. "Holy shit. Lizzy *really* moved in."

I look around the room over her shoulder, a warm feeling growing in my chest when I see her pink pile of pillows and the room surprisingly clean.

"Yeah, you could say that."

She looks at the pile of pillows, shaking her head and laughing. "Did she bring all of those?"

"No, I got those for her right after she agreed to stay over."

My sister turns and looks back at me, a wide, shit eating grin plastered on. "You definitely love her."

Yes. Yes, I do.

CHAPTER 39
LIZZY
I DON'T WANT TO TALK TO YOU

I WAKE up with a sinking feeling settling over me when I realize I'm back in my condo. It's familiar, a place I've woken up in so many times. But it doesn't feel right waking up here and not in Clay's arms. Did I do the right thing? Should I have stayed with him? My eyes adjust to the light and I see a cup on the nightstand, a nitro cold brew from Finch.

I bury my face into a pillow and groan. "Please go away. I don't want to talk to you right now. I told you, I need space. This isn't something you can fix."

"But it is something I can fix." A woman's voice, not Clay's immediately jolts me up. I look over to see Kayleigh, sitting in the corner chair of the bedroom.

I look at her in disbelief. Of all the people I would have expected to see right now, much less wanted to, she wouldn't be at the top of the list.

"What do you mean?" I say, my voice shaky and groggy, half from irritation, half from being half asleep.

"I know you may have doubts, but we're just friends. That's it. You *can* trust him."

The thing is, I do trust him. Everything in my heart says I can, but my mind doesn't want to believe it. "I saw you two. He loves you."

She sighs and drops her head and rubs her temples. "It's not like that. But you're right. He does love me and I love him, but only as friends."

My heart sinks at that admission. I knew what I saw, the connection between them. But only as friends? "Why did you need to see him right then, right in that moment?" I ask, desperately wanting to know what Clay wouldn't tell me last night.

"I've been going through some relationship drama. It finally ended. Charlie broke up with me yesterday. I just needed to talk to him."

"You realize that doesn't exactly make me feel better. That the first person you rush to when your boyfriend dumps you is the man I'm madly in love with, right?"

"Lizzy." She closes her eyes and takes a deep breath. "*She* ended it. *She* broke up with me." She looks up, her eyes meeting mine and I see the pain there. Charlie. Shit. I just assumed. But my family even calls my own sister *Charlie* sometimes. Suddenly, so much more makes sense.

"Kayleigh. I... I didn't know." I've heard about her for years. She's a public figure, featured in global ad campaigns and on posters at almost every ski resort in the country. "How-"

She wipes a tear from her cheek before cutting me off. "No one knows except for Clay and Grace. I finally realized it right when I was eighteen, almost nineteen. It was right around when Clay was recovering from his first injury, right around when he lost his mom."

I feel a tear welling in the corner of my eyes when she continues. "I never told anyone else. Not my family, not my coaches or trainers. No one. Growing up in Utah, in a very public family, I didn't want anyone to know, except for Clay."

My thoughts drift to Clay being worried if I scrolled up when I read her messages last night. Even in that moment, he was protecting her, worried for her.

"We were always so close and we were both such a mess then, it just felt natural to tell him. We leaned on each other so hard. Eventually, I told Grace too. The long distance thing worked for so long, but I guess Charlie and I just grew apart. Clay knew - he was the only person I could talk to and not keep it bottled up when it ended."

My heart breaks wide open for both of them. "Why are you telling me then?"

She turns and looks at me, her face hardening. "Because you're right, I do love him - like a brother. I care about him so much and he's helplessly in love with you. He's never been willing to open himself up to being hurt, until now, until *you*."

Those two words, *until you,* hit me like a punch to the gut.

"I never thought I would see this day. And somehow that boy, that man, trusts you." Her throat bobs. "And if he trusts you, I trust you with this."

I'm at a loss for words. I stare back at her in disbelief at everything she's just opened up to me about. "I don't even know what to say."

"Just... please do not ever doubt Clay. There is no one in the world I would trust more than him. I see the way you look at him. He needs that, someone who will make him look out for his own happiness for once. Shit, he was willing to break his own heart and ignore his own happiness to protect me. I wasn't going to let him do that."

I watch as more tears stream down her face. I pat the bed next to me. "Come here."

She gets up and sits next to me and I wrap her in a hug. She sniffles into my shoulder. "Please don't hold this against him. Do not doubt him. He doesn't think he's allowed to be happy. He doesn't think he deserves to want things just for him in his life. He's been more of a friend and ally than I could ever ask for, but it's his turn to be happy."

"Thank you, Kayleigh." I squeeze her tight, overwhelmed with everything she just told me. "Thank you for telling me. All of it."

Suddenly, I feel a flood of relief. I know that my heart and my mind were both right. I knew deep in my heart I could trust Clay. It just felt right. But my mind was right too. There was something there. But more than anything, I'm so relieved that I feel like I can trust myself.

I wipe the tears from my eyes, the happy tears for once. "Where is he now?"

"He's out with Grace." She laughs and looks at me. "You really must be rubbing off on him because they're out shopping. He'll be at the banquet tonight though." She looks down and frowns for a second. "After yesterday, I told him to take Grace as his plus one."

"Oh." I say, thinking that makes sense, but I just want to see him.

"You know, I still need a plus one though. Will you be mine?" She looks back up at me smiling brightly with a wink. "Strictly as friends, of course."

"Of course." I pull her back into a hug, before letting her go. "I can't wait to see him."

She laughs and shakes her head. "I'm going to need to find a new date to these things in the future. We always let people think we might be more than friends. We never really did anything to stop those rumors."

I shrug and smirk at her. "I might be able to loan him out to his best friend from time to time."

She lets out another soft laugh, wiping away another tear. "It's funny. That first night at dinner at your condo? Clay brought me because of you. He had no clue how to act around you. He was obsessed and terrified. So naturally I wanted to meet the girl he wouldn't shut up about."

My heart warms at the thought. "Thank you for telling me that. I'm glad he has had you."

She smiles softly and nods. "I'm glad he has you now too."

And now all I want is to be close to him, to feel his warmth. But another thought creeps into my mind, something that's been nagging me.

"Speaking of tonight, I need to talk to you about something."

CHAPTER 40

CLAY

HER

"I DON'T KNOW why you're complaining. You look great." My sister stands in front of me in the valet circle of the Grand Lodge, straightening my tie.

I jab a finger at her in the air. "You better be right about this. You talked to Kayleigh, right?"

She throws her head back in exasperation. "For the hundredth time, yes. I texted her this morning. They'll be here. And for the one hundred and first time, loosen up already. I swear, I don't know what Lizzy sees in you." She gives me a playful smirk.

I grin at her and laugh, feeling my shoulders relax. "I can think of a few things."

She glares at me. "Ew, stop."

I smile back at her warmly. "Seriously, thank you for helping."

She fiddles with my bowtie one more time before looking up at me. "Glad to help. You two are going to be fine. Just keep your head out of your ass and be you." She hums in consideration. "Well, at least the part of you that Lizzy likes."

Yep, she's definitely the wisest of the Chapman siblings. I look at her, taken aback by my little sister that reminds me so much of our mom. She looks up at me with a questioning expression. "What?"

"Look at you." I run my hand up and down in front of her. She's tall like our mom with the same flowing brown hair as her. My baby sister is just as smart and wild spirited as she was too. "Remind me again how you're single?"

She scoffs. "I haven't met a man special enough yet. It's just trust fund babies and wannabe ski bros around here. Too many boys, no men. I know what I'm worth." She tosses me a wink before looping her elbow into mine. "Just promise me you won't let us drift apart again?"

I nod, looking her right in the eyes. "Chapman Promise. Now let's go inside and get this shit show started."

I GRIP the hand of the man I used to look up to, pumping it in my definitely too tight grasp in a handshake I wish would end. I don't know when I started to resent him, but Lizzy was right. Standing here just inside the entryway to the event hall in the line of customers and clients waiting to greet him, I see him differently now. He's not the former ski legend that the impressionable eighteen year old me was eager to listen to and desperate to please. I should have seen through his bullshit years ago. He tore me down even further at my lowest point, just so he could build me into a tool to use for himself.

"Glad you're here, Clay." He's wearing that eerie smile that I hate. And now I know why it's never sat right with me, seeing him in a whole new light, recognizing just how much he's been manipulating me.

"No problem. Just part of the job." I squeeze his hand one more time before letting go.

He turns to Grace. "And if it isn't the youngest Chapman. It feels like it's been years since I've seen you."

She puts on a bright, but obviously fake smile. "It *has* been years, Ralph."

He frowns awkwardly and I bite back a laugh, knowing damn well that she knows that's not his name. I wrap my arm around her shoulder, steering her inside. "We'll see you inside, Mr. Jensen." He nods and immediately puts facade back up and turns to the next person to greet.

Once we're out of ear shot, I turn to my sister. "You're a trouble-maker. Ralph? Really?"

She hums and shrugs. "What? Lizzy's right. Dude's creepy. Someone needs to give him a reality check."

I snort a laugh. "Alright, killer."

She grins and tugs me by my elbow further into the huge room. "Come on, let's get a drink. You said it's an open bar, right?"

I nod and she pulls me along towards the bar on the back wall.

"Good, because I want to drink on his dime."

We get to the bar and flag down the bartender over the noise of the crowded room.

"What are you having tonight folks?" he asks, looking at Grace first.

"Champagne, please."

He looks to me and I think to myself, Grace is right. We should have a little fun.

"What's your oldest bourbon?"

He smiles back knowingly. "We've got a great single barrel of Wasatch Whiskey Twelve Year bourbon."

"Perfect. Make it a double."

"Go ahead and make that two doubles," a voice from behind me says. A voice that sends sparks up my spine.

I turn around to find Lizzy standing behind me, with Kayleigh at her side.

My eyes rake over her body, from her skin tight, strapless black dress, all the way down to her red heels. Her nails are done in red instead of her trademark pink that's grown on me, matching her kiss-able lips. Her hair is in her always perfect ponytail. She's pure, fierce, radiant perfection.

There are a thousand words I want to say, but when our eyes meet, only one comes out in a low, raspy breath.

"Princess."

She steps toward me, wrapping me tightly in a hug. "Shut up, Clay."

I've only been away from her for one night, but I already missed her touch and her presence so much. I pull her tighter into my chest, feeling her head against my pounding heart. I can finally settle down now that she's in my arms.

This is where she belongs.

My eyes look up to meet Kayleigh's, who's smiling back at me. She steps over to Grace, sipping her champagne.

"Why don't we give them a minute?" she says to Grace, ordering her own glass.

Grace laughs. "It was just getting good though. Princess? Come on, let me have this."

Kayleigh gets Grace to begrudgingly turn away towards the bar and I feel Lizzy mumble into my chest. "Ok, you can let go of me now."

"Never in a million years," I rasp against her hair, breathing in the scent I craved when I woke up alone this morning.

"Seriously, I don't want to ruin my make up."

A low laugh rumbles from my chest and I let go. This time, her eyes rake over me and the tip of her tongue darts over her lips. Her eyes work their way up and snag on my neck and a smile takes over her face. An infectious one that cuts right through me.

"I thought you said this was a *black tie* event?" She reaches up, straightening my pink bowtie. Her finger tips graze my neck and her nails scrape over the tattoo she always traces, sending another jolt of electricity through my tense body.

"I figured I would try to match you."

"Did you figure that or did Grace?"

I huff another low laugh. "Mostly her." I rest my hands on her hips, looking into her deep blue eyes that are sparkling back up at me. "But I see that you went black and red instead."

She crooks a finger at me to bring my ear to her lips. Even with her heels, I still have to bend down for her to whisper into my ear.

"I still wore pink, you just can't see it."

With that image in my head, it's a helpless struggle to ignore my cock twitching in my tight dress pants. "I hope I see it later, but can the heels stay on?"

She laughs before she pulls away. I look back into her eyes, remembering the feeling of watching a tear stream down her cheek when she left last night.

"I'm sorry. I'm so sorry. I wanted to tell you. I-"

She shakes her head at me, a serious look in her eyes. "No, don't apologize. I'm glad you didn't. The fact that you didn't tell me, that you protected someone you love even when it was making you fall apart, is exactly why I'm so fucking in love with you."

Those words. I know she said them last night, but hearing them now, again, lights a raging fire deep inside me. That someone like her, this fiery, vibrant, determined woman would love *me* is more than I could ever ask for.

"I love you too." I run my hands up her back, my fingertips settling on the bare skin just below the nape of her neck. Her lashes flutter and her lips part at the sudden, skin to skin contact. I crane my neck, bringing my mouth to her soft, waiting lips. That sweet taste, the feeling of her tongue grazing mine, her breathy, adorable little whimpers - all of it is perfection.

She is perfection.

I pull away, feeling her teeth tug at my bottom lip and her warm breath on my chin when I press my forehead to hers. "Are we good?"

She lets out a soft hum of approval. "Yes, more than good."

I trace my finger over her bare neck and she leans into my touch. "That's good, because Grace is about to move in and take over your room if you don't come back."

"When I come back, I'm moving into your room." She looks up at me and I see a nervous, excited glint in her sparkling eyes. "Also there's something I want to tell you. Something I wanted to say last night."

I soften my gaze, asking her to continue. She starts to talk when the bartender clears his throat. "Here are your doubles."

In unison, we both glare at him as we reach to grab our drinks. He snorts a knowing laugh before leaving to help another guest.

I take a sip of my whiskey, watching Lizzy's pouty red lips part, drinking the amber liquid, wondering what I ever did to deserve her.

"You were saying?" I ask, leaning back against the bar. I can see that excited look come back from just a second ago before we were interrupted.

She throws back another sip and wipes away a stray drop from the corner of her mouth. "Actually, there were two things I wanted to tell you."

"Oh, there you are." A man I don't immediately recognize comes up, hugging Lizzy, instantly making me tense wondering who would be touching my woman. "I've been looking for you all night, sweetie."

Lizzy looks at me, her eyes going wide for a second and a cute pink flush rolls over her cheeks. "Ok. Make that a few things." She hugs him back before he lets go.

He turns to face me, eyeing me up and down, smiling kindly and warmly. He's average height, well built and fit, probably in his early sixties. "And you must be Clay, the boyfriend she told me so much about last night."

This time, it's my turn to blush as I feel my cheeks go red. This must be Mr. Frank. I wasn't expecting to meet her dad tonight. And fuck, what did she tell him last night? I look back to Lizzy. She must sense my what-the-hell-is-happening anxiety because her eyes say *relax, it's ok.*

I set my glass down and reach my hand out. "It's a pleasure to meet you, Mr. Frank."

He grabs my hand and shakes it firmly. "Likewise. It takes a special man to win her heart and tame her."

Her eyes roll back and that pink flush returns. "Dad, seriously?"

I laugh. "With all due respect sir, there's no taming her. That's what I love about her."

He nods and smiles, patting us both on the back. "Well, don't let me keep you two from having fun. I'm sure we'll find time to talk again soon."

He brings Lizzy into another short hug, whispering something into her ear that makes her smile before he turns and works his way into the crowd.

I let out a long breath and look at Lizzy.

"Well, that was a surprise."

She shrugs, laughing nervously. "Yeah, sorry about that. I didn't know he was in town until last night."

"Seems like you two are in a bit of a better place?"

She smiles and nods. "Yeah, I was such a mess last night." She looks down at her drink, tracing the rim of the rocks glass with her finger. "With everything else going on, I just kind of went off on him. It was good though. We needed it."

My lips pull together in a half-hearted smile. "I'm glad you two talked, but I'm still sorry about yesterday."

She reaches out, grabbing my wrist. "I meant it. Stop apologizing."

"Alright. So what were the other things you wanted to tell me?"

She sets her glass down and steps toward me, resting her hands on my shoulders leaving just inches between us. She looks up at me, pure excitement and joy in her bluebird day eyes. "I took a full time job with Fischer, based here in Utah."

My heart pounds. This is really happening. We talked about how she could work here indefinitely and we could sort things out, but there were still some unknowns. But her being here permanently is music to my ears.

"That's amazing, so amazing."

She grins back at me and I can see the giddiness in the way she's practically bouncing on her toes. "It's a promotion. I'll still be doing some of my old job. But this isn't just about us, it's about me. I needed this fresh start too. And when I told Jessica the other night at dinner, I sort of got the feeling this was some grand scheme of hers because she hardly seemed surprised. But I wanted to wait to tell you until it was finalized with HR and-"

I flick my eyebrows at her, holding her eyes. "Lizzy, stop rambling. I'm so excited for you."

She steps closer, erasing the distance between us. "Me too. I'm glad this gives us a chance to do this for real." She stands on her toes, planting a whisper of a kiss on my lips.

I reach up, tucking a stray strand of her golden blond hair behind her ear. "So what else did you want to tell me?"

She starts to open her mouth right when the sound of silverware tapping a glass cuts through the room, signaling that it's time to take a seat.

I laugh and look down at her, shrugging one shoulder. "I guess the rest will have to wait until after dinner."

CHAPTER 41

LIZZY
FULL LIZZY

AFTER DINNER, I find Grace and Kayleigh at a high top over by the bar, sipping flutes of champagne while I'm on my second double of whiskey. I'm not sure why I'm surprised Clay has great taste in whiskey, like everything else.

Grace is in a dark forest green, silk slip dress that matches the color of her eyes. It hangs effortlessly off of her tall, thin and fit frame. She looks every bit of a Chapman, complete with dark brown hair pulled into a perfect pair of Dutch braids that I now look at very differently.

Kayleigh looks the part of the professional athlete. She's in a sleeveless, high neck ice blue dress that makes her black hair pop in contrast. Although it's floor length, it has an elegant slit that ends just above her knee, accentuating her long, very toned legs.

"You ladies look stunning tonight." I stand between them at the table, suddenly very aware that even heels don't make up for being 5'3" around them.

Grace scoffs. "Um, girl? I watched my brother's jaw practically hit the floor when he saw you. That dress kills it." She smirks at Kayleigh before looking back at me. "And don't even get me started on the princess thing. I'm never going to let him live that down."

I feel a flush creep across my neck up to my cheeks, knowing just how much I love it when he calls me that.

"I still can't believe someone finally brought his soft side back out," Kayleigh says, looking at her champagne flute.

I raise an eyebrow at her. *"Back out?"*

They laugh in unison before Kayleigh goes first. "He was the biggest teddy bear when we met in high school. Much less scowling."

Grace shakes her head with a grin, looking up like she's lost in a memory. "Yes! Way less scowling. See if you can get him to tell you about how excited he was when his first ski team sponsor was a cell phone company whose colors were pink and white."

Kayleigh snorts a laugh, covering her mouth. "Oh! I forgot about that. That boy in a pink racing spandex ski suit was a sight."

"I thought he skied moguls? You mean he didn't always wear twenty shades of black?" I ask.

Kayleigh nods. "He still did some racing when they first moved here, but he settled into moguls as he got older and competition got more serious."

My mind races with so many thoughts.

First, Clay in all pink spandex hugging that muscular frame.

Yes. Please.

But more importantly, I hope I get to see more of that soft side.

"Wait." Grace's almost squeal brings me back to the conversation. "I think I have pictures."

She pulls out her phone and starts scrolling before stopping and grinning wickedly.

A second later, my phone buzzes in my purse. I pull it out and look down to see I've been added to two new group chats, *Clay and the Girls*, and another called *Brunch Babes*.

I see that she's already sent an old picture of Clay and his mom on the slopes, with him in his very pink spandex.

> Grace: Look what I found. Told you that pink works for you.

Grace looks up at Kayleigh and me. "The one is for us to tease him. The other is for us to plan brunches and happy hours, especially now that you'll be around here in Park City more."

"I like the sound of that." I'm already feeling more and more at home here with these two. Veronica will always be my bestie, but Grace and Kayleigh make me feel so welcome and I know we can be just as close.

"Me too," Kayleigh says, raising her glass over the table. Grace and I clink our glasses to hers.

I scan the room, spotting Clay at another high top talking to a couple with Kayleigh's dad. I watch him reach into his pocket and pull out his phone. He flicks a thumb across the screen and even from across the room, I can see him toss his head back and groan.

All three of our phones buzz and we look to see a message in the new group chat.

> Grumpy Roommate: Please. No.

I watch Grace and Kayleigh type away with matching giddy, mischievous smiles.

> Grace: Too bad, so sad.

> Kayleigh: Pink was a good color for you, Clayton.

I giggle looking down at my screen before I chime in.

> Me: Yes, please. More pink!

I look across the room to see Clay, hanging his head and palming his face. Even from here though, I can see one of his dimples flash in a playful smile.

> Grumpy Roommate: I'm going to regret
> bringing you three together, aren't I?

"Alright, I'm going to go check in on him. But brunch tomorrow?" I ask.

Kayleigh and Grace both nod and I can't help but feel this is the start of a great new chapter in my life with them. This is exactly the fresh start I wanted.

I leave them at the table, watching them start to scroll through the camera reels on their phones. As I walk over to the high top that's now just Clay and Mr. Jensen, I laugh to myself along the way. Looking at my phone, they're already flooding our group chat with Clay, sending more embarrassing yet cute pictures of him from his high school days.

Looking at the pictures, that same chiseled jaw, those heart melting dimples, and that tall, imposing stature were there. But now when I reach the table, I'm still in awe of the man I'm in love with. Even in a tux, there's no hiding the rugged, rough, and devilishly handsome man he is today. From his neck tattoo popping out of his collar to the tattooed hands dwarfing his rocks glass. All of it is the pure, masculine sexual energy that sends molten heat to my core.

I walk up beside Clay, wrapping my arm around his waist, settling against him, craving his warmth even through his tux. He wraps his arm around my waist, pulling me into him.

He looks down at me smiling, his dimples popping before he turns back to his boss.

"Mr. Jensen, this is my girlfriend, Lizzy." Hearing him say that with so much pride only magnifies the molten heat inside me he commands so easily.

I take in Mr. Jensen, the man I've heard so much about. In person, he's obviously athletically built, even in his late fifties. His dark, short and straight hair, is peppered with grays and he's clean shaven. He's very much the image of old school, traditional Utah.

But the second he smiles at me and stretches out his hand to shake mine, I see what Clay means. That smile is weird and, frankly, this man gives me the creeps.

Knowing what Clay's told me about him in passing and how he trained him into a self-loathing robot lights a different kind of fire in me. And after talking about him with Kayleigh this morning, I do my best to hide my distaste for him. I will save that for another time because I do have things to say to him.

He eyes me curiously when I grab his hand and shake it firmly before letting go.

"Glad to finally meet you. I was wondering who could distract my best employee enough to make a mistake like forgetting to run the heaters at a job site." He smiles like he's making a playful, off the cuff comment, but his tone is mocking and condescending. It immediately turns my stomach. I feel Clay tense next to me and his thumb rubs the dip of my waist through the fabric of my dress.

I feign a laugh with a dismissive flip of my hand. "Oh it's not that bad. Mistakes happen. People are human, they're not robots. It's why businesses have insurance." I grin back at him, leaning hard into Clay. "Besides, it brought us together and I'm certainly not mad about that." I feel Clay's body relax into mine.

"Well, when you build your own company, you care about those things." He laughs dismissively again before continuing. "It was a costly mistake. Definitely one he knows better than to make."

He raises his soft drink, taking a sip before looking at Clay with an annoyed glare. "That's why we spent years learning to stay organized and focused, right Clay?"

I feel Clay tense again and I look down to see those tattooed knuckles tighten around his glass. If he squeezes any harder, it's going to shatter. He nods and gruffly replies. "Yes, Mr. Jensen."

This is the kind of condescending asshole I deal with every day. But to see someone talk like that to Clay, *my Clay*, is a whole other level of entitled boomer male that I can't stand.

I'm done playing nice with this dirtbag.

He looks back to me with that dismissive, fake grin. "That's the kind of thing I like to make sure doesn't happen to keep my share-holders happy. Something I'm sure you know all about in whatever business you're in." There he goes with that tone, talking down to me again. "What is it you do exactly, honey?"

Clay's hand slips from my side and he steps forward. I watch his posture go from tense to downright predatory as he steps toward his boss, putting himself between us.

"That's my girlfriend you're talking to, the woman I love. I know we go way back and that you've done a lot for me and I will always be grateful for that, but show her some respect and apologize right now and maybe I won't quit."

Mr. Jensen gives Clay an incredulous look before his eyes meet mine.

I step around Clay, brushing him back with a hand on his chest. "I love your enthusiasm and the whole protective thing is definitely doing it for me, but hold that thought. I got this." His eyes go wide and he holds up his hands, taking a step back, clearly seeing I'm a woman on a mission, not to be disturbed.

Yes. Clay, I'm going *Full Lizzy* - something I wasn't planning on doing tonight.

"It's funny you mention shareholders." I smirk at him with a wry, grin, batting my eyes innocently.

I love it when these self-righteous idiots make it easy and walk right into their own mistakes.

His nostrils flare in irritation as he eyes me with open disdain now, any semblance of his carefully crafted, polished veneer gone.

"I work in corporate accounting and finance, specializing in auditing." I take the last sip of bourbon and set the glass on the table, feeling more emboldened than ever. "And funny enough, your *extremely* capable employee here thought something was off with all of your GJF Inc. invoices on your most profitable, under budget projects lately."

I look at Clay, who quirks his head at me, wondering where I'm going with this. I wink at him, flipping my ponytail over my shoulder before turning back to his boss.

He glares at me, pure rage in his eyes, probably miffed that the little blonde princess is about to skewer him. "You better watch yourself," he says through gritted teeth, not wanting to draw more attention to the unfolding scene than we already have.

"Nope, I'm good," I tease playfully. "I wasn't planning on bringing this up tonight, but you just had to go and be the asshole everyone says you are."

He looks back at me, then to Clay, and now Kayleigh and Grace standing behind us.

"Bringing what up?"

"Oh." I bring my fingertip to my lips in mock thought, drawing out the syllable. "Just the little issue of you stealing from your shareholders. It was pretty clever, always swooping in at the end of your jobs that come in under budget. Pocketing the profits for yourself by paying the *consulting firm* you conveniently own. It was almost always the exact the amount you came in under budget too. Then you skip out on paying your shareholders and investors their portion of profit."

I smirk at him, relishing in the deer in the headlights expression.

"I'll admit, it took me a second to figure out what GJF Inc. was, but someone just reminded me of the *Golden Jensen Family* legacy. You really should have come up with a better name."

"You little bitch," he snarls, stepping towards me as that bewildered look turns to rage.

And that's when shit goes sideways.

I wince as he comes towards me, then I hear the thud of flesh and bone crunching and a gasp from someone nearby. All of a sudden I feel the sensation of something wet all over my chest.

I open my eyes to see that prick on the floor, grabbing his jaw in dismay with his empty glass shattered next to him. To my pleasant surprise, Clay is standing at my side, his arm pressed to my front protectively. This close to me, I know he wasn't the one to deliver the blow. He would have been justified in every way to lay this scumbag out, but my heart pounds knowing his first instinct was to put himself in front of me.

When I raise my eyes, I'm shocked to see my dad standing over Mr. Jensen, rubbing his fist. His eyes are blazing in a way I've never seen.

"Dad?"

He looks at me, his eyes softening before looking down at the asshole on the floor.

"What the hell are you doing, Charles?" He grabs his jaw and rubs it, his eyes flickering back and forth between my dad, me, and Clay.

"It's Mr. Frank, *Randall*," my dad replies in a tone reminiscent of the one used to scold Charlotte and myself when we were worse than usual. "And anyone that talks to my daughter that way has no business being a part of my company. I don't care if you're a minority shareholder or not, you will have nothing to do with this company any more."

He looks up in pure stunned disbelief and I savor the moment the realization settles in. I look at Clay who has an equally stunned, albeit much more pleased look on his face.

"Remember how I said I had a couple more teensy things to tell you?" I raise my hand between us and shrug, holding my thumb and forefinger apart with the tiniest gap between them. "Well, I found out my dad bought the majority stake in the company and I also pieced together what this shit bag was doing thanks to what you told me earlier."

Clay wraps his arms around me. He looks at me softly, his big, well worn hands rubbing my bare shoulders. "I knew you were the smart one between us."

An angry voice on the floor behind us interrupts the moment and we both turn to see Mr. Jensen staring at my dad. "Your daughter? I had no idea. I'm sor-"

My dad waves a hand at him to shut up. He's somewhere

between full on business mode and this new, protective dad mode. "I honestly don't give a shit if you knew she's my daughter or not. No one should ever talk to a woman like that." My dad looks at me softly and I nod, a grin spread across my face, watching him do all I've ever wanted, just be a dad.

STANDING AROUND outside the Grand Lodge at the valet circle is an interesting vibe to say the least. The last guests are filing out, whispering about the events of the night. Kayleigh and Grace are going on about our new group chats. Even after Clay got me a towel, I'm still a sticky mess from the soda but I hope dry cleaning will rescue my dress. But honestly, I don't really care because I can't take my eyes off the two men that make me feel so protected.

My dad walks over with Clay, both of them smiling at me in a way that melts my heart in one fell swoop.

"So I think I convinced your boyfriend not to quit." My dad tilts his head to Clay, who lets out a low laugh. "And maybe take a promotion to do a little more design work since I hear he has quite the hidden talent for it."

"Good, because he's probably the best asset in your new venture and he's damn good at design." I smile at Clay, who for the slightest moment has a pink hue in his cheeks as he wrings his hands.

"But we also have a proposition for you." He turns to Clay before they both look down at me, sporting matching grins again. I'm in for a lot of heart melting moments if these two keep doing that.

"We?" I ask, arching a brow.

Clay nods and clears his throat, looking at me. "You wouldn't just be working with your dad, you'd be working with me. Would you want that? You're so damn smart and after everything you figured out, the company could use you - I could use you."

My dad smiles proudly at me. "I know you've turned me down every time I've asked you to work for me before, but I think this would be a bit different. You'd have free rein and I think you'd like your coworkers." He winks after the last line. "Who knows, if you're as good as I believe you are, I could see this expanding to other ski areas, maybe even Jackson."

This is definitely not how I expected my night to unfold. I was ready to patch things up with Clay, especially after talking to Kayleigh this morning. But another job offer in Utah? Dad's right, for years I've turned down his offers that felt like handouts because I didn't want to be seen as the pretty little girl with rich parents. But this feels different. Maybe it would be a chance for us to reconnect.

I step forward, hugging my dad. "Sorry, still a little sticky." He lets out a chuckle before I continue. "But I will think about it, seriously. I just accepted a promotion yesterday, but maybe I could do some part time work at JSC and see how it goes."

He wraps me in his arms and I feel the same comfort I did last night when I poured myself out to him. "That's fine, sweetie. I'd like that. How about we get you home and cleaned up?"

I step back, brimming that it feels like he's really trying. But I look at Clay and my heart explodes.

"I'm going home, but that's not the condo." I grab Clay's hand, my favorite hand, running my thumb over the back of it. "Home is with him."

My dad looks at me with that same prideful look as before, like he finally sees me exactly the way I want to be seen. His nod says everything.

"But how about dinner tomorrow?" Clay says in unison with me, reading my mind. I flick my head to him, rolling my eyes as my dad laughs.

"You two are something, I can already see that."

I lean into Clay's warm body, squeezing his hand tighter.

Yes. I know my dad sees me - sees us - now.

AFTER SAYING goodbye to Lizzy's dad and I guess my new boss, I walk her towards the passenger side of my car.

When I pull out my keys and unlock it, Lizzy stops and quirks her head when she sees the lights of the sporty German coupe flash.

She turns to me, mouth gaping open. "That is *not* your truck. Are you a secret billionaire or something? When did you get this? I was only gone one night."

I step towards her, grinning down at her as I open the door for her. She stands there, her eyes flitting back and forth between the car and me.

"Well technically, the truck is the company's. I've had *this* for years. It was literally next to your Bronco the whole time, under the cover, since I don't drive it in winter. And no, we've covered that. I'm still just a guy that saves his money for the things he really wants."

I reach out to her, cupping the back of her bare neck in my hand, feeling her lean into my touch, freeing the softest whimper from her lips. One that goes straight to my cock.

"And right now, what I really want is to get you home and out of that dress."

She pops up on her toes, pecking me with a playful kiss. "Good, because that's exactly what I was thinking. It's also still very sticky with soda."

I grab her hand to help lower her into the car, but she pauses.

"I do have one question though."

"Anything, princess."

"Why this color? It's not what I would have pictured you owning."

"You mean it's not black?" I chuckle.

She narrows her eyes at me before tracing a finger tip along the top of the sapphire blue car. "Yes, I like this color."

I look into her eyes. "So do I, it was my mom's favorite, and now it's mine because it reminds me of your eyes."

Her parted lips curl into a warm smile as she lowers herself into the car and I shut the passenger door behind her.

"SO THAT WAS A NIGHT," I say, watching the road in front of us from Park City back to my house, *our home.* Something about hearing her tell her dad that my house was her *home* filled my heart in a way I can't ever remember feeling.

She laughs softly. "Yeah, you can say that again. Definitely not how I thought the night was going to go."

I peek over at her and her eyes still have a look of giddy disbelief. "You mean you weren't planning on skewering my boss in front of all his rich friends and investors and then having your dad promote me?"

She furrows her brows and glares at me sarcastically. "No. I didn't even know my dad bought JSC until last night when I talked to him at the condo. But I'll admit it was fun torturing Mr. Jensen."

I grin at her, my eyes darting between her and the road. "I have to say I enjoyed that too. Thank you."

She rests her hand on my thigh, sending a jolt of electricity through my spine. "For what?"

I drum my fingers along the steering wheel, rowing through the gears, shifting with my other hand. "Piecing all of that together. I knew something seemed funny, but you went next level digging in. I hope I can finally move on now, not having a daily reminder of so much baggage."

"What do you mean?"

I sigh, letting out a long breath. "You were right. He was a piece of shit. I always saw it as him helping me, but now I see how much he was breaking me down. It's already such a weight gone, like I can breathe again."

"I'm glad you feel that way." She pats my thigh, humming to herself. "But really, it was nothing. I'm glad I could help. Thanks for trusting me with it."

That word, trust. It means so much to both of us.

"I trust you with everything, Lizzy. Even my heart." My voice is strained. "But I'm still so sorry about the texts, about Kayleigh. I wanted to tell you and it was killing me not to."

I feel her hand squeeze my thigh. "I know. I saw how much it hurt you that night when I went back to the condo. But I'm only going to say this one more time: don't apologize for that." I hear her clear her throat and her fingers rub the fabric of my pants over my thigh. "Trust is hard for me. I haven't had the best luck with the men in my life. They've never been there for me like you have. I see how you're there for Grace and Kayleigh. You were ready to give up your own happiness to protect her. I understand what trust means to you now. I know I can trust you, *always*."

Hearing her say she trusts me means the world to me. I know what she's been through and how hard it is to earn that. I know I'll keep working every day to keep it. I look over to see her eyes fixed on me, soft but serious all at once. "But, Clay? I also need something else from you."

I nod. "Anything."

"I need to know that you can put yourself first for once. I love you because you make me feel good about being myself, exactly the way I want to be, excessive amounts of pink and all." She tosses me a playful wink and I feel the mood lighten a bit. "But I want to be that person for you too. I want to see you thrive and be happy like you have been these last few weeks. I want to see you make choices just for you. I don't want to see you be afraid to be happy again or think you don't deserve it."

I take my hand off the shifter, squeezing hers tightly, rubbing my thumb over the back of her soft skin. "I know I can do that. I want that part of me to be my past, not my future, because you're my future. I want everything that comes with that."

"Good, because I want that too." She smiles and lifts my hand to her lips, kissing my knuckles. "Ok. I like watching you drive my Bronco, but this might be better. Any more secret cars I should know about? Because I love being your passenger princess." My eyes flick over to Lizzy in the passenger seat, but hers are locked on my arm, rowing and shifting through the gears as we make our way up the windy road to my driveway.

"I'd hardly call this a secret. Again, you literally just had to lift that cover and it was there." I flick my eyebrows at her in a taunt. "But no, no more secrets. Period."

She nods and her smirk grows into a wide smile. I reach over, watching the road but rubbing her thigh at the hem of her dress. I could get used to nights like this with her, driving, talking, literally anything with the woman that makes me feel like it's ok to lose control.

That's all I want in my future, endless time with her.

WHEN WE WALK in the door from the garage, we throw our coats, keys, bags, everything down in a flurry of emotion. I don't care where shit is in my house any more as long as she's in it.

My hands hug the dip of her waist, pulling her into me. Her lips crash to mine and it's hard to tell who's more desperate for the other's heated touch.

It was only one night apart, but it felt like an eternity. We may have talked things out, but our bodies haven't.

She pants into my neck. "Can we finally get me out of this dress?"

"Thought you'd never ask." I reach down, hiking her dress up to her hips and lifting her up in my arms as she giggles in surprise and wraps her legs around me. The feeling of her soft, bare legs and ass in my hands makes my erection borderline painful in these dress pants. Holding her, feeling her, will be something I crave until my dying breaths.

I carry her down the hall, past her room, barely taking a second to breathe when our mouths aren't hungrily searching each other's. Her hands roam my body, practically ripping my bowtie off and unbuttoning my shirt, letting it fall to the floor in our wake.

She pulls her lips from mine. "Wait, we're going to *your* room?"

Last night when Grace stayed over, it finally dawned on me that we slept in Lizzy's room every night.

"Yes. You're never spending another night out of *my* bed," I growl into her neck. I open the door to my room and take a step inside before setting her down and flipping on the lights.

I watch as she looks around the room. Her gaze drifts to my bed, now covered in her pink pillows, to the leather chair in the near corner with a small book shelf next to it, to the soaking tub in the far corner by the windows looking out over the mountains.

She turns around to face me. "You've been holding out on me this whole time."

I quirk my lips and shrug. "I guess I wasn't ready to totally give up this last piece of my space."

She nods, her eyes full of understanding, like they always are, seeing right through whatever walls I put up.

I watch as she turns her back to me again, facing the room as her fingers tap the zipper between her shoulder blades. I step towards her, brushing her ponytail away with one hand, unzipping her dress with the other.

"You know, if you were really sorry about flooding my condo, you would have offered me this palace instead of the guest room."

I chuckle, but my breath lodges in my throat when I reach the bottom of her zipper and see the pink lace thong underneath. I let the dress fall to her feet and savor the view of her backside when she steps out of the dress. She looks back at me over her shoulder, those sapphire eyes sparkling like the stars in the night sky.

That's it. For the rest of my life, she gets what she wants. I don't care if she asks me to drive a pink truck, she gets what she wants if she looks at me like that.

"You're always such a brat." I lean down, placing a kiss on her bare neck.

She lets out the softest, hair raising whimper against my cheek. "Yeah, but you love it."

"I do," I say into her ear. "I love everything about you. I love you, Lizzy."

I run the back of my knuckles down her ribs, over her waist, settling just inside the lace of her thong. I hook my finger inside, shimmying it down her thighs until she steps out of it.

"I love you too." She breathes the words against me and I soak them in.

"Say it again."

She nuzzles against me. "I love you too."

I don't know what I did to deserve this. I don't know what I did to make someone like her choose me, to trust me, but I'm never going to question it. I erase that doubt in my mind and plant a kiss to the top of her head. "Now, let's get you cleaned up."

She leans into me, wrapping an arm around my neck, running her fingers through my hair. The scrape of her nails over my scalp makes my need for her rage. She pulls us closer and heat courses through me as she presses herself into my body.

I begrudgingly pull her hand off of my neck, palming it in my hand. I lead her through my room, past the soaking tub to the bathroom. Reaching into the shower, I start the hot water before turning back to find her eyeing me hungrily. We stand in front of the shower while I pull my belt off and drop my pants to take off my boxers. Her eyes watch in appreciation and she gives me a playful look when I catch her.

"Get in the shower." I point and follow her as she steps into the shower.

We stand there, letting the hot water run over us, feeling it wash away the aches and pains that the last twenty-four hours brought. I hold her against me, massaging and washing every last inch of her delicate skin.

"You know I'm never going to get tired of hearing you say that."

She laughs, her eyes looking up to meet mine through her wet golden hair. "Say what?"

I tuck away the damp strands, looking into her eyes, seeing the love and desire sparkle. "That you love me."

She smiles so warmly and wraps her arms around me before pressing her head into my chest. "Good, because you're stuck with me now."

That's music to my ears because there's no one else for me. "I'm not stuck with you. No one makes me feel the way you do. No one *could* ever make me feel so free. I'm never going to get tired of saying it either. I love you, so much."

I guide her to sit down in front of me on the marble shower bench and grab the shampoo. She drops her head against my stomach, her hands holding onto my waist while she lets me wash her hair. I work the shampoo in, eliciting soft whimpers and outright moans that I savor while her head stays pressed against my stomach.

Her touch, the feeling of her body against mine, has been addictive since that fateful night at Roxy's. *She's* been addictive since that night.

I've spent years telling myself, convincing myself that I was fine alone. I thought I was content not wanting more in my life. But now, with those perfect blue eyes looking back up at me like I'm the only thing in her world, I'm ok with wanting things for myself, like her.

I'm more than ok with needing her touch, her smile, her eyes on me every second of every day.

This smart, beautiful, fierce, defiant woman has made me damn sure of that.

But even if she wants me to put myself first for a change, I'm always going to make sure I'm there for her, however she needs me. She's always going to be my everything.

Whatever I can do to keep that sparkle in her eyes, I will. Whatever I can do to make her smile like that, I will.

And I'm going to show her that right now.

CHAPTER 43
LIZZY
YOU'RE RUINING IT

"WHAT ARE YOU DOING?" I watch as he stands in front of me, the steaming water beading down his rippled stomach, his hand gripping the base of his hard length.

I raise my eyes to his to find that the soft, gentle look on his face from moments ago is replaced by a divinely wicked grin. His emerald green eyes send hot, fiery need throughout my body with how they devour me.

"Something I said I would never do, because I love you, probably an unhealthy amount." His voice is low and husky, rough and ragged. I can practically feel how much he wants me, needs me in it.

I can't believe that less than a year ago, I was ready to settle down into a cookie cutter, suburban life. I was ready to accept passionless and boring. Now I have *this man* that sees me and loves me like I'm his entire world. Nothing about being with him feels cookie cutter. It's rough and raw, but so real. I want to feel the heat of his gaze, to feel his hunger for me for the rest of my life. I want to be looked at like this every day - no filters, no masks, nothing between us. I know it will never be passionless or boring.

I take in the site of him looming over me and my eyes widen as his grin grows and his dimples pop when he starts to grip his cock harder.

"Oh my god, yes!" I pull my hands from his thighs, bringing them together clapping and practically squealing. "It's happening! You're going to do it?"

I watch his hand work slowly, up and down his shaft and I can see the veins throb as the blood rushes into his cock. His grin widens and I shamelessly watch him stroke himself inches from me, the hot steam of the shower all around us. My eyes go back and forth from the perfect, dimpled grin to his abs to the private show he's giving me. I've dreamt about seeing him do this and it's better than that. I feel my tongue dart out over my lips and chuckle. "Why? You like what you see?"

I nod up at him eagerly.

He reaches for my chin with his other hand, forcing me to hold his gaze instead of watching him jerk his perfect cock. "That's good, because I told you, I'm yours. All of me is yours."

My heart pounds hearing that confession again in this moment. I know how hard it is for him to be vulnerable and he's giving me everything he has. His thumb traces my bottom lip and they part like a reflex to his touch as I whimper. My body hums, each nerve ending overstimulated. The feeling of the cool marble bench, the warm steam, the scorching heat of his gaze, the callouses of his thumb on my lips. All of it builds a tight coil of tension in me that only he can release.

"But since you did lose that bet on the river after all, you're gonna have to give me a show too, princess." He leans forward, grabbing my neck, his thumb tracing my parted lips as a gasp escapes them. I feel the column of my neck shift in his grip when I smile back at him eagerly. "Now spread those thighs and play with yourself for me, like you do when you're thinking about me. Show me how much you need me, how much you love me."

I smirk up at him, leaning into the grip of his hand. "Awfully bold of you to assume I do this thinking about you." My thighs open and I drop a hand to them, circling my already swollen and aching clit. I cup a breast in my other hand, rolling and teasing the tight bud. "But it might look something like this."

His eyes dart from mine to my breasts to the hand between my legs. I watch as his grip tightens and he works himself harder and faster. The sight of his abs tensing and the veins running down that V is a work of art.

"Fuck," he grits out. "You're so perfect. So damn perfect, princess."

I preen with his praise and he strokes my cheek with his thumb. "You're already so close for me."

"You're awfully confident. How do you know?" I look up at him, batting my wet lashes, still taking him in.

His hooded eyes peer into me and his thumb traces my still parted lips.

"Because your lips do that."

I nip his thumb, smiling back up at him. He grins back at me and I feel that knot of tension in me build under his gaze and the pressure from my fingers, circling my needy swollen bundle of nerves faster and faster. I know he must be getting close because I hear his breathing quicken and watch his muscles tense.

"And your cheeks get this pretty little shade of pink." His thumb goes back to rubbing my cheek and I whimper at the touch.

"And your eyes." The deep forest green eyes that I will always feel seen by burn right into mine.

"What about my eyes?" I pant.

He strokes himself harder and more erratically. "They get glassy, just like that."

"How do you know all of that?" I feel myself barreling over that cliff of ecstasy, breathing harder with each flick of my clit, each stroke of his thumb over my cheek. This man feels like he's part of my soul, part of me. I've given him that last little piece of me, the one I thought was broken and lost and he's cherishing it like his life depends on it.

"Because you're my everything. I haven't been able to take my eyes off you since the moment we met. I take in every breath, every step, every word." Those eyes. Those damn eyes hold my gaze. "Every time you tap those lips with those pink nails. Every time you flick that ponytail. I breathe it in. I drink it in. *You consume me.*"

"God, Clay." I come undone, wave after wave of pleasure coursing through me like the chorus of his words, his declarations of love. I melt into a puddle of bliss on the cool marble, knowing this is where I was meant to be, with him.

"Yes. Princess. That's it. So beautiful." I look up just as he bucks into his fist and his sculpted body clenches. He lets out rope after rope of warm cum on my chest, letting go of my neck and bracing himself against the wall behind me.

This is even better than I fantasized.

We stay there just like that, the hot water running over our bodies, for what feels like forever before he tilts my chin up to look at him.

He reaches next to me on the bench, grabbing the soap. "Let's get you cleaned up again."

He grabs my hand and pulls me to my feet. I turn around, leaning into his body and let him wash my chest. He takes his time, massaging and kneading. I lean back into him and he cranes his neck to bring his lips to mine for a perfect, heart stopping kiss.

Yes.

He's better than anything I could have ever dreamed of for myself.

I LAY IN BED, still giddy thinking about the show he put on for me in the shower, practically vibrating. It was the very show he said he would never give me. "So can that be an every shower thing?"

A low hum rumbles from his chest and he drapes his arm over me, lacing his fingers into mine. I pull his hand to my lips, kissing the back of his knuckles, grinning at the word *OVER* spelled across them.

That's just it. Just when I thought the idea of me being able to trust, of me being able to open myself up completely to someone, was *over*, Clay Chapman walks right into my life. He walked right into my favorite dive bar. He walked right into my condo. He walked right into my heart and now it really is *over*, I found the person I've always wanted, whether I knew it or not.

"What are you thinking about in that head of yours?" His deep voice pulls me back to the moment, a moment I want to happen countless more times.

"I'm thinking that should definitely be an every shower thing. You were hot, like so hot," I tease.

He mock groans, pressing a kiss to the top of my head. "You're ruining it, princess."

I push myself back into his big, warm, comforting body, melting when he wraps his arms around me tighter.

I knew I didn't need someone to make me better or stronger. I've never been a hopeless heroine that needed someone to prop them up or define them. I just needed this, a man that loves me exactly the way I am and will be by my side, hand in hand, through everything.

And that's who Clay is.

My partner. My equal.

My eyes flutter shut and I fall asleep with one thought on my mind.

Nothing could ever ruin this.

EPILOGUE
CLAY

Seven Months Later
Jackson, Wyoming

"YOU TRUST ME, RIGHT?" I peer at Lizzy, standing at the top of a place I thought I'd never be again, much less with the love of my life.

I watch her look at me, then back down into Corbet's Couloir. I still remember the first time I skied the rocky chute in Jackson, Wyoming with my brother and Mom by my side as a teenager. It was that same night that Tanner took me out to get the outline of the Tetons tattooed onto my wrist, just like him and Collin, after Mom signed the paperwork for the studio of course.

I still can't believe I was ok with giving up this part of my life that meant so much to me for so long. Somehow, Lizzy working her way into my life has brought me closer to my family, to my mom, to so many good memories I blocked out for so long. So when Tanner and V said they wanted a winter wedding in Jackson, I knew exactly what I wanted to do with my spare time back in my hometown.

"Yes, I trust you. But aren't there better ways to show that? I don't think this is what Tanner and V had in mind when they said we should go enjoy the day without wedding stuff together." Lizzy's voice cuts through the cold, frosty air at the top of the mountain peak.

"You're such a brat," I tease. Even through her goggles, I can feel her glare when she drops her head. I shuffle closer to her on my skis, putting my hands on her hips. She looks up at me and her little blonde slut strands that drive me wild float in the light wind. "But trust me, you got this."

She nods and looks down at the run again and I can tell by her posture that she's ready. But just for good measure, I poke my bear.

"Besides, you can't let Grace and V keep holding this over you."

Yep, that did it. She whips her head at me and let the long, blonde braids I did for her this morning flick over her shoulder. This time, I know without a doubt she's glaring at me. "See you at the bottom."

She takes off down into the rocky chute and my heart freezes in my chest as she takes the first turn. It's dangerous. Deserving of its title as one of America's scariest ski runs. She's not the most graceful, but she still nails it and gets down the run. I've never felt more alive on the slopes, watching her, knowing she trusts me, seeing just how determined she is. My perfect, untamable Lizzy.

"OH MY GOD. Are you going to be a brat all day?" I look at Lizzy in the stall next to me, smirking back while she gives me a death glare.

"Seriously, this sucks. I don't know how you have half your body covered in tattoos." She winces as the tattoo artist working on her finishes the outline of the Teton mountains on her ribs, the same place Veronica got hers done.

I chuckle to myself, prompting the tattoo artist working on my chest to scold me.

"Well, you'll finally be able to show off your first tattoo to the rest of the gang."

She gets up from the bench after her tattoo artist cleans up and bandages her freshly inked piece. I haven't even seen it on her, but I already know I'm going to be obsessed with it every time I see it, reminding me of how much she trusts me.

Honestly, I'm surprised it was this easy to get her into the little tattoo shop in Jackson. But when she's determined to do something, she does it and I love that.

She walks over to my stall and saunters towards me.

"Nope. Turn around. I already said you don't get to see it until tonight." I smirk at her and she rolls her eyes.

"Come on, just a peek," she pleads, clasping her hands together.

"Nope. That was the deal." I lift a finger, circling it in a turn around gesture.

She huffs. "You're no fun." She begrudgingly turns away, sitting in the open chair in the stall.

I'll admit, it's killing me not to let her see it right now. The second I had the idea for this tattoo in the center of my chest, I knew I wanted it. I couldn't think of anything else that reminds me of her more.

"All done." The tattoo artists cleans and wipes down my chest, handing me a mirror.

Lizzy looks back in surprise. "Wait, yours barely took longer than mine and you said it was way bigger?"

I shrug and laugh. "Yeah, well I'm not a fidgety brat. Goes a lot faster."

She turns away while I hold up the mirror, admiring the broken heart in the center of my chest. Down the center of the heart is an open tear, covered with a bright pink bandaid, because that's exactly what Lizzy was to me, helping me repair so many old wounds.

I feel my lips curve into a smile when I see it, the perfect reminder of *my princess*. The one that I want to spend the rest of my life with.

❄

"I STILL CAN'T BELIEVE you and Lizzy are a real thing." Tanner pats me on the back.

I clink my stubby yellow beer bottle to his. A warm smile spreads across my face and I don't miss the way Tanner, my dad, or my grandpa watch me. "Yeah, but she's perfect. I think you'll be seeing a lot more of her."

Tonight's their last night in town before going on a three week ski honeymoon with their dog, Rex, in their Sprinter van. So when he said he wanted everyone to get together at the old dive bar down the street from his cabin, it was an easy thing to say yes to.

My grandpa, Samuel, claps me on the shoulder. "As long as that means we'll be seeing more of you smiling like this, that sounds perfect. And your grandma thinks Lizzy is a hoot."

"Thanks, Grandpa." I pat him on the shoulder and look around the bar. Grace is sitting at a table, chatting with TJ, who was nice enough to let Tanner and V use his house and guesthouse here in Jackson to host their small, cozy wedding.

My grandma and V's parents are talking at another table with Lizzy's parents who came out for the occasion. I have to admit, the last six months working with him have been every bit of the change I needed. And I'm so happy to see that Lizzy and him are closer now, with Lizzy working two days a week for JSC.

Then I spot Lizzy, sitting at the corner of the bar, wearing those damn pink cowboy boots and that black sweater dress. She's every bit of the perfection she was that first night we met. What I'm more afraid of is the faces Benjamin and Alexis, the bartenders, are making at her while she's glaring at them, flailing her hands around.

I walk over to them.

"Been a while, Benjamin." I prop myself up on the bar next to Lizzy, while Benjamin groans in frustration.

"Can you tell your girl to order anything besides a piña colada?"

I look at Lizzy who's rolling her eyes and now turning her glare to me. "Don't give me that look. Just because I like bourbon doesn't mean I can't crave a fruity drink sometimes. I don't know how a bar can't have what they need to make them."

I smirk at her and reach into my jacket pocket, pulling out the small can of coconut cream. Her eyes go wide when I set it on the counter.

"I'm assuming this is what you don't have?" I turn to Benjamin who scrubs his face with his palm and groans. "So can you make one now?"

He grabs the can and mutters under his breath. "Always something with the Chapmans." I shake my head as he walks to his drink station at the other end of the bar and starts making her drink.

"Why on earth did you have that?" Lizzy looks at me, a delighted but incredulous look on her face.

I shrug. "You and V were talking about them all week. You kept going on about how you'd want a warm beachside honeymoon if this was your wedding and you'd crave a piña colada." I watch the smile, the one of pure delight that I love, spread across her face. "So I sort of had a hunch you might want one tonight."

She props her elbow up on the bar, resting her cheek in her palm. The way she looks at me, like I'm her world, makes me know I'm more than right about her. That she's the end for me. "You're something else, Clay Chapman."

Smiling back at her, I rasp knuckles against the bar. "I need to check on something, but I'll be right back." I toss her a playful wink and get up to head towards the hall in the back of the bar to the patio. I look over my shoulder to see her still watching me hungrily from the bar as I walk away, just like that first night.

I turn the corner out of sight and stop. If I know my girl...

One.

Two.

Three.

"I swear, Clay, we can make out in the bar but we are not doing anything else here. This place is dirt-" I hear her already going into a rant when she turns the corner to follow me, but she stops mid-sentence when she sees me kneeling on the floor.

"What are you doing down there? I was just saying these floors are gross."

Her eyes go wide when I reach into my other jacket pocket, pulling out the small light blue velvet box.

I flip open the box and her hands fly to her mouth when she sees the princess cut diamond.

"What do you say, princess? Want to make me the luckiest man on earth and be my queen?"

Her hands go to her hips and a playful smirk crosses her lips. "First, don't call me queen. It makes me sound old." Her smirk turns into a beaming smile and her sapphire eyes shine down on me. "But I will be your princess, forever."

Standing, I step towards her and smile. "Is that a yes then?"

She stands up on her toes, looping her arms around my neck and bringing her lips to mine for a short kiss. She tugs at my bottom lip as she pulls away just enough to whisper. "Just be a good boy and put the damn ring on my finger."

ACKNOWLEDGMENTS

There's a long list of people I could thank for their support.

First and foremost, I can't say enough about everyone that read and enjoyed Full Send. Seeing your reactions meant so much and gave me the boost I needed to keep going and write Fall Apart. And this goes double for the early ARC readers of Full Send, thank you so much for taking a chance on an indie author's debut novel.

Next, my beta readers. Jo, Stephanie, Abby, and Kelsey - you all helped so much with taking a book I already loved and turning it into something even better. I enjoyed getting your feedback and hearing how excited you were to read it. I still enjoy your spirited debates about chapter 27 and 33.

To my partner, your constant support and enthusiasm for these books has been everything. You've been there every step of the way as my alpha reader for Full Send and now Fall Apart. You've helped with editing both books and let me bounce all my ideas off of you at the most random of times.

To my friends that have continued to humor me and be a sounding board or just someone to vent to, I can't thank you enough.

And to my bookish friends I've met along the way, chatting with you has been a welcome treat every day. This community has been so kind and I cherish being welcomed into it.

ABOUT THE AUTHOR

I grew up in and around the city of Cincinnati, Ohio, graduating with a degree in Engineering.

I'm an avid skier and traveler, spending almost all of my free time traveling and enjoying time outside, ideally in the mountains. More often than not, I'm with my partner and our fur babies.

There isn't much that brings me more excitement or joy than getting in a car (or maybe a Sprinter van) and driving across the country and exploring. And besides, twenty-something hour long road trips means we have lots of time to cross plenty of wonderfully smutty romance novels off our TBR list. And who doesn't love that?

instagram.com/dforestwrites

goodreads.com/dakotaforest

threads.net/@dforestwrites

ALSO BY DAKOTA FOREST

Full Send

www.ingramcontent.com/pod-product-compliance
Lightning Source LLC
Chambersburg PA
CBHW050520110726
47899CB00005B/1527